Also by Steven dos Santos

The Culling
The Torch Keeper: Book One

THE SOWING

THE SOWING

The Torch Keeper: Book Two

STEVEN DOS SANTOS

Woodbury, Minnesota

First Edition
First Printing, 2014

Book design by Bob Gaul
Cover design by Lisa Novak
Cover illustration: Chris Nurse/Début Art

Flux, an imprint of Llewellyn Worldwide Ltd.

Library of Congress Cataloging-in-Publication Data
Dos Santos, Steven.
    The sowing/Steven dos Santos.—First edition.
        pages cm.—(The torch keeper; book two)
    Summary: "A year after winning The Establishment's brutal Trials and becoming a soldier, seventeen-year-old Lucky Spark's mission to undermine this totalitarian government is upended when he becomes an Incentive in the next round of the Trials"—Provided by publisher.
    ISBN 978-0-7387-3540-5
[1. Survival—Fiction. 2. Contests—Fiction. 3. Soldiers—Fiction. 4. Orphans—Fiction. 5. Government, Resistance to—Fiction. 6. Homosexuality—Fiction. 7. Science fiction.] I. Title.
    PZ7.D73673Sow 2014
    [Fic]—dc23
                                                        2013041657

Flux
Llewellyn Worldwide Ltd.
2143 Wooddale Drive
Woodbury, MN 55125-2989
www.fluxnow.com

Printed in the United States of America

To my dear brother, Edward dos Santos, who helped sow the seeds of imagination and creativity in my childhood by introducing me to the awe and wonders of *Star Wars* for the very first time. Even though you're gone now, Eddie, you will never be forgotten. Until we meet again, in a galaxy far, far away...

PART I

HOMECOMING

ONE

I squint through my protective goggles against the maelstrom of swirling sand and blinding neon lights closing in on either side of me, trying to crush me in their rainbow vise.

This is it. The Avenue of Longing. Home of the Pleasure Emporiums, the place where every appetite can be satisfied— for a steep price.

How many thousands—no, *hundreds of thousands*—of patrons have had their dark fantasies fulfilled behind these brilliantly lit facades, all at the expense of countless kids with no one to care, no one to fight for them?

Until now.

The sandstorm moans in my ears, its winds buffeting my body as if trying to hold me back.

But I won't be denied. Not after coming so far.

Adrenaline burns through me like lit kerosene. The familiar rush that I've nicknamed the *crush*—a mixture of fear, defiance, and justice, with a heaping dollop of vengeance. After months of sneaking off from my unit and risking execution, you'd think I'd have gotten used to it.

Still, each act of sabotage, each betrayal of the Imposer uniform I wear, seems just as exciting as the first and has made me even more daring. But it never seems to be enough.

Not until I've made the very government I serve pay for all the hurt it's caused.

I pull the chronometer from my pocket. Sand covers its face, obscuring the digital display. I brush it away and study the readout.

Less than an hour left. If I don't accomplish what I came here to do and get back to my unit, I may never get another chance.

Stuffing the timepiece back in my pocket, I pull my cowl tighter against the sudden chill of the desert night, fully hiding my Imposer uniform. It wouldn't be good for anyone to recognize Lucian Spark, the Establishment's newest Recruit and member of the Imposer elite squad. Especially since I'm AWOL.

I push through the gusts and down the paved concourse, leaving the yawning wasteland in my wake.

There are only a few stragglers here and there, lurking in the shadows, ducking down side streets. Probably just servants, valets of the Establishment's elite, hidden from the public's gaze. Weaving among the buildings, I pull out a few of the silver discs stuffed in my pocket and make sure to scatter them at random. If anyone sees me, they'll assume I've had one wanderer's brew too many.

I've never been more sober in my life.

I round the corner and spot my target.

Harmony House.

Its vulgar turrets and arches, bathed in the glow of sweeping, multicolored spotlights, are a fitting monument to the Establishment's corruption. A pathway of red carpet, flanked by golden rails, leads to the arched double doors.

This was the place that ultimately destroyed her. The place that's destroyed so many.

I stride up the pathway, burning with purpose. A hover carriage, propelled by gravity boosters, nearly collides with me.

"Watch where you're going," an electronically modulated voice shouts from behind the tinted windows obscuring the identities of the passengers.

But I ignore it, reaching the entrance at last. Before I can knock, the doors slide apart of their own accord. I enter and they squeal shut, sealing me inside.

It takes a few moments for my eyes to adjust. Wisps of stale smoke swirl through the shafts of dim gaslight, flickering down from the vaulted ceiling. The cloying stench of incense, sweet perfumes, alcohol, and sweat is suffocating. The sounds of wind instruments weave their way through the chamber.

"Welcome," a throaty voice croaks from the shadows.

A tall, sinewy figure slinks out of the darkness, wrapped in form-hugging leather. It has short, dyed-blue hair and skin pale as chalk. Even from here I can see the thick concealer caked on that face, drawing attention to the wrinkles and blemishes it's trying desperately to hide.

My eyes flick to the silver tablet clutched in one of those

bony hands—the master control unit. As subtly as I can, I press a notch in my utility belt, activating the computer virus that'll hack into the security system at Harmony House and reprogram it—that is, *if* my black market source earned his hefty fee.

I nod. "Evening."

The figure circles once before sidling up to me, hot breath snaking up my left ear. "Raja Featherbone here, carnal caterer extraordinaire. Your pleasures are *my* desire." The proprietor takes a puff of the long cigarette clutched in the other hand, smiles, and exhales a wave of concentric circles that ring my head and throat like a smoky noose. "So tell me. What does it take to make your *clock* chime, young man, hmmm?"

I smile back, fighting the urge to cough. "I'm looking for something...*fresh* tonight." I force a wink to hide my disgust. "I hear that's your specialty."

A chuckle bursts from Featherbone's throat. "Oooh! Yes indeedy! But that will cost you an extra premium. You know, supply and demand and all."

I wave these concerns away. "Not a problem." The computer scanner in my belt vibrates once, signaling that the hack is about one third complete. A genuine smile coats my lips this time.

"Oooh, Goody-goody!" Featherbone shoves the cigarette in place between yellowed teeth and presses a hand against the control unit's screen. There's a *buzz* as Featherbone's fingerprints are scanned. A split second later, a green light on the device blinks.

Featherbone nudges me with a pointy elbow and a lewd

glance before tapping the keys with the speed of a scavenger. "We have quite the selection tonight, oh yes we do, yes indeed!" The music cuts off. A rising hum fills the room, tingling through my ears, rattling my teeth. Panels in the ceiling stretch open with a bone-crushing grind. With the whir of motors, transparent tubes descend, each containing a body. One by one, these capsules rotate just above me, allowing me to get a good look at their cargo.

They're just children.

I can see the fear in their faces, particularly the younger ones, imploring me with saucered eyes. But what's even more chilling is the jaded expression of the older ones. They're maybe fourteen or fifteen years old at most—just a couple of years younger than me. It's as if they've been through this selection process hundreds of times and are almost bored with it. All of them are wearing blinking red bands around their wrists—security restraints. If they try to escape, a remote signal will deliver instant pain and death.

I want to reach out and snap Featherbone's scrawny neck. But that would be too easy. I'd be taken down by security quickly, and then this whole operation would have been in vain. My belt scanner vibrates twice. The security hack is halfway complete. I just have to hold this scum off a little longer.

"You certainly have a lot to choose from." I push the words through my mouth even as I struggle to push the bile back down my throat. "I guess you've been doing this for quite some time."

Featherbone's fingers tiptoe up my back. "I'm not *that*

old, lovie." He squeezes the words through his cigarette-clenched teeth. "Well? Care to taste any of my treats?"

I purse my lips. "Actually, I was wondering if you had someone that looked more like *this*."

Reaching into the folds of my cloak, I pull out the small, triangular holographic display cam and switch it on.

A three-dimensional figure of a little girl is projected before Featherbone's face. A beautiful little girl of six with long, raven hair and striking green eyes.

The proprietor's cigarette dangles from a pouty lip. "Seen a lot of pretty faces in my line of work, oh yes I have, yes siree! But *there's* one I've never forgotten." A smirk cracks the plaster of makeup. "That little crumpet was quite popular while she was here." Featherbone sighs. "Pity she had to get careless and breed. Ruined a good product. Often wondered what ever happened to that one, oh yes I have."

"Maybe I can satisfy your curiosity." Each beat of my heart blasts my blood with molten fury. "This is what she grew up to look like." I flick another button on the holocam. The image of the little girl disappears, replaced by that of a young woman. Even though her features look older, the hair and eyes are unmistakable. Memories flood my brain … a freighter, an island, two small children … all smothered in friendship, pain, and loss. "Her name is—*was*—Cypress Goslin."

Featherbone guffaws and points the cigarette stem at the grainy image. "I recognize that wench. She was one of the five—those Recruits from the Parish that were drafted last season!"

My eyes are riveted on the image. "Yes."

"I remember her well, yes, oh my yes! Business was slow and I bet a small fortune on missy here, hoping to recoup some losses if she beat the others during the Trials. Just look at the fire in those eyes."

But the holographic eyes pale in comparison to my memory of the real thing branded in my brain.

I shut off the holocam and jam it in my pocket. "She was my friend."

"Pity-pity. She had a good thing here. Indeed she did. I guess once she failed at the Trials she got sent to the mines. Serves her right."

The scanner in my belt vibrates three times: Security hack complete. Surveillance cameras disabled.

Molten steel pulses through my veins. This is it.

I whip out the blade hidden within my boot and thrust it toward Featherbone. "She's *dead*. Just like you'll be if you don't hand over that master control unit."

But Featherbone only stares at me and yawns. "Naughty-naughty. I hope they don't get too much blood on the carpet when they're through with you. Just had it replaced."

I lunge for the device but the slaver claws at me, knocking my hood away and exposing my face.

Featherbone's eyes bulge. "*You!* You're the one that *won* the bloody Trials! You're an Imposer for the Establishment, on *our* side! Your name is—"

"*Lucky*," I finish. "But unfortunately, not for you."

Featherbone backs away, jabbing at the controls on the unit. Lights flash. Alarms blast through the air.

Above us, the children stir in their transparent coffins,

cheeks and palms pressed against the glass. Even the older ones seem restless now.

"Oopsy! Security will be here in a minute," Featherbone hisses. "And you'll never make me give you access to the system before then, lovie, oh no you won't!" A triumphant glare pierces me.

"Then we don't have much time." I shrug. "Either you hand over the unit or you force me to take it from you."

The glint of strobing emergency lights douses my raised blade with splashes of crimson. I move in.

My shadow shrouds the flesh dealer, whose shrill screams are muffled by the blaring siren.

"Open up in there!" The rumbling voice vibrates through the other side of the parlor wall.

I dig my knife into Featherbone's arm. The cut's nowhere near as deep as I could go, just enough to draw a scarlet streak and an even higher-pitched yelp before I wrench the master control unit away. If the virus I uploaded has done its job and infiltrated the Emporium's computer network, this master unit now controls not only the security for Harmony House but every house in these pleasure pits. All I have to do is select one command to free all these kids and get them the hell out of here.

Bony arms clamp around my neck. The control unit drops from my hand as my vision blurs and the cold metal of my own ID tags digs into my throat like a garrote.

"What's this?" Featherbone croaks in my ear. "One tag says *Spark*...the other *Tycho*? You have a sweetheart, yes?" The cackle drowns out everything else and coats my ear with warm spittle. Everything's going dark. My knees buckle. The room's spinning. "Never see that one again, oh no you won't!"

No. I'll never see him again.

My head tilts so that my lips graze Featherbone's ear. "Cypress … sends her regards."

I rip the still-protruding blade from Featherbone's arm and jam it deep into the slaver's neck, feeling it cut through artery and sink into bone. Then I fling the twitching, grisly body off me. It thuds lifeless to the floor, inches from the master control unit.

BLAM!

The parlor doors burst open. Shrapnel torpedoes through the room, slicing through my hand. Before I can lunge for the control unit, a squadron of about a half-dozen black-clad security personnel swarms into the chamber, brandishing weapons that glisten in the flickering gaslights. They cut me off, standing between me and the master control.

The lead officer nudges his companions in my direction. "If he tries anything, shoot to kill."

I drop and roll. Electric charges pierce the ground inches from me. I spring and vault behind the bar. A volley of blasts strikes the shelves above me. Bottles rain down, some shattering against the floor. I spit out the taste of metal.

No cover. No weapon. No time. It's the Trials all over again.

"We have him cornered!" yells the leader.

"Nixter, take him alive for interrogation!" shouts another.

The glint of a steel toe rounds the bar. I grab one of the few unbroken bottles of alcohol lying next to me.

Nixter thrusts her weapon toward me like a skewer.

In the flickering shadows, she resembles a wiry, bug-eyed insect. "You're gonna need more than booze when we're done with you." She cocks the trigger.

I stare her down. "I wasn't planning on drinking it."

I hurl the bottle toward the closest gaslight and dive through the still-smoking gap in the bar, just as she fires.

Glass shatters. Sharp pain nicks my leg. I have just enough time to register the shocked looks of the guards on the other side of the bar as I slide toward them.

A loud explosion roars through the parlor. We're all hurled against the far wall. Rousing myself, I take in the carnage. From the looks of their contorted bodies, at least one of the guards broke his neck, while two others lie unconscious and bleeding. Above, the mechanisms holding the translucent prisons buckle under the impact. Children teeter inside their oval pens. The alcohol on the bar ignites. Soon the entire room is blanketed in a mantle of smoke that burns through my lungs.

I catch sight of the blinking green of the master control unit, just a few inches away. I reach for it.

Steel-like pincers clamp around my ankle, yanking me backwards.

Through the haze, I can make out one of the guards standing above me, holding my leg. His jaw is set in a grimace, blazing firelight reflecting in his eyes. He presses the butt of the weapon against my forehead.

I kick up, hitting him in the groin. His face twists in pain. I hook my foot around his, tripping him. He smashes into the floor next to me. Another guard aims her weapon at me and fires.

Instinctively, I hoist the first guard on top of me and the blast hits him instead.

Then in one fluid move, I grab the fallen guard's weapon, roll him off me, and let loose a barrage on the second guard. She collapses face-first, her nose crunching and popping against the floor as I take out the guards who are still stirring.

The weapon clicks empty and I toss it.

By this time the entire room's covered in a thick blanket of filthy mist. To my right, a curling tongue of flame laps the underside of one of the cylindrical prisons. Inside their capsules, the children are screaming, pounding against the reinforced glass, falling to their knees, gasping for breath.

Their cries jolt me into action. I scoop up the master control unit and activate the fire suppression system. Water jets from the sprinklers throughout the parlor and smothers the flames into submission. As soon as it's clear, I engage the activation button for the slaves' capsules and restraints.

Instantly the display tubes are lowered to ground level, dozens of them, row upon row of living cargo. They creak open, spilling out waves of dazed and coughing children. Clanking metal echoes through the chamber as the security bracelets spring apart and drop from their wrists, clanking onto the floor.

I kneel and grab a gun from one of the fallen guards, expel the spent cartridge, and jam in a fresh one. Then I stand to face them. "We're getting out of here. By now, reinforcements should be on their way. I want you to grab anything that looks like a weapon and empty the cash coffers behind the bar. Once we exit Harmony House, head west past the city limits until you reach the canyon. You'll be able to find shelter there and barter for provisions with one of the trading caravans I've arranged to meet you." They're all staring at me, hanging on every word. "I've hacked into the system and disabled every security bracelet in the city. The others in the different houses will be free as well, but confused by everything that's going on. Grab as many as you can on the way out and take them with you. Let's move!"

They scuttle like a colony of ants, intent on their mission to ransack the parlor for weapons and currency. In minutes, they're done gathering and stand ready.

A tall boy, almost my height, nudges the barrel of a pilfered weapon toward the doors. "How are we gonna get through the city? There'll be too many of 'em out there by now."

I reach into my pocket and pull out one of the last remaining silver discs. "I've taken care of that. Trust me. They'll have their hands full."

I slide the goggles over my eyes and drape my hood over my head.

Suddenly the gaping entryway is filled with more armed personnel, their weapons blazing. I toss the disc toward them and hit a button on my belt. "Everyone down!"

They follow my lead and dive to the ground. A fireball erupts in the doorway, rattling the building to its very foundations. A blast of hot air punches through the room. I scramble to my feet, pulling as many kids as I can onto theirs. "Move!"

En masse, we push toward the entryway, firing, stabbing, and slashing anything in our path, past the smoldering edges of the doorway, trampling over the bloody clumps of flailing guards on the other side. Some of the former prisoners pause to pry weapons loose from dead and dying fingers before moving on like a swarm of locusts.

Once we're clear of Harmony House, I press another button on my belt, triggering the other silver discs I've scattered throughout the city to detonate in a pre-programmed sequence. Explosions shake the ground like the tremors of an earthquake. One blast. Two. Three. Four. Five...

The Pleasure Emporiums are in chaos. The air is layered with thunderous blasts, a symphony of shattered glass, screaming, shouting, weapon bursts, hundreds of feet pounding the pavement. Cement and brick groan as the structures implode all around in a thick deluge of dust and debris.

I pump blast after blast of cover fire as the ragtag caravan of former-slaves-turned-warriors maneuvers through the carnage, past the confused and panicked masses, and disappears toward the western horizon.

Reaching into my belt one last time, I pull out a small tube of flammable liquid and then sign the initial on the ground by the Pleasure Emporium's entrance. Just one letter.

A giant T, which begins to blaze.

Then I'm trudging out of the city in the opposite direction, into the wasteland.

My glide cycle is still hidden under a tarp behind the dune where I left it. Hopping onto the seat, I flick the lever on the handlebar. I'm jostled by the familiar vibration as the wind, harnessed by the propulsion system, churns the props on the vehicle's wings. It sputters into the air with an asthmatic wheeze.

I pause once to look behind me.

The Pleasure Emporiums glitter brighter than they ever have against the shimmering canvas of night sky. Only this time, they don't paint the horizon in rainbow shades of seductive neon.

Gunning the throttle, I swerve and speed away into the night, away from the brilliant streamers of red and orange that dance behind me, content that by morning they will finally whither into oblivion.

TWO

"Rough night, Spark?"

"Just five more minutes," I groan. It seems like only seconds ago that I activated my black market bio-shroud—which I keep hidden in the heel of my boot to cloak my body's heat signature—crawled under the security fence, and crept into my bunk at the trainee outpost.

Of course, that was all after rappelling hundreds of feet down the funnel-shaped desert canyon and crawling through one of the camouflaged openings that are embedded in the craggy walls, hiding the base from view.

How long was I out for?

There's a firm tug on my arm and I wince when I pull it free. The aches of my recent skirmish pulsate through to the marrow.

"What's going on?" I croak, through the dry desert of my throat. Rubbing my eyes, I gradually focus, the first slivers of daylight slicing through my knuckles. Arrah's face fades into view like a disembodied specter.

"We've got visitors."

The lines on her smooth caramel face snuff out my drowsiness. I jolt up and swing my bare feet from the bunk to the ice-cold floor. "Who? When?"

She nudges her chin toward the window where our three other bunkmates—Dahlia, Leander, and Rodrigo—are clumped, peering outside.

My fellow Imposer trainees. Previous Recruits, winners of the past few seasons of the Trials. Arrah is the most recent inductee before me. The five of us are housed and trained together, with the logic being that the more experienced grunts in the group will pass their knowledge on to the others. Each year the oldest—in this case Dahlia, who's First Tier and practically a full-fledged Imposer—graduates to full Imposer status, leaving a vacant spot for the winning Recruit from that year's Trials.

"Convoy," grumbles Leander, who's second in line of succession after Dahlia. He keeps his massive, freckled back to me. "Pulled in 'bout an hour ago." He's built like a series of pale cinder blocks, wedged together into the shape of a mountain.

Dahlia wipes a swatch of window with a meaty palm and presses the expanse of her forehead against it. "All the way from the Citadel, by the looks of it."

My nails dig into the bed frame. If they've sent in troops from the Parish, that can only mean they suspect . . .

"Any idea why?" I coat my words in idle curiosity, hoping she won't notice.

Rodrigo yawns and drops to the floor and into a series of push-ups. One of his obsidian eyes winks at me. "Probably just an envoy…sent to…escort us back…to the Parish…in style…" He spits out each word out with the flex of his lean, tan muscles, which thrust his arms and chest toward and away from the floor with the fluidity of a well-oiled piston.

"That's it!" Dahlia snorts, giving Leander a wink and punching the mounds of his arm.

He snickers as if she's merely tickled him and swallows her hand with his. "We're the elite that can't be beat!"

Then they're roughhousing like Canid pups.

I suppress a sneer. This is all a game to them. They're only a few years older than me, but I can already see that the Establishment has branded its mark into their souls. I wonder which one of their loved ones they were forced to send to their deaths in order to get here.

I wonder if they even care anymore.

When I first arrived here, I thought for sure Dahlia Bledsoe and I would reconnect. After all, our families used to be close back in the Parish. Her mother even acted as a surrogate parent for my brother Cole and me after Mom and Dad passed—before being killed by our so-called Honorable Prefect, Cassius Thorn, all for daring to care about us.

So I could understand Dahlia's coldness and contempt and accept the blame, under normal circumstances. Her mother had been her only living family member, and she was dead now because of her involvement with me. Fine. I get that. But Dahlia had shunned her own mother as soon as she was recruited, even going as far as to deny her the privilege of living in the luxury camps at Haven, where all remaining "Incentives" from the Trials are sent for the rest of their lives—top-notch accommodations, plenty of food, fresh air, a virtual paradise. Instead, Dahlia condemned Mrs. Bledsoe to a life of squalor and disease. That's what ultimately killed her. Not Cassius. Not me.

Rodrigo, who's Third Tier, is still straddling the fence between immature bravado and cruel arrogance. He pauses now in mid push-up, backflips onto his feet, and spins to attention.

But Arrah, she's … she's still pliable, a piece of clay that hasn't hardened yet. I can see it in her eyes, the one ingredient that's missing from the rest: compassion. In another life, we might have been friends.

I stand and stretch, trying not to appear too eager as I saunter over to the window to get a look for myself.

Three transport vehicles are nesting on a landing platform that's rising from the bottom of the canyon: a drifter-class Terrain Trampler with an exposed bed, a refueling air-escort Squawker, and the much larger Vulture-class transport. It's this last one that twists the conduits of my nerves together, making them spark. Vultures are usually used for combat assaults on enemies of the state.

I walk over to Arrah, ignoring the others, who are too busy telling each other what badasses they are. "They wouldn't have sent an envoy all the way to a trainee encampment in the Fringelands just to escort us back to the Parish, would they?" I ask. "The Ascension Ceremony's not for another—"

"No." She sighs. "Sorry to disappoint you, Sparkles, but I

don't think this has anything to do with a handful of trainees getting rank promotions." Her voice drops. "Besides, rumor control has it that there was an incident at the pleasure pits last night."

"Oh?"

She's studying my face as if it were a map. "Not sure what happened, exactly, but one of the sentries let it slip to me that supposedly there were deaths involved."

My eyes retreat from hers. "Sounds serious. But what does that have to do with our unit?"

She shakes her head. "*That*, I can't help you with. I guess we'll find out soon enough."

I glance at the ships again. "Shouldn't they have called an assembly and told us something by now? That's been standard protocol since we've been assigned here. Why are they just sitting there? Something's not right."

"Maybe they're trying to figure out just what type of classified intel we should be privy to. Who knows?" Her eyes narrow. "By the way, you wander around camp last night?"

I grab my crumpled tank top from the foot of the cot and pull it over the twilight bruise setting on the ridges of my abdomen. "No. Why do you ask?"

Her lips purse. "Thought I heard someone come in. Must have dreamt it."

Does she somehow suspect me? Did any of them see me? Did I slip up? No. I'm just being paranoid.

"You should get dressed," she says. "It's visitor's day, remember?"

I sigh. "Who could forget the one day a month we get

to video chat with our surviving Incentives for ten whole minutes?" Although not in my case, since my surviving Incentive—my five-year-old brother Cole—hasn't been sent to Haven yet. I just get to receive clinical status reports on how he's holding up, from some stuffed-shirt bureaucrat. But Cole's scheduled to be sent to Haven this week. So maybe today will be different.

Arrah knows this, and she grins at me. "Maybe you'll get a nice surprise this morning." She marches over to the chair I draped my uniform over last night and grabs my fatigue pants. I can hear the jingle of the two remaining concussion discs from inside one of the pockets.

I grab the pants from her and slip them on. "Thanks."

I'm not sure if she heard the discs or if it's just my anxiety getting the best of me, but all I can obsess about as we bustle out of the bunkhouse is the Citadel convoy nesting in our midst. Each second that goes by with nothing happening only convinces me that something *is* happening. Something big.

———

The com room is pretty stark. Curved gray metallic walls enclose a series of booths; inside each booth is a seat, which juts from the wall in front of a rectangular holopad that projects the caller's image and voice and houses its own cam and mic to transmit. Once you're inside the booth, an invisible soundproof shield is activated to maintain some semblance of privacy.

I'm the last to arrive, and I pass Leander, Rodrigo, and

Arrah on my way to one of the end booths. Though I can't hear a word they're saying, I'm almost moved by the animated expressions on their faces. All that arrogance and Alpha-Canid posturing is replaced by warmth and flashes of genuine emotion that can only come from giving a damn about someone.

The irony is, that very same caring is what makes the Imps so ruthless. You'd think they'd be consumed with hatred toward the Establishment, since it put them in a situation, during the Trials, of likely being forced to choose which one of their Incentives would die a horrible death. And maybe they do hate it. But by rewarding the victorious Recruit's loved ones with a life of relative ease at Haven, the Establishment also gives its elite soldiers something to be grateful for.

Not to mention, it retains hostages—which ensures fierce loyalty from the Imps.

I've sometimes wondered what would happen if the top-secret location of Haven was leaked and the Incentives were released. Would the Imposers really want to go back to their old lives? Could they?

And would their loyalties shift away from the Establishment, as a result?

I quickly avert my eyes from my fellow trainees. I can't afford to humanize them—at least not Leander and Rodrigo. When it comes down to it, they're the enemy and will be crushed along with Cassius and the rest of the Establishment if I have my way.

The only other person not teleconferencing with a family member is Dahlia, who's busying herself with an extra set of morning calisthenics instead. No surprise, considering her dad perished as an Incentive during her trials and her mom died as a result of being *my* Incentive during my own ordeal. I wonder what keeps Dahlia in check? As I slip into the last booth, I can feel her eyes on me, burning through my uniform and into my skin.

In seconds, I've activated the privacy shield, submitted to the biometric scans, and placed my own call.

"Private Lucian Spark. Identity confirmed. Now connecting..." the synthesized computer voice announces.

The three-dimensional image begins to materialize in a swirling storm of crackling static. For a second I let myself hope that this'll be the moment I finally get to see and talk to Cole again.

But it's not my brother. The image has formed, once again, into the familiar face of Percy Favell, the beak-nosed rep from the Child Assimilation Services. He proceeds to update me on Cole's physical and mental well-being.

Although it's always reassuring to hear that my brother's doing okay, it's just empty words without being able to see for myself. When Favell pauses from his droning to finally take in some more air, I seize the opportunity to interrupt.

"When can I see my brother? He was supposed to arrive at Haven this week."

Favell looks up from the tablet screen he's been reading and regards me with his beady little eyes. "I'm afraid your brother's transfer to Haven has been delayed."

"What are you talking about?"

Favell grins. "Cole's been selected to take part in a very special program."

Before I can react, the image disappears, the lights come on, and the door to the com room whooshes open. A torrent of stark artificial light cascades through the room and I squint against it.

Then the light is eclipsed by a familiar hulking shape. "Officer on the floor! ATTEN*TION*!" he barks, barreling through the doorway followed by his squatter twin. They station themselves on either side of the entrance like two concrete columns propping up the structure.

Great. My old friends Styles and Renquist. They must have arrived with the convoy.

I spring from my booth to join Leander, Rodrigo, Arrah, and Dahlia, planting myself beside them at attention like a rigid stalk.

Styles's eyes crawl across the room and pounce on me. "Long time no see, Spark," he mutters.

Renquist's tongue flits across his lips. He winks at his companion. "Looks like someone's ripened into manhood."

"Assholes," Arrah whispers through clenched teeth.

"Big time," I whisper back.

"Quiet!" Styles snaps.

Styles and Renquist have got to be two of the most corrupt and sadistic Imposers I know, and that's saying a lot. If they've been sent all the way from the Parish to this outpost at the ass-end of the Fringelands, it's a good bet that Cassius has something to do with this—and that it involves me somehow.

If Cassius walks through this door, it'll really be a test of willpower not to pounce and tear his throat out.

The shadow that falls across my fellow trainees and

me doesn't belong to Cassius Thorn, but rather to another of the Establishment's decadent agents, one I'll never forget. She's tall, with amphibious slits for eyes and small, sharp teeth like rough gems mined from the quarries.

My old drill instructor, Sergeant Slade.

Her smile is a crooked slash across the pale stone of her face. "At ease, Flame Squad."

In spite of the audible release of breath around me, my muscles remain tense, on alert, ready to spring at a moment's notice. The last time I actually saw Slade was during the Recruit graduation ceremony at Infiernos, right before the Trials started. But I'll never forget the sound of her sadistic voice guiding us through the hell of each trial. I have no intention of giving her the upper hand again if I can help it.

She paces the floor, taking us all in. "I regret that we had to cut your family time short this month, but I'm sure you're all wondering why a detail has been sent from the Parish to such a remote station as this." Her eyes impale each of us in turn, like darts. She pauses, in between Leander and Dahlia. "Some of you have shown a certain degree of proficiency in your posts and have proven that you actually might have what it takes to serve among your fellow officers." She cuffs Dahlia's cheek with an audible slap and beams at her.

"Thank you, Sir." Dahlia nods, her face turning a slight shade of red.

"Unfortunately," Slade continues, "it appears that late last night there was a terrorist attack on the Pleasure Emporiums." She sighs. "As you know, the Emporiums play a vital role in curbing the baser instincts inherent in human nature, providing a safe and secure outlet for our citizens to embrace their natural tendencies without interference from the rabble who possess no self-control."

All I can see are the faces of the kids in those tanks at Harmony House. But I just nod and take deep breaths until my muscles relax.

Renquist lumbers over and hands Slade a small packet before returning to his post by the door.

She holds up the packet. "This was found in the wreckage of Harmony House."

Tearing open the packet, she pours something into her open palm. Her fist uncurls, revealing a charred silver disc—one of the concussion charges that didn't detonate during my attack on the Emporiums.

She waves the disc for all to see. "Forensics will be reconstructing this specimen, and then checking the markings and serial numbers against our arsenal inventory." Her face radiates pure hatred. "It's only a matter of time before it leads us to the terrorists."

I never break eye contact.

Slade stops directly in front of me and her eyes narrow. "This isn't the first of such terrorist attacks. Several weeks ago, someone set a fire at one of the plants supplying power to the Fringelands' generators, and a month before that, a precinct office was fire-bombed. In each instance, a lit torch in the shape of a T was set ablaze at the scene of the crime."

I suppress a satisfied smile. Looks like they've been taking note of my messages.

Good.

My eyes hold against Slade's. "How tragic … *Sir.*"

She glares at me. "Yes. Quite tragic, Spark."

Dahlia clears her throat. "Permission to speak freely, Sir?"

"Permission granted, Private."

"What can our unit do to help apprehend these criminals?"

Slade smirks. "Spoken like a true leader, Private."

"Yes, Sir!" Dahlia puffs out her chest.

"It seems last night's terrorist act was part of a coordinated effort," Slade announces. "At the same time the Emporiums were being hit, a team of insurrectionists overran a medical research facility in Asclepius Valley, murdered the officers on duty, and commandeered the station in their first open action of sedition. Even as we speak, there's a small group of Imposers who were delivering supplies who are now trapped and engaged in a firefight with the traitors. But communications have been lost."

Asclepius Valley? Why would the rebels hit a community of peaceful researchers and their families sequestered on the borders of the Parish … unless they were looking for something?

"This base is the closest to the station," Slade continues. "Unfortunately, the bulk of your personnel have been deployed to investigate and deal with an emerging threat on Infiernos."

Slade can vague it up as much as she wants. "Emerging threat" is code for the Fleshers. Whatever those things were that I encountered while training for the Trials, they're still out there. And growing stronger.

"With time being of the essence, that leaves only Flame Squad to conduct the raid on Asclepius Valley, with a handful of fighter pilots to provide air support." Slade turns her head. "Styles! Renquist! I want these grunts prepped and boarded for the war zone, stat."

Around me, there are hushed murmurs, glances cast around the room. This is it. After all our training and Sims, we're going into real combat.

Slade's eyes sweep the room. "I assure you, the Trials were nothing compared to what you are about to face." She turns her back on us. "Get them loaded for immediate departure."

"You heard the Sarge," Styles growls. "Asses in motion!"

The next thing I know, we're hustling to gather our gear and scrambling up the ramp that leads into the belly of the Vulture craft.

As much as I've been longing to escape this hole and get hands-on into the struggle between the Establishment and the freedom fighters, I never thought it would be under these conditions.

How am I going to face off with rebels, and not murder them while also not giving myself away?

THREE

The Vulture craft swoops down into the canyon of Asclepius Valley, jostling us with its bumpy landing.

My old nemesis Captain Valerian, her lean body already clad in a form-fitting gray envirosuit, bustles through the cockpit door. For a split second, I flash back to that time in the alley with Digory when we watched from the sewer grates as she unleashed a Canid on that poor kid. I can still hear those screams.

Everyone snaps to attention, but Valerian barely acknowledges us, as if we're specks of dust to be flicked away.

She points to the overhead compartments. "Listen up, Flame Squad. Your mission is multifold. Fight your way past the traitors until you get into the research facility. Once inside, dispose of any opposition and retake the labs until reinforcements arrive. Do not touch a thing. It is vital that the insurrectionists not smuggle any of the research out of the valley.

And finally, be careful not to trigger the facility's failsafe. If you do, you'll only have fifteen minutes to get your butts out of there. Now suit up, kiddies. We wouldn't want any blemishes on that sensitive skin. No telling what bio-weapons those insurrectionists have been cooking up."

Reasonable. Except I don't think it's the insurrectionists who have been dabbling in bio-warfare.

Arrah pauses and turns to Valerian. "Permission to speak, Captain?"

Valerian glares at her. "What is it, Private?"

"What about the civvies? Won't they be in the line of fire?" She glances at me, then back. "How are we supposed to know the dif—"

"*Any* civilians in your way are to be considered collateral damage," Valerian snaps. "Now get moving. Keep helmet coms on channel three." As she rumbles past me, she sighs. "One day you'll learn."

The cabin's filled with the creaks and clicks of harnesses being disengaged. For the next thirty seconds we all scramble into our envirosuits and snap on our oval helmets equipped with built-in scanner shades.

"Thanks for backing me up, Spark," Arrah grumbles as she zips up her suit. "I thought *you* understood."

"Ooh," Leander chuckles. "Poor little Arrah's afraid we might hurt somebody."

Rodrigo slaps him on the back. "I say bring 'em all on—civvies included."

Dahlia smirks and shoots me a look. "Just more target practice."

Ignoring them, I lock my helmet into place and stare down Arrah. "Just keep your mind on the mission. You're not going to be helping anyone if you're dead."

Grabbing my own pulsator rifle, I follow the others down the gangplank and into the carnage of Asclepius Valley, which has been transformed from a quaint borough of neatly paved streets into a scorched landscape of pathways littered with bodies.

"Stay in formation!" Leander shouts.

I can barely hear his voice through my helmet over the shrieks and weapon fire. We scramble down a side street toward the research facility.

When we emerge into the remnants of an intersection, the smoke becomes less dense. Searing sunlight bleeds through the dark plumes that smudge the morning sky, providing vivid snippets of the devastation looming all around us. Downed power cables hiss and crack, snaking across the ruined sidewalks. Dark pools have formed in craggy potholes—filled with fuel? Blood? I can't be sure. Most of us are panting like a pack of Canids, drenched in sweat even with the temperature regulators in our suits.

A woman shambles out of an alleyway in front of us. The once-white lab coat she's wearing is drenched in blood. I wince as I catch sight of crimson handprint stains.

"Thank the Deity," she wheezes as she stumbles closer. "We *need* help…"

My mouth goes dry as she staggers toward me, her eyes bleeding and her yellowed skin ravaged by oozing pustules. I can't help but think of what happened to Digory.

"Stay back!" Leander shouts.

But I'm frozen in place as the woman collapses against me, her grip surprisingly strong, her face desperate.

"Please stop the pain..." she croaks.

"Don't worry. We're going to take you back to MedCen and—"

Black blood bursts from her cracked lips, spraying my helmet.

Instinctively, I swipe at my faceplate with a gloved hand as she begins to scream.

"It hurts," she wails. "Stop the pain. STOP THE PAIN!" She digs her fingers into her eyes, clawing, twisting them into clots of gory pulp.

"Move away from her, Spark!" This time it's Rodrigo who's yelling.

Arrah rips me free as the madwoman begins to laugh, hysterical, drawn-out blubbering. "That's better." She grins through blood-caked teeth. "Now it's *your* turn..." Her still-dripping fingers curl into claws and she lunges, grabbing for my suit.

I whip my pulsator toward her, but before I can fire, a searing burst of heat soars over my shoulder and engulfs the woman, turning her into a writhing torch of human flesh.

She doesn't scream. Doesn't make any sound.

Behind me, Dahlia lets loose another blast from her flamethrower before releasing the trigger and shifting the still-smoking nozzle in my direction. "You're welcome."

Rodrigo's holomap lets out a plaintive beep. "The research center's up ahead!"

Leander slaps me on the back. "C'mon! Let's roll!"

The roar of Squawkers zooming overhead drowns out the rest of his words. We run after him, trying our best to keep formation. Explosions rip chunks from the ground and remaining buildings, spraying the air with a deadly mixture of glass shards, blinding grit, and flaming projectiles.

Refugees scramble around us, dodging debris, clutching bloody stumps. One young woman is staggering around, a gore-soaked hand pressed to her abdomen.

Just ahead, another explosion rips through a half-dozen fleeing people. Screams are cut short as heads burst, spewing brain matter like over-ripe melons.

I grit my teeth. No Simulation has prepared any of us for this. At least these people died quickly.

The front of the research lab is a smoldering crater of debris, blocking the entryway.

"Damn it!" Leander spits.

"Any other ways in, Rod-Man?"

The holomap is a blur in Rodrigo's palm as he scans through it. "There's a subterranean loading ramp they use to ship supplies, about a hundred and fifty yards around the corner. From there, we can splice into the freight elevator bank, bypass security, and hitch a ride into the main complex."

"Then I guess we better not waste any more time." Dahlia sprints in that direction, the rest of us on her heels.

The loading ramp dips down at a steep forty-five degree angle, into a thick wall of blackness.

"Great," Rodrigo mutters. "Power must've been knocked out by the blasts."

"Or cut deliberately," Arrah says.

Leander punches a button on his helmet. "Everyone switch to shadow-imaging tech."

The blackness is replaced by a sea of sickly green infrared images. A couple of freight sleds lie crashed into piles, their cases of med supplies strewn across the bay floor.

"Dahlia," Leander whispers. "You and me take point. Arrah and Rod-Man assume flanking positions. Spark—"

"Yeah, I've got caboose duty."

A series of sounds squirm through my headpiece, raising all the hairs on my body. Then something eclipses the sunlight. I turn to glance behind me.

The top of the loading ramp we just came down is jammed with festering people.

"We've got company."

Just like the infected woman who attacked me, this horde is filled with hemorrhaging eyes, some dangling from strings of dripping tissue, some with noses torn, exposing gaping nasal cavities gushing dark ooze. One young man, his clothes a tattered mass of blood-soaked rags, grins through split lips, revealing teeth caked with who knows what.

Then the entire pack is rampaging toward us.

"Open fire!" Dahlia shouts.

The first wave of diseased attackers disappears in a spray of limbs and guts as we hit them hard with volley after volley of blasts from our pulsators.

Rodrigo and Leander make it into a game, deliberately shooting off body parts to cripple first rather than shelve, in a sick attempt at prolonging the *fun*. Dahlia joins them, choosing to fry people with her flamethrower instead of firing kill shots.

Aiming for the heads and chest, I do my best to put these poor people out of their misery as quickly as possible, just like Arrah's doing. No matter how many we shoot or maim, though, they just keep coming, wave after wave.

"Fall back into the loading bay," Leander commands.

That's when the infected who've been lurking in the darkness begin to drop from the ceiling pipes and lumber out from behind pillars. We're trapped and outnumbered.

"There're too many of 'em!" Rodrigo yells.

"Get to the freight elevator!" I cry.

Droves of infected people swarm into the bay, forcing us to scatter. I dive behind an overturned supply crate and something brushes against me, causing my muscles to tense until I realize it's Arrah, crouched beside me.

Crack!

A man crouches on the crate right above our heads, what's left of his nasal cartilage sniffing the air. Beads of saliva drip from his open mouth onto my faceplate.

Gripping Arrah's gloved hand in mine, I tiptoe one hundred and eighty degrees around the crate and spot Rodrigo hugging one side of a downed freight sled to our right. On the opposite side of the sled that Rodrigo's hidden behind, an obscene mass of groping, sniffing, clawing people is slowly making its way around to him from his blind side.

"Rod-Man! What're you waiting for?" I hiss into my helmet mic. "Move, damn it."

But he doesn't move a muscle. No reaction at all.

The contaminated horde is practically nipping at Rodrigo's boots. In a few seconds, it won't make any difference whether we warn him or not.

"His com unit must be damaged," I say to Arrah. "I'm going after him."

I lunge forward but snap back as if bound by a giant rubber band. It's Leander's steel arm around my waist, pulling me back into the shadows against the brick wall of his chest. "You'll give away our position, Spark."

A skull peers at us from our left. No. It's Dahlia, her eyes deep canyons, her mouth opened in a silent shout. She jabs a finger in the direction of the freight elevator and the expression on her face is clear.

We gotta move. Now.

I thrust my hand into the darkness and pick up the first thing I touch. I wince. It's a severed foot. At least it's still encased in a ragged work boot. I hurl it across the gulf. My grisly projectile grazes the side of Rodrigo's helmet.

A twisting shadow falls over Rodrigo. He whirls, weapon raised. *Die, Mother F—*"

BLAM! BLAM! BLAM!

The deadly spray of Rodrigo's weapon fills the claustrophobic space with a deafening roar. Body parts fly as our attackers scatter in every direction.

"Get your asses to the freight elevator!" Leander shouts as he sprints from our hiding place. I start after him, but turn when I hear a moan behind me.

Arrah's on her knees, clutching her left thigh. Dark streaks spill from the wound onto her hand.

"Friendly fire," she groans.

Right behind her, the twisting bodies of more infected people approach, making those sickening sloshing, slurping, and crunching sounds that drown out everything—the weapons blasts, the pounding of the blood through my veins...

Aiming my own pulsator, my finger tightens on the trigger repeatedly. Energy bursts find their targets and the survivors scramble.

Arrah and I collapse into each other's arms.

Through the swirl of emergency beacons, I see the contaminated horde all around us in a nightmarish strobe, wriggling out of the walls and ceiling, more and more, too many to stop before we run out of ammo.

I can't get my brain around it. It's all wrong. Slade said the rebels had taken over the facility, but these are obviously victims. And I'll bet my life that this outbreak is the Establishment's doing.

"Rip out their livers and make them eat!" a voice bellows, prickling every hair on my body.

I'm not sure who shouted that, but we're not sticking around long enough to find out. I pry myself from Arrah's grip and drag her to her feet. "We're outta here!"

"Spark! Arrah!" Dahlia cries from up ahead. "We haven't got all day!"

Slinging Arrah's arm over my shoulder, I start running toward the freight elevator. I can hear the awful sounds of our pursuers not too far behind us, grinding through my brain, getting louder and louder.

"*What* have they done to these people?" Arrah's voice

flares in my helmet speakers. I'm too breathless to respond, and just as concerned with the *why*.

Up ahead, Leander, Rodrigo, and Dahlia are waiting for us by the elevator bank. Rodrigo's got the access panel open and is busy rewiring it, trying to bypass security, while Dahlia and Leander flank him, firing at any contaminated that venture too close.

Leander barely stops firing when he recognizes Arrah and me. His eyes bulge. "*Don't* look back! Keep running!"

A pang of guilt hits me. Leander and the others are Establishment, and they're waiting for me. Would I hesitate to leave any of *them* behind?

As Arrah and I reach them, Rodrigo connects two sparking wires together. "That's it, baby." The elevator doors grind open and we spill inside, just before dark shadows smother us.

Rodrigo jams his gloved palm against the elevator's key pad and the doors clang shut, sealing the horde out.

Leander grins through a blood-speckled face and elbows me in the ribs. "Everyone having fun yet?"

FOUR

With a stomach-curdling lurch, the elevator begins its descent into the bowels of the research center. The lights flash on the floor indicator at dizzying speed, creating a strobe effect. I shut my eyes. A brief flash of memory assaults my senses. I'm on a different elevator, descending into the depths of the Skein on my way to begin the Trials. Instead of my fellow trainees, I'm surrounded by the four other Recruits, all with bowed heads. Cypress, Gideon, Ophelia, and...

Digory.

This time my chest lurches. My blood's like a mallet pummeling the inside of my temples. Dead. They're all dead. And there's nothing I can do for them now but exact justice on their murderers.

My eyes spring open.

An alarm blares.

I brace against the side of the car. "What's *that* all about?"

"Everyone remain at attention!" Leander barks.

The elevator brakes suddenly, bouncing to a stop and jostling us around the car.

The overhead lights flicker and dim.

The doors *swoosh* open. A crimson glow spills into the cramped car, drenching us in emergency lighting.

A voice bursts from speakers in the walls: **Attention! A security breach has triggered the research facility's failsafe device. The entire complex will self-destruct in T-Minus fifteen minutes. All personnel proceed to evac stations immediately. This is not a drill. Repeat. This is not a drill.**

I can't help but notice the disdain in Leander's face flicker into…something else. Is it fear? His hand coils around his sidearm.

A guttural scream that sounds like it came from just outside the elevator doors shatters the silence, piercing my flesh like a skewer.

"Back up!" Leander shouts, drawing his weapon in a flash and aiming it at the opening.

We huddle behind him, drawing our own guns, our backs pressed against the rear and sides of the car. Arrah and I exchange a glance.

I prod her shoulder with mine. "It's going to be okay. Just remember our training."

Leander snorts and gives me a wink. "That's cute, Spark. I'm deeply touched."

Arrah pushes away from me. "I've had more training than you, Spark. You just worry about taking care of yourself." She looks away, her eyes focusing outside the car, her expression unreadable.

Another scream reaches a crescendo, then echoes down the corridor. The crackle of several energy bursts follow it. Someone's firing. But at who? And why?

Dahlia takes a few steps forward until she's standing at the opened elevator doors. "Stay put!" she says to us.

Another yowl stretches through the corridor, followed by several short energy bursts.

Then nothing but the sounds of our breathing and the steady thrum of my own heart in my ears.

Crackle! A burst of static from Leander's wrist com shatters the quiet.

"Flame Squad, what's your position? Over." Even over the static, I can feel the tension in Valerian's voice.

Dahlia peers out the doors. "At the sub-level three south elevators, Sir. Over."

"Now that the failsafe has been activated, your directive has changed. It is imperative that you elude attack, make your way to Med Lab 10, and take Project GX07 into your custody. Then proceed to the emergency escape lift to the rooftop for evac before the station is neutralized. You now have fourteen minutes—" The radio hisses and sputters. "You must—"

Valerian's voice cuts off, replaced by the earsplitting whine of feedback before going dead altogether.

We all stare at each other in silence as the seconds tick by.

"Here's what we're going to do." Dahlia's eyes sweep over us. She reaches into her cache of ammo. "I want Leander and

Rodrigo to assume flanking positions." Before she's even finished, she's tossing them new cartridges.

Leander's grin splits his face like a crescent moon as he catches his. "Yes, Sir!"

He nudges Rodrigo, who locks and loads his with a sharp *click*. Then they both assume their positions at Dahlia's side.

"I want…" Dahlia's eyes bounce back and forth between Arrah and me. "I want *Arrah* providing rear cover." She reaches into her satchel again, tossing wristbands to the other four but not to me. "We won't be completely blind. Activate holotrackers."

She touches a button on hers and a palm-sized, three-dimensional image appears. There's a steady unsettling sound, like a heartbeat, as sonar waves bounce back, revealing a series of heat signatures that represent Flame Squad. Soon the cramped elevator car is filled with five distinct glowing cubes and abuzz with five heartbeats in deep sync with one another as we move toward the corridor.

I wait for my instructions, but after ten seconds or so, it becomes obvious none are forthcoming.

"Aren't you forgetting someone, Sir?" I interrupt at last.

Dahlia's eyes slash across me. "I don't have time for this, Spark."

"But what are *my* instructions?"

Leander sneers at me. "You're too green, Spark. We don't trust you. You're to stay put *here*. Out of the way, and keep the elevator primed and ready to go topside." He tosses me a holotracker. "You can monitor our activity with this."

I stare at the tracker, watching as their heat signatures

move farther away from my position—five meters, then ten—until they disappear from range.

That's when I spring into action. I activate the emergency brake on the elevator car to keep it from going anywhere. Leaning out the doors, I peer first left, then right, down the crimson-hued corridor. There's no way in hell I'm staying put, not when something's going on in sub-level three that could point to a potential weakness for the Establishment.

Pressing against the cold, steel walls of the hallway, I slink along quietly, passing empty laboratories on either side. Maybe it's because of all the medical equipment and refrigeration, but the temperature feels noticeably cooler. I pause at a fork. A cloying medicinal smell snakes up my nostrils. I check the holotracker.

But the hologram is empty, like a three-dimensional tomb. No movement—just the steady beats of the sonar pulse racing to catch up to the rhythm of my own heartbeat. I decide to go right this time.

Still nothing on the tracker. How long have the others been gone? Five minutes? I'm about to turn around and head in the opposite direction when the pulse of my tracker quickens and a low *bleep* penetrates the quiet. My blood turns to antifreeze and I drop it. I fumble for the tracker and grab it before it can skitter away into the dark.

But it's not displaying the four distinct heat sigs of the others. Instead, only one signal flutters on the display. Whoever it belongs to is fading fast. Dying.

According to the distance readouts, it's only five meters away, just around the next junction. Wiping away the cold sweat pooling in my brows, I turn the corner. Directly ahead of me, the corridor dead-ends into a door. The sign above it reads *Medical Records*.

As I skulk toward the door, I struggle to apply the brakes to my speeding heart and lungs. I can't let my emotions get the best of me. I can't afford to be that person anymore.

The tracker's heartbeat pulses faster and faster.

I reach out and grip the icy handle. Maybe it's locked. Maybe the decision to confront whatever's inside will be taken out of my hands after all—

CLICK!

The door opens with a drawn-out creak that chisels up my spine with ice picks.

I pause at the threshold, taking in the neat rows of storage cabinets and banks of computer monitors, all dark except for one, flickering in a far corner and creating shadows that crawl across the room.

I can sense it. There's someone else in here. I can hear the shallow rasps of breathing intermingled with the low hum of the equipment. And they're right on the other side of that working monitor.

I peer around the edge of the workstation. The only sound I can hear now is my own heart thudding in my ears.

And that's when something grabs my foot.

It's a man wearing surgical scrubs, maybe in his late thirties, early forties—hard to tell in this light. His short hair is plastered against an ashen face. A hypodermic needle juts from one of his arms. His eyes are glazed with a milky film.

I hunch down and cradle his head in my palm. His skin broils under my touch. "Don't worry. I'm going to get help—"

Both sets of his fingers dig into my arm. "There's no time. The virus... it's too... you... have... to... stop..." He gasps for air.

"Stop *what*? *Who* did this to you?"

His rasps turn into a wet gurgle. His nails claw at my suit. Those eggshell eyes roll back into his skull. Then one last breath wheezes from deep in his throat and he slumps over. Silent. Still.

I choke back a flash of the past... it's the same thing that happened to Digory. The memory of him lying there in my arms, saying our goodbyes.

This is not some random coincidence. There *has* to be a connection.

I lunge for the monitor, hoping against hope that I'll be able test my theory. The terminal is still logged onto the central system. Whoever jabbed the med tech must have snuck up on him while he was entering data, which now gives me access to some of the Establishment's secrets.

My fingers fly over the keyboard, accessing menus, sub-menus. But it all might as well be in another language. Projects and names that mean nothing to me. If only I had enough time. There's a trove of information here that could help me strike strategically at the Establishment's weakest links, as opposed to the random targets I've selected up until now. When I get to an alphabetized list, I begin to scroll down to search for intel about the virus, past the *A*s, *B*s, *C*s, further and further down the list, my eyes flitting back and forth between the screen and my holotracker, hoping I have enough time to find what I'm looking for and escape before I'm discovered or the building self-destructs.

I'm at the *Ss*. Only a few more to go…

Two words stop me cold.

Spark, Cole.

My heart surges. All thoughts of the virus are ripped away. As much as I'm thrilled by the prospect of maybe learning my brother's whereabouts, seeing his name in stark bold-face in an Establishment roster feels like a knife in the gut.

I press the tips of my fingers against the keys, which for some reason feel more resistant to the touch. I press harder and highlight the entry before hitting "enter."

I hold my breath. The screen goes dark. For a second, I think the connection has been severed.

An image of Cole fades into view, accompanied by a block of text. Key words jump out at me. **Brother recruited. Orphaned.**

Every muscle in my body tenses. He's *not* an orphan. He has *me*.

I continue skimming, hoping to find some information on how he's doing, why he's in the medical research database. And that's when I see it. Almost near the end. Highlighted in red.

Scheduled for U.I.P. on 12-24.

That's less than a week away. What the hell does it mean?

The last line in the entry says: **Currently under the tutelage of the Priory.**

The Priory—the guardians of the Establishment's mandated state religion. The ultimate hypocrites. The Priory's creed might be to serve the Deity by demonstrating compassion for the poor, the sick, and the less fortunate, but their only true masters are the Prime Minister and the corrupt political parasites feeding off her power.

The thought that my brother is being brainwashed by this crazed and sadistic cult—and facing this mysterious U.I.P. procedure by the Establishment—turns my blood into an icebreaker plowing through a glacial wilderness. They won't have him. I'll crush every single one of them with my bare hands if I have to. At least now I know where to find him.

Ta Dum! Ta Dum! Ta Dum!

I scramble to inspect the holotracker, which is now displaying a solitary heat signature. Someone's approaching. Coming down the corridor toward this lab.

I jam my index finger on the scroll key, whizzing through the last of the *S*s. But before I make it very far, my finger springs from the keyboard, pausing the entries on the last of the *T*s.

Tycho Syndrome—U.I.P.

Tycho?

Digory.

And once again, the same mysterious U.I.P. designation.

Just underneath this entry, there's another one marked in red: High Level Classification. Bio-Weapons Division. Infiernos. Containment Lab 5.

The ball of my finger highlights Tycho Syndrome and jabs the enter key once more.

Footsteps shuffle on the grates just outside the lab.

Instead of a static image arising, the screen dissolves into grainy black-and-white video surveillance footage that only takes a moment to register. It's *me*. Crouching down beside Digory, holding him in my arms as we're saying our last goodbyes in the darkened corridors of the Skein, just before I left him there, alone. Just after he sacrificed his life so that I could complete the final Trial and save Cole. Just before we told each other how we felt about one another.

At the time, Cassius said that all the surveillance in that sector was shut off. So where did this video come from?

As Digory and my lips touch onscreen, I can feel my mouth burning with the power of that moment. I brush my forearm against my eyes, trying to wipe away the feeling of violation.

I'm glued to the screen, my emotions asunder. As soon as the footage shows me running off, I watch as three figures converge on Digory. The two burly, sadistic Imposers Styles and Renquist, and—

No. Not him.

Cassius Thorn.

He kneels by Digory. My fingers curl into claws and my skin crawls as I watch him grip Digory's wrist. He's listening for a pulse. The bastard's making sure Digory's dead. Then Cassius is up and barking orders that I can't hear. The next thing I know, a medic team moves into camera range and lifts Digory's body into a hovering, transparent cryogenic tube, the kind used for injured elite and military personnel who have suffered grave injury and are frozen until they can be safely revived at a medical facility. Such as this one.

Cassius had Digory placed in cryo? But why? And does that mean his body's *here*?

My heart's trilling at a million beats a minute.

Oomph!

Something slams into me from behind. The impact shoves me into the monitor. It plummets from its stand and smashes in a shower of glass, sparks, and smoke.

Pain jolts through my shoulder when it smacks into the ground. The holotracker flies from my grip. Then I'm rolling on the floor, locked in a scuffle with a nightmarish, ghost-white form. A set of gloved hands grips my helmet, trying to tear it off my head and expose me to the contaminants polluting this place. I grasp the steel-like fingers, trying to pry them loose as I force my eyes to focus on the face above me.

It's a boy no more than twelve or thirteen, clad in a rag-tag envirosuit that looks like it's been patched together from various castoffs. What I can see of his face is as pale as a burial shroud; his dark eyes are cold and expressionless, mere slits cut into face. His teeth are gritted and the veins in his temples pulse.

Before I can reach for my weapon, he kicks it away from my hand. It clatters into a dark corner of the room. What this kid lacks in size he makes up for in skill. But unfortunately for him, I don't have time for child's play.

Ignoring every instinct screaming in my brain, I let go of one of the kid's hands and grope at the med tech's corpse, ripping out the hypodermic needle still sprouting from its wound. I slash an arc in the air with the needle, stopping just short of plunging it into the thin layer of suit protecting the boy's neck.

The boy releases my helmet and I fling him off me. His eyes bulge as he stares at the gleaming hypo. He knows that whatever's in this ampule is lethal. Perhaps he's the one that killed the med tech.

I don't wait. I slide away backward, never taking my eyes from him. My hand crunches against the remains of the holotracker, a casualty of the scuffle. I frown and toss it aside. Leaning against one of the file cabinets, I can feel the energy flowing back through me. I pull myself to my feet.

"I'm not going to hurt you," I say. "Aren't you a little young to be part of the resistance?"

The kid's still sprawled where I left him, amidst the remains of the monitor and the med tech. Eyeing me. Unblinking. Still, except for the rise and fall of his chest. That's when I notice the case tucked under one arm.

Before he can stop me, I hunch over him and rip it free, staring at the text stenciled on its face.

GX07.

This is it. This is what Valerian sent us here for. This is what they want to make sure doesn't get into the resistance's hands. The others are looking for this in Med Lab 10. This kid beat them to it.

The speakers crackle to life again with the warning message: **Attention all personnel. The self-destruct sequence will be initiated in T-Minus five minutes. Proceed to evacuation vehicles at once.**

The boy lunges for the case, but I push him back down,

straddling him until I have him pinned and he's squirming beneath me. What if it's all connected to the same virus that Digory and I were infected with during the Trials? What if Digory's in this facility, in cryo, and whatever's in this case is a cure for the virus?

Running feet approach. There's no time to speculate.

The only thing I know is that if the Establishment wants the contents of this case, this GX07, I mustn't let them have it, even if it means giving it up myself.

I pull the boy to his feet and thrust the container back at him. "I'm on your side. I'm the one that shut down the Emporiums. Now go on! Get out of here!"

He stares at me for a split second with a mixture of suspicion and confusion. Then he grabs the case and flees.

As fast as I can, I backtrack the way I came, through the maze of blinking emergency lights and dimly lit passages, darting into the elevator just as the others round the corner and dash inside with me.

"Spark!" Leander shouts. "We didn't find it. Get us the hell topside now before this bitch blows!"

Behind him, Leander, Dahlia, Rodrigo, and Arrah form a grim tableaux, breathless.

I release the elevator brake and jam my fist against the button that will take us to the roof. We brace ourselves as the car begins zooming up at a breakneck speed.

Rodrigo shoves me. "Where the hell were you coming from? You were supposed to stay put!"

"I heard some shots. Thought you guys might need backup."

Arrah stares me down. "I tracked movement coming from Medical Records. Two heat signatures."

I shrug. "Instead of you guys, I found one of this station's personnel. But he'd been mortally wounded and died pretty quickly before he could tell me what happened. Then I high-tailed it back here."

"This is Flame Squad," Dahlia barks into her wrist-com, mercifully interrupting. "We're on our way topside to the rendezvous point. Requesting confirmation. Over."

A burst of static. "Affirmative Flame Squad," Valerian responds. "On the way. We're not sure we're going to be able to recover you in time. Requesting confirmation that you retrieved the biological agent. Over."

Leander and Rodrigo look at each other and sigh, all trace of bravado gone. Arrah's face looks grim. Before Dahlia can answer, I grip her wrist-com and smash it against the railing.

She glares at me. "What the hell did you do *that* for?"

I shake my head. "Do you want out of here or not?"

The car lurches to a halt and the elevator doors burst open. Then we're all scrambling outside and grabbing onto the transport harnesses dangling from the Vulture that's hovering above us. As soon as we've all grabbed on, the aircraft zooms us away—just as the research facility disappears in a deafening roar and a blinding ball of fire that singes through our suits.

If Digory's body was in cryo in that facility, it's gone now. Forever.

Once we've been hauled back on board, we're greeted by Valerian's anxious face. "Where is it? Did you get the case?"

Dahlia shakes her head. "That's a negative, Sir. By the time we got to Med Lab 10, it was already gone. We searched a few of the surrounding labs but found nothing."

Valerian looks like she's been physically struck. No doubt *her* superiors won't be happy either.

I clear my throat. "I'm sorry we failed, Sir. At least it's nice to know you would have come back for us no matter what."

Valerian surveys the room, then pins me with a glare. "Quite right, Spark. The important thing is that the station and the insurrectionists who attacked it have been destroyed." Her words drip with disdain. "How fortunate for us all."

My gaze wanders to the others, then out the cabin windows to the destroyed facility, then back to Valerian.

"They don't call me *Lucky* for nothing."

FIVE

Along with my fellow trainees, I spend the next few days back home in the Parish under quarantine at Imposer headquarters. We're confined to the stark medical ward of CKT, the centralized knowledge tower located in the Citadel of Truth. I lie flat on my back, tethered to a series of IVs that burrow into my skin like icy worms. Although Valerian and the medical staff assure us it's just a precaution, since the infection that contaminated the research facility isn't communicable except through direct contact with the bloodstream, the concern chiseled into the stone of their expressions doesn't necessarily inspire confidence. Nor does the fact that every time I ask just what disease, exactly, was set loose in Asclepius Valley, all I get is some mumbled gibberish about viral anomalies.

If anything, everyone—ranging from Valerian and the other Imposers to the doctors to my fellow trainees—seems more concerned about what I was doing in Medical Records and what exactly I saw there.

"So when you found the body of the med tech," Valerian asks for the umpteenth time after the incident, "you were never exposed to any viral agents, Spark? Nor did you see any evidence that any data was compromised, correct?"

No matter how many different ways she or any of the others phrase that question, my answer remains the same. "No, Sir. I picked up a stray heat signature on my tracker, heard gunfire, and when the others didn't return, I left my post to investigate and provide backup. The sector was in disarray and the med tech died a few seconds later. Then I returned to rendezvous with the rest of Flame Squad."

In spite of some eye-narrowing here and there, extensive jotting of notes in pads and com screens, I get a lot of nods and "*I see's*," so I figure I'm in the clear. For now.

Pellets of ice *ping* against the window by my bed; hail that melts into slush, frosty tears that trickle down the glass. From up in this tower I can take in the familiar sight of huge, rusty pipes coughing up plumes of obsidian smoke that stain the fresh-falling snow. By the time it reaches the cobblestone streets, the white powder will look more like flecks of grime.

Yep. I'm home.

The other trainees have barely talked to me. The general consensus seems to be that somehow my inexperience and recklessness might have caused me to be exposed to the biological agent, and I'm responsible for everyone having to spend their first couple days back home in the sick tank. This completely ignores the fact that they were all busy wandering around sub-level three, possibly exposed to the same contagion that infected all those other poor souls.

But I think their mood has more to do with the unsettling ramifications of what Valerian said, right before I prevented Dahlia from informing her that we didn't find the GX07.

I can't worry about any of that right now. My head's still reeling from the information I saw on that computer. I press my palms against my forehead. Cole, being held by those crazies in the Priory. And who knows what this U.I.P. procedure will do to him.

And that video of Digory. He was actually alive for at least a few minutes after I left him. But if he was being kept in that research facility for study, then I just witnessed him die all over again. It's overwhelming.

The doors to the ward slide apart, startling me out of my reverie. A lone figure enters, holding a tablet. Dr. Marquez, whose snow-white hair contrasts with his youthful face.

Marquez glances around the room, consults his tablet screen, then turns his attention to the display of chart holos projected in the corner. His face is immersed in their shimmering, greenish glow, as if his head's underwater. He waves his hand in the air regularly, leafing through the images as if they were printed pages, using his fingers to highlight and zoom in and out as he studies the readouts. A smile flits across his face that seems as perfunctory and planned as his perfectly pressed cobalt scrubs. Then he's striding toward us.

"So what's the scoop?" Rodrigo calls.

"Yeah, when do we get out of here?" Dahlia chimes in.

Marquez ignores them and stops at the foot of my bed,

which is closest to the door. "How are we all feeling this morning?"

Reaching over the side of the bed, I thumb the button that elevates the headrest until I'm at eye level with him. "Hmmm. Let's see. Other than all the bruising and aching from being attacked by infected psychos at that research facility, barely escaping incineration in the mushroom cloud that destroyed the station, not to mention being sore from all the needle poking and prodding and being confined in a place that increases my possible exposure to contagion, I'm doing great. How 'bout you, Doc?"

A thin smile splinters across his face. "You forgot to deride the quality of the hospital food. It has quite the reputation for being inedible."

"Food's actually pretty good," I say.

"Your tests came back," Marquez says, nodding at the charts. He pauses.

"And?" Arrah gestures with her hands as if she's trying to scoop the rest from him.

Marquez waves a palm and the charts blink out. "Everything checks out. You're being discharged today."

The ward erupts with cheers, applause, whistles, and palm slaps.

Marquez holds up his hands to quiet us down. "The nurses will be here momentarily to remove the IVs and bring you your uniforms. Your squad leader will arrive within the hour to collect you." He pauses on his way out and turns ... to me. "Oh! I almost forgot. All except *you*, Spark."

My abdominal muscles clench as if trying to crush my internal organs. I bolt upright. "Excuse me, Doc?"

"As soon as you're dressed, you're to report to the rotunda on the observation level." His eyes are like two sharp pinpricks. "It seems you have a visitor."

Then he's gone, the doors knifing through the air and sealing behind him with a loud whisper.

The silence that follows is palpable. Even Leander and Dahlia, who'd normally make some crack about the Fifth Tier being coddled, don't utter a word, which in itself speaks volumes. I sit still and avoid their gazes, confident that they're all thinking the same thing that I am.

Who'd come to visit Lucian Spark? And why?

I stare at the nearly drained IV bag still lodged in my vein, imagining that each drip is laced with dread that slowly invades every cell, every artery, in my body until I'm literally burning with anxiety.

What if they suspect what I've been up to? What happens to Cole then?

———

The fact that there are two armed Imposers flanking the lift to the observation level when I approach does nothing to neutralize the acid burning through the lining of my stomach. We trade silent salutes, then I enter, taking in a deep breath as the elevator zooms up and stops.

As soon as I step through the parted doors, they slide shut behind me and the light fades up. The entire room is comprised of clear windows that provide a breathtaking, three-hundred-and-sixty-degree view of the entire Parish as the chamber slowly rotates. Above me, a high domed ceiling of glass shifts from a reflective state to a transparent one, revealing an unobstructed view of the gray sky. The horizon is already soaked in a deep orange twilight bruising to a vivid purple. A flurry of snowflakes flutters toward me, and—to my shock—seems to go through the glass and right into the rotunda with me, sprinkling the room as if with a giant, invisible salt shaker.

I hold out my palm. Instead of a few flakes pooling there and giving me the frosty sensation of holding a handful of slush, the flurries go right through my hand, fading away once they reach the floor.

A computerized simulation. How cozy.

"Hello, Lucky."

The voice freezes me. I turn.

And look Cassius Thorn dead in the face.

He hasn't changed much since the last time I saw him— both of us standing on that ramp, his thick auburn hair writhing in the wind. His eyes, which before his recruitment had sparkled like emeralds, were rotted over with reptilian green. He'd pleaded with me then, his hand outstretched, beckoning me to leave Digory to a gruesome, lonely death and join him instead.

I'd almost succumbed, in order to save Cole's life... *almost*...

Until I realized that aligning myself with Cassius would only have damned my brother.

"I should have known it was you," I finally say. My eyes hold his. Cassius is the one that flinches, a millisecond twitch of the cheek that's gone before I can even blink. He must sense the change in me. Maybe he shouldn't be here without his trusted bodyguards to protect him. Then again, I'm probably being watched by unseen eyes. This *is* Cassius, after all.

"You're looking well. Seems like trainee life agrees with you." His lips curdle into a thin smile.

And to think there was a time when the thought of those lips against mine—I shove the vile memory back in its niche.

"It's not like I have much choice in the matter," I say.

He shakes his head. "That's not true. There's always a choice. If memory serves, I seem to remember you making quite a few during the Trials."

If he's trying to goad me into an emotional reaction, he's wasting his time. "What's so important that it would drive the Prefect himself here? It couldn't be concern for my health."

His footfalls gouge a deliberate path across the stone floor until they stop directly behind me. "Despite whatever you may think, you're always in my thoughts."

The words are like alcohol poured into a gaping wound. A chuckle escapes my lips. "Is that why you let Ophelia try to kill me after I refused your little *offer?*" I snap. "Your *thoughts* don't seem to be a good thing for my health. Do me a favor and forget I ever existed, *Sir.*"

His fingers clamp around my shoulders like talons, spinning me to face him. "I was angry. *Hurt.* I would never have let anyone harm you."

He's so close I can feel the hot flecks of his saliva peppering my face. I wipe the offensive matter away with the palm of one hand and prod him in the chest with the index finger of the other, punctuating each word with a jab. "Don't...touch...me...again...*Sir*."

He releases his grip and backs off. "You think you've grown so much, but you're still that same naïve little boy who couldn't even tie his shoes without my help." His smoldering features cool into a smile at the memory before turning to stone. "You're no better than anyone else. No better than I am."

I sigh. "It's not about being *better*, Cassius. It's about *compassion, humanity*." For a second I remember the boy who fed me his scraps even though he was starving, who shielded me from the cold with his own shivering body. Before the Establishment erased him. The muscles in my face become more pliable. "I went through the Trials myself. I know what you experienced and what was taken from you."

His expression looks wounded. And weary. The silver chain around his neck glints in the light: a pendant bearing two clasped hands. Behind him, the horizon rotates, casting his silhouette in alternating shades of gray and fiery sunset. I spot the banks of Fortune's River, frozen over now, like my feelings for Cassius. The halo of deep red surrounding him gives way and plunges him into the darkness of night.

"You shouldn't pity me..." He pauses and purses his lips. "Save it for all the poor people that died in those mysterious fires that wiped out the Pleasure Emporiums."

He *knows*.

For a moment we just stare at each other in silence. The room continues to spin like a macabre carousel.

"What's the matter, Lucian? You're as stiff as the marble bust of our illustrious founder, Queran Embers, standing in the Citadel's great hall."

"What do the Emporiums have to do with me?" I finally ask, my voice disembodied and tremulous.

"Funny you should ask that. Especially in light of the fact that it's not the first heinous crime that's occurred within the past, oh"—he scratches his temple—"six months or so, is it? Around the same time frame you started your training…"

"I'm not sure what—"

"Now let's see … hmmm … " The muscles of his face contract. "There was that explosion in the outland refinery, which hampered the government's communications systems. Then, about a month later, that mysterious electrical fire that disabled the surveillance and security systems in the agricultural plants." He frowns and shakes his head. "Nasty business. The breach allowed countless food storage containers to be stolen from right under our noses."

He's ticking points off with his fingers now, circling me counter-clockwise even as the room continues to revolve in the other direction.

"And we mustn't forget that horrid incident with the railroad tracks being tampered with on their way to the mines— what? Two months ago?" He shrugs. "Lost a whole squadron of troops in that one." His eyes fix on mine. "Miraculously, the car carrying the prisoners went unscathed and they all managed to escape. If I were a religious man, I'd question the Deity's sense of divine judgment on that one." He brakes directly in front of me. "And finally, the most recent incident at the Emporiums."

I bite my lower lip. "Such an unfortunate loss, to be sure."

"The general consensus seems to be that it's all the work of the insurrectionists we've been trying to flush out."

"But you have a different theory?"

He nods. "I believe it's the work of only one, a terrorist with a single-minded purpose to disrupt our way of life. Do you know that at every crime scene we keep finding a lit torch that would appear to be this terrorist's signature? Despite our attempts to keep these incidents from the public and stir further unrest, news of many of them has leaked, prompting the insurrectionists to begin referring to their new hero as the Torch Keeper." He pauses. "I seem to remember you having a fixation with torch-carrying ladies once."

I turn away from him and press against the glass, focusing on the now-darkening sky. The snow's picked up, pooling on the turrets and streets below like white caps breaking on a dark sea. "I still don't see what any of this has to do with me."

"Each crime scene was within a ten-mile radius of *your* trainee outpost. Talk about a coincidence."

So that's it. He's called this meeting to taunt me before he has me arrested. My muscles clench.

I turn to face him, resolved, calculating how much time I'd have to choke him to death before reinforcements arrived and killed me. "Coincidence isn't proof of anything."

"You're quite right. I've been conducting discrete investigations into each of the barracks you've been posted at to see if anything turns up. So far nothing has. *Yet*."

Now it's my turn to smile. Good. Looks like my efforts to cover my tracks worked out after all.

"You're wasting your time. There's nothing *to* find," I say.

"You can't imagine how relieved I am, Lucky."

The com-link band wrapped around his wrist *bleeps*. He glances at it. "Ah! Couldn't have timed it better."

My elation evaporates. "What do you mean?"

"Regarding the incident in the Medical Records room on sub-level three, I asked to be notified as soon as the analysis of the video surveillance was complete. Before the results are sent on to the Prime Minister."

"What analysis?" My eyes narrow.

"You claimed the med tech was already dying when you found him and that none of the data on the computer system was tampered with before you were forced to flee and return to your squad to evacuate. The facility's video logs are automatically transmitted off-site in the event that the station's integrity is compromised. I had the techs pull the feeds to verify your account. Assuming your version of events checks out, you have nothing to worry about and will be returned to active duty." He sighs. "However, if it doesn't . . ." He lets the thought hang in the air like a blackened cloud.

There's no way out of this. He's going to know I lied. I can't stay here, not with so much hanging in the balance. Even if I have to kill him now and somehow break out, I need to get out of here.

As his eyes scan the data on his tablet, I move in closer, ready to pounce, to dig my fingers in his throat, to make him pay for all the pain he's caused, for murdering the person he used to be…

"Interesting." He looks up, his expression unreadable.

I move in closer, just a foot away, my body tense and coiled, ready to spring…

"It appears the data has been corrupted. Completely unrecoverable." He flashes the message my way so I can read it for myself. "Looks like someone's watching out for you after all."

He puts an arm around me, and I'm still in so much shock I don't have the energy to pull away.

"I'm glad there's no proof against you, Lucky. I've kept my suspicions under wraps. Believe it or not, I don't want to see you go down the wrong path. Because of this, I've decided to keep you close. It will ensure that you don't fall under the scrutiny of others, such as Prime Minister Talon, who won't have your best interests at heart. So I've added you to my personal staff, as an Ensign."

That breaks me out of my trance. I pull away. "What do you—"

"Tonight you'll be assigned your new quarters at the Citadel. Get a good night's rest, because tomorrow you return to active duty." He claps me on the back. "After the Ascension Ceremony, you'll be reporting directly to me, and I'll be able to keep a close eye on your every move."

SIX

"Spark! Hold up!" Arrah calls after me from the alcoved entrance of the Citadel.

But I'm too wired to stop. Ever since the conversation with Cassius last night, I've been desperate to get to the Priory. Cole's running out of time, and the Ascension Ceremony is just a day away. Once I'm trapped under Cassius's relentless scrutiny twenty-four/seven, I won't have another window to make my move. He suspects too much.

Ignoring Arrah, I forge on like a freight train, huffing and puffing clouds of frosty breath instead of smoke. I pull my parka tighter around me, but it's not enough to shield me from the wailing wind's razor teeth that nibble on my exposed skin. I never thought I'd miss the desert as much as I do at this moment.

Arrah's gloved fingers lock onto my arm and pull me to

a stop. "*Slow down*. We're on recon patrol not a relay race, remember?"

My eyes search the horizon. Ghostly outlines of buildings and towers fade in and out in time with the howling breeze. The sky's coated with grayish sludge—smog from the mines and the sewage and electrical plants mixed with swirling snow.

"We've got a lot of ground to cover," I grunt. "If this weather keeps up, it might whiteout soon. I don't know about you, but I don't want to get caught outside if it does."

"I agree. And it could be worse. Leander, Dahlia, and Rod-Man are training on Worm interrogation." Arrah shakes her head. "This is probably some kind of endurance test. But it's not like we have a choice. We have our orders. Valerian was really clear: conduct a sweep of the area, make sure no one's violating curfew, and report back in. Then we can take the rest of the day off." Her eyes flit from her chronometer to the streets, as if she's looking for something, then back to me.

I shake my head, trying my best to appear casual. "If we freeze to death, we don't pass and move on to the next tier."

She smiles and her eyes dart back to her chronometer. "Gotcha." She reaches up and swats frost off my brow. "Nice to see you haven't lost your sense of humor. You've barely said a word since we've been placed back on active duty. What's going on?"

If only I could tell her. She's the closest thing I have to a friend. But there's too much hanging in the balance. And there's something about the way she's been checking the time. What's she waiting for? What's *her* agenda? Trust is nothing more than a set-up that makes you weak. Sometimes it's hard enough not betraying yourself.

I rub my gloved hands together like I'm trying to start a fire. "Can we talk about this later, over a hot meal in the commissary, before frostbite sets in?"

Arrah backs up and points a finger at me. "I'll hold you to that."

I nod and check my chron. "We'll meet back here in . . . let's say . . . two hours and file our reports."

She gives me the thumbs-up. "You got it. First one back treats the other to a hot chocolate with whipped cream smuggled from the officer's lounge."

"Right."

Then we move off in opposite directions.

No sooner is she gone from sight than I duck into the mouth of the nearest alleyway, turn onto Liberty Boulevard, and make my way through the mazes of streets and sewers that cut through row upon row of dilapidated tenements. It's hard to believe I used to share one of these boxlike dwellings with my parents and Cole. That was someone else's life. Someone who no longer exists—like my parents, like Digory. Melted away and evaporated like one of these snowflakes.

And finally I see it.

The Priory.

The stone relic presides at the top of a hill, looking like a charred skull against the stark white horizon. Windows of angled glass cut through the granite, burning with flickering light. The arched entrance oozes darkness down the sloping pathway to the base of the mound. Five spires claw at the sky.

For a place that was built to repel sin, it seems like a natural magnet for it.

And somewhere, swallowed up by this terrible place, Cole waits for me.

The memory of the last time I was here cuts through my brain like slivers of hail. Dad had just died. Mom was left to take care of infant Cole and twelve-year-old me. She'd swallowed her pride and begged the Prior to help us give Dad a proper burial and provide a few meals until she could get back on her feet.

I remember how Prior Delvecchio's face frightened me, his toothy grin, the way he looked at Mom and licked his lips as if he were hungry. There was an electrical storm raging that night and each flash seemed to take an x-ray of his angular face, making it look more like a corpse. Cole wouldn't stop crying despite how much my mother rocked him. When Delvecchio asked to speak with her in private, she handed him to me and he wrapped his tiny fist around my finger.

My mother and Delvecchio disappeared behind a partition. All I could see were distorted shadows, accompanied by the awful sound of Delvecchio screeching at my mother to get down on her knees and pray for strength. Then the sound of ripping fabric, and my mother's screams, followed by a slap. The next thing I knew, Mom came racing around the partition, one cheek red, blood dripping from her nose, her torn work overalls exposing a naked shoulder. Delvecchio followed, his eyes bulging and four claw marks across his face. My mother scooped Cole and me into her arms and as we ran out into the torrential rain, Delvecchio's angry curses drowned out the storm. *You stupid bitch. You could have had it all. Now you'll rot like your husband.*

Dad never got his proper burial. His body was incinerated by the state and disposed of in a mass grave. Of course, Mom hadn't wanted me to see, but I'd snuck away, hidden among the rank piles of garbage, my eyes glued to that wavering heap of tangled, twisted limbs, searching for my father's face, too afraid to find it and hoping it was all a mistake.

Less than a year after watching my father burn, and probably as a result of the extra shifts she pulled in the mines, breathing in all those toxins, after Delvecchio refused to help us, my mother was dead too.

I wipe the icy slush from my burning eyes. The muscles in my legs strain with the effort of propelling myself up the mound of snow toward the Priory.

Cresting the top of the hill, I pause and stare at the monstrosity squatting before me.

It probably won't be a good idea to march right through those wrought-iron gates. I'm sure the Anchorites are under strict orders not to let me see Cole. Fine. I've gotten through more heavily guarded places than this before.

Although a monastic order that thrives on other people's pain could prove to be far more dangerous.

I skirt the abbey's perimeter to a side entrance, then duck behind a cluster of brambles. The prickly branches skewer the falling snowflakes.

Two hooded figures emerge from the door, clad in bright red robes that bleed against the stark snow. Between them they pull a wooden cart heaped with what looks like piles of garbage, including a cache of old robes. They proceed to dump the refuse in a bin and disappear back inside.

My eyes dart to my chron. I still have time before I have to report in. No one will be missing me—yet.

Checking my surroundings to make sure there's no one else in sight, I scuttle over to the bin and open it. My nose wrinkles. But foraging through trash is something that's been a part of my life so long, I barely notice as my hands dive in and pull out an Anchorite garment. A few stains, maybe a tear or two, but hopefully no one will notice before I find Cole and get him out of there.

Slipping on the cassock and drawing the hood over my head, I approach the door and try it. Locked. No problem. Good thing it's one of those ancient jobs, splintering wood and rusty keyhole. A minute later, after a few quick jabs with the pincers in my utility kit, I'm rewarded with a click.

I pull the door open, cringing as it squeaks and creaks. I pause and hold my breath, listening for approaching footsteps. There aren't any. I exhale a plume of frost and inch the door open a little more, just enough to squeeze my body through, and ease it closed behind me as quietly as possible.

After the blinding brightness of the snowstorm, it takes me a few seconds to get my bearings.

There's no one around. All's quiet except for a mournful cadence of far-off chanting that weaves through the shafts of light radiating from the stained-glass windows. Vaulted ceilings tower overhead. As my feet pad against the plush carpet, the flickering of sweating candelabras stretch my shadow down the long, wide corridor—past grand fireplaces with gilded mantels, elaborate hand-knit tapestries, and glass cases filled with jewel-encrusted diadems. The trinkets in this place alone could feed the entire population of the Parish indefinitely.

I wind through spiraling stairs, searching, ducking into the occasional alcove for cover from hooded passersby. The Anchorites glide along on hover discs like bloody specters, exchanging wordless nods with one another before floating past me.

The deeper I travel into the Priory's bowels, the louder the chanting becomes. I finally find myself on a balcony that overlooks a gathering of the monks. I hide behind a pillar. They look like a mass of flames, all on their knees facing an altar of sparkling gold. Above the altar, a stained-glass mural depicts a flowing figure in white, arms outstretched.

The Deity.

Below this figure, tumbling into a pit, the mural shows two mythical beasts. One resembles the galloping caballus, except that it seems deformed somehow, smaller—with tinier hoofs, no flowing mane, longer ears, larger eyes, and a sparse tail except for the tuft at the end. The other beast is much larger, a grayish behemoth with large, flapping ears, sharp tusks, and a long curling snout.

The stained glass comes to life as the holographic projectors embedded in the crystal panes are activated. The two animals bite and tear at each other, even as they fall into darkness. The glass turns black as night, then burns bright with an intense white light.

"Behold," says a hooded monk from the pulpit. "The Great Deity cast down his mightiest angels, whose lust for power and greed led to the Great War of Ashes that destroyed the Holy Land of Usofa. As punishment, they were transformed into the Beasts known as Asinus and Elephantidae, forever condemned to the eternal darkness. Because of their grievous sin, no one shall ever reap any rewards that set them higher than the rest. So spaketh the Deity."

"The Deity's words shall bind us," the gathered Anchorites chant in response.

I shake my head. Nonsensical stories, used to frighten and control the ignorant.

Darting between the stone columns, I pause at the landing of a spiral staircase just in time to hear a hovering sentry Anchorite whisper to his companion, "The child upstairs..." before they glide past and disappear round a bend.

It feels like a hammer is pounding nails into my heart as I dart up the steps. Two of the monks are standing sentinel beside the entrance to an open room that's filled with beds. A dormitory. I pull the hood farther over my head and nod, striding inside as if I belong there.

Unlike the rest of the Priory, the décor is sparse in here. Empty beds line the walls on either side. My eyes strain through the gloom as I cut between them, searching for some signs of life.

I reach the last bed, which is likewise empty. He's not here. I feel crushed, as if someone's cast *me* down a dark pit with no hope of ever climbing my way out again.

That's when I hear the soft sound of sniffling. I look up.

Cole is wedged into a corner of the room. He's sitting on the floor, staring out the window at the snow-smothered landscape.

Suddenly everything else—my training, the covert hits on Establishment targets, even the business with the virus—none of that seems as important.

I close the gap between us, resisting the urge to startle him from behind with a huge hug. "Cole," I whisper. "It's me. I'm here."

He turns away from the flurries glancing off the window and fixes his gaze on me, rubbing his large coffee eyes as if he were awakening from a dream. "Lucky?"

Then I scoop him up into my arms and squeeze him tight, whirling him around for good measure. "You're getting heavy, buddy!"

"What took you so long?" he whispers in my ear.

"You know me. I'm always getting lost."

"But you still always find me." He squeezes me back.

"I missed you so much!"

"Missed you *more*!"

I set him on his feet and kneel in front of him, stroking his hair, examining his face, holding his hands. "Are you okay? Did they hurt you?"

He shrugs, something I don't remember him doing much of. "I'm okay. They try to be scary, but it only works a little bit. So then I think of the stories you told me and it gets better."

He looks so grown up. Like a little man. I'm elated, but saddened at how much I've missed and how fast he's had to mature in my absence.

"Cole, we don't have much time. I need to take you away from this place. Tomorrow, after the Ascension Ceremony, we're leaving the Parish. Do they watch you every minute?

The Ascension Ceremony will be done by noon, and the crowds will give us a diversion. Do you think you can sneak down and meet me by the side entrance at noon? That's when the—"

"I know! I know! That's when the sun's bright and both arrows are pointing at the one and the two and the clock gongs twelve times! I'm not a baby! I'm *five*!"

I grin and ruffle his hair. "Of course." I reach into my pocket and pull out a spare chronometer. "Sorry I missed your birthday. This is for you."

His eyes flare. "Oooh! What's that?"

"This will make it easier for you to remember. Just in case you don't hear the gongs. When the display says One Two Zero Zero, I'll be waiting right outside and I'll take you with me." I place the chronometer into his small palm. "But you have to hide this and make sure no one sees it."

He stuffs the chron into a slit on the side of his mattress. "I know how to hide things! Remember when we used to hide the story of the Lady under the floorboards back home?" His eyes are glistening with the memory now and he wipes them with his arm.

"Yes, I remember." How could I ever forget reading Cole his favorite tale—the forbidden story, which I'd found in the library archives, of the regal queen who presided over the magical city? Especially after I discovered the towering statue of her during the Trials and realized that she wasn't a myth. She had once existed, just like the now-ruined city she protected.

I hug him again, kissing the top of his head. Then I break

the embrace and hold him at arm's length, looking deep into his eyes.

"Someone's coming," Cole whispers.

I duck into an alcove.

"There you are, Spark. I've been looking everywhere for you, boy. You can't hide from me."

The sound of that voice wriggles around my spine like it did before. Suddenly, I'm twelve years old again.

It's Prior Delvecchio.

SEVEN

My heart catches in my throat. Delvecchio still looks pretty much like the specter that's haunted my memories and stalked me in nightmares over the years. Perhaps a little more gaunt, the grooves in his face a little deeper.

The Prior's dark shadow falls over Cole's bed. "I checked on you earlier and you weren't in your lessons. I was informed you were ill."

Cole sinks into his pillow. "My head hurts."

Delvecchio sits on the bed. His knobby fingers press against Cole's forehead, rubbing it, lingering too long before pulling away. "You feel just right to me, boy. No fever. But we cannot be too cautious. If you are not feeling well, there's no sense in wasting your dinner. I'll have it withheld until you've recovered enough to keep it down." He smiles.

Cole's eyes open wide. "But—"

The cleric leans in, the tips of his fingers edging closer to the chron's hiding place. "I worry for the fate of your immortal soul, young Spark. I hope you aren't lying to me about being ill. Lies are the instruments of sin. I would hate to think of what would happen to such a naughty child in the afterlife." He shakes his head in mock sorrow. "Fire and pain for all of eternity."

All my muscles tense. If he touches Cole again, I'll kill him.

The Prior stands up. "Actually, I came to inform you that you'll be leaving us very soon. It seems there are great plans for you. However, I believe you've been treacherous, and a cleansing of your mind and body is in order."

Delvecchio pauses. The only sounds are the thudding of my own heart in my ears and the moaning wind, setting the windows creaking and melding with Cole's soft breaths. Time is running out. I have to get back before Arrah and Valerian question my absence.

Delvecchio sighs. "During the remainder of your stay here, you will be remanded to a regimen of fasting, coupled with increased chores and the sting of the lash. This will do wonders to clear the mists that can shroud one's conscience." He strides toward the exit and turns. "We shall see just what it takes to purge the evil from your young heart."

Then he's gone.

I wait a few minutes just to make sure it's clear. Arrah must be wondering what's taking me so long by now. Creeping from my hiding place, I slink back to my brother's bed.

He buries his head against my chest. "Please don't go," he whispers.

"I'll be back for you tomorrow, Cole. I promise," I whisper back, tucking the sheet in around him like I always used to.

I kiss his forehead and steal down, excited that I'll soon take him far away from this hell.

———

A few minutes later I've made my way through the maze of echoing hallways and staircases, folded my robe and hidden it just in case I need it again, and am back outside tramping through the snow, my breaths puffing out like bursts of exhaust as I rush to meet up with Arrah. All the while trying to formulate our escape plan.

Late tonight, I'll sneak out of my bunk at the Citadel and make contact with one of the barge operators at the port. He owes me a favor for freeing his brother from the mines in a railway crash I caused. Tomorrow, after the Ascension Ceremony, I'll pick up Cole and we'll hide aboard the ship. Once we've sailed beyond the Parish limits, we'll debark and head west. I've saved enough money that we should be good for a while. Not what I had planned, but with Cole scheduled for this mysterious U.I.P. treatment instead of Haven, I have no choice.

I turn into the alley, just in time to see a figure emerge from the shadows behind Arrah and reach out for her.

"Arrah! Look out!" I sprint and leap, soaring through the air and crashing into them.

Next thing I know, I'm rolling in a heap of tangled limbs, banging against trash bins, spinning in garbage. When we come to a stop, I'm straddling the figure beneath me.

It's a girl around my age. Fair-skinned, with brown hair strangled into a long braid. She's clutching something in her hand and I snatch it from her.

It's a cluster of fake IDs. I've seen this before—she's a Worm. Someone so desperate they'll assume the identity of potential Recruits' loved ones and risk dying as an Incentive, just to have enough money to survive. I'll never forget the screams of the last Worm I encountered, begging for his life as that slobbering Canid tore him apart limb from limb.

I turn away from the girl and look back at Arrah. "Are you okay?"

Arrah's face is rigid. "She came out of nowhere. I never saw ..."

The girl's face brims with desperation and fear. Her body is trembling.

I can't turn her in. The punishment for being a Worm is public execution. But if I let her go, Arrah will know.

Cassius's words taunt me. *You're no better than anyone else. No better than I am.*

"What's your name?" I ask the girl.

"Dru-s-illa," she manages through quavering lips.

I squeeze her shoulder. "You're going to be all right, Drusilla." I move off of her and help her to her feet.

As much as it pains me, now all I can do is sneak up behind Arrah and knock her out. Incapacitate her long enough for the girl to get away. Then take my chances and blame it on a phantom attacker.

We turn toward Arrah. "We'll have to take her in," I say,

hating the thought of what I'm about to do to my fellow trainee.

"Right," Arrah responds, her face colder than the snowflakes in the gap between us.

The girl tenses.

"I'm sorry," I say to her.

She rips free and lunges toward Arrah—

—who gathers her into her arms. The next thing I know, they're cupping each other's faces tenderly, kissing each other passionately.

Arrah looks at me. "I'm sorry too."

I have just enough time to register the gleam of her firearm pointing at me before a loud blast rips through the air, flinging me backwards.

The pain's intense—

Then nothing.

EIGHT

Voices drift in and out of the smothering blackness.

Why did you bring him here?...I panicked. Didn't have much of a choice... Too bad you didn't finish the job... Will he live?... It's too late. He's seen. He knows too much... He has to die...

My eyes spring open. Harsh lights overload my vision, intensifying the throbbing in my head. I'm lying on a table of cold steel, each of my limbs manacled to its surface. Ignoring the aches, I struggle to pull free, but it's no use and I slump back against the slab. The head of the table is elevated, and the glare of lights is making it difficult to distinguish my surroundings.

From what I can see, the room I'm in is small and cramped. Low ceilings. Brick walls. A single arched door, iron by the look of it, lined with bolts and rivets. There's a head-sized opening cut into it at eye level, complete with bars.

A prison cell.

Nothing as sleek or high-tech as those in the Citadel of Truth.

A draft blows through the opening, carrying cool air and the echo of murmuring voices. My head's spinning, and not just from dizziness and pain.

The loud clang of the bolt unlatching knifes through my senses, followed by a drawn-out creak of hinges as the door swings inward. I see her familiar silhouette imprinted on the door's surface a moment before she enters.

Arrah.

She walks up to me but doesn't say anything. She just stands there, expression unreadable but with the occasional tell of a twitch on her lips.

I break the silence. "Come to make sure I was dead? Sorry to disappoint."

The resolve in her face fractures. "Lucian. It's not like that."

I can't help but let out a hollow laugh. "It certainly looks like *that* from where I'm lying."

She sighs, more like her old self again, whoever *that* really is. "If I'd wanted you dead we wouldn't be having this discussion now. I purposely aimed at the awning right behind you, which collapsed and sent you smacking into the wall. Just some bruises, contusions, and a minor concussion. I'm a pretty decent shot. *You're* the Fifth Tier, remember?"

"Where am I?"

"I can't tell you. It's ... complicated."

I pull against the cuffs for her benefit. "It looks like I have the time."

The expression on her face turns grave. "Actually, you don't. Not much, anyway."

"What are you talking about?"

She leans in closer and lowers her voice. "They'll be coming to take you for questioning in a few minutes. Your fate depends on what you know—or don't know." She turns away. "I'm so sorry. I didn't mean to drag you into all of this, but I didn't have a choice."

There's always a choice.

I shove Cassius's words from my mind. "This is all tied into that girl, the one I tackled—Drusilla." The image of them embracing and kissing comes back to me clearer than ever.

She nods. "I couldn't let you arrest her. We love each other. But no one in the Establishment must ever know or they'd use it against us. She's up for Recruitment."

The irony of the situation almost makes me burst out laughing, if it weren't for the pain in her face and the seriousness of it all.

"Hate to break it to you, Arrah, but I never checked in with Valerian after our rounds. They'll be looking for me."

She shakes her head. If I didn't know any better, I'd swear she looks ashamed. "After bringing you here, I slipped back into the Citadel and used your log-in password to check you in, as well as a set of your fingerprints, which I took the liberty of lifting while you were knocked out. Since we're both off duty for the remainder of the day, no one will miss you until tomorrow morning."

Now it all makes sense. The feeling that Arrah was hiding something from me. The fact that she's so different from the other trainees. How she acted nervous earlier, like she was waiting for someone.

No wonder Arrah attacked me. I would have done the exact same thing.

"This place," I say. "It's a rebel safe house, isn't it? You're both part of the movement."

She shakes her head. "I've already said enough. I'm sorry I can't tell you any more."

Someone's approaching down the hall. Several people, from the sound of it.

Arrah's palm presses against my cheek. "All I wanted was for them to treat your wound. I was going to try to make up a story. But you saw me with a gun. They think it's too risky to let you go."

"They? The resistance leaders?" I ask as the approaching footsteps get louder. They're almost right outside the cell. "Arrah, *listen*. I wasn't going to arrest Drusilla. I was going to knock you out and let her go. Believe me. I swear!"

"I want to believe you. I really do. But there's too much at stake. The final decision's not up to me." She hesitates, her face a battlefield of conflicting emotions. "I'm so sorry, Spark. I think you're okay. Even for a Fifth Tier."

"Gee, thanks."

She leans in so close, I can feel her hot breath on my ear. "I'm not sure what your relationship to Digory Tycho was, but I suggest you think very carefully before you answer their questions about him."

The mention of Digory's name triggers a geyser of adrenaline. "What the hell are you talking about?"

Before she can answer, the cell door bursts open and she moves away from me to join Drusilla in the corner. Four figures bustle in, all wearing black hoods over their heads. Three of these people keep their distance, while the one in the center approaches me. Male, by his shape and size. He pulls out a familiar object and dangles it in front of my face.

My ID tags. Mine and Digory's, the only tangible remnant of him I have left.

"These were found in your possession after you were shot." He speaks through an electronic modulator that disguises his voice.

"What does Digory have to do with any of this? He's..." The word catches in my throat. "He's *dead*."

Hoodie stuffs the silver tags back into his pocket. "It doesn't matter. Any bloke associated with Digory Tycho, especially during the Trials, is suspect."

"Suspected of what?"

"Being a traitor to the cause. Conspiring with the enemy."

"The *enemy*? You mean the Establishment, don't you?"

Hoodie tilts his head as if he's puzzled. "Strange words coming from an Imp trainee."

I cock my head toward Arrah. "I don't know about that. Maybe you can get our other trainee here to weigh in on the issue."

Arrah doesn't say a word. She just stares hard, as if willing my mouth to remain shut.

Hoodie ignores my sarcasm. "You were one of the four others recruited with Tycho. The only one who survived, to our knowledge. We need you to tell us how and why Tycho perished."

It's all starting to make sense now. The last time I saw him, Digory told me how he and his husband Rafé, a fellow resistance fighter, had married as part of their plan to be each other's Incentives and not put anyone else's lives at risk during the Trials. Digory had sacrificed Rafé's life, and his own, so that Cole and I would have a chance. But at what cost to his reputation? His tortured words still ring in my mind: *We knew what we were getting into, what the risks were … but Cole's just an innocent child …*

How would the resistance react if they knew Digory let one of their own die for personal reasons? Would they view Cole's life as worth more than Rafé's? Or would they view Digory's decision as a betrayal of their cause, since Rafe's survival as a rebel could be considered more important to the greater good?

If I tell them that Digory did what he did out of love for me, they might not care about his reasons and harbor resentment at his choice. The truth could seal my own fate, and Cole's fate as a result.

But why would any of this matter now?

Unless they, too, suspect he's still alive and want justice.

I shake my head, trying to maintain my composure and smother the emotions swirling inside me. "Look. I don't know what it is that you're after, but Digory died because he was a victim of the Trials, like we all were. I only wish there was some way I could have saved him—"

The words slip out before I can reel them back in. I try

to contain myself, but by the look in Hoodie's eyes, which are growing wide behind the slits of his hood, I've failed miserably.

"So you admit that you and Tycho got to be cobbers during the Trials, did you? Perhaps even closer? Was he secretly working for the Prime Minister? Following orders from the Prefect? Tell us what you know."

I look deep into Hoodie's eyes without so much as a blink. "I don't know anything, except that Digory was horrified by the atrocities we saw committed during the Trials. He seemed like one of the most decent and compassionate human beings I've ever met." I choke back the riptide of emotion crashing against the walls of my chest. I have to be strong.

Hoodie doesn't break my gaze. "So how did Tycho supposedly cark it?"

Splinters of memory embed themselves deep in my skin, tearing through, leaving gaping wounds. "The three of us remaining Recruits were infected with a virus. There were only a limited number of antidotes. Digory was trying to get the last one so he could save his husband's life." Hoodie seems to tense at these words. "I..." I take a deep breath. "I beat Digory to the last one and...left him there alone to die."

And left a part of myself with him to die, too.

"So why were you wearing his ID tag?" Hoodie finally asks.

For the first time during this little interview, I feel like I can finally be a hundred percent honest.

"Digory had no other family that I know of. It wouldn't be right if he were forgotten."

Hoodie is silent for the next minute or so. Then he proceeds to barrage me with questions for the next thirty minutes. Or is it an hour? Two? It's hard to tell. I'm emotionally drained and physically exhausted. He grills me regarding Imposer troop movements, security protocols, weapon caches—but I can sense it's more of a formality at this point. I don't have any vital information to give them, and they know it.

Finally, Hoodie turns and huddles with his companions, muttering and whispering out of earshot. At one point I hear him tell the others, "If we do this, it'll make us just like those mongrels."

My eyes find Arrah, her hands entwined with Drusilla's, her expression grave. We both know what's coming next. A heavy cloak of silence drapes over the motley assembly.

Then Hoodie surprises me by tearing off his hood, revealing the handsome face of a young man close to my age, with pale skin stretched over high cheekbones and an angular jaw. His long wavy brown hair is pulled back and tied. He clears his throat.

The fact that he's letting me see his face can only mean one thing.

His charcoal eyes pierce right through me. "A decision has been reached. You are to be executed immediately."

NINE

I struggle against my shackles. "Please..." But my mouth grows numb and I can't form any other words. The three captors who are still hooded wheel the slab I'm shackled to out into a small auditorium jammed with people, some whispering to each other, others pointing, and more than a few glaring at me. An older, rugged man with a salt-and-pepper beard appears and holds out a hypo to the young man who's been interrogating me. "Make it quick and painless, Micajah," he mutters.

"I will, Dad." Micajah hesitates, then takes the hypo. He turns to me, stone-faced, his eyes locked onto mine as he slowly approaches me. I can feel my life slipping away with each step he takes, and the fear that I've managed to contain behind the wall of pain and anger is breaching it at last, sending a rampaging surge through me.

"There *has* to be another way!" Arrah shouts.

"Arrah!" I gasp. "My brother. Cole. He's being held at the Priory. You have to get him out of there before—"

Two of the hooded figures grab onto me and hold my struggling body in place while the third rips up my sleeve. I can see the vein in the crook of my elbow throbbing, my fear betraying me, pumping the blood so hard it's as if it's trying to invite the lethal invader.

"Let go of me!" I yell.

The one named Micajah stands before me, needle raised. "Sorry, mate."

"*He* was the one that let me get away in the Valley."

This declaration sparks a wave of muttering throughout the crowd as they turn toward its source.

A figure emerges from the shadows. Even without the envirosuit, I recognize him.

It's the boy I let escape. The boy I gave the GX07 to.

The whole chamber erupts in gasps and murmurs of surprise.

Micajah's laughter is filled with warmth as he turns to me. "So *you're* the terrorist that has the Establishment chasing its own tail? You're the Torch Keeper?" He smiles ear to ear. "I was expecting someone a tad older."

"Sorry to disappoint," I manage.

"No sweat, mate." He cocks his head toward the kid. "Looks like the ankle-biter just bought you a reprieve."

The kid glares at him and flicks him off.

Micajah chuckles and turns back to me. "You've proven to be somewhat useful to the cause."

There's an uncomfortable moment of silence. Micajah looks away.

"Release him," the young man's father barks.

In seconds, I'm free of my bonds, rubbing my wrists and prompting more murmuring from the crowd. If there's anyone more shocked at this turn of events than I am, it's Arrah, who runs over and throws her arms around me. "For a Fifth Tier, you never cease to surprise."

"Name's Jeptha Argus," Micajah's father says, clasping my hand. "Please accept our apologies. We had no way of knowing who you were."

The kid takes a step forward. "Corin's the name." He gestures to the figures behind him, who have now removed their hoods. Two guys and a girl, all around my age.

"Boaz," mumbles the tall, lanky one with a slight case of acne.

The other male, shorter, stockier, and powerfully built with a bald tattooed head, comes forward and offers a beefy hand. "Crowley's the name. Nice to meet you, Mister…uh…*Torch Keeper*, Sir." He busts out into a chuckle, but it doesn't sound mean-spirited, so I grip his hand firmly and return the handshake.

The female eyes me with suspicion and hesitates before stepping forward herself. She has short bobbed hair, jet black except for a scarlet streak cutting across it. "Whatever. I still don't trust him."

"Get over yourself," Corin mutters. He turns to me. "Her name's Preshea. But we like to call her a lot of other things." He smirks.

"Keep it up, kid," Preshea says through gritted teeth.

I attempt to ruffle his hair, but he moves away and fires a dirty look my way.

"Enough yabbering, dipsticks," Micajah grunts.

These people are part of the insurrectionist movement? That Deity everyone likes to invoke sure has a sense of humor.

The crowd begins to disperse, moving about like worker ants on a mission. I clear my throat. "Look. I'm not here to interfere with operations. I'm just someone like all of you, fighting for what's right."

"You couldn't have come to us at a more crucial time," Jeptha says. "Now that you're with us, there's a better chance our plan will succeed."

My eyes shift between Jeptha and Micajah. "What do you mean?"

Micajah clears his throat. "Before you got here, the plan was for Arrah to undertake the most difficult part of the mission, since she was the only person we could place close enough to the target."

Arrah shoots me a look. "I'm more than capable of handling myself."

Jeptha shakes his head. "Arrah, you've never undertaken an assignment of this magnitude." He gestures to me. "Spark here has a proven track record of operating under extreme conditions and thwarting the Establishment under their very noses. We can't afford to fail. It should be him, with you as his backup."

"What are you talking about?" I repeat.

"Of course." Jeptha turns back to me. "Tomorrow, during the Ascension Ceremony, we're going to assassinate Prefect Thorn and the Prime Minister herself."

TEN

The night seems endless. I lie on my bunk in the Citadel dorm wearing only my underwear, bathed in a cold sweat. The sheets are a rumpled valley of hills and canyons wedged around my prostrate body. I can only stare straight ahead. Vertigo overwhelms me. I haven't had such a sleepless evening since the night before I was recruited last season.

And now here I am, on the eve of the Ascension Ceremony—the event that will culminate with me assassinating Cassius, along with the Prime Minister and anyone else unfortunate enough to be within a ten-meter radius of the dais.

Ascension Ceremony. I stifle a hollow laugh. The irony isn't lost on me.

Ever since Cassius betrayed Cole and me, I've wanted nothing more than to inflict payback on him. But this assassination attempt is a cold, calculated exercise in premeditated murder.

Sure, I've planned and executed strikes against Establishment strongholds for months now—the attack on the prisoner convoy, disrupting the communications tower, the siege on the Emporiums—all without batting an eye. I was burning with a single ice-cold purpose, blocking out all my emotions...and becoming someone else. Someone who didn't care whether I lived or died in my attempts. After all, the lines between the two were already so blurred, I guessed it was all the same either way.

It was all so much easier when I shut off my emotions and became Lucian Spark, Imposer trainee, the number one terrorist on the Establishment's *Most Wanted* list. But I was a fool to think I could hide behind that persona for too long. No matter how hard you try, how much you delude yourself, you can never escape who you truly are.

The thing is, I'm not sure just who I am anymore.

The briefing I received before I left the rebel cell tonight replays in my head, over and over again.

Jeptha held up a small gold pin, a perfect replica of the Fifth Tier trainee insignia that's pinned to the breast of my uniform. "Even if they sweep for weapons before the ceremony," he told me, "you'll be able to get this through without being detected." He handed it to me.

I turned it over and over in my fingers, examining every inch of the gleaming pin. "What is it, really?" I asked.

He took it back, pointing to a tiny groove in the base that would only appear as a miniscule imperfection to anyone who'd actually taken the time to scrutinize it. "It's a BMP."

"A Bio-Magnetic Pulse? I've heard rumors about those."

Jeptha nodded. "The biological equivalent of an EMP, except this one sends out a microwave signal designed to compromise heart, lung, and brain functions."

"*Compromise?* You mean terminate. As in instant death, don't you?"

He pursed his lips. "Yes. It's quite lethal. The perfect way to kill your enemy while not creating collateral damage or subjecting the environment to the after-effects of messy biological warfare. Just another of the Establishment's insidious creations that we are using against them."

I shook my head. "These are supposed to be in the planning stages, just experimental at this time. How did the rebellion come by them?"

Jeptha hesitated. I sensed he was uncomfortable.

That's when Micajah stepped forward. "That explosion at the munitions factory. The one the Torch Keeper—*you*—set off."

"What about it?"

"During the chaos, the prototypes were stolen and sold on the black market. We managed to get ahold of a few."

I buried my face in my hands. "So basically, who-knows-what weapons might be out there and in whose hands, for sale to the highest bidder. All because of me."

Jeptha gripped me by the shoulders then. "And tomorrow, things will change for the greater good, all because of you."

My eyes remained fixed on the pin. "What exactly do you want me to do?"

Micajah handed Jeptha a large roll of paper, which the older man unfurled on a round stone table. Arrah, Drusilla,

Boaz, Crowley, Preshea, Corin, and I all gathered around to take a look.

A set of schematics. From the looks of it, detailed blueprints of the Citadel of Truth, highlighting the dais in the Town Square below the Prefect's balcony. I didn't need to see those floor plans and layouts. The entire area was ingrained in my mind the day I was recruited.

Jeptha jabbed at an area on the plans, indicating the dais with his index finger. "If the Establishment follows standard protocol for an Ascension Ceremony, and there's no reason why they shouldn't, the five trainees will be gathered here, just in front of the stage. Once the ceremony begins, they will each be called, one by one, to come up to the podium, where they will be greeted by the Prime Minister and the Prefect and have their rank pins exchanged for ones corresponding to their next level of training." He then looked directly at me. "As the Fifth Tier, you will be the last one called up to the dais."

I nodded, understanding exactly how things were going to play out from there. "Once I walk up and receive my congratulations from the Prime Minister, I'm to hand Cassius—Prefect Thorn—my old pin, while he pins the new rank on me. Only I won't really be handing him my pin, but the BMP device."

"Exactly," Jeptha responded. "Quite simple."

I shook my head. "But how does the BMP get activated?"

Micajah cleared his throat and leaned over the blueprints, brushing against me. "A small group of us, composed of Crowley, Preshea, Boaz, Drusilla, and myself, will be positioned right *here*"—he traced an area on the diagram—"by the fountain with the statue of Queran Embers, the Establishment's founding father." He winked at me. "I think it's appropriate that the monster who started it all should witness its destruction firsthand." He turned back to the diagram. "We'll activate the BMP with a remote transmitter." He held up a small black box.

I shook my head. "So the whole square will just drop dead?" I wrinkled my nose in disgust.

Micajah's warm hand moved to blanket mine. "Relax, mate. We measured the circumference of the dais. The BMP has been calibrated to affect only that particular radius. No one in the crowd will be harmed."

His smile radiated genuine warmth. I pulled my hand away, suddenly angry at myself but not knowing why. "Wait a minute. Something doesn't make sense with this plan. "Arrah and I will still be standing on the dais when that BMP goes off." I glared from Micajah to Jeptha and back again. "You didn't say anything about this being a suicide mission."

Jeptha clamped a hand on my shoulder. "It's not."

"But you said—"

He reached a hand into his pocket and pulled it out, opening his palm to reveal two yellow tablets. "Just prior to the ceremony, you and Arrah will take these."

I studied the pills. "What are these, some kind of antidote?"

Jeptha pursed his lips. "More or less. While testing the BMPs, the Establishment figured they'd need a way of counteracting its effects in order to safeguard their own personnel during their use. So they came up with the compound that you allowed Corin to escape the labs with—GX07—which, once ingested, will shield the body's vital organs from the effects of the pulse during limited exposures. We have enough of this antidote to safeguard the team who will be in range of the BMP."

Micajah nodded. "It's kind of like the potassium iodate pills our ancestors used to ward off the effects of nuke radiation during the Ash Wars. And we've confirmed that there isn't any other source of the GX07 for the Establishment to immunize themselves with."

"So you hope," I muttered. But there was something else that was bothering me, more than the possibilities of what could go wrong. "The three other trainees—Dahlia, Leander, Rodrigo. They'll be up there with us. What's going to protect *them* from the BMP?"

I already knew the answer even before Jeptha replied.

"The other trainees are virtually Imposers already. Who knows when we'll get this opportunity again? I'm afraid there's nothing we can do about that."

Leander was already a sadistic bastard, taking pleasure in bullying and hurting others. He'd fit right in with the likes of Styles and Renquist. Rodrigo wasn't much better. But what about Dahlia? She was Mrs. Bledsoe's daughter. How could I be complicit in her death after all her mother did for Cole and me?

I shook my head then. "No. I won't do it. They're just as much victims here as everyone else trampled under the Establishment's boots. They're . . . they're my *friends* . . ."

And in some sick definition of the word, they were. The

closest thing I'd had to friends since the deaths of my fellow Recruits during the Trials.

Jeptha sighed. "We can't force you. But we urge you to remember just what's at stake here. It's your choice."

I hated him in that moment. First the Establishment, now the rebellion. Always forcing me to make hateful choices.

I snatched one pill from his palm, along with the BMP, and jammed them in my pocket without saying a word. I didn't want to look any of them in the eye for fear I might pummel them.

"I'll do my part." I squeezed the words out even as I squeezed past Jeptha and the others, not caring that I still didn't know exactly where I was or how to get the hell back to the Citadel.

Once out of the main room, I was blindfolded by Boaz and Crowley—to protect the location of this cell should I be found out—and led through a maze of passages until they finally removed the blindfold and released me into the catacombs of the sewers. I braced against a wall, ignoring the slime seeping through my clothes and remembering the last time I was down here. I was with Digory; he'd challenged me to look beyond my personal circumstances and take a stand to do what was right.

If only I'd listened to him then, not gone to Cassius... then maybe we could be together now.

Would assassinating Cassius and the Prime Minister in cold blood be what Digory would want me to do? In the end, even with all his talk of fighting for the greater good, he'd let his personal feelings for me cloud his judgment, hinder his duty.

At that moment, faced with tainting my hands with the blood of my fellow trainees, I understood exactly how torn he must have felt—and how much he must have loved me in order to ignore the inner voices screeching about honor and loyalty to the cause.

I would have done the same for him.

Finding the nearest ladder, I hoisted myself up the rusting rungs, slid open the manhole cover, and peered both ways to make sure no one was looking before crawling out into the snow. The refreshing coolness of the flakes was welcome, ridding me of the stench of the sewers. I opened my mouth, relishing the wetness against my dry tongue.

I figured I'd better get moving, if I was going to have time to reach my contact at the port and make arrangements to get Cole and myself away from this hellhole.

The grate squeaked behind me, followed by soft footfalls on the snow-covered cobblestones. I spun. A figure loomed in the alley behind me, eclipsing me with its long shadow.

"It's me, mate." Micajah stepped forward, his smoldering charcoal eyes cooled to ash. "I called to you before, but I guess you didn't hear me." He half-chuckled. "I figured someone better make sure the Torch Keeper didn't get lost on his way home."

I studied the moon hovering through the mottled skies. "Sorry. Lot on my mind."

"It's a lot to ask of someone. I understand."

I shot him a look brimming with all my frustration and confusion. "Do you *really*?"

He held my gaze without so much as a blink. "You think

you're the only one who's had to make difficult decisions? I thought the Torch Keeper was made of stronger stuff than that." He whirled, his hair coming loose and whipping behind him, his torch cutting a flaming rainbow through the gloom before he slammed it into the packed snow and snuffed it out. Then he ignored me and tromped through the side streets.

I plowed through the maze of alleys after him. "Wait a minute. Who the hell do you think you are, turning your back on me? Hold up! Are you listening to me? Stop or I'll—"

He stopped at last, under a torn awning swaying in the wind. "What are you going to do, arrest me, Imposer, *Sir*?"

Our eyes met and held for a moment.

Then his face, stoic up until then, trembled with effort and he broke at last into a chuckle and a lopsided grin. "Now *there's* the fire I've heard so much about."

I sighed. "Yeah, well, keep it up and you're liable to get burned." I glanced around the corner. "I think I can find my way from here."

I turned to go, but he reached out and hooked my arm. "Wait," he said. "I know how hard this is for you. I want you to have this." He thrust a little pouch into my fist. "Maybe this will help make things easier."

I opened the pouch and dumped the contents into my palm. I exhaled a cloud of misty breath.

Three yellow pills. Three more doses of GX07.

Ones that had been meant for Micajah and his crew.

He was willing to sacrifice his own safety, and that of two of his comrades, to ease my conscience.

I shook my head. "I don't think your team would approve, and I don't need to give Preshea another reason to hate me."

"She doesn't hate you, mate. She's just a little overprotective of me. We had something going once, but it didn't work out. She was too afraid of getting close and losing someone else. Hurt like hell, but I eventually forced myself to move on and connected with Rafé—"

"The same Rafé that married Digory?"

He grinned, but I couldn't help notice the dew in his eyes. "Very same bloke. I mean, I know it wasn't a romantic thing between those two. Still, took its toll on us. Ended even before Rafé carked it during the Trials." He shrugged. "Guess meeting the right girl or bloke isn't in the Deity's plan for me. Love is a luxury when there's war on the horizon."

"I can't take this." I pushed the pills back into the pouch and tried to give it back.

But Micajah engulfed my trembling hands with his warm large ones, curling my fingers closed around the antidote. "It'll keep the other trainees safe, and you focused. I'm sure you'll figure out a clever way to get the blocker into their systems."

"What about you?"

"No worries, mate." He smiled. "It was purely a precautionary measure for us. We'll be outside the pulse radius. We don't need them. Why waste these pills on us? Besides, what my dad and the others don't know won't hurt them." He shrugged. "I bet your oldies are overprotective, too."

"My parents are dead."

His smile disappeared. "Sorry. Any other rellies?"

"Just my brother, Cole. Look. I can't take your stash of the antidote. What if something goes wrong?"

He laughed. "With the Torch Keeper at the helm of the ship, what could possibly go wrong?"

Instead of easing my mind, his words filled me with dread. I tried to give him the pills again, but he was already backing away.

"Micajah! I can't accept this. It's too much of a risk," I whispered.

"It's *Cage*."

"Excuse me?"

"Call me *Cage*. Everyone does, except for my dad."

"Look, Cage—"

"Get your sleep, mate. Big day tomorrow." He tipped his fingers to his forehead in salute.

"Why would you do this? You barely know me."

He paused and shrugged. "Like I said. I've been following your brief but impressive career. I like what I see so far. Maybe you're more than a show pony after all." His eyes fixed on me. "Besides, Digory Tycho and I were cobbers. He spoke very highly of you before he was recruited."

I tried to swallow but it froze in my throat. "Digory...was a very special guy."

"His blood's worth bottling, I thought." Cage paused then, eyes narrowing, lips pursing, before reaching into his pocket and taking out one more item: a small, circular holo-disc. "Take a squizz at this."

Taking it, I couldn't help noticing the scratches marring its shiny surface. "What's on it?"

"Tycho kept a journal. After his recruitment, I found it hidden among his personal effects. The final portion's been damaged. Been working on restoring the bloody thing, but no luck so far. That's what's kept me from showing it to anyone else—I need to be sure." His eyes burrowed into mine. "Maybe *you* can make sense of it, mate."

Then he turned and disappeared into the veil of snow.

————

And now, after hours of tossing and turning, I remove the holodisc from where I've hidden it under my bunk. I jam it into my holocam, pop in an oval earpiece so none of the sleeping trainees can hear it, and slide under the sheets. My trembling finger hesitates before hitting the play button.

There's a burst of three-dimensional static as the image begins to glow, and I take a quick peek from under the covers to make sure everyone else is still asleep. Then I turn on my side and position the holo off the edge of my bunk, which is right next to the corner of the room. For a second, there's just eddies of electronic artifacts, and I worry that the disc has been damaged beyond repair.

But then it begins to morph, and I inhale sharply as Digory's face appears.

His bright blue eyes are so full of excitement, so full of life. Unlike the last time I saw them, wrapped in that sickly caul. I shove that memory aside. His tawny hair hangs wildly about his handsome face and he's dressed in the same tattered coat he was wearing the first time we connected in that dingy alley.

As Digory's hand reaches out to adjust his recorder's lens, I can almost imagine he's extending it to me, and I catch myself before reaching out to touch the image.

"Not much time left before the Recruitment Ceremony," he says.

The sound of his voice reignites so many emotions I've forced myself to let freeze over. I'd never thought I'd ever hear him again.

"I can't risk this recording falling into the wrong hands, which is why I'll destroy it after the ceremony," he continues. "I've just made contact with Lucian Spark. I opened up to him about the rebellion—tried to convince him to join." He shakes his head and a slight grin appears on his face. "But Lucian's a stubborn one. I remember the way he used to give instructors a hard time in classes, always pressing them, always questioning the facts." His face goes serious again. "He *really* loves his brother. That's all he has left." Digory's eyes seem to pierce right through the image and into mine. "If Lucian gets recruited today, I have no doubt he'd die trying to save Cole."

Now it's my turn to smile, although it's laced with heartache. Even back then, he already knew me so well.

Digory shoots a look behind him, and, when he turns back to the cam, anxiety fills his face. "I've got to get to Town Square for the ceremony. Hopefully I can make contact with Lucian again before things start." He leans closer to the cam, until his entire face fills the image. I can almost feel the warmth of his breath on my face. "I'll do whatever it takes to get him to join our cause. I just need more time—"

The lights in the dorm flare, cutting through the darkness

like a supernova. I quickly shut off the holocam and stuff it under my mattress.

"Rise and shine, maggots!" Renquist blares from the doorway. "Ascension Day has arrived!"

As Leander, Dahlia, Rodrigo, and Arrah scramble to their feet, I pause for a moment, Digory's face still burned into my vision. When they've left to go shower, I retrieve the yellow pills and the retrofitted Fifth Tier pin from under my bunk.

I'll *never* give up, Digory.

Today is for *you*.

ELEVEN

That morning during breakfast in the commissary, the five of us are treated to a celebratory Ascension Day feast. Everyone's so excited by the festivities that it's easy to slip the powdered residue of the crushed GX07 pills into the orange juice before we toast.

My fellow trainees are all in great spirits. Dahlia actually compliments me on how I look in my uniform, and even Leander and Rodrigo—after all their bullying and verbal abuse—tease me in a brotherly way. I sense something different; a grudging respect that's never been there before. They see me as someone who's paid his dues. I'm one of *them* now.

After we're done with breakfast and Dahlia pulls out her holocam to snap one final group picture commemorating the event, we march single file from the Citadel into Town Square. The growing sounds of the assembling crowd buzz in my ear like a hornet's nest. But no matter how loud it gets, it can't drown out the one thought bombarding my brain over and over again like a strategic military campaign: *Cassius is about to die and I am his murderer.*

Good thing I was able to reach my contact at the barge last night before sneaking back into the Citadel. The barge operator was so grateful for how I saved his brother that I had to insist he take the money I offered. My plans are set: as soon as the Ascension Ceremony is over, I'll slip away in the chaos, pick up Cole at the Priory, and board the ship. We'll head west and disappear for good. Arrah and Cage will never know what happened to me, and it'll be better that way.

The memory of Digory's face floods my thoughts. I wish I'd had time to watch the rest of his journal. But I will, soon, when Cole and I are far away from this terrible place. For now, there's comfort in knowing that not only am I carrying Digory in my heart and memory, but literally, in his ID tag, which is once again intertwined with mine under my uniform. The holocam with the disc is stuffed into a hidden pocket of my uniform. I know it's risky to have it on me, but if all goes according to plan and we manage to escape after the assassination, I *need* to have this, the only image of his face and sound of his voice I'll ever have.

Styles leads Dahlia, Leander, Rodrigo, Arrah, and me through the throng surrounding the dais, Renquist bringing up the rear. I squint against the hazy morning light that's assaulting my sensitive eyes.

The heat pylons embedded throughout the square hum with activity, keeping the area clear of snow. It melts into clumpy rivulets that slosh through the perimeter before seeping into the drainage grates. The moaning wind is crisp and bitter cold. At least it's not snowing. But from the look of the grays and blacks tainting the horizon, it's obvious that another storm is on the way.

We stride past the grand fountain of Queran Embers that Cage showed me on the diagram, and my eyes can't help but dart to the onlookers surrounding it. There's Cage. And Drusilla, Boaz, Crowley, and Preshea. Nearby, the kid Corin is tossing pebbles into the water. Then we're striding past and they're behind us.

They're already in place. Now it's up to me to deliver.

The throng of spectators surrounds us on either side, glaring. It's like they know what I'm about to do. In spite of the cold, sweat beads on my neck and trickles down my spine.

I loosen the collar of my uniform.

Focus. Breathe.

When we reach the first row of the cordoned-off seats right in front of the dais at the far end of the square, we file in and sit down.

The last time I saw this platform was during my recruitment for the Trials. Then, I'd been detached, removed from the entire process, watching from Cassius's balcony and on the jumbotrons surrounding the plaza.

Now it all feels more real. More visceral. It was to *this* very platform that Digory, Cypress, Gideon, and Ophelia were led when Cassius announced their names on Recruitment Day. It's fitting that it should all end in this very same place—before a new batch of sixteen-year-olds are chosen during tomorrow's Recruitment Day ceremony.

Arrah nudges my arm and I turn to follow her gaze. Lurking in the shadows of the turrets and gargoyles of the Citadel, overlooking the dais, are dark figures wielding gleaming weapons. Snipers, armed with assault rifles. Considering that most of the seats behind us are filled with squads of Imposers, this seems like overkill to say the least. I guess that with the Prime Minister making a personal appearance and the recent acts of sabotage against the Establishment, they're not taking any chances.

Ten Imposers trot up to the dais, each guiding a leashed Canid. The hulking black beasts pad up the stairs, and it's almost as if they're the ones leading their masters. They strain against the leashes, burying their large snouts in every nook and cranny of the stage. Searching for weapons, no doubt.

My hand reflexively tugs at my pin, almost as if I'm trying to shield it. Hopefully they haven't been trained to sniff out BMPs, or this little party will be over before it's begun.

After a few tense minutes, the beasts settle down and lead their masters off the stage and through the crowd. People scramble to give them a wide berth, despite being so tightly packed together.

I free the breath I've been holding.

The spotlights flicker to life and arc through the square. There's a burst of static from the jumbotrons as all of them fill with live feeds of the stage.

Trumpets blare, heralding the start of the Ascension Ceremony. All my muscles tense. This is it. Whatever happens, there's no going back now.

Everyone stands. In case anyone forgets to, there's always an armed Imposer around to remind and motivate them.

I crane my neck to look behind me. A procession of hover coaches winds down the pathway toward the stage. Even though their cabs are transparent, the occupants are protected by a safety bubble of repellent energy seals, designed to deflect even the most aggressive weapon's fire.

I flinch. Even through the ticker-tape blizzard I can make out Cassius's profile next to that of the Prime Minister. They're waving to the crowds, who are too terrified not to reciprocate.

Valerian is sitting in the row behind me, along with Sergeant Slade. Slade sneers and turns away, as if the very sight of me offends her. But Valerian's face is a marble bust of non-emotion. I swipe the sweat from my brow. What is she thinking? Does she suspect what I'm up to? *Shut up*, I tell myself. I'm just being paranoid. I try to break the tension with a nod, but her unyielding expression is too unnerving. I finally force myself to look past her.

As the cars get closer, the forced applause builds to a rumble. It feels like I'm at the summit of a volcano, unable to move, waiting impotently for it to erupt and engulf the entire Parish in a deluge of molten heat and ash.

Beside me, Dahlia, Leander, and Rodrigo are whistling and pounding their palms together with verve, as are most of the military personnel surrounding us.

My hands barely graze each other and, though I open my mouth, no sounds tumble out. My eyes snare Arrah's and I can tell she's doing her best to mimic the others, just like I am.

Then they flit to the fountain to catch a glimpse of Cage and his team.

Prime Minister Talon and Cassius are now standing on the dais, along with their retinue of government officials and at least a dozen armed security escorts. I stifle a satisfied gasp—standing behind them is Prior Delvecchio and a quartet of monks, their scarlet robes silhouetting the others like flames. My tongue caresses my lower lip. Good. The pot just got sweeter. If anyone deserves to be up there, it's *him*.

Cassius holds up his hands. Unlike at my Recruitment Ceremony, where he had his back to me the whole time he concocted his ultimate betrayal, this time Cassius is facing me head-on. At least I'll give *him* the courtesy of staring him in the eyes when I destroy his life.

He lowers his hands to grip the sides of the lectern. A smile snakes across his face, cutting across the stage and right through me. "Citizens of the Parish and honored guests," he begins. "As we gather here today to celebrate this time-honored tradition of Ascension Day, it is my great privilege as your Prefect to present the esteemed leader of our society, the person responsible for maintaining the legacy of the strong and just civilization established so long ago by our forefather, Queran Embers, and for forging the pathway to our future." He extends a hand to his right. "I give you Prime Minister Talon!"

The masses burst into applause and cheers, which reverberate through the square like the buzzing of a giant hive. Fear and starvation are truly amazing motivators.

Prime Minister Talon glides across the dais, her limbs long and lithe like an arachnid, the train of her silver, fur-lined gown unspooling behind her like a web. Her dress matches the gray of her hair, which is pulled back into a bun made of braided hoops that dangle at the sides of her neck like twin nooses. The deep wine of her lips contrasts against a canvas of frost-colored flesh pulled too tightly around the sharp bones of her skull—the artificial effects of ten-too-many age-rejuvenation treatments.

She smiles and grabs Cassius's hand with her spindly fingers. Leading her the rest of the way to the lectern, Cassius fades into the background as she stabs at the air with her index fingers and clears her throat.

"My dear Prefect Thorn. Thank you for such a warm welcome," she croaks. Her voice sounds like spinning tires on gravel. "I know that I speak on behalf of all the citizens here today when I commend you on what an exemplary job you've done in enforcing the laws of our government and maintaining order here in the Parish"—her face congeals into sorrow— "despite the continued onslaught of the insurrectionist vermin even now plotting to sow the seeds of discord among our people."

Arrah and I shoot each other a look. I can tell she's just as nervous as I am—even more so, because the girl she loves is here right now, exposed and vulnerable should anything go wrong.

"We need more young people like Cassius Thorn," Talon continues. "More young people to take pride in their government and join us to build a bolder future. That is why this ceremony means so much to me."

She takes a deep breath, as if trying to compose herself.

"The sight of the Imposer cadets we are honoring today, who are taking the selfless initiative to serve their country, fills me with pride as if they were my own children!"

Another tempest of applause. I shift my weight back and forth and swipe at the cold sweat blurring my vision. My eyes dart from Cage and his crew to the snipers, the exits, and then back to the dais, over and over again. The BMP feels like it's burning a hole through my uniform and seeping acid into my chest.

Cassius won't stop staring at me, and I force myself to hold his gaze so he won't suspect what's about to go down.

Once the clapping storm blows over, Talon continues. "Without further ado, I call upon the first cadet to graduate from First Tier trainee to Imposer level." She pauses to study the hovering teleprompter. "Dahlia Bledsoe!"

Cheers rumble like thunder.

Dahlia squeezes her way past me and trots up the stairs to the dais. Her face is unreadable.

Cassius steps forward and shakes her hand. Then he's removing her pin and replacing it with a brand-new insignia.

It's official. She's an Imposer now.

Leander and Rodrigo follow Dahlia in rapid succession, until only Arrah and I remain.

Talon fixes her sights on us. "The next trainee, who is being promoted to Third Tier cadet, is Arrah Creed!"

Arrah shoots me a nervous glance before heading up the stairs.

I glance casually toward the crowd, and see that at the

fountain, Cage is engaged in a heated exchange with two Imposers. He reaches into his pocket—

The Imposers raise their weapons—

My breath freezes in my throat. All I can hear is my heart hammering away at my ears.

But instead of the triggering device, Cage hands them a document. ID by the looks of it. One of the Imposers snatches it from him to study.

The other Imposer is on her radio. Is she calling for backup?

"I now call the final trainee we are honoring today: Cadet Lucian Spark!"

It takes me a moment to realize that Talon has just called me up onto the stage. Everything—her voice, the crowd—it all sounds muffled, as if someone has a pillow over my head and is suffocating me in my sleep. I force my limbs to move, but it feels like I'm slogging through a bog.

The bitter taste of blood oozes into my mouth from the teeth digging into my lower lip. It seeps down the desert of my throat.

I move toward Cassius. He takes my hand in his, but I can barely feel it. He leans forward, his breath against my ear. "I have a little surprise for you," he whispers.

I look up. Behind him, Prior Delvecchio and another one of the Anchorites move apart, revealing the figure standing between them.

Cole.

TWELVE

He smiles at me and waves.

The shock tears through the shroud of numbness enveloping me. Instead of everything moving in slow-motion, it's as if things are speeding up. *This can't be happening what have I done he's going to die right here in front of everyone and it's all my fault oh mother forgive me I failed you both I fucked things up murdered my own brother all my struggles to save him were for nothing I'm nothing but a dumb stupid shit oh sheesh oh no cole I'm so sorry I'm so—*

Cassius reaches in and plucks the BMP pin from my uniform. He may as well be ripping my still-beating heart from my chest.

I clutch at his hand. "No! You can't take that—give it back!"

He gapes at me as if I'm crazy. Maybe I am. "What's going

on with you?" He squeezes the whisper out through a gritted smile.

I risk a glance at the fountain. Cage's backing away from the Imposers. His hand's reaching into his pocket. The same pocket that holds the triggering device...

On the stage, Cole's looking at me, his eyes brimming with confusion and fear. He mouths the words *what's wrong?* The other trainees are fidgeting in their stances. Arrah's shaking her head at me.

Cassius tries to pull his hand away. His mild annoyance has turned to anger. "Let go of me, Lucian."

But I don't. I can't.

My eyes lock with Cassius's. I hear Prime Minister Talon's voice. "Is there a problem, Prefect?"

The wave of fury in her voice drowns out the hubbub of the crowd. Her bodyguards move in on me...

The Imposers at the fountain draw their weapons at Cage's team. Cage is nothing but a blur as he shoves one Imposer against the other and whips out the gleaming black remote.

"Stop him! He's got a bomb!" someone yells.

Screams and shouts penetrate the crowd.

"Give it to me!" I shriek at Cassius, even as my fist connects with his jaw and I rip the BMP free from his grasp. He tumbles backwards.

Cage's jaw drops. He stares at me in horror for a moment, then aims the remote at the stage. The guards lunge for me. But before they can tackle me, I hurl the BMP toward the only place I'm sure will prevent it from being triggered.

Right at the fountain. Right at Cage and his team.

They didn't take the blocker. If Cage triggers it, they'll die.

A heavy weight slams into my back. I collapse onto the stage floor, my head hanging over the edge, my body pinned in place.

Ignoring the pain, I raise my head, looking for Cole. But he's gone, along with Delvecchio. The Prime Minister's guards have already escorted her off the stage to safety. In the square, enforcements have arrived, ringing Cage and his team and seizing the remote from his hands. As the Imposers lead them away in energy cuffs, Cage glances my way, his face a mixture of disbelief and disgust.

I've betrayed him. I've betrayed them all.

I had no choice.

There's always a choice.

"Put him in the brig," I hear Cassius say.

Then I give into the pain, the dizziness, the nausea and close my eyes, wondering if I'll ever open them again, not caring if I ever do.

———

I wake up alone, in one of the Citadel's holding cells.

As I flex my jaw and finger the tender skin, all I can think about is Cole. Where is he now?

There's a bandage covering the crook of my elbow. Once I've checked to make sure nothing's broken, a panicked thought hits me and I check the hidden compartment in my uniform. Digory's video journal is still there.

Sighing, I pull it out and clutch it in the darkness, a

shield against the desperation creeping in. There's no reason they won't kill me now, and probably Cole, too.

What the hell can I do now?

After what seems like hours pass with no one making
an appearance, I decide to risk it and activate the holocam.

Digory's face appears once again, eclipsing the dread of
loneliness.

"There's no reason why Lucian has to be recruited," Digory says, continuing from where I shut the recording off before.
"He can be a very valuable ally."

Valuable ally? Me? We'd barely said two words to each
other at that point. Besides, I don't think Cage, Arrah, and
the others would agree.

Digory's face seems different now. More... I don't know.
Clinical. Detached. "All I need is a little more time with
Lucian and I'll be able to get results. One way or another, as
instructed, I'll find out where his loyalties really lie. If it turns
out he can be trusted to join our cause, I'll personally deliver
him."

My finger jabs the pause button, freezing Digory's face.

So Digory was working with the rebellion to actively
enlist me? And the meeting in the alleyway that morning
was scripted, not just random? But why am *I* so important
to the rebellion that they'd actively seek me out? What the
hell could I possibly have to offer? It makes no sense.

And if Digory meeting up with me that day wasn't
chance, then what about everything else he said and did?
What about the way he felt?

My head throbs and my mouth goes dry. I hesitate for an instant, and then my trembling finger presses the play button.

Digory's expression grows colder than the blood churning its way through my system. "If it turns out Lucian Spark can't be trusted, then I'll make sure he gets recruited myself."

I pause the playback again. Staring at Digory's face. Trying to reconcile those last words with the memories of what we meant to each other.

There has to be a rational explanation. Yes, he made this recording shortly after our not-so-fateful first meeting. He didn't really know me, didn't have deep feelings for me yet. But he told me, later, that he'd cared for me since way back in school, before we'd ever spoken.

Whatever the truth is, it doesn't change the look in his eyes. It's a look I've never seen before. Cold, emotionless.

Who is *this* Digory?

There's movement, right outside the cell, and I turn off the holocam and jam it back into the hidden pocket just as the cell door opens.

Styles and Renquist barrel in. "We've been ordered to take you to the Recruitment Ceremony," Styles hisses.

My eyes bug out of my skull. "The Recruitment? You mean I've been out a whole *day*?"

Styles snorts. "That's right. The Recruitment is already underway." He aims his weapon at me.

Renquist drags me out of the cell and shoves me into a line with Dahlia, Leander, Rodrigo, and Arrah. From the circles under their eyes and the bruises on their skin, they don't seem to be doing much better than I am.

Leander grabs me by the collar and shoves me against the wall. "This is all *your* fault! One second we're getting promoted, the next we're being hauled off and interrogated by our own people about some plot to assassinate the PM, all on account'a that stunt you pulled on stage! Start talking, Spark!"

"Don't forget the blood they drew!" Rodrigo adds.

This revelation has a sobering effect. "Blood?"

"Yeah, blood," Arrah hisses.

I can barely look her in the eye and turn away.

Dahlia nudges her chin in the direction of my arm. "From you, too."

So that's what the bandage on my elbow's about.

Leander shoves me again. "Just what the hell have you gotten us mixed up in?"

"Move!" Styles commands, leading us down the corridors.

"I give you ... this season's Recruits!" Cassius announces from his balcony to the cheering crowds below, just as we're escorted onto the observation deck behind him.

During the whole trek from the prison, I've been imagining all of the monstrous forms our punishment can take. Public execution. Private torture. Even being sent back into the Trials to compete against each other.

But that last possibility dissolves the moment I look at the jumbotrons—and see the faces of the five Recruits standing on the dais below.

Cage, Preshea, Boaz, Crowley, and Drusilla.

Tears stream down Arrah's cheeks and she turns to me, trembling with rage.

Prime Minister Talon steps forward and the crowd goes silent.

"It seems, since our last Recruitment, we have started a trend of *firsts*," she says. "Most of you witnessed the attempt on my life yesterday, carried off in part by the insurgents who have just been selected to partake in the Trials. Being the just society that we are, we have given them the chance to redeem themselves and embrace the principles we so cherish." She braces herself against the lectern, as if in great pain. "But a darker problem has been brought to light. It appears, through the actions of Cadet Lucian Spark, that our trainees also had knowledge of this plot, a fact that has been further corroborated by a blocker that was found in their bloodstreams."

Rodrigo nudges Leander. "What's she talking about?" he whispers.

But Leander only glares at me. "You should be asking Spark. Maybe he can offer you another drink while he's at it."

Talon extends a hand to Cassius. "Fortunately, Prefect Thorn has suggested a perfect way to deal with this distressing situation."

Cassius smiles and steps forward again. "Thank you, Prime Minister. Citizens of the Parish, in keeping with our principles and our commitment to instill a sense of justice in all of our citizens, we have decided that the five insurrectionists shall compete in the Trials to redeem themselves, as planned. However, only *one* of each Recruit's two Incentives shall be selected from their pool of loved ones."

My throat tightens.

"Their other Incentives," Cassius continues, "shall be comprised of the five Imposer trainees: Dahlia Bledsoe, Tyrus Leander, Valdin Rodrigo, Arrah Creed, and Lucian Spark. These former Recruits will now get the chance to experience the Trials from a whole new perspective."

The crowd erupts.

Leave it to Cassius to think of such an ingenious way to appear benevolent while disposing of his enemies at the same time. Cage and the others will choose my death, and the deaths of my fellow trainees, before their own Incentives' without hesitation. And whichever of the rebels prevails in the Trials will undoubtedly suffer a little *accident*.

We're all doomed.

Thanks to me.

Cassius raises his hands to silence the crowd again. "During the Trials, our new Recruits will learn"—he glances at me—"that there's always a choice. Which do they value more, their personal relationships or their misguided cause?"

I step forward but am immediately intercepted by the Imps and pulled back. "They're all innocent. It was all *me*!" I shout.

Cassius sighs. "You're making quite a habit of public spectacle, Cadet Spark."

I sag against the guards.

On the jumbotrons, Cage and the others' expressions seem to burn right through the crowd, singling me out.

By my side, my fellow trainees stare at me with nothing but hatred and contempt smoldering in their eyes.

I'm going back into the Trials.

Surrounded by former allies who want nothing more than to see me dead.

And this time there's no way out.

PART II

EXILE

THIRTEEN

The Eel-class submarine shoots through the dark ocean like a bullet searching for its target. I've been isolated in this tiny compartment on the berthing deck for days now. The sub has stopped at a few ports along the way, to restock supplies, before zooming onward toward Infiernos and the Trials.

I can't believe I'm headed back there again. I can still picture the enormous steel dome, the teethlike spires, the jutting pillars of the deadly sonic fence that surrounds the military training base. Last time, I spent a few months in training before being sent underground for the actual Trials, held in the subterranean labyrinth known as the Skein.

I thought that part of my life was over. But as horrible as it was, at least I had some control over my fate then. The idea that whatever happens to me now, as an Incentive, rests purely on someone else's performance and decisions just emphasizes how powerless I feel.

I never asked Cole what life was like for him as an Incentive, living in fear of the moment when I'd finish last in one of the rounds and have to choose whether to save his life or Digory's. After Cole's ordeal was over, he seemed to block out most of what had happened—a defense mechanism I'm sure—and I didn't press him. Better for him if he didn't remember.

But during those few days we spent together right after the Trials, I got to witness him waking up in the middle of the night screaming, and zoning out during conversations. Innocuous noises like the shutting of a door could send him into a tantrum. Classic symptoms of post-traumatic stress disorder.

Huddled here in the darkness, my brain is my own worst enemy. It grasps at every possible scenario, trying to focus on anything but the growing claustrophobia smothering me.

I'm not sure how much longer I can take being trapped in this tiny compartment without losing my mind.

What few meals I've received have been sent via the vacuum chute on the wall panel, mostly stale ration bars and lukewarm water. At this point, I'd relish the company of anyone, even those bastards Styles or Renquist. That's how lonely it feels.

The only other sound besides my breathing is the steady hum of the steam-driven turbines and generators of the nuclear reactor that's powering the sub's propellers. Then my stomach sinks as the cabin shifts. The air pops in my ears. There's a distinct change in the thrum as the nose of the craft tilts up. The stern planes in the rudder have been activated.

I press my face against the cool glass of the solitary porthole that separates the inner hull from the outer hull. My head feels like it's going to implode from all the tension. Up until now, I haven't been able to make out anything through the blackness of the murky depths that make everything feel like one endless night.

Now I see bubbles. The ballast and trim tanks must be expelling water.

We're preparing to surface at last.

Rising through the darkness are the remnants of an immense city comprised of massive structures; some look almost perfectly preserved. It's as if the inhabitants have just fled, never to return, leaving the buildings undisturbed.

This must be the Lady's city. Or, it *was*. Before the Ash Wars consigned it to the bottom of the ocean.

The Eel maneuvers through the once-towering buildings. Lights from the sub sweep over an enormous multileveled bridge with giant towers that crisscross like an insect's web. What a great civilization this must have been, to have built such a grand system of thoroughfares.

Next, we pass over what appears to be a huge coliseum. It must have seated at least fifty thousand people. But all those seats are empty now, barnacles clinging to them like a cancer, eating away at them until they're barely recognizable.

Then we're rising again. The lights grow brighter until I can make out the ramps and platforms of a docking bay looming all around the Eel.

We've arrived at Infiernos—the one place I'd hoped to never see again in my life.

I'm about to face them all. Flame Squad—Leander,

Rodrigo, Dahlia, and worst of all Arrah. What can I possibly say to erase what I've done to them? And how am I going to look Cage and the other rebels I betrayed in the eye again?

The cabin door bursts open.

Two armed Imposers stand at attention on either side of the doorway. Can't see how I'm much of a flight risk. Where the hell would I go on a sub?

Captain Valerian marches through the hatch and stands in front of me. The expression on her face is so cold, I feel like I'm getting hypothermia just looking at her. I haven't seen or spoken to her since I was arrested.

Though she's always looked at all of us trainees with contempt, I'm surprised to see a ripple of something else in her expression now—is it disappointment? Pity?

Why should I even care? She's one of *them*.

She sighs. "Despite my initial misgivings when you were recruited, I truly expected more from you, Spark. Even when you were a Fifth Tier, I could see in your training that your abilities far exceeded those of your elder trainees. I allowed myself to believe that you had what it takes to get things done. That you would come through under the most difficult of circumstances." She shakes her head.

I lean in closer so that we're practically nose to nose. "Begging your pardon, Sir, but torturing and dehumanizing people is more a measure of cowardice than it is strength."

She smiles, but there doesn't seem to be any pleasure in it. "Ah, an idealist. Not everything in life falls into neat little compartments labeled *good* and *evil*. Eventually everyone has to get their hands a little dirty to get things done."

Before I can ask her what she means, she motions to the guards, who step inside. One of them hands her a familiar-looking duffel bag. Mine.

She begins to rummage through it. "When you were taken into custody, Spark, you certainly didn't have that many items of interest among your personal effects. Just these." She pulls out a set of shiny Recruit ID tags, Digory's and mine, and lets them dangle in front of my eyes before shoving them back in the bag. "And this." She holds out the holocam with Digory's journal.

I feel sick. I knew they must have found it, but I'd hoped that somehow they'd bury it in some storage locker where I might one day get it back before they realized what it meant to me.

Valerian activates the recording, and Digory's face appears between her and me.

"I'm leaving for the Recruitment Ceremony now," Digory says. "I'm confident that before this day is over, I'll be able to gather intel as to Lucian Spark's true allegiances. I think I can get him to trust me…"

Again, that uneasy feeling grips me like a stranglehold. Why was I so important to Digory and the rebellion? No. I don't want to know. All I want is to rip the holocam from Valerian's hand before it can continue. But I'm paralyzed.

"I promise I won't fail you," Digory says, and for a crazy moment I think he's talking to *me*. I wish he were.

The recording bleeps and a small window opens in the lower right corner of the screen, with the words *Incoming Transmission* flashing inside it.

Then it hits me. This whole time, I'd assumed Digory was chronicling his private thoughts, when in fact he was communicating with someone else. Probably Jeptha or another one of the rebel leaders, maybe even his husband, Rafé—

There's a burst of static in the new transmission window, coalescing into the image of the mysterious second party.

The Trials may not have killed me, but at this moment, the image of Digory's superior does.

It's Cassius.

All the hurt, all the pain, the sorrow, the grief—all of it blends together in a molten avalanche.

It's all been a lie.

"Excellent work, Tycho," Cassius says. "I eagerly anticipate the filing of your next report. Your efforts to quell this insurrection from the inside will be duly rewarded."

Digory nods and smiles. "It's an honor, Prefect Thorn, *Sir*."

The image freezes on Digory's face, then begins to pixelate, obliterating any semblance of familiarity. But it's still seared into my brain.

Valerian shuts off the holocam. I half-expect her to be gloating over the pain she's inflicted. But she appears stern, like a parent who's just administered a harsh lesson to their unruly child. She holds up the holo and the ID tags. "Maybe I can get them to let you keep these in your cell."

I shake my head. "They're garbage. Possessions of a dead man. Toss 'em."

As she shoves the items back into the duffel bag, the two Imps shackle my hands together, shove the butt of their neurostim weapons into my lower back, and prod me out of the room.

At least I'm not shackled to false memories anymore. Digory Tycho is truly dead.

FOURTEEN

I follow Valerian through the bulkhead into the corridor. "Where are we going?"

"You're an Incentive now," she says without looking back. "Time to find out just who will be championing you this time."

Considering that I've betrayed every single one of the Recruits, I wouldn't be surprised if they've already made a pact that whoever I'm paired with will lose the first round of the Trials deliberately, just so they can all watch me die as soon as possible.

That is, unless my former trainee companions—now fellow Incentives—don't take me out first.

"Let's go," Valerian grunts.

After having been confined to that cramped berth for days, my limbs ache as I hurry to keep pace with her, the guards' neurostims digging into my back every time I start to fall behind. We head forward, down the narrow passageway, until we reach the hatch leading to the nerve center of the entire craft: the Control and Attack Center. I pause for a moment just outside the CAC hatchway before following Valerian through.

The chamber is much wider than the corridor, running the full width of the Eel. A myriad of screens and equipment banks blink and flash with activity as crew members seated at the consoles monitor screens and gauges.

To my right, several Imps stand watch over a disheveled group of five people who are shackled just like I am. They must be the family members of the rebel Recruits. The only one I recognize is Corin. The poor kid. The fear on their faces sends ice caps bobbing through my blood. That look is engraved in my brain. I saw the same look on Gideon's parents, the Warricks, and even on Ophelia's mother, Mrs. Juniper. It's the look of people who know they're going to die and are just waiting, wondering which second it will strike.

To my left, Arrah, Dahlia, Leander, and Rodrigo stand shackled as well. They look exhausted, their eyes bloodshot, shoulders sagging. But the moment our eyes connect it's like a wave of electricity courses through them, making them stand erect. It fills their eyes with crackling fire that burns right through me.

I look away.

Dead center, Sergeant Slade stands on a raised platform that houses the periscope, the eyes of the Eel. She sneers at the sight of me. "Good. Now that everyone's here, it's time to find out what the Incentive pairs will be." She pauses. "Of course, all the selections have been made randomly."

Her smirk says otherwise.

She taps a few keys on a control panel and the screen dominating the chamber flickers on. Half of it displays images of the five Recruits: Cage, Drusilla, Boaz, Crowley, and Preshea. The other half is a blur of shuffling images moving faster and faster, racing to catch up to the rhythm of my heartbeat.

The first of the Incentive images freezes, then slides into the slot next to Preshea's image.

It's Rodrigo.

Then Dahlia's image appears and moves into place besides Crowley's.

A few seconds later, Leander's face takes it's place besides Boaz's.

Just two more. Arrah and me.

Faces slide across the screen, right in between Cage and Drusilla, hesitating for an instant—and then my image glides into place besides Cage, the one rebel I *personally* betrayed. The Recruit who I'm sure would be more determined than any of the others to make me pay for what I did.

Arrah buries her face in her hands as her image connects to Drusilla's. I'd experienced that same feeling when Cassius informed me that my new second Incentive—replacing Mrs. Bledsoe—was Digory.

Of course, the Establishment has planned these pairings for maximum effect. We're all just pawns in a game for their twisted amusement.

"And there you have it," Slade hisses. Her eyes fix on me and her tongue darts across her lips. "This should make for the most intriguing Trials ever to take place." She motions to the guards. "Make sure our Incentives here are nice and comfortable, regardless of the length of their stay."

"C'mon! C'mon!" one of the Imps barks from behind.

A squad of Imposers herds all the Incentives single-file off the sub. From there we exit the docking bay and pass through an aircraft hangar, heading into a section of Infiernos I've never seen before. With the muzzles of Imps' guns pointed at our backs the entire way, we trudge over a narrow underground gangway. We've been placed in alternating order—each former-trainee Incentive followed by a family-member Incentive. Cage's other Incentive and I are at the end of the line.

I'd expected Cage's other Incentive to be Jeptha. A logical choice. After all, not only is he Cage's father, but he's also a member of the rebellion. But instead I'm unsettled to find myself teamed up with a teenage girl, maybe a year or two younger than me. From the color of her hair and tear-soaked eyes to her facial features, it's obvious she and Cage are related. His younger sister, I'd bet.

Even if Cage didn't already have reason to want me dead, I'm sure he'll do anything to protect his sibling.

After all, *I* did.

Hopefully that blood bond will translate into logical thinking and he'll put aside any possible thoughts of throwing a Trial just to get his revenge on me. The sooner disposes of me, the closer he brings his sister to death. And the longer he avoids getting the lowest score on a trial, the longer I have to plan my escape.

The girl's foot collides with the back of mine and she gasps. I turn just in time to see her teetering over the edge of the gangway, and I grab onto her.

For a few seconds, I'm staring into the abyss below, a landscape of twisting machinery and pipes extending hundreds of feet, flowing through and around the natural rock formations. I hold on tight as I pull her up, just as much to make sure I don't go over myself.

"Thanks," she half-sobs into my shoulder, her arms noosed around my waist.

I wonder if she knows that I'm the one responsible for what's happened to her brother, and for what's about to happen to her.

A dark caul descends over us.

Slade.

She leers at us like she's stepped in shit. "Spark! Of course *you'd* be the reason for the delay!"

I untangle myself from the girl and carefully rotate on the walkway so that she's now behind me, away from the sergeant. "She tripped and almost—"

The snout of Slade's gun shoves into my gut. Sparks of pain rip through me as if I've been stung with a cattle prod.

I double over, trying to snag a breath, wiping the blurry moisture from my eyes.

"I'm not interested in your pathetic excuses." Slade grips me by the hair and pulls me to my feet. Her eyes glance at the chasm, then back to me.

I take a deep breath. I can't make my move.

Yet.

When I look around, I catch a glimpse of the others staring at me. Arrah's face is cold, impassive. She'd probably push me over herself if she could.

Guess she'll have to wait her turn, in line along with everyone else.

I focus on the back of the person ahead of me as the queue continues moving forward.

We reach two massive gleaming doors on the far side of the gorge. They rumble open.

"Welcome to Purgatorium!" the Imposer at the head of the line grunts as we follow him through.

The massive cavern we enter resembles the insides of a behemoth's rib cage. Bonelike support braces made of metal are spaced a few feet apart. They curve up the walls and fuse at the ceiling. Between each rib is a small, transparent cubicle with barely enough room for two bunks.

Holding cells.

Appropriate that they should be located inside what appears to be the torso of a dead body.

As I look closer, I can make out wheels, pulleys and gears just above and below each cubicle, which rest on a series of tracks. Of course. In order to avoid the delay of having to transport all the Incentives to the location of each trial, this conveyer system is constantly moving through the Skein, keeping the Incentives readily available and accessible for disposal.

How efficient.

At the far side of the chamber, an enormous black screen

dominates the wall. Slade marches into the center of the room. "This area is known as the Pen, your home for the duration of the Trials." Her serpentine slits scan the room. "Of course, *some* of you will enjoy a shorter stay than the rest."

Some of the other Imposers chuckle at this, and Slade doesn't bother to discipline them.

"You will all be confined to this common area during the Recruits' rest periods," she continues, "but during each round of competition, you will remain in your cells unless otherwise instructed." She paces back and forth, stabbing each of us with her gaze. "Anyone who disobeys this regulation will be considered to be in direct violation of protocol and will be shelved immediately." She motions to the Imposers standing guard on the upper levels.

"One more thing." Slade clears her throat. "Due to the unusual composition of Recruits and Incentives selected for the Trials this year—namely, the better-than-average skills possessed by this distinguished group of candidates—the committee has agreed that the pre-Trial training and orientation, usually scheduled for a ten-week period, shall be considerably shortened." Her voice echoes through the chamber. "Any questions?"

Cage's Incentive lifts her gaze and clears her throat. It sounds like the last sputter of a dying engine.

Slade's eyes skewer her. "Yes? Speak up!"

"When ... w-will I ... " The girl drops her gaze again. "Get to see ... my brother Cage ... again ... "

Her words trail off into barely a whisper.

I was right. They *are* brother and sister. And I know exactly what she must be feeling.

Slade walks up and hovers over her. She smiles like a mother about to eat her young. "You miss your brother very much, don't you, my dear?" She grips her by the shoulders.

"Y-yes. Yes, I do."

"What's your name?"

"Tristin."

"And you'd like nothing better than to talk to your brother, if only for just a few moments, wouldn't you, Tristin?"

The girl looks up at Slade, eyes barely able to contain their wetness. "Oh, please…"

The Sergeant leans in, as if to whisper in her ear. "Be careful what you wish for. The next time you see him might very well be the last time you'll see him … or anything at all, for that matter."

She shoves the girl away and whips around to face the rest of us. "That goes for every single one of you suffering from a sentimental streak or"—her eyes penetrate mine—"the pangs of a guilty conscience."

GONG!

The sound of the deep clang reverberates throughout the chamber, drowning out the rest of Slade's words and sending a frost spiraling down my spine. I recognize that sound.

It's the call of the Fleshers.

Grisly images flash in my memory. Sitting around the campfire with Digory and the other Recruits during one of our training exercises … the legend of the Fallen Five … trekking through the island wilderness in search of the missing recon team. Then there was that canyon filled with mounds of human bones, skulls screeching as the wind passed through their gaping sockets, and the dark, barely glimpsed horde of Fleshers that chased the five of us.

The room is doused in the crimson glow of emergency lights.

Attention! a voice blares through the speakers. **Possible breach in quadrant seven. Repeat. Possible breach in quadrant seven. Initiating emergency containment procedure. This is not a drill.**

The smug look on Slade's face turns to concern. She jabs a finger at one of the Imposers stationed at the control console above. "Seal it!"

The officer jams his fist onto a switch embedded in the wall. A drawn-out *sssssshhhhhh* drowns everything out as all the cell doors slide open.

Slade gestures at us, then at the holding cells. "Each pair is to proceed inside the pen closest to you." Her panic disappears. "Now!"

Where the Fleshers are concerned, I don't need to be told twice. I grab Tristin's hand and pull her with me. "Everyone inside! C'mon!"

Then we're tumbling through the cell doors, just as they seal behind us.

"Are you okay?" I ask Tristin.

But she's not paying attention to me. Instead her eyes are glued to the scene playing out through the transparent walls.

Imposers dash to and fro, checking control panels, shouting into com units. Across the way, Arrah, Leander, Rodrigo, and Dahlia are pressed against the glass of their cells while their fellow Incentives cower in the corners.

They're all looking at me, and I can tell that they know I've got some idea about what's going on.

Minutes later, the emergency lights switch back to normal and the activity peters out. Slade nods to an officer nearby, who punches the keys of his terminal.

Attention, the voice blares through the speakers again. **Breach has been contained. The facility is secure.**

Slade takes the mic. "Time for you to get your rest. Lights out."

Then the cells are plunged into darkness.

As I lie on the cold floor listening to Tristin's quiet sobs, my mind races with possibilities.

I'm still not sure what the Fleshers are and why they scare the Establishment so much.

But they might just be the advantage I need to break out of this hell.

FIFTEEN

"Rise and shine, people!"

The booming voice is accompanied by a blast of light as powerful as a solar flare searing through the darkness of space. I squint and rub my eyes against the blindness, trying to focus.

The door to our cell opens and one of the Imps is standing there, amusement plastered all over his face. *Ensign Echoes,* his name tag says. It's the officer who was in charge of sealing the outer doors against the Fleshers.

Beside me, Tristin is hunkered down, hugging her knees to her chest. Her eyes are red and puffy, her cheeks stained like a dried-up riverbed. I'm not the only one who didn't get any sleep last night.

"Don't just sit there," Echoes grunts. "You have fifteen minutes to shower and eat." He checks his chronometer. "Fourteen and a half now. Hurry it up."

He steps aside and I force my aching limbs to piston my

body through the door. I can hear the soft pad of Tristin's footfalls behind me.

My Imposer training has taught me to survey situations very quickly. In a matter of seconds, I take in the guards on the bridge; the two exits to the control area, one on either side; and the number of guards on the floor, maybe half a dozen at present. Getting up to the control room will be difficult. But not impossible.

In the common area, the other Incentives are being herded out of their cells by Imps armed with long taser wands. One of the family members, a thin, middle-aged, haggard-looking woman with grayish hair, lags behind the others. A guard walks up behind her and shoves the weapon into her back. Sparks fly. She screams. Then she stumbles forward and follows the rest, disappearing through a passageway. If I had any doubts where to go, all I'd have to do is follow the stench of scorched skin marking her passage.

I risk a glance behind me before entering the corridor. There's only Tristin and Echoes. I don't see Arrah and the others. They must be leading the pack. Good. I'm still dreading what that confrontation is going to be like when it finally happens.

My boots clank against the floor as I examine the gratings both above and below. There appears to be a sub-flooring conduit located underneath me, and ventilation shafts located beyond the ceiling. Assuming the crawl space is big enough to accommodate me, these might provide alternate accessways to the control center, or maybe another way out. As the hallway zigzags on, I commit the maze to memory, filing it away for future reference. Hopefully I still have enough of a future left that it might come in handy.

"Do you know where they're taking us?" Tristin whispers. Every syllable quavers in the frigid draft seeping through the passageway.

"Don't worry," I whisper back. "It's going to be okay." Though I try to disguise the anxiety in my own voice, I'm sure she doesn't believe me. How could she?

Echoes strikes his wand against the wall, where it sizzles and pops. "Cut the chatter, you two."

We turn another corner and my stomach clenches.

It's another cell block. But instead of containing separate transparent cubicles, the walls themselves are enormous pens of reinforced glass, revealing a horizon of human suffering as loathsome as I've ever seen.

On both sides of me, bodies are strewn everywhere, some lying in heaps of tangled flesh, others huddling in clusters, surrounded by clumps of their own filth. Their expressions are so drawn and vacant I'm not sure if they can even see us, or if this glass is a two-way mirror, allowing us to see them, while reflecting the grimness of their living hell back at them and wringing out what little hope they might have in the process.

This is the Establishment's idea of justice. These prisoners' only crimes were probably petty theft due to starvation or standing up for themselves against abuse. Yet they're shipped here to be fodder for the Trials, medical experimentation, and who knows what else.

I swallow hard. This isn't the first time I've come across scenes like this. I still get nightmares of the time when I had

to wade through bodies during one of the trials to find loca-
tor bracelets. I tried not to focus on the agony around me as I
fought to save Cole and Digory's lives.

A little boy's face and palms press against the glass. I stop.
I can almost feel that he sees me. I turn away. There's probably
no hope for this boy. For any of them. All the acts of sabotage
I've committed over the last year—what good have any of
them really done? No matter how many people I might free
from the Emporiums, there are a hundred more that'll die.

Suddenly it feels like an enormous weight is bearing down
on me, squeezing my organs together until they're nothing but
bloody pulp. My skin burns from the rage and frustration well-
ing inside me. No matter how hard I try, I can't save them all.

Tristin's hand touches my shoulder.

A jolt of lightning surges through me, slamming me to
the floor. I look up to see Echoes hovering over me, his prod
still smoking. "I said keep mov—"

I spring up and snatch the wand from him, and his eyes
look like they're going to burst through his skull. I jab the
wand at his throat. "We're *not cattle.*"

Then I toss it at his feet and whirl past Tristin, continuing after the others before I can gauge his reaction.

I don't really care what it is.

The next corridor we enter opens into a yet-larger room,
this one covered in soap-scummed tiles. A series of pipes
jut inward from the ceiling like rusting tentacles. The entire
room reeks of body odor and disinfectant, battling it out for
supremacy.

A communal shower.

The others, including my trainee team, are already in various stages of undress, tossing their clothes in a heap in the center of the room.

"Strip!" The officer on duty spits the words at me like a glob of phlegm.

It takes a little time to pull my boots off my aching feet. Then I slither out of my jumpsuit, pulling down my underwear until I'm standing there naked, trying not to shiver from the cold blast of air prickling my skin.

"Spread 'em," the guard grunts. I extend my arms and legs as he circles my body with an icy steel probe.

Beside me, Tristin's being searched by another guard. Our eyes meet for a second before we both turn away to protect what little's left of our modesty.

The Imposer slaps me on the butt and smirks. "Hit the showers, Pretty Boy."

My bare feet pad across the frigid tiles and the next available showerhead. I hesitate. It's right between Arrah and Leander. I'm about to turn toward a spout on the far corner of the room when another Imp grabs me by the nape of the neck.

"We haven't got all day, traitor," he snarls.

The next thing I know, he shoves me forward. I slam into the porcelain wall, banging the side of my face against a broken tile.

Water jets from the nozzle above, piercing the numbness as every single one of my nerves is shocked. This is even colder than the showers in the trainee barracks were.

Leander's hulking body leans in close. The stream of water glistens on the muscles of his arms and chest as one of his hands flexes into a fist and punches his other palm. "That's nothing compared to what *we're* gonna do to you, *Lucy*," he snickers. "You're a dead man."

I turn away. Even though I'm shivering, I welcome the jets of ice. Grabbing the bar of lye soap embedded in the wall, I scrub my skin with vigor, trying to rid myself of the remnants of that probe's touch, the memory of those festering prisoners, the anger in Leander's face. I let the water reinvigorate my sore body.

"I understand why you thought you had to do what you did, Lucian," a voice whispers to my right.

Arrah.

I open my eyes.

She's just standing there shivering under the shower, her brown eyes staring at me, unflinching beneath the deluge of water pelting her. She looks so sad and vulnerable, like a little girl lost in a thunderstorm, wondering how, and *if,* she's ever going to find her way home again.

"Arrah. I swear I didn't mean to betray you or the others. I had no choice. I didn't know Cole was going to be there. I couldn't just let him die. Surely you can understand that?"

She nods, water dripping down the bridge of her nose. "I do understand." She purses her lips. "I know what it's like to love someone, to feel you have to do anything possible to protect them from danger. Unfortunately, you didn't think things through. What do you think is going to happen to your brother now that you've been arrested? You really think you saved him? At least if he'd died on that podium, he would have died for the greater good." She shakes her head, spraying droplets to and fro. "Now his death will be meaningless. As will all of ours." She steps away from the shower. "At least you won't have to live with the guilt for too long."

She walks away. The showers shut off. And this time I can't control the shakes that wrack my body.

"Get dressed," one of the officers barks.

As I step away from the shower, I notice that everything we were wearing is gone. In its place is a pile of tattered clothing, much like the rags that the prisoners in those mass pens were wearing.

I join the others in sifting through the stack of clothes, covering my nakedness with a pair of ragged pants that barely run from my hips to my knee caps, and a sleeveless shirt that's missing most of its buttons and fits more like a vest. There aren't even any shoes to protect our feet from the cold, hard floor.

"Time to eat!" the Imposer that frisked me shouts.

They jostle us into an adjacent chamber with the noses of their weapons. The steel and chrome fixtures remind me of the commissary back at the Citadel only a lot more threadbare, with just a few tables and no variety in menu items.

The Imposer smirks. "Grab it while it's hot," he snickers to his companions.

One by one, we take steaming bowls of grayish clumps. There aren't even any utensils. I'm the last one at the gruel station. The rest are already seated, divided between two tables. My former squad stares at me with looks that smolder more than the glop in their bowls, and Leander kicks the remaining chair at their table away. Tristin and the rest of the family members, at the other table, barely look up as they scoop the goo into their mouths. I decide to take my chances and sit with the latter group. At least they don't look like they want to kill me as much.

Tristin gives me a tentative smile as I set my bowl beside hers. Then I stoop and right the chair Leander kicked, scooching in close to the table.

"Hello," I mutter as I tilt the bowl to my lips, letting the noxious gunk seep past my tongue and throat. I churn it past my gums as quickly as garbage through the sewer treatment plants. I need the nourishment, not the taste. At least it's hot.

"What's *he* doing here, Jorgen?" It's the pale, gaunt, middle-aged woman with stringy brown hair I saw prodded by the Imp earlier. She's sitting across from me, loudly whispering into the ear of the tanned young man seated beside her.

Jorgen's dark eyes are as cool as the stew is hot. "Mrs. Grimstone, I've been asking myself the same question."

Tristin pushes her three-quarters-full bowl away from her. "Everyone, this is Lucian Spark." You'd think we were at a social affair. She half-smiles at me and I'm reminded of Cage's infectious grin.

The balding man seated on the other side of Tristin slams his bowl down, rattling the table. "We *know* who he is!"

Mrs. Grimstone and Jorgen nod their heads.

Corin glares at me and spits a wad of food in my direction. "He's the snake that got us into this mess."

I expected hostility from these people, so it doesn't surprise me. Scanning their eyes now, I wonder whether they distrust me simply because I'm a former Recruit or because they, like their recruited loved ones, are part of the rebellion and know that they're here because I betrayed the cause.

As if reading my thoughts, Jorgen clears his throat and stares me down. "You're not welcome here. Why don't you go sit with your little *friends* over there?" He nods his head in the direction of my squad, who, with the exception of Arrah, are staring at our table with amused smirks on their faces.

"Because even *they* won't have him," Baldy grunts through another swig of the slop.

"True, Mr. Ryland," Tristin says to him. "But we're not like Imposers, even those in training, are we?"

"They wouldn't show any pity on us," Jorgen growls.

Tristin grabs my arm to prevent me from leaving. "That's exactly my point," she continues. "What would the Deity ask us to do?"

The others drop their gazes.

I think of this poor girl at the mercy of slime like Prior Delvecchio and his minions. "You actually attend services at the Priory?"

She shakes her head. "Our family can't afford the tithing. And Cage thinks I'm crazy. But I still believe on my own."

There's something so profoundly innocent and tender in her demeanor and tone that I squirm in my chair. Lately, I haven't been the most compassionate person in the world, and my motives haven't been the purest. I've done what I've had to do. I'm not even certain if there is or there isn't some mystical Deity, whether everything we do is based on free will or some sort of divine determinism. The only thing I'm sure of is that we can't just sit around on our asses and wait for things to happen.

Mrs. Grimstone's cold fingers touch my hand. "Please. I remember when you were recruited. You've been through this before. Is my daughter…my Preshea…is she safe now? Are they torturing her? I *need* to know…"

The fear and worry on her face wrench my gut. I pat her hand. "Your daughter's fine right now." I turn to the others. "All of your loved ones are. They keep the Recruits strong and healthy so they can compete in the Trials. Just like they'll keep us alive."

"Thank you," she whispers, trying to stop the streams leaking down her cheeks.

All the edge seeps from Jorgen's face. Suddenly, he looks like a child. "But we'll never see them again, will we?"

I feel the weight of all their stares bearing down on me—Jorgen, Mrs. Grimstone, Mr. Ryland, Corin, and Tristin. Any anger and contempt they felt at my presence is gone, replaced by fear and the embryonic glow of hope. I gulp down my last mouthful of steaming gruel. "Yes. You *will* see them again." It's not really a lie. To say more would shred whatever comfort they can wring from my words, and I can't do that. There are plenty of things you can rip away from a person—their dignity, self-respect; hell, even a limb or two—and they can somehow find a way through it. People are strong like that. They've had to be. Even organs are replaceable with synthetic replicas if you have the cash.

But once you take away hope, that's it. Game over.

That's when people break for good and can never be

repaired. I've seen it happen over and over, ever since I can remember.

Corin taps me on the hand. "We're gonna die, aren't we?"

The kid's rough exterior is all but gone. This is the first time I've seen his true age in his eyes. I've managed to hold it together until now, but those five words hit me hard.

I stare at each of them for a few seconds before returning my gaze to Corin. "You're not going to die, kid. I promise." My eyes sweep my former comrades at the next table. "With the way the Establishment's set things up"—I raise my voice—"the Imposer trainees and myself are a buffer between you and anything bad happening. As long as we're around, you're all safe."

Mr. Ryland snorts. "Oh, yeah? What happens when the five of you are k—"

I cut him off with a glare that reaps the air between him and Corin.

Ryland clears his throat. "When the five of you are *no longer part of the Trials*?"

Corin glares at him. "You mean when they bite it."

I shake my head. "A *lot* can happen between now and then." I pause for moment before turning to the others. "You should all consider yourselves very fortunate under the circumstances. You're not just stuck in this hellhole with five other regular Incentives." I turn to face Leander's table. "You're in here with one of the best Imposer trainee squads ever to survive the Trials."

Through the icy stares I get back from my former squad I see something shift, if only for a second. Then it freezes over again in a blizzard of hatred and they all turn away again.

I'm going to need their help to get us all out of here. But

it's going to take more than words or playing to their egos to get my former allies to consider any kind of truce. And I don't have much time to make it happen.

SIXTEEN

This is it. After several weeks of being confined in the dark and cold, subsisting on gruel and enduring back-breaking labor, the Trials are about to begin.

This is the first morning that no one has said a word during breakfast. Everyone looks weary. From the look of the bowls around me, no one seems to be feeling particularly hungry either.

The mess hall doors burst open. "Chow time's over!" Echoes barks. "Let's go!"

This time, I'm the last one in the single-file line as we make our way back to the common room. Ever since our arrival I've been cataloguing the layout of Purgatorium in my mind, not only memorizing the order of the winding passageways but also committing to memory the number of steps to any given area. If I'm somehow able to gain access to the vent shafts, air ducts, and/or drainage systems, this will definitely help me with finding my way around. The one thing that's going to be a challenge is getting my hands on tools and some type of light source. Tricky, but not impossible; if I could make it through the last Trials in one piece, this shouldn't be too difficult. At least that's what I'm telling myself to keep from cracking.

Trying to get my former squad to work with me, though, has been less fruitful. Every time I attempted to talk to them, they either outright shunned me, gave me pissed-off looks, or grunted and muttered some colorful epithet. I'm going to need more time to win them over.

The problem is, time is not on my side. If Cage is the first Recruit to lose today, then all my strategizing, memorization, and self pep talks will die with me. I need to work fast, and not just to save my own life. For all I know, Arrah could be the first to die if Drusilla falters. It's impossible to say what decision someone will make when put under that kind of traumatic pressure.

Once back in the common room, I can sense a change in the atmosphere. It's as if it's charged with electrical particles just before a storm.

The Imps usher us toward our holding cells but don't force us inside, instead just leave us standing there as they disappear into the shadows. Then the lights dim and the whole room begins to glow as a deep hum vibrates throughout the chamber. Tristin's eyes are closed, her head bowed in prayer.

It's starting. And when it's over, there'll be one less chicken in the coup.

The light is blinding now, and I shield my eyes against its

intensity. Then it's gone, and I have to rub my eyes to make sure I'm not hallucinating. The entire chamber's been replaced by an outdoor landscape. The guards, the control room—everything's gone.

And standing right in the center of the room are Cage, Drusilla, Boaz, Crowley, and Preshea.

"Cage!" Tristin cries, rushing toward her brother.

Around me, Mrs. Grimstone, Jorgen, Mr. Ryland, and Corin also bolt to embrace their loves ones. But as soon as the Incentives converge on the Recruits, it all makes sense. As they wrap their arms around their loved ones, they find that their embraces cut right *through* them.

Of course. The Recruits are holograms. This whole chamber is a giant holographic projector broadcasting a live feed.

We're going to experience the horrors of this Trial right alongside the Recruits themselves.

Just like Cole must have.

Welcome Recruits! The Trials are about to begin.

The familiar voice blaring from the speaker system chills my blood. Last time, it was Slade's voice that guided us through the Trials. This time it's Cassius's.

The expressions on the faces of the Recruits' five family members turns from elated to crestfallen in the blink of an eye. Mrs. Grimstone sags into Mr. Ryland's shoulder, pointing at Preshea. "She *can't* see me. My baby can't see me." Then she's sobbing, and I can't help but be touched as the gruff man holds her up, patting her back, even as his own eyes well at the sight of his daughter, Drusilla. "Dru..." His words choke off.

Jorgen, on the other hand, stares at Crowley in silence.

Is that admiration on his face? Pride? They don't really look related, and I don't detect any romantic longing in that expression, so I can only assume they're friends or fellow rebels, both prepared for this eventuality, like Digory and his husband Rafé were. They're resigned to the fact that they're both probably not going to make it out of this.

After her initial enthusiasm at the sight of her brother, Tristin is the only one to seem calm now as she gazes at him. It's like she actually believes he's going to be all right and there's nothing to worry about. In some bizarre way, I envy her. Ignorance or divine enlightenment—it gives her an incredible edge in dealing with what's to come.

Poor Corin seems confused. His body is trembling as he stares wordlessly at the image of Boaz, directly in front of him but failing to acknowledge his presence. At one point he tries to tug Boaz's arm, his fingers slipping through to nothingness.

"Boaz raised him after his folks were killed," Tristin says to me.

Now I see just how devastating it can be to those standing by, watching their loved ones struggle. Knowing there's nothing they can do to help, nothing they can do but stand idly by and watch, hoping not to die.

I walk over and take hold of Corin's arm. "Don't worry. He can't see you, but he's definitely thinking about you. I was a Recruit just like Boaz is. And my little brother waited for me, just like you're waiting for him now."

He wrenches his arm away. "Stay the hell away from me or I'll kill you!"

Recruits, take your places.

I look up from Corin to see Cage coming right toward me, his face stern and menacing. Before I can move out of the way, he steps right through me. Cage takes his place at the starting line beside the images of Boaz, Crowley, Preshea, and Drusilla. Their expressions are like slivers of a broken mirror, cutting through their images with shards of fear, sadness, determination, and anger.

Arrah breaks off from the other trainees and walks over to Drusilla's image. The hologram casts a subtle glow, bathing Arrah's features in a shimmer of warmth like a shaft of starlight. She leans in and whispers a few words that I can't make out. The way her eyes study Drusilla's holo, it's like she's in awe of the most beautiful canvas she's ever seen. Her fingers lightly trace the air around Drusilla's hand and then cover it, giving the illusion that she's clasping her hand.

Leander, Rodrigo, and Dahlia stare at her, and I can tell they're confused. They had no clue about Arrah and Drusilla's relationship, obviously. I guess there's no need for Arrah to hide it anymore.

For this first Trial, Cassius's voice continues, **each Recruit will be asked to traverse the obstacle course ahead until they reach the other side.**

Obstacle course? Wonder what horrors they've conjured up this time.

Once all the obstacles have been cleared, each Recruit must successfully deactivate the transmitter that is programmed to detonate explosives placed within his or her Incentive. The last Recruit to make it through will only be allowed to deactivate one of his or her Incentives, making

the choice as to which. Good luck. And may the best Recruit prevail.

I feel like I'm disconnected from reality, as if a bomb has already gone off in my own head. All around me, I can see the meaning of those words dawning on everyone else's face. Corin takes a step closer and shoots me a panicked look.

Explosive charges within each Incentive? No wonder we were all so tired this morning, even though we were anxious about the Trials. They *drugged* us—probably spiked our meager dinners—to put us to sleep while they implanted micro-bombs inside each of us.

The lights of the obstacle course brighten. Spread over the entire field, spaced just a few feet apart from each other, are the writhing bodies of prisoners, at least a hundred. They sprout waist-up from the ground like a harvest of withered crops, battered and bloodied. Flashing silver discs are crammed into the spaces in the ground between them, bathing their faces alternately in rotting green and bloody red. Their cries and moans are amplified through the speakers.

You must time your steps through the course so as to only step on the circular discs when they are lit green.

Dahlia shoots me a look before joining Rodrigo and Leander in front of the projected images of the Recruits. Together they stare into the faces of the strangers who will decide their fate.

Commence … now!

DING!

Cage and the others spring forward.

The five of them scramble across the field, leaping from

one green disc to another as the prisoners shriek all around them. How they can concentrate with all that unnerving screaming, I'll never know.

My heart boomerangs inside my rib cage. So far, the five Recruits are neck and neck, with Boaz and Crowley at a slight advantage and Cage and the rest not far behind.

Drusilla leapfrogs across one of the prisoners to take the lead. Arrah lunges forward, never leaving Drusilla's side, tracking her progress. Drusilla lands on an emerald disc—

Just as it turns crimson.

Arrah drops to her knees and screams.

"Drusilla!" Mr. Ryland shouts.

Crackle!

Drusilla leaps up just as a burst of arcing energy erupts from the disc. It grazes her right foot and sizzles through the air like a whip, slashing through the surrounding prisoners and dismembering their bodies, which fall to the ground in clumps.

Then Drusilla stumbles onto the next green disc, clutching her foot, her face in agony. It looks like it's still attached, but who knows how deep it's been cut. She teeters, her body swaying to the left, right next to a blinking red disc…

Ryland clutches his chest.

"Be careful!" Arrah's scream pierces the chamber.

Drusilla drops—

"I gotcha!" Cage swoops in on the other side and scoops her in his arms. "Hang on!" Bearing her weight, he jumps to the next disc just as the one he was standing on starts blinking red.

Boaz emerges from a smoldering pile of body parts, nursing an injured arm with a long, ugly, smoking gash carved into it.

Unlike the time *I* went through the Trials, this whole thing's rigged for the Recruits to die. They're facing dismemberment and the rest of us are wired to explode. The prisoners are just a grisly bonus added to the mix.

On the field, Preshea is closing the gap between herself, Crowley, and Boaz, leaving Cage and the injured Drusilla trailing behind. I can tell from the exhaustion on Cage's face that the burden of leaping from sphere to sphere while carrying Drusilla is taking its toll on him.

"Can you walk?" he asks her.

She grits her teeth and nods. "Think so."

He sets her on the closest green disc and they both dive for the next one, narrowly escaping the lethal red flashes.

The discs are flashing faster now, speeding up with each passing minute, making it that much harder and deadlier to get across the field. The half-buried prisoners are wailing louder, their screams intensifying with each illuminating strobe of the discs in front of them.

Boaz lets loose a guttural yelp as he sails through more flying body parts, his cheek bearing a smoking scorch mark, the price of his temporary victory over death.

"It's okay … it's okay … " Tristin is clutching Corin close, trying to comfort him and keep his attention diverted, but the kid's in a frenzy now, all pretense of being a badass long gone.

Just ahead of Boaz, Crowley soars from a flashing red disc across the finish line.

Jorgen drops to his knees, hands in the air. "Yesssssssss!"

Then he's engulfed by a sea of holographic body parts, the remains of the nearby prisoners. He drops his face into his hands, his shoulders heaving.

Boaz leaps through him and disappears behind Crowley, in second place. Dahlia and Leander exchange a quick look of relief. They're both safe—for now.

"Don't worry, Boaz made it through. You're both going to be fine," Tristin coos into Corin's ear.

But the words are as hollow as the images being projected all around us. The discs start flashing faster ...

Only three Recruits left.

Including Cage.

Preshea moves into the lead, followed by Cage and the injured Drusilla.

"Please, oh, *please*, you can make it ... come on, sweet-heart!" Mrs. Grimstone's face looks like that of a madwoman illuminated by rainbow lightning.

Arrah's eyes are glued to the struggling Drusilla. She sinks to her knees, her forehead slick, eyes puffy, breaths short and quick. "C'mon, Dru ..." she whispers.

Leander grabs her by the arm and pulls her to her feet. "What the hell's wrong with you?"

She rips her arm away. "Let go of me."

Leander points a finger at Rodrigo, whose olive skin is pale as he stares at the field in silence. "You're as bad as your little traitor friend Spark. Rod's completely on his own and you're on a first-name basis with *Dru*? Just how tight are you with this insurrectionist scum? How long have you been doing each other?"

Mr. Ryland steps between them. "Careful what you call my daughter—"

"Shut up!" Leander shoves him away and Mr. Ryland falls flat on his back with a loud crunch.

I lunge at Leander, pushing him back. "Leave him alone."

His body's a blur as he leaps forward and topples me. Then we're rolling, fists connecting, my body exploding with the agony of his blows as I struggle to breathe. My knuckles crunch against his jaw, but he keeps pummeling me.

"Stop it, you two!" Tristin's voice. "You want to end up in solitary?"

Then hands are pulling me away—Arrah and Mr. Ryland—while Dahlia and Rodrigo try their best to contain Leander, who's snapping his teeth and spewing saliva like a rabid Canid.

"I swear I'm gonna kill you!" he spits, his voice muffled by his bloody nose.

Tristin points down the obstacle field. "Look!"

Preshea's almost at the finish line, Cage not far behind her.

But it's Drusilla that surprises us. Not bothering with leaping from one blinking disc to another, she's decided on the most direct path. Right over the prisoners themselves. Using their writhing and screaming bodies as a living pathway, she jumps from one to the other in a straight line, her boots tromping on foreheads, cheeks, wrists until she soars past Preshea and disappears over the finish line. Leaving Preshea and Cage behind.

Arrah lets go of me, half-sobbing, half-laughing. Mrs. Grimstone is on her knees, hands clasped.

Preshea prepares to leap for the final disc with Cage right on her tail. Her image blurs in a green and crimson haze as she crosses the finish line. Cage is just an instant behind her.

Tristin's hand feels warm against my ice-cold one as she squeezes it. She knows what's coming.

I'm dead.

Cage's jaw is set, rigid, his lips clenched. I'd have thought this would be an easy decision for him.

But Preshea's smile vanishes, her eyes suddenly confused as she looks down at her abdomen. Cage's eyes follow her gaze. Wisps of smoke swirl around her midsection.

Then the upper half of her body falls away at the waist, revealing a smoking stump of charred intestines that topples after it.

Mrs. Grimstone's shriek tears through the entire chamber as the rest of us just watch in stunned silence.

Recruit Preshea's poor performance has resulted in termination of her participation in the Trials. As such, both of her Incentives shall now be shelved.

Cassius's words barely have enough time to register when two metallic claws descend from the ceiling and grab Rodrigo and Mrs. Grimstone, pulling them toward their cell.

Rodrigo looks like a frightened child. "What's going on? Lee-Man! D! *Help me*...!"

"Hang on, Rod-Man!" Dahlia shouts as she and Leander try to grab his hands. But they're no match for the powerful steel pincers clamped around his body.

Mrs. Grimstone is wailing over and over again, "My baby. They *killed* my baby."

Then both Rodrigo and Mrs. Grimstone's bodies are flung inside their cell, which seals behind them.

Rodrigo presses his face and hands against the glass, so much like that little boy in the prisoner pens. He's sobbing. "*Please*. I don't want to die. I wanna go home, man..."

Leander's palms press against the space opposite his. "Don't think about it, Rod-Man. Just close your eyes, think about all those crazy times we had... we're the elite that can't be..." His voice chokes. "They're gonna pay for this... they're gonna..." His words fade with a whimper.

Grinding gears vibrate through the room and the cell rises, disappearing from view along with the hologram of the trial field.

Dahlia caresses Leander's head. She looks up at me, her tear-stained eyes icy slivers. "It should have been you."

On the big screen, the image of the cell rising into the actual trial field appears. Both Mrs. Grimstone and Rodrigo are sobbing and pleading, the severed body of Preshea now lying between them.

Commence shelving.

Mrs. Grimstone and Rodrigo burst into flaming clumps of flesh and gristle, which obscure the camera lens before the image fades to black.

SEVENTEEN

"You think you're all on some type of holiday with free room and board?" Slade's voice echoes through the silence of the common area as she makes her way through it, an armed quartet escorting her. "You're still going to have to earn your keep around here"—her eyes dart up to the one empty cell, darkened now—"no matter what happens."

Ever since that first Trial ended, all of us have just been sitting in our open cells, not saying a word, not even looking at each other.

Slade pauses in the center of the room. "Out of your cells, *now*."

I ache all over from sitting on the cold, hard floor, cross-legged, in the exact same position for who knows how long. The pain reminds me that I'm still alive and I have to fight, regardless of the odds stacked against us.

I shuffle after Tristin out of our cell and line up beside the others. I study their faces for the first time since the trial, and I can see the change there. Where once they looked confused and frightened, now there's something else there, a hardness just beneath the surface. For the first time since we've been here, I get the sense from those shell-shocked faces that they're finally starting to understand.

Slade eyes the room. "As you all witnessed for yourselves, the Trials can be quite messy at times." Her gaze lingers on the cell vacated by Rodrigo and Mrs. Grimstone. "As such, cleanliness is of the utmost importance."

She shares a wink and nod with the guards standing sentinel over us. "Beginning immediately, you are all assigned to clean-up detail of the competition fields, where you are to pick up all debris and scrub each area until it's spotless. Any performance that is lacking shall be rewarded with reductions and/or cancellation of rations."

It takes a moment to realize that she's talking about bodies. All those poor people who were sliced and diced by the lasers. She wants us to dispose of them and wipe out any trace of their existence. They could have automated drones do this, but that would be too easy. They want us toiling away among the stench of death and decay.

"What are you waiting for?" Slade barks. "If you start now, you'll barely have enough time before the next Trial." A smirk stretches across her face like a sail in blustery skies. "And I assure you, you won't want to miss it!"

She snaps her fingers and the guards step forward, prodding our line out of the chamber. Slade points a finger at Leander and myself. "*You* two wait here."

Both Arrah and Dahlia crane their necks, staring back at us as they follow the other Incentives out. The two of us stand alone before Slade and the remaining armed guards.

Leander's face is filled with venom. But behind his glare, I sense anxiety, if not downright fear. He's probably thinking the same thing I am.

This can't be good.

Slade's eyes move between us. "I figured, with such qualified and elite Incentives as yourselves, it would be best to put your leadership skills on display to set an example to the others."

She snaps her fingers and another guard appears, wheeling a bucket, an old mop, and scrub brushes, which he plunks down in front of us. Some of the water spills over the rim, splashing our feet and ankles with muddy ice.

"Some of the containment cells can get particularly grimy, so you have to make sure to get in between each crack and crevice," Slade whispers.

Grinding gears shake the room, rattling my teeth. Rodrigo's and Mrs. Grimstone's cell descends and I stifle a gag. The once-clear glass is coated with reddish gunk, some chunks still glistening with moisture as they drip from the glass in a symphony of loud plops.

She tosses me the mop. "Don't just stand there. Clean up your friend."

———

"I oughtta just kill you right now and mop you up along with Rodrigo." Leander glares at me. "He is—*was*—my best friend. Even before we were recruited. We went to school together. Lived in the same neighborhood. He had everything going for him. Would'a made a great Imposer if you hadn't come along." He wrings the scrub brush so hard, I can see the veins in his arm bulging. A stream of gore sloshes from his brush and into the bucket, spattering my cheek. It's going to take more than a shower to feel clean after this.

My kneecaps feel like they're about to pop from resting on them so long. "I'm sorry."

Leander plops the mop into the bucket. "You *will* be, Sparkles."

I grimace. "You do realize none of us are getting out of this alive—"

"Shut up!" He bangs the bucket against me, spilling a clump of gore on the floor with a loud plunk. "Everything out of your traitor mouth is a dirty lie!"

He shoves me aside and squats with the brush. It squeaks against the floor, reminding me of the sound of rodents.

It's no use trying to explain anything to him. He's too blind and brainwashed to understand. I'm just about to turn away when I notice that he's scrawling something with his index finger in the grayish matter under the bucket's shadow.

I crane my neck.

U were right

At first I think I must be seeing things. But one look at Leander and I can see this is no joke. His finger dips into the bloody sludge again.

They killed him, gonna kill us

His eyes pierce me, then dart to the ceiling just outside.

I follow his gaze.

Of course. There are cameras surveilling us, equipped with audio, not to mention an Imposer sentry making her rounds.

His eyes flash back to mine and he scrubs the message away. "You'll say anything to place the blame on everyone else but your rebel self!" He brings the brush back to the bucket, wrings it again, then continues to polish.

Now it's my turn to communicate with him. What if it's a trap? Should I risk it? Then again, what choice do I really have? I'm going to need help to get out of here.

I slosh some of the filthy liquid onto the floor and scrawl my own message.

We have 2 work together

"You're only getting what you deserve," I grunt, turning away from him.

"You can't even look me in the eyes, can you, coward?" His dripping finger scribbles another message.

What's ur plan?

After he's sure I've seen it, he scrubs it away again.

I fake a yawn. "I'd rather look at this mess than filth like you." I make a show of scrubbing harder, then I squiggle another note.

Vent shaft in my cell after dark. Access to compound. Need tools.

This time he's the one to wipe it away after reading it.

"Yeah," he snickers. "Take a good look at this mess, Sparkles. Before the end of the day you're gonna look even worse. That's a promise."

He doodles another message.

Already on it

His hand digs into a pocket in his pant leg and he slips something from it into his brush, continuing to scrub. His nod is almost imperceptible.

As I scrub, our hands brush against each other and we swap brushes.

Then I lean back and sit up, stretching for show again, and flip the brush over behind the bucket to get a better look.

Embedded into the brush's bristles is a rolled-up piece of torn fabric. I pluck it out and unfurl it.

It's a bone fragment about three inches long, jagged at both ends. Leander was probably thinking about using it as a weapon. It just might work to pry open that vent. I shudder. I can't tell if it belonged to Rodrigo or Mrs. Grimstone. No matter. Either way, something good may come of their gruesome deaths.

I tuck the bone into the lining of my waistband, hoping they won't search us before taking us back to our cells.

Leander scrawls another message.

Don't worry. Will get D and A on board. No one messes with our squad.

I nod.

"What's going on here?" Slade's voice startles me.

"We were just finishing up, Sir," Leander responds.

"Stand up, both of you," she hisses in reply.

We exchange a look and climb to our feet—

That last message is still on the floor.

Slade's eyes inspect the cell. "Hmmm. Not bad. Looks like you two deadbeats might be of some use after all." Her gaze digs into me. "What's the matter, Spark? You look ill. I'd have thought you'd be over your squeamishness by now."

"No, Sir," I squeeze out.

"What are you hiding behind that bucket?"

Leander's face turns red.

"Nothing, Sir." I feel my throat tighten up.

Slade takes a step toward us. "Out of the way!"

Just before she reaches us, I move, banging my foot against the bucket. It teeters and splatters the floor. Slade pushes past me and I turn. Most of the message is erased—except for the last word, which Leander quickly steps on and smudges away.

She stares at the slimy puddle a moment, then shoves us away. "Incompetents, both of you. Ensign! Get them out of here." A jittery soldier just a few years our senior appears and escorts us back to our cells.

As soon as he's gone, I pull the bone fragment from its hiding place and run the tip of my finger against its sharp, jagged edge.

We won't be here much longer, one way or another.

EIGHTEEN

I barely have time to wedge the bone into a corner crack in my cell when the others are herded back through the cell block at gunpoint by Styles and Renquist.

"We haven't got all day!" Renquist barks.

The six of them look as bad as I feel. Dark hammocks cradle bloodshot eyes. Their skin is mired in gruesome muck.

As they pass me, both Dahlia and Arrah make eye contact with Leander and me, a mixture of confusion and resentment. They're probably wondering why we were separated from the rest. At least the two of them look like they're keeping it together, still holding their heads high.

That's more than I can say for the rest of the Incentives.

Styles waves his weapon at me and Leander, who's also standing at the threshold of his cell, across from me. "You two! Get your asses in line with the rest of 'em!"

Leander and I join the formation. Soon we're trailing through the familiar maze like rats until we reach the showers.

"Strip!" Renquist orders.

No one says anything as we slip out of our clothes. Exhaustion is much more potent than modesty.

Styles lets out a sinewy whistle. He sidles up to Dahlia and tugs at the torn shirt draped over her bare shoulder. "Need any help with that?" he snickers.

She gives him a look that could cut and cauterize and turns away, flinging her clothes at his boots.

His walkie crackles to life. **Get the Incentives prepped and over to the tanks, stat!**

Cassius's voice.

Tanks? What is he planning on doing to us now?

Before we can head under the shower heads, Renquist steps forward holding a hose, which uncoils behind him like a monstrous serpent. He's grinning. "Sorry, folks. Haven't got time for anything else."

Styles lets out a *whoop* as if it's the funniest thing he's ever heard and spins the valve on the wall. They hose us down.

After what seems like forever, the onslaught stops and we're left naked and freezing, hugging our bodies, the chamber echoing with chattering teeth and rapid breaths.

"Let's go!" Styles snarls. He leads the way while Renquist follows behind. From somewhere ahead I can hear the soft sounds of sobbing, but I'm not sure who it's coming from.

As the passageway veers into a new direction, I again concentrate on memorizing it, the number of steps, every turn, every grate. The corridor finally opens into a large room with gangways crisscrossing pools of black water, almost like the hangar bay the Eel docked in when we arrived.

Instead of submarines, however, dark sacks hang from the ceiling by cables. They're like chunks of meat hanging in a butchery, except they're vaguely formed into the shape of a human body. I swallow past the knot in my throat.

There are eight of them—one for each of us.

Armored personnel hustle about like bees in a hive, checking gauges, observing monitors, checking printouts. Styles and Renquist lead us down one of the gangways until we're all standing directly below the ominous black casings.

A whir of grinding pulleys echoes through the room as the shapes descend until they're at eye-level. One is noticeably smaller than the others and I glance at Corin, trying to control my sadness and rage.

Then the pods open like metallic jaws. Inside the padded interior I can see a miniature screen at eye-level, as well as small speakers surrounding a headrest area.

The Incentives shall now enter the Bio-Pods.

"Inside," Renquist growls, shoving the muzzle of his gun into my arm.

Fear bores through my heart and into my stomach. I grip the sides of the pod. The material's coated with a slimy lubricant and feels like a giant, leathery tongue. I hesitate on the gangway.

"I can't go in there," Jorgen gasps. All traces of cockiness are gone. His eyes are riveted on the pod before him. Mr. Ryland looks like he's going to have a heart attack.

Tristin grips Corin's hand, both of them silent, expressionless. The kid looks almost catatonic.

Then I'm shoved roughly between the shoulder blades and into my own pod. I have just enough time to catch a glimpse of Leander, Arrah, and Dahlia, their expressions grave as they're jostled into their respective pods, before the enclosure seals closed with a soft pop, like a dark kiss. I'm plunged into pitch black.

My heart clatters against my ribs. The icy gelatinous mucus of the Bio-Pod closes in all around me, jamming into my ears, my nostrils, hardening against the contours of my body like drying cement. I'm paralyzed. My pulse thrums against the substance. Can't move. Can't see. Completely powerless.

Like being buried alive.

The infrared goggles I spied earlier have come online and I can make out the personnel scrambling to perform their duties in the hangar.

In one corner of the screen, superimposed over this image, are four thumbnail video feeds showing Cage, Crowley, Boaz, and Drusilla. They each appear to be barely clad, the guys bare-chested and in briefs, Drusilla in a tank top and shorts. All of them are standing on the bank of a dark body of water, just like the one the Bio-Pods are dangling over.

In the other corner of the screen is a display of readouts, with each Incentive's name listed. Next to each name is data listed under the headings Oxygen Levels and BPM.

Right now, everyone's O2 reading is exactly the same: one hundred percent. The heartbeat readings are another matter.

Mine seems to be holding steady at ninety-five beats per minute. Higher than normal, but not too bad.

I study the oxygen readouts once again. If they're keeping track of how much air we have in these prisons, it must mean we're going to start losing it during the course of this Trial. As the implications sink in, the blip on the screen next to my name increases its pace.

Ninety-eight BPMs.

One-hundred and two BPMs.

Welcome Recruits to your next Trial!

Cassius's hateful voice startles me in my cramped confines. Cage and the others stand at attention as Cassius continues.

In this Trial, each Recruit will be required to dive into the sea and retrieve the Bio-Pods containing each of their Incentives, which have been marked accordingly.

While the instructions are being relayed, I can feel my Bio-Pod vibrating as the pulleys overhead begin lowering it into the ocean. The bobbing hangar bay I saw before begins to pull away. My stomach churns. The lower half of my goggle screen fills with bubbles, then darkness that quickly devours the remaining light.

Then the black sea is all around me, gulping down my body, which rocks with sickening turbulence as I plummet into the depths.

This is a race. Each Bio-Pod has been equipped with a limited amount of oxygen. You must retrieve both of your Incentives before their oxygen levels become depleted ...

My Bio-Pod tumbles end over end, spinning me upside

down, right side up. I fight the urge to puke, concerned that if I do I'll just choke on it in this watery prison.

Choose the order of your retrieval carefully, Cassius continues. **Whichever Incentive remains submerged when their oxygen runs out shall be the losing Recruit's de facto choice to be shelved. If more than one Recruit is unable to retrieve both Incentives, that Recruit will also be considered to have failed, making a choice as well.**

With a thud, my Bio-Pod strikes the ocean floor. I'm resting at an angle, but at least I'm not upside down.

Onscreen, the Recruits stand at the water's edge, bodies arced, waiting to receive the signal.

Be cautious. The sea is filled with all manner of natural obstacles. Good Luck. Begin!

The four Recruits plunge into the water.

My eyes dart to the oxygen levels, which have all already dipped to ninety-nine percent. In the murky depths, I can make out the ghosts of some of the other pods, swaying like restless sleepers in the current, but I can't tell who's who.

A shadow falls across my shell. Something jostles my Bio-Pod, shifting its angle. Every muscle locks.

A hand appears at the faceplate of my pod, smearing the dark glass. I recognize Cage's face. His eyes are pools of desperation and fear as they dart back and forth, not a hint of recognition nesting in them.

He drifts from view. I glance at his monitor, which shows him hovering over the Bio-Pod next to mine, repeating the same frantic ritual.

Then it hits me. While *we* can track the Recruits via the

feeds from the cameras attached to the surface of the suits, *they* can't see *us*. Whatever choice each Recruit's making as to who to rescue first is purely guesswork.

My eyes flick to my vitals readout. Oxygen level: eighty-two percent.

Cage grabs Tristin's pod, and then mine, attempting to swim with both of us to the surface. My pod sways and bounces, then stops. Cage's face looks like he's straining, the veins in his forehead pulsating, his cheeks bulging. He's running out of air.

A second later he shakes his head and lets go of me, kicking his feet as he glides upward with Tristin's pod. He disappears in a trail of bubbles.

My Bio-Pod bounces to a rest on the ocean floor once again.

At least Cage will be pleased he made the right choice.

Oxygen level: sixty-eight percent. I squeeze my eyes shut as another wave of claustrophobia slams into me. I focus on the monitors and readouts.

Drusilla and Crowley are already making their way back to the surface, each towing Bio-Pods of their own. It could mean that Dahlia and Arrah are safe, but the bio-readouts for the Incentives are impossible to interpret. The racing heartbeats could mean elation at being rescued or terror at being left behind.

Boaz is in last place, just having picked one of his Incentive's Bio-Pods before scrambling after the others. Since that pod is smaller than the others it means that at least poor Corin is safe.

I hear a quiet sound. And then a steady stream, like the sewage sloshing through the sewer tunnels back home.

An even deeper cold slices through the numbness in my lower extremities and I force myself to look down. Ocean water is seeping into my pod, climbing past my feet, my ankles, my calves. The Establishment isn't taking any chances. At this rate, they'll drown us before the oxygen levels are depleted.

My anxiety levels kick into overdrive. The door in my mind blasts open, letting in a tsunami of ice-cold panic that engulfs everything in its path. "*Get me out of here!*" I screech, buckling against the confines of the capsule.

But it's no use. My throat's raw, my stomach twisted like a wrung-out washcloth.

Oxygen level: thirty-eight percent.

My breaths are quick rasps bursting through my ears like the chugging of a steam engine, growing faster and faster. I'm starting to feel dizzy, like I'm going to pass out. Lightning jets through my hands, feet, and lips. I'm hyperventilating, losing too much carbon dioxide. The realization makes me feel floaty.

Oxygen level: nineteen percent.

I think of Digory. Instead of the dark, cold waters drowning me, I'm bobbing in the warm blue of his eyes. He smiles, his flawless lips forming words that travel in concentric circles of perfect ripples until they cozy up to my ears and fill them with bliss.

Never give up.

My heart surges—

Until I remember Digory's betrayal and how much it

hurts. I've tried my best not to think of it during these weeks in Purgatorium.

But the rage works just as well.

Frosty sea water laps against my chin, jarring me back to reality. *Control yourself, damn it! Cole needs you to survive and get back to him!*

I force myself to imagine that each breath I'm expelling is pushing me farther and farther away from Cole, and I feel them begin to slow.

Oxygen level: ten percent.

On the monitors, Boaz has overtaken Drusilla and Crowley and is racing ahead of them to pick up his second Incentive. Seawater seeps past my lower lip, filling my mouth with salty ice that I spit back out.

Boaz scoops up his remaining Incentive and heads for the surface, followed by Drusilla. At least that guarantees that Corin, Leander, Arrah, and Mr. Ryland will make it through to the next round.

Crowley's left behind, trying to untangle his remaining Bio-Pod from debris. From the way his face is contorting, he looks like he's struggling to breathe.

My mouth's now completely submerged and I tilt my head up as far as I can, struggling to keep my nostrils free.

Crowley finally pulls the last of the debris free and grips his Incentive's Bio-Pod.

Cage darts into view, propelling himself like a fish. Gripping my pod, he heaves me from the ocean floor and begins the trek to the surface. Crowley's just a little farther ahead with his Incentive.

Oxygen level: four percent.

The water spewing into my pod is trickling past my nostrils.

Then Cage pulls ahead and takes the lead. Oxygen level: two percent.

An oblong shape zooms into view, dissecting the shafts of surface glow. It's a fish. A *big* fish with a long pointed snout, angular fin, gills like slashes in its side, and the blackest eyes I've ever seen.

A carcharian.

Crowley lets go of his Incentive and swims away, but Cage just freezes. *Wham!* The predator slams into me, teeth chomping through the monitors and gauges as it rips a large hole in my pod.

I manage to avoid the creature's teeth and slip through the opening. Cage grabs my arm and starts to pull me up with him to the surface. Beside us, Crowley's recovered his Incentive and is swimming neck-in-neck with us, just as the carcharian rips free of the remnants of my Bio-Pod and shoots toward us like a silver bullet. Its maw grazes one of Crowley's legs as it zooms by him, then circles around to attack him full force. Crowley clutches his wound and shoves his remaining pod toward the predator.

Tearing away from Cage, I grab Crowley, pulling him up with us to the surface as the carcharian devours Crowley's Incentive, Bio-Pod and all. Then I'm breaking through the surface, gasping, filling my starving lungs with glorious air, Crowley slumped against me. On my other side, Cage is bobbing in the water, hand clasped in mine, holding them both high for everyone to see we've made it.

"You okay, mate?" he whispers.

I nod.

The whine of feedback pierces my clogged ears:

Recruit Cage, you have rescued your second Incentive and completed this Trial in Third Place. Unfortunately, Recruit Crowley has finished last and his Incentive has been shelved accordingly.

On the platform above us, Drusilla and Boaz stand, anxious looks plastered on their faces.

"Crowley...needs...help!" I gasp.

Boaz pushes forward. "We got him!"

Then they're crouching at the edge, helping Cage and me haul Crowley onto the platform. Blood oozes from the wound in his leg, puddling at our feet.

Crowley's eyes are wide open and glazed, all the color drained from his flesh. "*Jorgen...*" he mutters through clenched teeth.

Drusilla cradles his head in her lap. "Is he even breathing?"

Cage rubs Crowley's forehead. "He's in bloody shock."

I'm gripping Crowley's leg, trying to apply as much pressure as I can. "He's losing too much blood."

"We need a medic here!" Boaz shouts at the spherical drones hovering above us like insects.

I lean in close to Crowley's ear. "Hang in there. It's going to be okay. Help's coming."

He moans and clutches my arm. "Please tell me I didn't just kill Jorg—oh, hell...what have I done...?"

"Stay away from him!" Boaz shoves me so hard I nearly fall back into the sea.

Cage grabs me and keeps me from going over. He springs up and shoves Boaz away. "Rack off! It's nobody's fault except the mongrels running this show."

Boaz ogles him. "How can you take this traitor's side? Crowley's one of *us*. And now he's going to die because of—"

"He's *not* going to die, you whacker!"

But even as he says the words, Cage's jaw clenches, his expression hardening like dried clay.

He turns to gaze at the recovered Bio-Pods, which are being picked up by metal claws descending from a conveyor belt in the maze of girders and beams above. "Tristin okay?" he mutters.

"She's hanging in there. Better than most." I try to crack a smile. "Why didn't you just leave when you saw who was in your other pod?"

He nods toward the drones. "Is that what *you'd* do, mate?"

Two Imposers appear and lift Crowley into a hovering med capsule, disappearing with him.

I can't help but think of that image I saw of Digory on that grainy surveillance footage.

Styles and Renquist emerge out of a side door and approach me with weapons drawn.

Drusilla touches my hand. "Tell Arrah...tell her...I *love* her..."

I nod. "I will."

"Let's go, Spark." Renquist grunts.

Then they're hauling me away, and I'm wondering if it's Dahlia or Jorgen who won't be there when I get back.

NINETEEN

I'm standing in the middle of a long corridor of arched black stone. Something's swaying back and forth, something metallic like dangling chains...

A Bio-Pod, torn and smeared with blood.

I grab hold and rip the faceplate away.

It's Digory. His skin's mottled gray, once-full lips shriveled and torn. His eyes pop open. Instead of that brilliant blue, they're white as eggshells. Tears of blood pool and drip from the corners down his hollow cheeks. His mouth opens with a sickening pop, as if his lips have been stuck together for a long time.

"You never came back for me like you promised." His voice is a throaty gurgle. His skin tears as his mouth stretches into a smile, oozing pus. "But soon you'll be dead, too."

———

I bolt upright.

"Lucian, are you okay?" a voice whispers in my ear.

I can't see anything but the thick cloak of blackness that smothers me. Panic jolts through me like a live wire. What have they done to me? I'm blind. Instinctively, my fingers grope my face to make sure my eyes are still in their sockets.

Then consciousness tears through the tattered vestiges of my nightmare. It was a dream. I'm in my cell. Must be after lights-out.

I sense breathing and my hands find the face near me, cupping the smooth, cool cheeks.

"Tristin?" I whisper back.

"Yes, it's me." Her hand touches mine. "When I got brought back, you were already passed out. Then they turned off the lights for the night. Looks like you were having some kind of bad dream. Heard you calling for 'Digory.'"

I let go of her face and grab her hands, anxious to change the subject. "The others, did you see them? Are they okay? Who did we lose? Was it Dahlia?"

She sighs. "I'm not sure. I only caught a glimpse of some of the others—Corin, your friends Leander and Arrah. That's about all I remember seeing before they switched off the juice. Sorry."

I nod, forgetting for an instant that she can't see me. The last image of Cage's face on the platform hovers into my memory. "Your brother. I've seen him."

"Cage? Is he okay? I couldn't tell from those monitors, and then they went blank, and—"

"He's okay. Asked how you're doing," I try to inject a little levity into my words. "How long was I out for?"

"Maybe an hour, hour and a half. Why?"

Good. That means I still have several hours before the morning guard shift arrives.

"Tristin, I'm going to need your help. There's something I have to do if we're all going to get to see the people we care about again."

"What do you mean?"

"I need to get out of this cell and find a way out of this complex. If we don't get out of here soon, we're all dead— you, me, your brother, everyone. That's the Establishment's endgame. No survivors this time."

There's nothing but silence for a few moments. I feel the weight on the cot shift. If she doesn't cooperate, there's no way I'm going to be able to pull this off.

"I'm in. What's your plan?" she finally whispers back.

"I'm going to try and get through one of the ducts."

Groping against the wall to orient myself, I reach into the crevice where I've hidden the bone fragment and pull it out. I climb back onto the cot and feel my way up the corner wall until I can feel the rim of the ventilation grate. My fingertips probe the metal slats on one side of it, finally finding the grooves.

From the mental blueprint I've been able to piece together, it seems our holding cells move vertically and horizontally on some type of gear system, so this grate must lead to a ventilation or maintenance shaft that runs parallel to the track system, at least when our cells are locked in their default ground-level position, as they are now.

Unless my theory's totally wrong.

I guess I'm about to find out. That is, if the bone fragment is thin enough to fit into the screw head. The fabric wrapped around my makeshift tool rustles as I unfurl it.

"What're you doing?" Tristin whispers into my ear.

"It's just a little gizmo Leander slipped me to help loosen these bolts."

The next couple of hours are an exercise in frustration and jangled nerves. While I'm able to wedge the bone fragment into the screws without being able to see, actually turning the heads to loosen them requires repeated attempts. I'm only able to turn them a millimeter at a time before my tool pops out and I have to repeat the process over again.

I'm all too conscious of every single creak from the grinding bolts, which pierce the muffled sounds of our breathing and the thudding of my pulse in my ears.

Twice, Tristin and I are forced to abandon the project and fling ourselves into our bunks when Imps making their rounds approach and shine a light into our cell.

The second time, the guard lingers and I keep my eyes squeezed shut, trying to control my breathing. I grip the sharp utensil like a weapon, hoping the guard doesn't decide to come into the cell and take a closer look, forcing me to use it.

But it's Tristin who breaks the tension by releasing a stream of soft snores, mimicking the sounds of deep sleep to perfection.

Moments later, the glare of the flashlight disappears and

the guard's footfalls echo down the corridor, leaving us in the thickness of black silence once again.

We spring back into action.

"Nice work," I whisper into her ear.

Finally, I've released all of the screws on the grate except for one. The last thing I need is for the grate to clatter to the ground and alert the guards. Also, I need to be able to slide it back into place in a hurry and not worry about securing it to the ceiling. Gripping the loose edges, I shove the vent to the side, having to push real hard against the rust holding it in place.

Without needing a cue from me, Tristin fakes a coughing fit to cover up the sound of the creaking metal. The sound makes me break out into gooseflesh as if it were nails scraping across an old chalkboard.

There's no way they can't hear this.

Once the grate is moved sufficiently, I pause, slumping against the wall, my ears straining for the first chords of booted feet heading our way.

Each second seems like an hour.

But no one comes.

"I think we're good," Tristin murmurs. I can hear the anxiety tingeing her words.

Releasing my breath, I whisper to her. "I need you to help boost me up."

It's awkward in the dark, but in a few minutes, she's cupping my foot in her hands and pushing me up and through the open duct and into the shaft. There's a panicked second where I don't think I'm going to be able to squeeze through, but after a little pushing and some scraped flesh, I'm in.

I poke my head back through. "I'll be back as soon as I can."

"Hurry," she mutters. This time there's no mistaking the fear in her voice. She slides the grate back into place.

Taking a moment to orient myself, I start to crawl through the duct, feeling my way past the transport mechanisms that connect to the pulleys and rails at the top of my cell. Once I'm into the network of ventilation shafts, I reconcile my direction with what I've already memorized of Purgatorium's floor plan and fit this journey to my mental schematics.

Up ahead, shafts of light illuminate my way as I pass by the mess hall, the showers, the other prisoners' cell blocks. I peer through the slats of each vent as I go by. There must be a skeleton guard crew on duty since I only spot a couple of Imps, silent wraiths haunting the corridors below.

It took so long to get up here. How much time do I have left? Surely it won't be long before the morning shift takes over and the entire facility's flooded with activity—

And my absence in the holding cell is discovered.

My pace increases. I ignore the pain in my bare kneecaps as I forge on. By my calculations, what I'm really looking for should be just around the next corner. A few feet away, I reach an intersection with a vertical shaft.

This has to be it. A way to access the upper control rooms located on the catwalks overlooking our cells. Fortunately, there's a maintenance ladder leading up, and I'm able to skirt the rungs in seconds and emerge into a horizontal shaft parallel to the one I just left.

As I start to crawl toward the nearest vent grate, I can hear the steady hum of machinery mixed with the murmur of voices. Being as careful as possible not to make any noise of my own, I inch my way toward the grating, staying as much in the shadows as I can while still being able to peer down into the control center below.

There are only two Imps that I can see, Renquist and Echoes. They're both kicked back in their glossy black chairs, feet resting on the console, staring absently at the monitors that flicker around them and create strobing patterns on their disinterested faces.

My eyes are drawn to the transparent locker behind them and the cache of weapons gleaming in it. Neurostims, seismic charges, knives, clubs, guns, grenades…a virtual treasure trove of destruction that can make the difference in the duration and outcome of our little stay here.

All I have to do is figure out how to get my hands on them.

Bleep!

One of the lights on the monitor hiccups a glow of red, and both Imps' postures stiffen.

I duck farther into the shadows and hold my breath.

Echoes presses a button and the intercom crackles to life. "This is control center one."

"Control center one," the voice on the other end says, "this is recon patrol four. We've finished our sweep. All pylons powering the sonic fence perimeter have been repaired and reinforced. We shouldn't have a problem with any more of them getting inside."

My pulse quickens. *Them*? *Inside*? Could the Fleshers have already breached security?

"Copy that, recon patrol," Echoes responds. "I'm showing no signs of activity on the cams and I've triple checked all locks and shields. Nothing's getting in again. And it'll be dawn soon. Looks like we all pulled an uneventful shift."

"Thank the Deity for that," Renquist mutters. "I'll rest more easy when our contingent is up to full strength and not this skeleton crew they have running the station."

"You got that right," the voice on the intercom crackles. "Whatever made them pull out the bulk of our troops must be pretty big. This is recon patrol, over and out."

The red light dies.

So Infiernos is operating with limited personnel. This definitely gives us the edge.

Renquist gathers his gear and heads for the door. "Speaking of dawn, shift's almost over. Time to squeeze in a little stress relief before I'm outta here." His wink to Echoes sends a chill worming up my spine.

Echoes grins. "That's right. You've got a two-day furlough coming. Who's it going to be tonight? Pretty boy, Spark?"

"Bledsoe." Renquist pauses. "You won't see me for another forty-eight hours. Try not to let anyone in while I'm away." Then he's gone.

So Jorgen's dead and Dahlia's alive.

Ignoring the throbbing in my hands and knees, I speed through the tunnel, navigating through the maze of ductwork, trying to get my bearings and make it to Dahlia's cell before Renquist does.

But the whole way, one thought jackknifes into my brain. Even if I do get to her first, *what* can I do?

I've finally made it to the ducts above the holding cells and my eyes barely register the sleeping forms below.

Finally, at the far end, I peer through the vent down into Dahlia's cell. Unlike the others, she's breathing heavy, like when she's exercising. She must be doing push-ups.

And she's still alone.

I press my face against the grate. "Dahlia!"

Rustling below me. "Who *is* that?" she whispers back up to me.

"It's me, Spark."

"How did you—?"

"I don't have time to explain. Renquist is on his way to your cell. He's going to . . . *hurt* you."

"What are you talking about? Lee-Man said I should trust you now, but—"

"Just shut up and help me unscrew the grate!" I thrust my hands through the grate and start unscrewing the bolt with my bone blade.

In the distance, the sound of footfalls reaches my ears, mingling with our heavy breathing. Each clomp of the boot heel against the floor is like a chisel to my heart.

In a flash, Dahlia joins me, her hands sweaty and trembling against mine, helping to twist the screws I've loosened. In seconds we have one side free, then another; all we need is one more and I'll be able to push it aside and help her escape, though I'm not quite sure where we'll go.

The bone shard slips from my hands and clatters against

the floor, disappearing into the darkness. Dahlia's hand tightens around mine. The footsteps must be no more than ten feet away now. Already there's enough light from Renquist's flashlight for me to make eye contact with her.

She drops to the cot and I duck into the shadows of the shaft, just as Renquist's hulking form stops outside her cell door. My heart's thudding in my temples.

As he reaches into a compartment for his security access card, Dahlia's arm darts underneath her bed and emerges with something clutched in her hand, which she tucks into the mattress.

It must be the bone fragment I dropped.

The door to her cell opens and Renquist saunters in. He pauses by her bed. In the sickly yellow glow of the flashlight he sets on the floor, I can see his face twist into an awful leer.

I'm not sure if the breathing I'm hearing is Dahlia's or my own.

"Rise and shine, beautiful." He reaches down and strokes her hair with his stubby fingers.

Dahlia bolts up. I see an ivory flash as her arm thrusts toward his thick neck.

But Renquist is too quick. He grabs her wrist before she can make contact and backhands her with the other hand. *Thwack!*

"*Ungh!*" Her neck snaps back and she hits her head against the wall. Her dazed eyes flutter open as she tries to focus. Then she yelps as Renquist's fingers tighten around her wrist and he plucks the bone from her grasp.

"I'm not sure where you got this, little lady, but there'll be time for questions after I'm done."

He lowers himself on top of her.

She spits at his face. "I ain't no lady."

In a flash, she raises her knee and slams it into his groin. Then her fist jabs him in the chin. He reels back and clutches himself. His bellows echo down the hallway.

I smirk as I think of his last exchange with Echoes about ignoring any sounds coming from the cell block. No one's going to be checking things out for a bit.

My fingers wrap around the final screw and twist harder and harder. I can feel the grooves cutting into my flesh, moistening my fingers with blood. The bolt begins to loosen...

Dahlia tries to scramble from the cot. But Renquist grabs her by the hair. His yelp of pain is turned into a howl of rage. His face contorts into a vicious snarl. "You'll pay for that, *bitch*!"

Then he slams her face-down onto the hard floor.

A long moan squeezes out of Dahlia's throat. Her body twitches and writhes.

Then Renquist's tearing off his belt and peeling away his clothes like a snake shedding dead skin. He grabs the bone fragment and climbs on top of her, slicing through her clothing.

My heart's about to tear free of its moorings. I twist the screw as hard as I can—

The sounds of ripping fabric pierces right through me. Flashes of Delvecchio ... and my mother ...

Below, their bodies are a blur of motion, punctuated by the loathsome sound of Renquist's rasping breaths.

Then Dahlia is screaming, a series of long, plaintive wails that burrow deep inside of me, ripping through my guts.

"What's going on in there?" someone yells, farther down the hallway.

Leander?

As I twist the screw harder, my whole body's trembling with rage at the violation below me. Hot moisture leaks down the corners of my eyes, stinging my cheeks with venom. I yank the screw free, heedless of the pain, shove the grate aside, and leap—

Then I'm on Renquist's back, fists pounding, clawing at him, tearing him away from Dahlia's convulsing body.

He shoves me aside, flecks of spittle flying from his foamy mouth. "Just wait *your* turn, *pretty!*"

Something inside of me breaks. I grab Renquist's belt and loop it around his neck. Before he can react, I'm pulling with all my strength, concentrating all my fury, my vengeance, on this one act, pulling tighter and tighter, watching the thick cords on his neck bulge as his body convulses, still attempting to dislodge me. But nothing he does can make me let go.

And then Dahlia plunges the makeshift blade of bone into his chest, once, twice, three times ...

Renquist's body spasms. Then his struggles begin to subside, until he finally stirs no more.

I fling his lifeless husk to the floor, staring at his glazed eyes, the puffy tongue poking out from between purplish lips. Kneeling by Dahlia, I try to arrange her torn clothing to cover her, but she flinches.

"*D-don't ... touch ... me.*" She covers herself.

"I'm sorry." I move away, not knowing what to do or say.

She's trembling, her eyes fixed on Renquist's body. "What are we going to do about *that*."

Pulling away from her, I stare back up at the grate. "We have to get him out of view, up inside the shaft."

She looks confused. "Won't they notice he's missing?"

I shake my head. "Not for forty-eight hours."

I scramble up into the shaft. As she helps me pull and wedge him through the duct, I explain about Renquist's furlough.

Once he's hidden away, I rummage through his uniform and utility belt. Aside from his security clearance card and flashlight, he's got infrared goggles, a chronometer, and a compact, hand-held version of a holocam that can be worn around the wrist and will be great for monitoring the facility's transmissions. He's also got a gun. I take these, and then help Dahlia secure the grate cover enough that no one will be able to tell it's been opened.

I check the time and stare down at her. "It's almost 0600 hours. The morning shift will be arriving soon. Gotta get back to my own cell. You going to be okay?"

She nods. "Thank you. I just need to get cleaned up." Plopping back down on the cot, she stares at the wall, humming some unrecognizable tune to herself as if I'm no longer there.

All the lights come on in the holding cells.

"Rise and shine, maggots!" an Imp croaks down the cell block.

I scramble away from the grating, squeeze past Renquist's

body, and scurry along the maze of ducts like a rat, my heart racing, my breaths rapid-firing. I'm breathless by the time I get back to the grate above my cell.

Tristin's anxious eyes find mine—just as Styles opens the cell door. He stares at the lump on my cot. Apparently, Tristin's bundled the sheet to make it look like I'm there.

He reaches for it. "Get your ass up, Sparky!"

Before he can touch it, Tristin bolts past him out the cell door. Styles turns and grabs her, and they begin to tussle.

"I have to see my brother!" she screeches.

She's positioned her body so that Styles has his back to the cell . . . to *me* . . .

Not wasting a precious moment, I move the grate aside and slip through, moving it back in place just as Styles tosses Tristin back into the room, where she collides against me.

"No ration privileges for *you* today!" he shouts.

Then he glares at both of us. "Now hit the showers. Both of you. Today's Trial is about to start."

I nod at Tristin as we join the others lined up outside their cells.

As anxious as I am about what they have in store for us today, I can't help but smile.

Things have changed.

TWENTY

The next Trial is about to begin.

Cage, Boaz, Drusilla, and Crowley are perched on the ledges of long cylindrical columns, which gleam like silver missiles ready to launch them into oblivion. Even through the unnatural flicker of the holo-projection, there's no mistaking the new lines carved into their haggard faces. Their arms and legs tremble as they struggle to keep their balance, their backs pressed against the smooth steel.

But as bad as the other three look, Crowley's fairing the worst. His flesh is leached of color, a sickly whitish yellow. His features are contorted, his cheeks and jaw clenched. Unlike the others, who are bracing themselves against the pillars with both hands, one of Crowley's hands is grabbing his leg, just above the bloodied bandage that covers his torn flesh. Every time he teeters, I hold my breath, expecting him to lose his grip, tumble off, and plunge down the twenty feet or so to the surface.

Dahlia is standing in the shadows of the common room with the rest of us. Her eyes remind me of the carcharian's—cold, empty sockets reflecting the dark emptiness within. I can't even imagine what she must be feeling—if she's even feeling *anything* right now. Maybe it's better if she isn't.

Welcome to your third trial, Recruits!

The lights in the chamber dim even further, until I can barely make out that the other Incentives are standing here with me.

Spotlights capture the four Recruits, washing out their features in a flood of cold light.

This next Trial is a test of endurance, requiring strength, balance, and the ability to withstand any natural threats you may encounter in hostile territory. Be the last Recruit to remain on your pedestal and you will be the victor. The winning Recruit must then select which one of their failed competitors must choose between their Incentives. However, if the victor is too weak to make this choice, then he or she will be deemed unworthy and immediately be shelved, along with any remaining Incentives.

My stomach knots. I remember how, during my own Trials, I was faced with the terrible burden of making a blind choice. The horror I felt when I found I'd selected Cypress—and watched her die alongside her two young children.

The choice is always yours. Good luck.

My eyes dart through the darkness, toward my cell.

Now. While this Trial is going on. I have to risk going back into those ducts to look for more weapons.

The signal blares through the chamber.

A low hum fills the room, vibrating through my teeth. Cage, Boaz, Drusilla, and Crowley are braced against their pillars, which have begun to shake as if they're suffering the aftershocks of an earthquake. Drusilla and Boaz's eyes are shut as they struggle to retain their balance. Crowley's face is a concoction of fear and pain. On the opposite end, Cage is staring straight ahead, stone-faced, as if he's a sculpture etched out of his pillar.

Something brushes against my arm and I whirl. It's Leander. In the dimness, I can barely make out his silhouette as he nudges his chin toward my cell, then back at the holos. But there's no mistaking the nod he gives me.

He moves off to the center of the room.

"Boaz!" he shouts at the images. "You can do this! Don't punk out on me!" He shouts obscenities at Boaz's holo that would make even the most hardened Imps blush.

The perfect diversion to keep the focus off me.

None of the others seem to notice, their eyes glued to the three-dimensional projections as they agonize over whether or not they're about to receive their own death sentences.

Now's my chance. I sink deeper into the shadows, melding into the darkness until I'm feeling my way back into my cell. Once inside, I waste no time springing onto the cot, pushing the grate aside, and wedging myself up and through, ignoring the cold metal clawing at my skin.

After groping through Renquist's things near Dahlia's

cell, I grab his flashlight and flick it on the dimmest setting, careful to keep it pointed away from the cell below. Good. This makes it much easier to pull on his uniform over the rags I'm wearing. Though I've packed on a lot of muscle during my Imposer training, Renquist's uniform is still too big—I hope whoever spots me won't look too closely.

Checking the weapon to make sure it's loaded and ready, I holster it to my belt. I wedge the earpiece of Renquist's hand-held holo in my ear and flick on the device. I adjust the audio level so it's loud enough to hear, but not so loud that it would drown out any other warning sounds I might encounter. Then I start to crawl, keeping the hand-held in front of me so I can monitor the Trial as I slither through the twisting maze of ducts.

Crowley is shaking so bad, it's like he's having a seizure.

"Hang on!" Cage shouts at him. The veins on his forehead are pulsing from his own effort to stay aloft. "You *got* this. Don't give up now, mate!"

But it's useless, and I can tell Cage knows this by the panicked look plastered on his own face. Crowley is teetering like a top sputtering out of control.

I creep along faster, pushing myself to the limits.

Crowley turns to Cage. His wide eyes are coated with fear. "I...I *can't*..."

He drops off the pedestal like a felled bird.

"*Crowley!*" Cage cries.

Even through the earpiece I can hear the thud of his body as it slams onto the floor. Then he just lies there, his body twitching.

They're just going to leave him there like garbage until it's all over.

I hurry along faster.

Recruit Crowley has been eliminated in this Trial. But for those of you that are left, the test of endurance has just begun. Out in the wilderness during actual combat conditions, you never know what types of natural elements you may encounter.

I whip around a corner as fast as I can. The duct leading into the locker room is just ahead. I pause to get my bearings and study the images projected on my palm.

"What's going on now?" Drusilla screeches, echoing my own thoughts. She and Boaz are barely hanging on, alongside Cage, but now have their eyes pried open.

Boaz nudges his chin toward the side of her pillar. "Your pedestal's *opening!*"

"So's yours!" She whips her head around to Cage. "That goes for you too, Cage."

I reach the duct and fumble with my utility belt, whipping out the compact blow torch and aiming it at the slats in the grate. There isn't time to twist open screws. But even as I turn it on and the wavering tongue of blue fire casts flickering shadows down the shaft, I can't help but glance at my hand-held.

Things are crawling out of the openings on the pedestals.

Hundreds of them. Maybe thousands. Twisting, worm-like insects, like rotting grains of rice, wriggling and headless, engulfing the three Recruits. Some form of mutated maggots.

"*What the hell?*" Boaz tries to flick them away, but he almost loses his balance and manages to steady himself at the last moment. "*Get them off of me!*" His shriek pierces my eardrum.

"Stop it!" Drusilla cries. "Just hold still. They only eat *dead* tissue!"

I cut through the slats as quickly as I can, hoping no one below can hear them as they clatter onto the floor. Then I kick in the last of the slats and drop down.

Getting my bearings, I check my gear and look around, making sure no one's seen me. But the chamber is clear and I spring to my feet, straightening out my uniform, my belt, my helmet, and trying to look as presentable as I can. Once I'm done, I kick the melted pieces of the grate into a corner and hope no one will discover them.

I have no choice but to deactivate the com unit.

Then I make my way to the door, take a deep breath, and open it, emerging into the corridor. The control center should be to the right. No sooner do I start out in that direction than two Imps round the corner and head my way.

"It's only a matter of time before one of those things gets through the perimeter and into central control," the taller of the two is saying to his shorter, thicker companion.

"All the more reason we should take out the lot of 'em before they get the chance," the other responds.

Who are they talking about? The Fleshers? The Imps are just a couple of feet away.

With the brim of my helmet low, I keep my stride measured as I march past them, offering a salute, which they return absently.

Dead ahead is the entrance to the control room. I dig

into my pocket for Renquist's access card. Whipping it out, I slide it into the slot by the side of the door.

Ping!

The light blinks green. **Authorization accepted.**

Then I slip inside. The good thing is that the control room is dimly lit, thanks to the Trial in progress. There are maybe half a dozen Imps there. I brace myself for an onslaught of questions, anticipating the lies I'll have to weave, working up my conviction.

But all their eyes are riveted to the main screen. I take a sharp breath.

The three Recruits are completely covered in maggots.

"Hang on, Boaz!" Cage spits the words and I can see flecks of the wriggling larvae spray out. Boaz teeters on his pedestal. The maggots are covering his lips, squirming their way into his nostrils…

"*Help!*" Boaz cries through a mouthful of slimy invaders. His hands fly to his face, tearing at it, scraping as many of the insects off as he can—

And he loses his balance, plunging off the pedestal to join Crowley at the bottom.

Recruit Boaz has been eliminated from the competition.

"*Son of a bitch!*" One of the Imps shoves the other.

"Pay up! I want my cash *now*, Bartesque!" The other Imp shoves him back.

Bartesque plunges his hand into his uniform and whips out a wad of bills. "Double or nothing the girl takes it!" He slams the money down on the console.

"You're on!" his companion snorts.

While they're all preoccupied, I march straight toward the supply cabinets and begin loading my satchel with all the weapons that I can.

On the screen, an onslaught of arachnids has joined the horde of maggots engulfing Cage and Drusilla, their hairy, spindly legs creeping over them as they skitter out of the gashes in the pillars.

"I can't take much more of this!" Drusilla cries. "Please! You gotta let *me* have this, Cage!"

Cage shakes his head. "I can't! Tristin needs me... and... I'm sorry, I *can't!*"

I continue stuffing my satchel. A few more guns, some thermal charges, flame thrower.

A big hand clamps around my shoulder and I nearly piss myself. "You're sure packing some firepower, aren't you there, sonny?"

It's Styles.

All my muscles stiffen. I keep my back to him. "Heading out to Quadrant seven," I grunt, lowering my voice.

He chortles and claps me on the back, nearly sending me through the cabinet. "I hear you. Those things are getting out of hand. You must be part of the reinforcement squadron."

"Uh-huh." I zip my satchel shut.

His fingers remain on my back, pressing into my flesh like iron. "What did you say your name was?"

My stomach sinks. This is it. It's all been for nothing.

"Wahoo!" Bartesque's companion bellows.

Styles releases me and I can feel him turning away. "What's up?"

"Seems like the little lass has lost her grip, which means *I* win, double or nothing!" the Imp says. "Pay up, Barty!"

Recruit Drusilla has been eliminated. Recruit Cage, you have emerged victorious in this Trial. You must now select which Recruit will have to make their selection in the next sixty seconds.

Styles shuffles away from me. "How about a little wager as to who he's gonna choose?"

"You're on, buddy!" Bartesque snorts.

Without wasting a precious second, I grab my bag and slip out the door, trying to move as fast as I can through the corridors without arousing suspicion before Styles decides to sound an alarm.

Then I'm in the utility room and scrambling up the shelves into the ceiling, pushing the satchel containing the weapons ahead of me as I crawl as fast as I can back toward my cell. Breathless, I flick on the hand-held as I scuttle through the ducts. Cage has been lowered to ground level and a drone is just finishing spraying off the last of the vermin from his body. His face is a struggle of emotions.

Recruit Cage. Make your selection now.

I reach my cell.

Cage's eyes are glistening with moisture. "I'm so sorry. I can't eliminate Crowley. He's too weak to even talk—it'll mean his death. And if I choose Boaz and he chooses Leander this round, then Corin dies if Boaz fails again. Can't chance that.

I'm sorry. I have to choose *you*, Dru. Please . . . forgive me . . ."
Anger flashes across his face as he wipes his eyes.

"*It's not fair . . .*" Drusilla sobs.

I tear off my uniform and drop down from the vent shaft into my cell, emerging into the holding area and rejoining the others just in time to see two Imps grab Arrah and Mr. Ryland, shove them into their cells, and strap them into chairs.

Then that terrible, familiar rumble as the entire cell is lifted and disappears, reappearing on the holographic projection of the trial field.

No. We're not ready yet. And if we try to escape now, we'll be caught before we even get started.

"It's all right, baby," Mr. Ryland calls to Drusilla. "Whatever you decide, I can accept it. I'm proud to have you as my daughter."

Drusilla is sobbing uncontrollably. "Daddy . . . I love you *so* much . . ." She turns to Arrah.

"Oh, Arr . . . I love you too . . . I *can't* . . . I can't do this . . ." She looks up to the sky. "*Please . . . don't make me do this . . .*" Drusilla sinks to the floor. "I . . . I choose . . ."

Mr. Ryland clears his throat. He gestures toward Arrah. "The one thing I want more than anything else is for you to get out of here and live your life. You have a better chance with her, Drusilla. Choose *me*."

Arrah's sobbing, too. "No, Dru. He's your father. I understand. I love you too much to make you choose him."

Recruit Drusilla. Make your selection now.

Drusilla's eyes bounce between them. "I choose . . . my

father!" she screams, burying her face in her hands and collapsing to her knees. "Daddy, I'm so sorry ... I'm so sorry," she wails over and over again.

Cage tries to hug her, but she shoves him away.

Metal spikes thrust from the ceiling above.

Mr. Ryland smiles. "I love you, honey."

Then the metal slams down, impaling him. His head slumps over as a fountain of blood erupts from the wounds.

The holo fades, and we're herded back into our cells in silence.

TWENTY-ONE

My eyes and nostrils are stinging from the stench of the rotting corpses filling the cart. Every bone in my body aches from all the stooping and lifting.

For hours, we've been wading through the heaps of dead inmates that litter the stockades. We drag them into the wagon, haul them to the crematorium, and pile them into the incinerators. Back and forth, back and forth—a grisly conveyor belt of human tragedy.

If we don't get out now, those of us who are left will be making this journey very soon.

Arrah finishes shoving the body of a middle-aged woman on top of the pile. The woman's arm swings off the side, swaying from side to side like a grayish-blue pendulum warning that time is running out. No rigor. Must've been dead for a couple of days already, from the look and smell of it.

Arrah turns, smearing the sweat and grit from her brow

with her forearm. She looks at me with eyes so dark they're like twin black holes that have swallowed the light, after everything they've seen.

I know that look very well. It stares back at me whenever I happen to catch my own reflection.

"Did you see the look on Dru's face, Lucian?" she asks. "She looked so frightened. So *lost*..." I almost get the feeling she isn't talking to me. Just trying to make sense of the horror in her own head.

But how do you rationalize a nightmare?

"And I couldn't do a thing." She rolls the wagon over to a body set apart from the others.

It's Mr. Ryland.

His remaining eye has rolled up into his head and looks like a bloodied eggshell. The other socket is a craggy cavern where one of the spikes pierced it.

Arrah stares at him. Her lips are quivering. Tears mix with the soot on her face, streaming down her cheeks like black blood. She drops to her haunches. One of her hands touches Ryland's face, caressing his cheek before closing his remaining lid.

I stoop beside her, covering the dark craters torn through Ryland's chest with the tattered remnants of his shirt. Arrah smooths his hair. "He was going to be my father-in-law. Dru and I—we were going to be married. Right after I finished my training and she wasn't in any more danger of being recruited. Why didn't she let *me* die instead? *Why?*"

I grimace. "Trust me. I know, it's hard. I've lost people

too … " I glance away. "Drusilla and you still have the possibility of a future. She loves you. Just like you love her."

A bitter laugh bursts from her lips. She grabs Ryland by the arms and I take my cue and grab his feet. Then we're lifting the body between us.

She stares at me across the corpse. "Even if we do make it out of here, every time Dru looks into my eyes, she'll know that I'm the reason her father is dead. And I'll *know* she knows. How can you have a future like that?"

I don't answer. What can I say that won't sound hollow?

We maneuver Mr. Ryland into the cart. "Careful," she says.

Then it's done. We return and load up for another trip to the furnace.

I grip her hand. "We're breaking out today," I mutter.

She squeezes me back. "Who's *we*?"

"All of us."

I nudge my chin toward Leander and Dahlia, who are trundling their own loaded cart toward us, followed by Tristin and Corin wheeling a smaller one. As soon as they're close enough, I grip the handlebars of our cart and keep pace with them as we head toward the crematoriums.

Leander and Dahlia draw up alongside us. "Did you tell her yet?" he mutters through heavy breaths.

Arrah's eyes dart back and forth between the two of us. "Tell me *what*?"

As we roll through the utility corridor and into the crematorium, I fill Arrah in on my excursion to the control room and the cache of weapons now hidden in the duct.

The glazed look in her eyes turns to surprise, and then the familiar Arrah starts to seep through. "You've been doing all that while the rest of us have been napping?" Her smile fills me with warmth. "Not bad. Looks like the Fifth Tier has a few surprises left in him."

I smile back and nudge Leander. "I had a little help from the Second Tier over here. Leander's not completely useless."

"Keep talking, Sparkles, and you'll see how useless my fist is." Even without looking I can tell he's smiling when he says this.

My eyes connect with Dahlia. "And of course I couldn't have put this little Op together without our First Tier."

She nods. "Thank you."

When we reach the furnace, Dahlia helps me open the heavy iron door. Waves of heat emanate from the crackling, spooling flames. One by one we toss the bodies inside.

"We need to get away *before* the next Trial, or one of us ain't gonna be along for the ride," Leander says.

"Maybe we should rethink this," Tristin interrupts. "It might not be safe. We have to have faith that—"

"*Faith?*" Dahlia whispers. "The only thing I believe in is putting a bullet in each of these bastards' brains."

Leander nods. "You got that right, D." He turns to Tristin. "It's great that you're all in tune with the higher powers and shit. But nobody's coming for us. The only thing that's gonna save our asses is *us*."

Staring at Corin's vacant eyes sends chills through me. I muss the kid's hair. "How's *he* doing?" I ask Tristin.

"He's not saying much these days." Her smile is laced with

sadness. She looks up at me. "But he's hanging in there for now."

Yeah, but for how much longer?

"That's why we need to get out of this hell-hole now," Dahlia murmurs, as if reading my mind.

Tristin pulls Corin closer to her. "I hope this plan of yours, whatever it is, will work. Does it include the Recruits? After all, what happens to them without any Incentives to fight for?"

"They get Shelved? Sent to bed without supper? Who gives a damn about *them*?" Leander pushes past Dahlia and gets in Tristin's face. "Look. I don't give a crap about your religious-pacifist bullshit. You, your brother, and the other insurrectionists are the reason we're all in this mess in the first—"

I grip his arm and pull him away from her. "Leander. *Lay. Off. Her.*" My voice is steady, in control. "It doesn't matter how or why we got here. It's going to take *all* of us to get out."

Dahlia shoves him with her shoulder. "You're forgetting what they did to Rod-Man...what they did to..." She closes her eyes for a moment and grits her teeth. "What they've done to *all* of us."

Leander's demeanor flicks like a switch. He backs away. "Sorry, D. Just trying to wrap my head around this whole..." He runs a palm over his buzzed hair.

She shakes her head. "There aren't any rebels, any Imps anymore. Only those who are getting away. And those who are going to die."

Arrah steps forward and touches Dahlia's shoulder, caressing it, trying to quell the fire. "I agree that we're all in this together—rebel and trainee alike. But Tristin *does* have a point. The Recruits are victims just as much as we are." Her eyes find mine and I can see the desperation there. Of course she's worried about Drusilla. Just like I worried about Digory once.

"Dahlia and Tristin *both* have good points," I say. "I've taken the Recruits into account. I'll fill you in on all the deets later. But the short version is, we're outta here before the next trial. During our escape, we'll set off explosive charges. I've already planted them throughout the ducts. That ought to keep the Imps busy and provide a diversion. The chaos will give the Recruits a chance to make a break for it."

The furnace doors squeal as I slam them shut. I turn to face the others. "I don't know about you, but I'd rather go out on *my* terms. What do you say?"

They move in, until we form a circle. Arrah nods. "I'm in." She holds out her hand and I reach out to clasp it.

"So am I," Tristin murmurs. Her own hand touches ours.

Dahlia adds her grasp to the mix. "As long as we get to kill them."

Leander smiles at me. "For Rod-Man." His grip is firm.

A smaller hand reaches out. Corin's. His fingers feel cool as they rub against my own. "Let's kick their asses," he whispers.

Someone's coming down the corridor, and we separate.

"What do we have here?" Styles marches up to us, along with a couple other Imposers, hands on their holsters. I shift into a slouch.

He sneers at the bodiless carts, then back at us. "If the garbage has already been taken care of, what the hell are you sorry lot doing just standing around? Move it back to your cells unless you want to join the rest of the trash in the smoke box."

His companions snicker alongside him as they herd us from the crematorium back through the corridors. I have to try to control the fresh spring in my gait. Whatever happens, this will be the last time we'll have to burn bodies and walk down this path.

Instead of leading us to the showers first, Styles and his crew lead us right back to our cells. "Inside," he snarls. Using the butt of their weapons, they prod us inside.

I stare him down. "Is that our punishment? No showers? I wouldn't think you'd miss a chance to see us naked."

He smirks at me. "Soon. But unfortunately, there's no time."

It feels like vermin are gnawing at my gut from the inside. "*No time?* What are you talking about?"

He leans in real close and leers. "Timetable's been moved up. The fourth trial is about to start."

TWENTY-TWO

We're taken from our cells and deposited on top of a circular field of sand, which is shaped like a giant ant hill with spiral pathways etched into the sloping sides. Our half-naked bodies are shackled together at the wrists by a long length of chain that's embedded in a stone pillar at the top of the mound. Metal bands, containing a thin slot and a blinking red light, have been clamped around each of our necks. The lump in my throat is not solely due to the tightness of the band digging into my neck.

Directly ahead, on the far side of the field, Drusilla, Cage, Crowley, and Boaz emerge—in the flesh this time. They're standing on a circular platform that rose up from beneath the sand, the hole sealing behind them with a serpent's hiss as they step off. Just like us, they're barely clothed.

Welcome Recruits, and congratulations on making it to round four of the Trials.

In spite of Cassius's greeting, the four of them look anything but thrilled.

Scattered throughout the field are keys that will unlock both the collars around your Incentives' necks and their manacles. There are only three keys available, and four Recruits. The collars have been equipped with a lethal neurotoxin that will be dispensed if not removed in time. The last Recruit to complete the task will be required to select which one of their Incentives will receive the toxic dose. Good luck!

BUZZ! The shrill sound of the starting signal ricochets through the Trial field.

Drusilla tears away from Cage and Boaz, who take a few seconds to disengage from the ailing Crowley before sprinting off after her. Crowley teeters as he struggles to maintain his balance. This whole contest won't even be close.

My hand finds Dahlia's and I expect her to flinch and pull away, but her fingers slip into mine and squeeze firmly.

"It's not over yet," I mutter through clenched teeth.

"It will be soon," she mumbles back.

Cage and Boaz have caught up to Drusilla. The three of them look feral, like cornered animals tearing through the crevices in the sand in a fight for survival. Then Drusilla's arm emerges from the rubble holding up a flashing beacon. Dangling from it is a long, golden key.

"*I got it!*" Her elation is almost choked by a sob. But the wide smile on her face is eclipsed as the shadows of Cage and Boaz fall upon her.

Boaz holds out his hand. "Let me have it, Dru." The calm in his voice is unsettling. He takes a step closer to her.

She backs away. "I *need* it." Her glance shoots in Arrah's direction, pleading, before boomeranging to her two fellow Recruits.

"It's not for me." Boaz softens his tone. "It's for Crowley." He turns for a second toward their companion, who is slowly limping along in their direction. "He needs our help, Dru. Let him have this one and you can take the next one."

Drusilla shakes her head. "I'm taking *this* key. If you find the next one, you can give it to him yourself."

The anger returns to Boaz's face. "It's because of that girl. *That Imp bitch!*" He jabs a finger toward Arrah. "First Cage here, and now you. Whose side are you really on, Dru? Huh?"

"It's not about sides. I *love* her."

A harsh sound approximating a laugh bursts from Boaz's lips. "*Love?* This coming from someone who murdered her own father."

Drusilla recoils. I can feel Arrah flinch as if the chains that bind us are a string of nerve endings.

Boaz continues his rant. "These Establishment bastards are slaughtering our people and you're too selfish to care." He lunges at her, grabbing her throat and pulling the key away.

"Boaz, no!" Cage leaps for him. But Drusilla knees Boaz in the groin.

"*Ungh!*" He doubles over.

Drusilla yanks the key back and rushes over to Arrah. The chains connecting us rattle and pull taut as she grabs hold of her. Their foreheads meld together as Drusilla cups her face, laughter mixed with sobs. "I never thought I'd get to hold you again." She fumbles with the manacles a few seconds before slipping the key into first one lock, then the other. *Click! Click!* The chains binding Arrah clatter to the ground.

Arrah throws her arms around Drusilla, planting kisses all over her face until their lips meet, first tenderly, then passionately, as if they're sharing one final breath that will dissipate the moment they pull apart.

"I'm so ... so sorry about your dad ... " Arrah chokes on her words.

"We can't ... not now ... " Drusilla's tone is tender but I can sense the sharp edge, like a paper cut, barely scratching the surface but deeply painful.

I finally turn to Drusilla. "Get Arrah out of here. *Now*."

Drusilla jams the key into the collar's slot and turns. The device pops open. Arrah rips it off and turns to me. "Lucian—"

"Remember what we talked about at the furnace." I force a smile. She's still looking at me as Drusilla hauls her off to the safe zone.

Recruit Drusilla has released her Incentive and is the victor in this trial. Only two keys remain.

Out on the field, Crowley stumbles around while Cage and Boaz circle each other. If it weren't for the occasional loud crunch of fists against flesh, you'd think they were dancing; their swaying, twisting bodies maneuver around each other in a spray of sweat and blood. Dark crimson trickles from their noses and mouths. Boaz speeds up his jabs. But even though

Cage's lip is swollen purple, he's taking a defensive stance, holding back, not hurting Boaz as much as he could.

On the ground between them, another key glistens.

"I need it too, mate," Cage rasps, sounding more desperate than I've ever heard him. "My *sister*—"

"And that *traitor*!" Boaz takes another swing, but Cage blocks it. "You think I haven't seen it in your eyes? If you lose this Trial you could *still* save Tristin. But you won't sacrifice him, will you? Even after what he *did* to us?"

"Shut up," Cage rumbles.

Boaz takes advantage of Cage's temporary distraction and bashes him in the face. Cage reels backward and Boaz lunges for the key.

Cage isn't down yet. He grabs Boaz by the shoulder and hauls himself up. His fists are a blur. *Thwack! Thwack!* I can't help but recoil from the sound of each impact. It's as if he's venting all of his rage at last.

"Cage!" Tristin screams.

But her brother doesn't seem to hear her. Or doesn't want to.

"They're just playing it up for the higher-ups." Leander nudges Corin in the shoulder and steps forward, shielding his view.

But the kid ignores him, pushing past Leander to get a better view. "Leave him alone, Cage!" Corin screams.

Boaz collapses, his face pulpy like potter's clay.

Cage steps over him. He staggers over to us almost as if he's on auto-pilot. His chest is heaving.

Tristin falls into his arms. "You shouldn't have ... "

228

"It's … going … to … be … okay." His hands leave bloody prints on her skin as he pulls her close.

Our eyes meet for a second over her shoulder, and he turns away. Ashamed of what he's done? Or that I know how he feels about me? Does he know I can never feel anything for anyone ever again?

Cage unlocks Tristin's bonds, then turns and unlocks mine. "Thanks for looking after my sister," he says as my neck band falls away.

I nod. "Cage—"

He turns away and hustles Tristin to the safety zone.

Recruit Cage has released his Incentives. Only one key remains.

I grab for Dahlia's hand but she shakes her head. "Don't worry about me. It's better this way." Her eyes glisten and I see relief there.

Then I'm pulled away by Cage and thrust into the safety zone, helpless, as my foster mother's daughter waits to be murdered.

A few feet from where Boaz lies, Crowley crawls across the sand, his pale body covered in grit and scrawling a bloody streak like the tail of a comet about to burn out. He slumps beside Boaz.

Boaz reaches out and touches Crowley's head. "Aren't we both a mess." He tries to chuckle, but it turns into a cough and he spits out a mouthful of bloody saliva. His face turns serious. "Don't worry. I'm going to get you some help."

But Crowley's barely stirring now.

Boaz raises himself on hands and knees. Suddenly, he digs

into the ground. A high-pitched laugh echoes throughout the field.

He raises his hand.

In it rests the last key.

My whole body tenses. This is it. Now Dahlia dies.

But instead of staggering over to the Incentives, Boaz stoops, grabs Crowley in his arms, and half-carries, half-drags him over to them.

To Dahlia.

Her eyes open wide. There's confusion there at first. And then, regret.

Boaz thrusts the key into Crowley's hands. "*You* have to do this, brother."

Crowley's eyes flood. He mouths something to Boaz. Even though I can't hear it, I know he's expressing his gratitude. Boaz is giving him a chance to live.

A chance for Dahlia to live.

Crowley steps over the line and almost tumbles.

Leander catches him in his arms. "You're almost there," he says. His voice sounds different than I've ever heard it before. Compassionate. Tender. Gently, he guides Crowley's hands toward Dahlia's bonds, holding them steady while Crowley unlocks her hands, then moves to her collar.

Dahlia is shaking her head. Tears stream from her eyes. "What the hell are you doing?"

Leander smirks at her. "You've always been First Tier, D." He shrugs. "Guess this is one time *I* get to be first."

The collar drops to the floor.

Recruit Crowley has released his Incentive. Recruit

Boaz, you have emerged last in this Trial and must now make your choice.

Dahlia drags Crowley over to the safety zone. They stand silently beside me.

Leaving only Boaz and Leander and Corin.

Corin takes Leander's hand. "I'm not going to leave you."

Leander swallows hard. "Thanks, kid."

Recruit Boaz. Make your selection now.

Boaz turns to Leander with what appears to be genuine regret in his eyes. "Sorry."

Leander looks in our direction and nods. "Not as sorry as these bastards are going to be when they find out what we're made of. Flame Squad to the end." He salutes us and Arrah, Drusilla, and I return it.

"I choose Incentive Leander." Boaz's voice breaks, losing its earlier bravado.

"I'll be with you soon, Rod-Man."

Then the smile on Leander's face disappears, turning into a grimace. His body convulses and his hands fly up to his temples. Fountains of blood spring from his mouth, his nose, his ears. His eyes swell, then burst, spattering his chest with gobs of pulp. He collapses. Corin crouches down and cradles Leander's head in his lap.

Dahlia stiffens beside me.

Around me, the others stare at the corpse.

The last thing Leander saw before he died was *us*.

That's the same thing all the other Imposers at this installation are going to see.

TWENTY-THREE

We've been running on pure adrenaline for the last couple of hours since Leander's death.

Down in the crematorium, my eyes water from the stinging heat of the furnace. Inside, resting on the metal rack, Leander's body blackens as his crisping skin shrivels away to the bone. A recently virile and vibrant human being, reduced to nothing but a smoldering pile of ash in minutes. I've grown so used to the stench of roasting flesh that it barely registers anymore.

I feel like I'm the one that's burning.

Tonight's the night we either break out of this shithole, or go down taking as many of them with us as we can.

Either one works for me.

Since we've been under constant watch ever since the last trial, I have to dish out the details of the plan piecemeal—as we load more bodies onto the carts, mop out the grime from the cells, take our shower, and finally sit down in the mess hall, sharing what could be our last, meager meal.

Where once there were two tables, now there's only one.

"So, you said you and Tristin are gonna come get us tonight?" Corin asks through a mouthful of gruel.

My eyes flick to Ensign Echoes, the lone Imposer, who's standing by the doorway stifling a yawn.

"That's right," I reassure him. After everything Corin's been through, I'm just glad he's speaking again. The fire I saw in his eyes way back during our first encounter at the research facility is coming back. "After lights-out, Tristin and I will crawl through the ducts and set the timers on the charges I planted."

Tristin gives him a hug and smiles. "Then we'll come back and use the access card Lucian and Dahlia stole from Renquist, to unlock the cell blocks for you guys to slip out."

Dahlia swallows, her eyes staring ahead into nothingness. "Like I said before, opening the cell doors will transmit a signal to the duty guard in the control room. They'll be on us in seconds. We have to be ready to take them on."

I glance again at Echoes, who's scratching his nose. "Don't worry. I told you, we'll have some firepower on our side. You'll get your chance."

Arrah lifts her water cup to her lips, covering her mouth as if she's going to sip. "And you're sure you have enough weapons?"

I stir the slop in my bowl with a finger, not looking at her. "At least enough to take the skeleton crew by surprise before they send for reinforcements." My eyes sweep across them.

"The explosives will distract any guards long enough for us to slip through the ducts, into one of the aircraft hangars, commandeer a Vulture, and get the hell out of this place."

Corin is staring at Leander's empty chair. "Where will we go?" he whispers.

I reach out and muss his hair. "Anywhere's better than here." I smile at him, but I've been thinking the same thing. Flee to where? We'll be fugitives. If the Establishment doesn't find us first, there are other things out there.

"Finish up!" Ensign Echoes calls from across the room. "Time to get going!"

The squeak of chairs fills the room as the five of us push away from the table as one. We give each other one last, knowing look. Within minutes, we're back in our cells. The doors hiss as they seal shut. Moments later the lights are extinguished.

The only thing I can hear are the mingled sounds of Tristin and my breathing, and the throb of my own pulse.

Time passes. Maybe twenty minutes. Maybe thirty. Can't be sure. I strain my ears. Footfalls in the distance. More doors closing. The low rumble of voices fading.

"Time to move," I whisper to Tristin.

Climbing on top of the cot, I reach my fingers up through the darkness of the cell until they brush up against the slats of the grate leading into the vent shaft.

The lights flare on, flooding the cellblock and momentarily blinding me. My heart misses a beat, then shoves a couple of extra ones in to compensate.

Tristin and I stare at each other in shock, not moving a muscle.

"Lucian, what's—"

I shake my head, cutting her off. They found out what we're up to. Somehow, they *know*.

Do they have us under surveillance that I'm not aware? I've searched this cell from top to bottom, hundreds of times, and never found any hidden cameras. What else could it be?

Did one of our very own betray us?

No. After all we've been through, that's something I refuse to believe. Even though it wouldn't be the first time.

I glance at the vent shaft overhead. Whatever's happened, now might be our only chance.

But before I can move, the cell doors spring open.

Attention Incentives, an unfamiliar voice blares from the cell block speakers. **You will now exit your cells and gather in the main holding area. We have a special announcement to make.**

Special announcement? This can't be good.

Several Imposers, including Styles, are milling around brandishing their weapons. Judging from the grogginess on their faces, it looks like everybody's rest period was cut short.

But why?

I follow Tristin out. Arrah and Corin look my way. They both have the same look on their faces—a blend of fear and curiosity. Arrah's eyes are asking me what's going on, but I can only shrug and shake my head.

Only Dahlia seems unfazed. She takes in everything with dead calm—no panic, no contempt, no rage—nothing. It's as if Dahlia Bledsoe abandoned her body, leaving only a gutted shell. The only sign of life is the slow sawing of her ragged nails against her arms, digging deep enough to dredge up thin rivers of glistening red.

Cassius Thorn's face fills the screen.

He nods. "Greetings, Incentives. I know that you are all wondering why your rest period has been interrupted in such an unexpected manner." He pauses for a moment, as if he's waiting for us to agree. "As you are aware, Recruit Crowley sustained an injury during one of the Trials."

"Yes. We *know*," I respond.

"Recruit Crowley's condition," Cassius says, "continues to steadily decline." He sighs. "In fact, he is not expected to survive more than an hour or two at most."

"He wouldn't be in this shape if you'd given him medical atten—"

Styles shoves me with the butt of his weapon. "*Shut up!* You will not address the Prefect—"

Cassius waves him off. "It's all right, Officer. Let him speak." His eyes drill into me. "Actually, what happened to Recruit Crowley could have been completely avoided had his performance during the trial met acceptable standards."

"Acceptable standards?" I scoff. "There's nothing acceptable about any of this."

"Crowley had the opportunity, just like all the other Recruits, to train and make the right decisions—"

"But—"

"His well-being and ultimate fate is in his own hands. A fact *you* of all people, Spark, should be well aware of, given your own brush with illness during last season's Trials—oh!" His fingers massage his forehead. "Forgive me. *My* mistake. You didn't obtain those antibiotics on your own. You relied on the pity of a fellow Recruit—what was his name?" He shakes his head and flicks his hand as if he's shooing away dust. "No matter."

"You know his name," I say. "After all, wasn't he on your payroll?"

"Enough time has been wasted," Cassius says, not taking the bait. "Rather than waiting for Recruit Crowley to expire, thus eliminating himself as well as his sole remaining Incentive from the Trials"—his eyes prey on Dahlia for a moment—"we have decided to preserve the integrity of the Recruitment process and incorporate this unfortunate situation into the next Trial, which will take place immediately."

My mind reels. Holding the Trial right now, especially given Crowley's condition, means Dahlia, like Leander and the others, is as good as dead. No more reprieves.

Unless we don't waste another second and make our break for it right now.

I scan the room. There are only three Imposers. Maybe we can take them out and make a break for the weapons cache hidden in the vent shaft—

Tristin's hand brushes against mine. When I turn to her, she's looking at me as if she's read my mind. The shake of her head is barely perceptible but it's there. I follow her eyes to where Corin's standing, frightened and teary-eyed, just a few feet away from Style's massive bulk.

She's right. As much as I'm dying inside at the thought of losing someone else, there are still three other people counting on my help to get out of here. This time, I can't put my personal feelings above everything else.

The screen showing the image of Cassius dissolves, replaced by a holo of Cage, Drusilla, Boaz, and Crowley, all lying in cocoonlike capsules. Tentacles of wire are wrapped around their naked bodies, which are strapped down to gleaming silver slabs as if they are about to be autopsied. The wires are connected to humming, blinking machinery. I can tell from some of the digital readouts on the display that all bio-functions are being monitored, just like they were when we were trapped underwater in the pods. While I would expect that the heart rate and breathing of the Recruits would be accelerated under these conditions, there's one readout that's too slow, barely blinking.

Crowley is fading fast.

As you can see, Cassius's disembodied voice says, creeping all around us, **the Recruits are incapacitated and tethered to neurostimulators. These are connected to pressure points throughout their bodies, and are capable of delivering sensations of the utmost pleasure—and the most agonizing pain.**

As if on cue, a sharp pain stabs my gut. I can see where this is going.

This Trial will test each Recruit's resilience and ability to withstand pain, in the event that one day they are captured by enemy forces and subjected to the most barbaric interrogation methods.

Each Recruit will be subjected to jolts of pain that will be inflicted in increasingly potent increments via the conductors attached to them. When the Recruit reaches the

limit of their endurance, they will issue an indication for the exercise to terminate—usually in the form of a verbal plea, either spoken or screamed. Thus eliminated, they will either choose between their Incentives, or choose the form of termination of their remaining Incentive. In the event that the Recruit is unable to make their wishes known due to their own death—the holo pans across the Recruits—any living Incentive associated with said deceased Recruit shall immediately be shelved.

But don't be alarmed, Cassius goes on. Undoubtedly, some of you are feeling that this trial is unfairly skewed, that the ability of some of the Recruits to endure pain has been severely compromised, as in the case of Recruit Crowley.

Even though I can no longer see Cassius, I can feel his eyes crawling all over me as he says this, as if it's for my benefit alone. The holo shifts to a close-up of Crowley.

We have taken this factor into account when designing this challenge. That is why the Incentives will serve as a deciding factor that will affect the outcome.

At this, my throat runs dry. I turn to the others and we exchange a look that conveys more than words ever could.

There's a hum from above, followed by the grinding and squeaking of under-oiled gears lowering devices in front of each of us.

I force myself to look at the shiny black box that's hovering before me like a deadly arachnid dangling from its web. The names of the remaining three Recruits are embossed on its surface. Beside each name are two buttons, one green, the other red. It doesn't take a genius to figure out what they're for.

Before you are remotes that control the sensory outputs to each of the Recruits. Your task is simple. Once the commencement signal is given, you are free to select a Recruit of your choosing and provide them with a dose of either pleasure stimulation, via the green button, or pain, via the red button. If you pause for more than five seconds between each selection, or do not make any selection at all—as some of you may be tempted to do—then the particular Recruit representing you will receive a double-dose of the pain option, making him or her more susceptible to failing the challenge and therefore putting yourself at risk of being shelved.

Cassius pauses before continuing. **Just one other caveat. If you decide to simply flood each Recruit with pleasure stimuli and forgo using the pain option, be cautioned that if there is no clear endurance winner after ten minutes, every single Recruit will be automatically eliminated, along with their remaining Incentives, and these Trials will come to a close.**

I can tell from the crushed expressions around me that I wasn't the only one planning to use this strategy.

I urge you to choose strategically and wish you the best of luck. Begin!

Instinctively, my finger jams against Boaz's red pain selector. I cringe when his body spasms and his face contorts; it's as if I'm also hooked up to the neurostims. I can't inflict more pain on Crowley; Cage's fate is tied to Tristin and my survival;

and poor Drusilla and Arrah have been through so much, what with Mr. Ryland's death.

Boaz is strong, he can take it—

Then it hits me. Boaz's fate is tied to Corin's, who in spite of being part of the rebellion is still a kid.

This is impossible.

I've wasted too much time. I have to choose another—

A buzzer pierces the room and Cage's body convulses like a fish wriggling on a hook.

"Cage!" Tristin wails. "*Stop hurting him!*"

Out of the four Recruits, it seems like Cage is the one being bombarded with the most pain. Arrah, Dahlia, and even Corin must be gunning for him as their only viable option, since every hit Crowley and Boaz take brings Dahlia and Corin closer to death.

"Tristin!" I call without turning. "Concentrate every other move on delivering healing impulses to your brother. I'll take care of the rest." I don't care that the others can hear me. I'm sure they have strategies of their own, and I don't blame them.

Each jab of my finger against Drusilla's red button fills me with self-loathing. Over and over again I strike, watching as her body buckles violently against her straps even as Cage's begins to relax.

My eyes flit to my periphery. Arrah's eyes are wide and overflowing with tears. She seems so desperate. I can't even imagine what I'd be feeling if it were someone I loved strapped to that slab.

Then her eyes connect with mine, burning with molten

accusation. She *knows* it's me. She knows I'm hurting the girl that she loves more than anything in this world—

And she has no choice but to try and stop me.

"Dahlia!" she shrieks. "I *need* your help. Concentrate all your blasts on Cage."

Tristin turns on her. "No! You can't do that! My brother can't take much more of this, please..."

Arrah shakes her head. "I'm sorry...Dru's in too much pain..." She whirls. "*Do it, Dahlia!* I'm begging you!" she half-sobs, half-screeches.

Dahlia glances at her, then at me. Not too long ago, she would have glazed me with contempt. But now I can see the conflict on her face, the guilt. The shame. She looks away, as if the very sight of me is a slap across her face. Her eyes lower to her remote unit. Her fingers work the keys.

I'm not sure what she's decided.

"Lucian!" The panic in Tristin's voice courses through me like a live wire.

I look up from my remote. Cage is going into seizure mode again, his body thrashing back and forth, froth pooling at his lips and spraying from his mouth.

However much Dahlia has softened toward me, she's made her choice.

While Cage has the benefit of receiving healing stimuli from Tristin, it's no match for the combined punishment being inflicted upon him from Arrah, Dahlia, and Corin. As strong as Cage is, he's going to break any second—unless he dies first, in which case I'll be dead moments later, and so will Tristin.

There's only one thing left to do.

And I hate myself for it.

My finger hovers over Drusilla's button a split second—before jamming down on a different button, the only other option I have, the only other person who is in a weakened-enough state to succumb to his injuries before Cage does.

Crowley.

"Forgive me..." I whisper over and over again. The pain button on the remote blurs until it's nothing but a blotch of red, consuming my vision, devouring everything in its path. My temples throb, my heart pounds like a mallet, each beat a reverberating gong that drowns out the sounds around me until all I can hear are my own breaths, chugging and hissing like a steam engine.

They've won. They've turned me into the kind of monster that would torture a dying man.

I release the button, flinging the remote across the room. It slams against the wall, smashing into a million pieces.

Just like my chances of getting out of here alive and rescuing my brother.

The machinery buzzing around Cage sparks. The hum dies out. Cage has reached his limit and bowed out.

It's over.

It appears that this Trial has now ended. Cassius's voice is as cold and emotionless as ever. **Recruit Cage's participation has been terminated. He must now make his choice.**

Styles and Echoes appear out of the darkness and grab Tristin and me. The others' faces are a blur of stunned expressions as we're hustled away.

"Lucian," Arrah sobs. "I'm *sorry*." She rushes forward but is intercepted by a couple of other Imps who block her and Dahlia from following us. "*Let go of him!*" Her shouts sound like they're so far away.

Styles and Echoes shove Tristin and me into our cell and strap us in. Styles's lips graze my ear. "Looks like it's finally the end of the line for you, pretty. Shame we never got the chance to get better acquainted."

The doors clang shut and the entire cell begins to rise up the dark shaft. I crane my neck. Above, there's a light shining in the distance, growing brighter and brighter.

I turn to Tristin. She's sobbing quietly. I wish I could reach out to touch her hand. "It's okay. You're going to be fine. Promise me you'll help the others get the hell away from this place."

She squeezes my fingers. "Don't worry. We're going to stop them from doing this to anyone else. I promise."

We share a smile as the grinding gears reach their apex. Light floods into the cell as it lurches to a halt.

We're here.

Just outside our cell, the backrests on the silver slabs rise, elevating the Recruits, including Crowley, to a sitting position. They all look haggard, exhausted. Cage is pale as snow, his lips torn from where he bit into them. A thin red stream flows from them, glistening as it trickles down onto the bobbing nub of his throat.

All my struggles—the separation from Cole, losing Digory and then finding out that he was using me, my vigilante attacks against the Establishment, my involvement with the rebels—every struggle and setback now comes down to this one last moment.

The moment of my death.

Recruit Cage. You must now make your choice.

Cage opens his eyes. They glisten with moisture as he stares at us long and hard. "I wish it didn't have to be like this. But I can only make one choice," he says.

I nod. "It's okay." I almost break out into a chuckle. Nothing has ever been so *not okay* in my whole life. "Do what needs to be done, Cage."

"I swear it, mate."

Your time has expired. Make your selection now.

His eyes fix on me. "I choose ... " His voice chokes. "I choose *Lucian Spark*."

I hear my name as if from the fragments of a dream. Everything feels so disconnected, as if I'm no longer in my own body, but a puff of vapor caught in a swirling eddy that's slowly tearing me apart until everything that's me will fade into nothingness.

The metal grapplers around my arms and legs screech to life, tugging my arms until they're opened wide and my legs are spread-eagled. I look up, staring at the gleaming hydraulic cables coiled like a beast poised to spring at any moment. Drops of oil trickle from the mechanism like dark blood, mixing with my sweat as it oozes down my neck, over my heaving chest.

They're going to rip me apart like a rag doll, tear me limb from limb while the others watch me bleed out right before their eyes.

I struggle against the clamps holding me in place, but it's

no use. Every second is an excruciating blur, waiting, wondering when it's going to happen, what it'll feel like when my tendons and ligaments snap like rubber bands, when my muscles are torn to tattered shreds, when my bones pop free from their sockets, gouging out chunks of flesh...

I'm so sorry I failed you Cole.

I look up and face my unseen audience. "*Do it!*" The words singe my throat.

The hydraulics rattle. My limbs grow taught as the tension in my restraints builds...any moment now...

The hydraulics whine to a halt.

The pressure in my joints relaxes as the restraints go slack.

Why are the lights going dim? What's happening?

A crazed thought boomerangs through my brain. Am I already dead?

With a crackle, the speakers come to life once more.

We regret to inform you that Recruit Crowley has succumbed to his injuries. It would appear that the sensory overload of this last trial has proven too much of a challenge to his weakened system, and he has expired.

Crowley dead? Of course he is. And *I* did it. *I* pushed him over the edge because of my own selfishness. And it was all for nothing.

"Not Crowley, too." Drusilla whispers. Boaz looks stunned. Cage buries his face in his hands.

Of course. Before any of this, Crowley was their friend, their comrade. They were going to change the world together, make it a better place—until I came along.

"It's not your fault," Tristin whispers.

But I won't look at her—can't look at her. At anyone. Why couldn't the Establishment have killed me *before* making this announcement?

Because it's all about making us suffer to the bitter end. My body tenses.

And because—

As Recruit Crowley's participation in these Trials has been concluded, his one remaining Incentive shall now be shelved alongside Lucian Spark.

They're going to murder Dahlia, too.

In seconds, Tristin is released from her confines beside mine and hustled out of view. She's screaming and turning, trying to get a look at me before she disappears.

The next few minutes are the longest, as Dahlia is brought in to take Tristin's place. The sound of each of her restraints being clamped into place shatters through the fog in my brain.

"Dahlia. I didn't mean for it to be like this...I tried so hard..." My voice breaks off. Going to my grave with two more deaths burdening my conscience is too much. It's overload.

She shakes her head. "And just when I thought I might want to live again." She smiles, but her face contorts as she chokes back tears. "Don't blame yourself, Spark. You've done so much for everyone. So much for me. My mother loved you very much. I guess I started resenting you when I was taken away from her. You had something so precious, time with her that I only dreamed of having. I'm sorry."

"This one's ready!" Styles barks. He turns and gives us

a smirk before slinking out of the chamber after the other Imposers.

Leaving Dahlia and me alone … for the last time.

"Just think of your mother," I say to her.

She lowers her voice to a whisper. "My jealousy of you wasn't why I shunned my mother after the Trials. I didn't want her to go to Haven like the other surviving Incentives." She fights a sob. "It's not the paradise that everyone's been led to believe. It's—"

The hydraulics grind to life again.

"—Must stop this at once!" a familiar voice commands, out of my field of vision.

Cassius has left the control room he's been hiding in and is here in the flesh, barreling in with a squadron of Imposers that includes Valerian and Sergeant Slade. His cloak whips behind him as he pushes his way toward us.

When our eyes meet, his face flinches for a moment, but he turns to address the nearest soldier, jabbing a finger in our direction. "We cannot shelve them before we extract useful information from them. Get them down at once!"

"Yes, Sir!" the officer responds, nearly toppling over his companion as they come forward to unlock Dahlia and me from our bonds.

We exchange confused looks as we're released and dragged down to join the other Incentives. This time, Cassius doesn't make any eye contact with me.

But Slade does. She reaches out a leather-gloved hand and grips my jaw, her cold fingers digging into my flesh. Stalactite eyes pierce right through me. "Don't worry, Spark. This is only a brief reprieve. Once you've answered our questions, you'll be shelved." She leans in until our noses are practically touching. "As a matter of fact, I'll be pulling the switch myself."

She shoves me aside.

Styles comes bustling to the forefront with the rest of his squad. He salutes Cassius, Slade, and Valerian. "What's going on, Sir?"

Cassius turns to him, still avoiding eye contact with me. "It appears we've located your companion, Renquist—dead. In one of the vent shafts. Along with a cache of weapons."

"Renquist...is *dead*?" Styles's stance falters. He looks confused.

But he can't possibly be as confused as I am.

"I'm afraid it's true, Styles." Cassius pats him on the shoulder. "It would appear these Incentives have been busy, possibly working in tandem with the Recruits and a traitor in our midst, right under your noses, in fact."

He finally turns to me, his eyes bitter with frost.

"And they're going to provide us with some answers, before they are *all* executed."

TWENTY-FOUR

My aching lungs revolt against the cold water flooding them, cutting off the air. My nails scrape against the metal armrests, cracking, tearing. Can't take it in. Can't spit it out. I flail in the chair I'm strapped to. My body convulses as if jolts of electricity are ripping through it. Drowning, struggling for a single breath...nothing but a big blur. Colors. Shapes. A dozen times already and the fear's worse each time. It's not going to stop this time—oh, shit. Fuck. No....

Swoosh!

The water filling the face mask that covers my head is sucked out once again by the vacuum tube.

Dark shapes move into view, blocking out the hot glare of the floodlights trained on me.

Sergeant Slade and Captain Valerian.

Valerian rips the mask from my head, her nose wrinkling

from the stench of my throw-up. But other than that, she seems just as bored as she did when this whole interrogation began.

The same can't be said for Slade. Her eyes are twinkling like fireflies. Her thin lips pull back to her ears in a half-moon grin. She's relishing every moment of my degradation and suffering.

She leans in conspiratorially. "I am going to ask you for the last time, Spark. Who were your accomplices in the murder of Officer Renquist?"

I clear my throat of the lingering mixture of acid and puke. I lift the burden of my eyes until I'm staring her dead on. "I've already told you at least a dozen times, you stupid bitch." My voice sounds ragged, hoarse. Every syllable hurts. "It was only me. Get it? *Me*."

I'm going to die anyway. No sense dragging anyone else down with me if there's even the remotest of chances—

Smack!

The force of her blow snaps my head back. In seconds, the side of my face is throbbing. My tongue scrapes against my gums, tasting metal. My back molar rattles in its socket.

In spite of the pain, I conjure up a smirk. "You don't have much to give, huh?"

The words hit her like a seismic surge. Her smile cracks and sinks. Tremors rock her reddened face. She tears the helmet from Valerian's hands and slams it back over my head. It still reeks of vomit.

"I think we need to try this again." She marches over to the control panel. Her hand hovers over the release valve.

Buzz!

The sound shatters my already-shredded nerves. A transmission is coming through the com system. The large screen flickers to life.

Slade twists the valve shut. The dark gunk in my mask freezes less than an inch away from the faceplate, sloshing with a sickening wetness.

Cassius appears on the monitor.

Behind him, the others—Cage, Boaz, Drusilla, Arrah, Dahlia, Tristin, and Corin—are barely standing, their faces and exposed parts of their bodies covered in bleeding cuts and bruises. My eyes linger on the kid's hands. Even from this camera angle, I can see the blood oozing from the tips of his fingers.

They pulled every single nail out.

My hands and feet strain against their restraints.

"Has he confessed the conspiracy to you yet, Sergeant?" Cassius asks Slade.

Is that a squirm? This must be the first time I've ever seen Slade this nervous. "Prefect Thorn, Sir. Spark insists on the lie that he was solely responsible for the murder and theft." Her eyes shoot hate my way, then return to Cassius. "But I can assure you, I was just about—"

Cassius's tsks silence her as effectively as a shout. He shakes his head. "No, no, no, sergeant. I'm disappointed. I would have thought someone with your expertise would understand that there is only one thing Lucian Spark cares about." He sighs. "*Others.*"

He holds out his hand to Styles, who is standing behind the group. "Give me your sidearm, Officer."

Styles unclips the gun from its holster. His expression alternates between bloodlust and disappointment, as if he's being robbed of another opportunity to inflict pain on the innocent. He slides the weapon into Cassius's palm. The long, gleaming, black eel contrasts against alabaster flesh.

My heart trips over itself as, one by one, Cassius's long fingers coil around the grip. He holds the gun out and begins to pace along the haphazard line of haggard Recruits and Incentives. They're sandwiched together, terror and exhaustion spread over their faces, eyes pleading through the cameras at me.

Cassius studies each one as he passes, the barrel of his weapon tracing lines of sweat, blood, and grime across their foreheads. "What is it going to be, Lucian? Are you going to cooperate, or am I going to be forced to *motivate* you?"

"Don't bother, Spark." The sound of Boaz's voice surprises everyone, like the dead calm of the eye of a storm that rages around it. "They're going to kill us either way."

The cock of a trigger cracks loudly, like the sound of splintering bone. Cassius shakes his head. "Our first volunteer."

Before words can erupt from my throat, Cassius jams the gun against Boaz's temple. I can almost feel the cold steel pressed against my own head and I flinch—

BANG!

A bright flash obscures the image for a split second. Then a spray of red and gray confetti spatters Cassius and the prisoners closest to Boaz.

The blast propels Boaz's body into Dahlia and Corin. His body teeters for a few seconds, then crashes to the ground.

Someone's cry penetrates my shock. It's Corin, now sobbing uncontrollably.

Cassius turns to look right into the camera again. Flecks of Boaz's blood and brain trickle down his face like obscene tears. He swipes at the gore sprinkling his uniform. "I wish you hadn't made me do that."

Just as quickly, his expression changes into one of rage. He shoves Dahlia out of his way and grabs Corin, jamming the muzzle of the weapon into the child's mouth.

"No, don't hurt him!" Arrah shrieks.

Cage springs forward, but Styles slams the butt of his gun into the back of Cage's head and he falls to his knees.

Cassius's green eyes target me. "What is it going to be, Lucian? As always, the choice is yours."

It feels like I have that mask clamped over my head again—I can't breathe, my stomach twists as it tries to repel an invisible invader.

"Let the boy go." My voice is hoarse. "I'll tell you anything you want to know."

"I knew you would." He pulls the gun from Corin's mouth and pats his head. "Styles. Take this boy back to his cell...for now."

"Yes, Sir. What about the other prisoners?"

Cassius casts a disinterested glance their way and stifles a yawn. "This lot is guilty of conspiracy and treason. Take them down to the furnace and execute them. It will save you the trouble of having to drag the bodies down and burn them."

"Right away, Sir."

Styles and the guards surround the others, dragging them away.

My chair nearly topples over and I buckle against it trying to break loose. The restraints dig into my skin, drawing blood. "Cassius! I said I would tell you whatever you wanted to know. We had an agreement!"

"I said I wouldn't harm *the boy*. The others are expendable collateral. Really, Lucian. You always seem to hear what you want to."

I slump against my chair. It's hopeless. The plan we spent so much time putting together, invested so much of our sweat and hope into, has failed. No second chances. Boaz is dead. The others will follow in just a few minutes. And after I tell them what they want to know, Corin and I will be murdered too.

There's no way out.

"Slade." The Sergeant snaps to attention at the sound of Cassius's address. "A team is on its way to your location to retrieve Spark for further debriefing."

"As you wish, Prefect, Sir. I will make sure—"

But he's already dismissed her with his eyes, focusing instead on Valerian.

"Valerian," Cassius continues. "I need at least one person I can count on. See to it that the custody transfer goes smoothly and is not bungled."

She salutes him. "Everything will be taken care of, Sir."

The transmission ends. The images are snuffed out.

Slade and Valerian exchange glances.

I can tell Slade is bristling with anger at having her judgment questioned. She scowls at Valerian. "Unstrap him."

Valerian hunches over me, using her key to unlock the manacles on my legs first. Then she reaches for the ones on my hands.

I blink as the light of her sidearm reflects in my eyes. No. It's not over. Not until I'm dead.

Snap!

The last manacle clicks open.

In a flash, I'm ripping Valerian's gun free. Before either she or Slade can react, I kick Valerian in the gut. She slams into Slade, throwing off the Sergeant's shot.

BAM!

A burning hot bullet nicks my ear, and a smoking hole rips through the chair. I roll off it in a spinning arc.

BAM! BAM! BAM! The chair explodes into shrapnel. Then there's a loud series of clicks.

Slade's out of ammo.

Before she can reload, I'm letting loose a round of my own. The two officers dive behind an equipment cabinet, scrambling to escape the shower of sparks and chunks of plaster raining down all around them.

Click.

Damn it. The chamber's empty. I hurl the now-useless weapon across the room, where it clatters against the wall.

I might have missed *them*, but at least I've taken out the com unit.

"You'll never get out of here alive, Spark," Slade sneers.

Snap. The ominous sound of another ammo clip locking into place.

I dive for the door. My body slams into the floor and continues to slide on its own momentum—three feet away, two feet, one...

Slade's body is a blur as she leaps from her cover, her weapon blazing.

I don't give her a chance to come to a stop before I spring, head-butting her. Then we're rolling, grappling for the gun clutched in her hand.

Instinctively, my free hand shoots up and grips her fingers, tearing them free of my face, bending them backwards... and backwards... away from the palm...

Her face contorts in pain and rage. "*Argh!*"

SNAP!

The bones in her fingers give way with a piercing crunch.

A shadow eclipses the light above us. We both twist our necks to look. Valerian's standing over us, weapon held at the ready.

Somewhere beyond the doorway and out into the hall, alarms are blaring and the clatter of boots are approaching. The rush of energy I had evaporates, replaced by a tightness all over my body.

Slade leers down at me. "Game over, Spark. I don't care what Thorn says. You're too much of a liability to keep alive." She turns to Valerian. "What are you waiting for? Shoot!"

Valerian's eyes narrow at me. "As you wish."

I close my eyes and tense for the impact as she pulls the trigger—

BANG!

TWENTY-FIVE

I look up to see Slade's face, a look of surprised confusion carved into it. And a smoking hole in her forehead. She releases her grip and slumps over, her body collapsing on top of me.

I shove Slade's corpse off me and spring to my feet. Valerian stands stone-faced, aiming the gun at me. I look at the body at my feet and back to her. "*What the hell?*"

Instead of firing, she tosses the gun to me. In spite of my surprise, my reflexes kick in and I catch it.

She sighs. "Try not to botch this mission too, Spark."

"What?"

But she's already moving, snatching up a familiar looking rucksack from the corner of the room.

The one containing the weapons I stole.

And the detonator.

She lobs it to me. I catch it and look inside. Everything's still intact. But there's a notable addition: a charred silver disc.

It's the remaining concussion charge from my attack on the Emporiums. The one Slade was going to have analyzed by forensics, which would have exposed me. Valerian covered for me…

"I saved these for you, too." She pulls out Digory and my ID tags from her pocket, as well as the holo recording of Digory's transmission to Cassius. "I've recovered the corrupt data on the disc. You may want to take a look.

Now I'm really pissed off. "I told you to trash those. Why the hell would I want—"

"Shut up and *listen* for once, Spark. When you get out of this, you'll thank me."

Reluctantly, I shove the items into the rucksack with the weapons.

The clatter of boots comes to a halt just outside the door. Someone tries the lock but the door remains closed. Fists hammer against it.

"Sergeant Slade! Captain Valerian! What's your status?" someone shouts on the other side.

I cross the room to Valerian. "What's going on here? Why did you—"

She shakes her head. "There's no time. *Hit me.*"

"*What?*"

"I need you to hit me. *Hard.* And make it look convincing. Not like those childish blows you traded with Slade."

Battering against the door, rattling it from its hinges.

Valerian grips my arm. "Do it *now!*"

I swing at her, knuckles connecting with her face, her nose. *Crunch!*

Bone shatters. Blood flies. Her head whips back. She staggers against the wall. When I reach for her, she pulls back, wiping the blood, smiling. "Maybe Jeptha was right after all," she whispers.

"Jeptha? Cage's father?" I stare at her as I dig into the rucksack, finding the detonator. I pull it out, slip it in my pocket, and sling the bag's strap over my shoulder.

The door bursts open.

A half dozen Imposers spill in, weapons aimed. Taking in the sight of Slade's body, Valerian's bloody face, and me standing there holding a gun on her.

There's a series of clicks like the chattering of rodents as every weapon is trained on me. "Drop your weapon!" Ensign Echoes shouts.

I fling the gun to the floor.

One of the officers is communicating via his hand-held. To Styles.

"Just about ready to begin executing the prisoners," Styles reports. I can see the flickering images of Cage, Drusilla, Tristin, Arrah, and Dahlia just beyond him.

"We've got Spark in custody," Echoes responds. "Proceed with shelving immediately."

My finger jams down on the detonator in my pocket. I can hear multiple explosions rock the complex like a massive earthquake. The room teeters, and everyone falls to the floor. The lights go out, plunging everything into total darkness.

"What the hell was that?" Echoes's voice pierces the blackness.

The sound of grinding, screeching metal cuts him off,

echoing down the hallways. It's followed by a series of deafening clangs and a series of smaller explosions.

There's the sound of running just outside the door as soldiers sprint past us.

"Defenses have been breached!" someone shrieks. "The enemy's entered the base! Prepare for ground assault!"

The enemy. I know who they mean even before that dreaded sound shatters my thoughts—

GONG!

The Fleshers have penetrated the outer wall. Infiernos is under attack.

Just like I planned.

I'm ready for the mass confusion. In no time, I've donned a pair of infrared goggles from the rucksack and shoved my way past the web of bodies, out the doorway, and into the corridor.

Trying to catch my breath, I careen down the corridors. All around me, the sounds of screaming and weapon fire assault my ears. Imposers run to and fro. Some even slam into me. But they don't bother to stop, don't seem to care about my presence at all, and that's even more disturbing.

I see Corin, dazed in a corner, curled up in a fetal position. The Imps escorting him to Cassius must have just abandoned him here during the explosions and ensuing panic. He jumps when I touch him.

"It's okay, kid. We gotta move." Then I'm pulling him to his feet and we're both running.

Rounding another corner, we spy a cluster of Imposers,

their backs to us, firing weapons at something just around the bend that we can't see.

But we can hear it.

Clacketyclacketyclacketyclacketyclack . . .

Whir . . .

The chilling sounds of the unseen Fleshers crawl up my spine. Obscene shadows scrawl the walls as something approaches the huddled squad.

We're on our own now.

We take off in the opposite direction. My mind is dizzy with disorientation. In the vent shafts I knew exactly where I was going. But the sights and sounds of the unseen invaders are wreaking havoc on my senses.

More explosions rip through the stairwell above. Shards of metal and concrete rain down on us. We burst through the doors of the lower level, narrowly avoiding being skewered.

Through the greenish haze, I can make out the entrance to the crematorium. Part of the wall is caved in. I brandish my weapon and we tear up the distance to the entrance.

Arrah, Drusilla, and Dahlia are struggling against the group of Imps who brought them down here. Corin bursts from my side and jumps into action, flinging rocks and kicking out at those around him. The smothering dark has robbed anyone of an advantage. As I glance off to the side, my elation turns to concern. Cage is lying in the rubble, obviously in pain. Part of him is trapped under a mound of debris. Tristin is hunched down beside him.

Aiming my weapon, I take out the Imposers trading blows with Arrah, Dru, and Dahlia.

"Lucian?" Arrah shouts. A grin rips across her face. "That *you?*"

"Who else?" Then I'm dashing over. "Take these!" Reaching into the rucksack, I scoop out more goggles and weapons, thrusting them into each of their hands, even Corin's.

For the next few seconds, everyone's busy strapping on belts with guns and grenades.

"We thought you were d—" Drusilla stops midsentence, snapping a fresh clip into her gun instead.

I reload my own weapon. "Yeah. Thought you were, too."

Dahlia's eyes flit to Cage and Tristin. "Can you move?"

Tristin shakes her head. "His hand's trapped."

I squat beside them. Cage looks like he's fighting the pain. The lower half of his arm is buried in the rubble almost up to the elbow. I reach for the surrounding debris, straining as I try to dislodge it, but I only succeed in making Cage inhale sharply and wince.

"Sorry," I say.

He tries to smile but it's a real effort. "S'okay. I've still got another one."

GONG!

Clacketyclacketyclacketyclacketyclacketyclacketyclackety!

The horrid sounds are approaching our position.

Fast.

Tristin hugs Corin close. "What *are* those things?"

"Right now, they're our chance to get out of here," I whisper. The others are crowded around us, trying to lift the rubble trapping Cage's arm, but it won't budge.

And the Fleshers are getting closer.

Cage's free hand locks around my wrist and he pulls me close. "Spark. There's no time left. This is the chance we've been fighting for. Take my sister and get the hell out of here. *Now!*"

Tristin claws her way between us. "We're *not* leaving you behind. We would *never* do that!" Her shaded eyes search the group, and I try to avoid doing the same so I won't see their expressions.

And so Tristin won't see my own.

She clutches my arm. "Don't you have anything that can blast through this rubble?"

Instead of answering her, I rifle through the duffle bag, searching for something—a low-impact charge to blast the rubble, some sort of chisel—*anything*.

But there's nothing. Except for . . .

My slick fingers brush against the cold metal of the blow torch.

A low hum fills the cramped space. The tip of the torch glows, bathing our exposed skin in purplish orange. It'll cut and cauterize simultaneously. Destruction and healing all in one slice.

Cage's firm hand locks around my forearm. He nods. "*Do it*, Lucian."

Dahlia rips off one of the rucksack's leather straps and places it next to Cage's lips. "Bite down on this."

He does.

I plunge the laser tip down onto Cage's wrist. His body convulses. An agonized moan squeezes past the leather in his teeth. He whips his head back and forth. Arrah and Drusilla struggle to keep him steady. The last of the bone gives way and I nearly stumble backwards.

I barely catch a glimpse of the still-smoking stump of Cage's arm before Tristin is wrapping a piece of torn fabric around it.

BLAM! Something crashes through the wall behind us.

"We gotta move!" Arrah shouts.

Without sacrificing a precious moment to look back, I help her haul the pale and shivering Cage to his feet.

The next few seconds are a blur of strobing lights and discordant sounds. We run, climbing up a mound of rubble to the torn entrance of a vent shaft.

"Arrah!" I shout. "You take point. I'll take backup and keep you covered!"

Arrah squirms through the opening, helping hoist Corin behind her. Tristin climbs through next, turning to help Drusilla wedge Cage through. Clutching his wounded arm to his chest, he grunts as he squeezes his bulk into the narrow passage and disappears with them inside it, leaving just Dahlia and me.

"After you!" Before she can protest, I push her through the opening.

Slinging my weapon over my shoulder, I grip the edges of the shaft to heave myself inside—

Something clamps my shoulder.

My blood clots. Then my body's spun around and a massive weight settles on top of me, knocking my breath out. A shadow looms above, eyeing me with burning hatred.

Styles.

He shoves the cold barrel of his weapon against my temple, his face trembling with rage and fear. Streaks of blood line his features and stain his torn uniform.

"You killed Renquist," he croaks. "And you're responsible for everything that's happened here." His eyes leave me and dart around the room. He cocks the gun; the click rips through my ears.

CLACKETYCLACKETYCLACKETYCLACKETY-CLACKETYCLACKETY!

Darkness smothers us. Styles whips his head around to look. And in that instant, I jam my knee into his groin as hard as I can.

He recoils. Seizing the advantage, I tear the gun from his hand. My fist right-hooks into his jaw, and I feel it crunch beneath my knuckles. Then I'm rolling out from underneath him and crawling into the vent. Unslinging my gun, I aim it toward the shaft entrance in case he decides to follow.

My breath catches.

I see metallic tentacles ensnare Styles, lifting him off the ground. His eyes saucer as they take in a nightmare beyond my field of vision. He looks up at me, fear flooding his eyes. "Spark! Please…help…me!"

His screams almost drown out the mechanical sounds… that terrible slurping and squishing…

No one deserves that. Not even Styles.

Aiming the gun at him, I let loose several rounds into his chest until all that's left is the ghost of his last horrific scream, echoing behind me as I scramble down the shaft to catch up with the others.

Breathless, I nearly collide into Dahlia, who's waiting just around a bend in the duct.

"Spark! I was just about to go back for—"

"Keep moving! They're right behind me!"

My words are like vocal adrenaline. Everyone picks up speed as we scurry through the tunnels. In the flashes of weapon blasts that penetrate the slats in the grates we rush by, I glimpse Imposers scuttling every which way, all semblance of order gone as they retreat from the Flesher forces. Human screams mingle with that horrific biomechanical cacophony in a symphony of fear and destruction. Blast after blast rock the complex, vibrating through the shafts, rocking them so thoroughly I'm convinced the entire tunnel will collapse, trapping us under layers of twisted metal.

C'mon. C'mon. Not much farther.

"I can see the grate to the transport platform up ahead!" Arrah's shout echoes over the din. "We're almost home free!"

If there are still any ships left . . .

"Arrah, wait!" I shout.

Everyone halts in front of the grate. Behind us is a loud thumping, followed by screeching and grinding.

They're coming.

I let loose a volley of gunfire into the darkness. We can't stop them, but maybe that'll slow them down. Then I squeeze past the others until I'm pressed against the grate beside Arrah.

"No activity," she whispers.

The hangar bay is a shambles. Scorch marks line the walls like pox. Mounds of broken and shattered equipment litter the floor. But there appears to be one Vulture intact. And a few rows over, a Squawker that looks like it was abandoned during a maintenance check.

"I'm on it." Dahlia's already cutting through the grate with the blow torch and my eyes inadvertently flick to Cage, who's leaning against Tristin and Corin.

The grate tumbles into the hangar.

I clap my hand to Arrah's back. "You go down and get that Vulture prepped for liftoff."

Her eyes narrow. "What about *you*?"

I nudge my head toward the opposite vent. "The detention center's just below. We can't just leave people behind. There's enough room in that Vulture for many others."

"I'm coming with," Drusilla says.

Arrah pulls her close and plants a tender kiss on her lips. "Don't take too long."

Drusilla smiles, gives her another quick kiss, and eases from her embrace. "I won't."

Dahlia tosses me the blowtorch. As the others scramble down into the hangar bay, I cut through the grate leading to the prison. Seconds later, I drop through, Drusilla right behind me with her weapon drawn.

The first thing I notice is the wave of heat. The other side of the hallway is ablaze. Clouds of smoke billow toward us, making it difficult to breathe.

"This way." I dash over to the door of the cellblock, Drusilla at my heels. Instinctively, I try the door controls, knowing they'll be sealed. "We have to cut through. Cover me."

I hold the blowtorch to the panel and activate it. Embers fly as the cutter slices through the wiring.

"Spark!" Drusilla's voice is laced with panic. "We're running out of time!"

Through the crackling of the blowtorch, I can hear the mechanized throes of the Fleshers getting louder ... louder ...

"They're right on us!" Drusilla's eyes drop to the ground. "They're in the subflooring!"

No sooner does she sound her warning than the floor erupts about a dozen yards away. Shards of metal fly. I catch a glimpse of those metallic-looking tentacles that seized Styles slithering through the opening, grasping for anything in their path—

The door panel shorts and the prison doors slide open with a gust of putrid air.

A pack of prisoners tumbles out, their faces twisted in confusion and terror.

I rip a fire hose from its wall socket and hoist Dru up the vent shaft, so she can secure it as a means for the escapees to climb out. But the sounds of the Fleshers approaching are getting too close and we decide to abandon the idea, opting instead to take the long way around, which leads to the doors of the hangar bay.

I grab hold of an emaciated youth. "This way to safety!"

Then we're all dashing away from the Fleshers toward the hangar bay. Drusilla and I fire blast after blast behind us, trying to buy time. But those awful sounds keep getting louder, as those dark shapes flit through the smoke and flame in relentless pursuit.

We round the corner. The door leading into the hangar

bay is wide open. Beyond it, I can hear the rumble of the Vulture's engines waiting to take off. "Through there! There's a transport!" I herd the prisoners through, and then Drusilla.

But I don't follow.

Arrah, Corin, and Cage are standing by the boarding ramp, their faces anxious as the prisoners flee into the ship.

Drusilla whirls. "Spark! Why aren't you—?"

I shake my head. "Someone has to seal the doors and buy you time."

Digging into my pack, I pull out one of two tiny transceiver units, set both channels on the same frequency, and toss one to Drusilla. "Keep in touch."

Arrah and Cage start running toward me. "Lucian! You get aboard that ship right now!" Arrah shouts.

I smile at them. "You did good. All of you. Now get them home."

The door to the hangar slams closed behind me when I hit the release. Then I'm welding it shut with the blowtorch.

Just as I finish, a tentacle slams into the door just an inch from my head, denting the thick metal as if it were clay.

I whirl, just in time to see a massive shape emerging from the flame.

Clacketyclacketyclacketyclacketyclacketyclacketyclackety-clacketyclackety!

I dive and roll down the adjacent corridor, springing to my feet and running as fast as I ever have. Tentacles slam the floor behind me as I lead the Fleshers farther and farther away from the others.

From my friends.

The other side of the corridor is a dead end.

Containment Lab 5.

My heart races. This is it. The location that the computer back in Asclepius Valley mentioned. Right under the entries about Cole and Digory and the mysterious U.I.P. procedure. The place where the Establishment's highly classified bio-weapon is being kept.

If I'm going to go out, I may as well take whatever it is with me rather than risk it getting into the hands—*tentacles*—of the Fleshers.

Of course, the lab is locked.

Grabbing the torch, I start cutting away at the lock and almost have it open when a tentacle wraps around my leg and drags me from the door, slamming me into the ground and ripping my gun from my grasp.

The Flesher emerges from the smoke. It's at least nine feet tall. The face is roughly humanoid, with bleached, hairless white skin and a bald head lined with throbbing veins. Instead of eyes, a dark, reflective strip is grafted into its flesh. Sinewy membranes cover the nose and mouth area, feeding into a twisted mass of wiring that's coiled around its skull and protruding into its throat.

Metallic armor, simulating an exposed skeleton, covers its upper torso. These bones continuously shift, exposing appendages that seem to be individual tools. An amber light engulfs me from the tip of one, while a cutting blade whirs to life on another one.

While it has two bony arms that end in claws, as if the fingers have been surgically grafted together, metallic tentacles like the one grasping me now emerge from the bones of its forearms. Its legs have been grafted, mid-thigh, to a complex set of servo-motors and gears that allow it to alternately roll or climb, depending on the terrain.

Crash!

A blur comes through the door of the lab behind me, slamming into the Flesher.

It's a young man, naked except for the remnants of a hospital gown. His muscles gleam in the firelight as he swings around to the Flesher's back, wrapping one of his thick biceps around the thing's throat as his thighs lock around its waist. The Flesher releases my leg as both tentacles lash around, striking at its attacker. But the youth's head is a blur of long, scraggly hair as he whips his head out of the way, catching one of the tentacles in his hands.

I scramble to snatch up my gun, aiming it toward them, but it's impossible to get a shot without risking the young man's life.

Whir!

The cutter comes to life, reaching toward the youth's throat, closer, closer ... only an inch away ...

BAM! BAM! BAM!

My rounds glance off the Flesher's protective armor, but it's all the distraction the guy needs. He seizes the cutting arm and plunges it into the Flesher's own throat. Dark fluid—*oil? blood?*—spurts from the creature's neck.

Clacketyclackety ... whir ... whir ... vroom ...

The Flesher begins to spin, out of control. The young man leaps from it.

272

I fire the remainder of my ammo, striking the most vulnerable target, its head, ripping holes through the tubules connecting from its nose to its skull.

The thing lunges for me—

Click! Click!

I'm out of ammo—

Then the thing teeters and collapses at my feet.

But its body is convulsing. As I watch, horror-struck, I can see the flesh mending. Whoever built this monstrosity employed some kind of regenerative tech.

I back away from it and turn to the young man.

But he doesn't move. Doesn't say anything. His massive chest pushes in and out with heavy breaths. Sweat trickles down it, past the sculpted ridges of his abdomen and narrow waist.

"This thing's not dead yet, and there are more of them coming!" I shout. "We've got to get the hell out of here. Follow me!"

GONG!

The sound explodes right behind us. I whirl, vaguely aware of my rescuer in my peripheral vision. Then we're both running back down the hallway, snaking up the still-dangling fire hose leading into the vent shaft and dropping down into the hangar bay, the pursuing Fleshers threatening to overtake us at every moment.

Dashing into the lone Squawker, I hit the ignition switch as soon as we're both aboard. My heart stammers as the engine sputters.

The door to the hangar bay bursts open. A horde of Fleshers rips through the chamber, heading right toward us.

I pound the control console as the first of the Fleshers closes in.

The engine roars to life. As I hit the throttle, my back slams against the pilot seat. In the rear monitor, I see the craft's exhaust set Fleshers on fire. Then we're airborne, shooting out of the hangar and into the dark skies.

Below, the Infiernos military installation is just a smoking husk of debris, completely overtaken by the swarm of Fleshers crawling all over it until it's smothered in living darkness.

No one will ever endure that hell again.

The Establishment better beware. This is just the beginning.

I settle back into my chair, tears burning down my cheeks, as the Squawker is swallowed by the clouds.

Finally, I have a few seconds to spare for the stranger who, I'm vaguely aware, is in the copilot's seat beside me. "Thanks for your help back there. Are you okay?"

No response.

I turn toward him. He's slumped in his chair, his long, wild hair still obscuring his face and falling across his powerful pectorals.

I *know* that profile.

"Can't you hear me?" I move closer and grip his rock-hard shoulder.

He flinches and pulls away, and the moment he does, the hair cloaking his face in shadow falls away from his face and I see those piercing eyes.

Those piercing *blue* eyes.

He looks away.

My hand drops. No. It *can't* be.

A blizzard of emotions engulfs me. Shock, unfathomable joy, wholeness, deep betrayal—my brain is short circuiting. I can't breathe as I revel in this miracle. Or is it a curse?

Maybe I'm finally losing my mind.

Reaching out a trembling hand, I push the hair from his beautiful face.

It *is* Digory.

PART III

REUNIONS

TWENTY-SIX

Dusk's rays filter through the cockpit window, bathing the cabin in a soft purplish glow. "I can't believe you're really here," I whisper. "Why? Why did you do it? Was it *all* a lie?"

Digory still won't answer me. Won't even look at me. He just stares out the window, his blue eyes like glassy seas reflecting the dying light until pools of liquid orange form there.

Losing him was one of the deepest pains I've ever felt. But finding out he betrayed me was worse than death. Now, having him so close, yet so far away at the same time, I feel an unbearable mixture of joy and agony. I just want to scoop him into my arms, hold him as tight as I can, never ever let him go again—or throttle the last breath from him.

Below us, a familiar silhouette rises from the rippling whitecaps. The statue of the Lady. Even though she's canting deeper into the ocean than I remembered, she's still standing. The sight of her fills me with memories, longings for home, for Cole. She's still holding her torch high, and with the fiery red sunset burning behind her, it's as if she's lighting a path through the desolate seas just for Digory and me.

Digory and me.

No. There is no Digory and me. Not anymore. There can't be.

At that instant Digory turns, almost as if he senses me staring at him. The exhilaration of gazing at his face once more sends a rush through me. I reach out my hand to him, then pull it back.

A series of angry *bleeps* pierces the quiet.

The fuel gauge is blinking red. Shit! I checked it when we first took off. One of the Fleshers must have ruptured the lines as we were taking off.

My hands grip the control yoke, fighting against the jarring vibrations.

Digory places his hand over mine, helping me to keep the yoke steady. The Squawker's engine sputters and it banks from side to side, jostling us back and forth in spite of the safety harnesses.

"We're almost out of fuel," I say. "I'm going to have to set her down."

I bank the craft in an arc around the Lady's face. For a moment, her large stone eyes fill the cockpit windows, calm, reassuring. Then we're around her, pointing in the direction of her gaze.

At the dark remnants of her ruined city.

I veer the craft as best as I can as we half-glide, half-plummet toward the skeletal structures looming before us like the corpses of long-dead behemoths. "Hang on!"

Most of the city is half-submerged in the dark waters. Massive structures whiz by us in a blur of broken concrete and twisted metal. The streets that aren't completely submerged are cracked and broken by craters, jammed with all manner of rusting vehicles.

The tallest building I've ever seen is directly in our path, getting closer by the second. Our only chance is to eject. Unhooking my restraints, I lunge for the overhead compartment. There's only one glider chute. As much as I hate what he did to me, I can't bring myself to leave Digory to his death. Not without answers. Wasting no time, I strap on the chute and make sure the rucksack is still strapped to my body. "Digory! *Let's go!*"

Remaining silent, he springs to my side—lithe, like a creature acting on instinct rather than a comprehension of my words—and grabs me tight.

I jam my fist into the control panel. The escape hatch blows open and we're sucked out, tumbling into thin air. Behind us, the Squawker slams into the building and ignites in a fireball.

I can feel the heat singeing my skin as I pull the rip cord. The glider's wings spring forward, halting our descent with a jolt.

Just ahead, a large canopy of trees covers a vast area, a mossy shroud shielding the area from prying eyes.

We crash through the underbrush. Branches scratch my face and hands, snapping and cracking all around us. Then our bodies slam into something solid and rough. The bark of a tree.

I feel lightheaded and disoriented. My body is swaying upside down, dangling from the remnants of the glide chute. We're lodged in the branches of a massive tree, the long, tangled limbs writhing in the gusts of chilled wind.

It takes me a few moments to get my bearings.

A low purr from below vibrates through the air. My skin erupts into gooseflesh. Two glowing yellow eyes are staring up at me, attached to a sinewy, fur-lined shape as dark as shadow. Some kind of felis, but larger than I've ever seen before. Sharp claws glisten in the moonlight. Its muscled legs flex, and its body coils as it prepares to spring.

It leaps for me. My body tenses as I try to curl up and away. I'm just out of its range, but the tip of its huge paw grazes my shoulder, tearing a gash through it. The pain is searing, but not as potent as the fear of what it would feel like to get eaten alive.

The branches above me snap with a loud crack and the glide chute drops another foot, putting me into the creature's range. It lets out an ear-shattering growl, ready to spring again.

Out of the corner of my eye, I see Digory spring past me to the ground. He grabs the creature in a headlock with one arm. In his other hand, he's clutching a long stone shard, which he drives halfway into the animal's skull.

Rip!

When he tears it out, it's dripping with blood, splattering darkness all over his heaving bare chest.

Digory lets out an unearthly sound—part anguish, part guttural savage—that prickles every inch of my skin. The way the moonlight catches his eyes, they seem to glow, too, just like the creature's.

Snap!

The glider crashes through the tree and I drop—

TWENTY-SEVEN

Light.

My eyelids feel like a burden as I struggle to finally pry them open. I squint against the dawn's first rays, streaks of pink and yellow stretching tentatively over the fresh canvas of a new day. Unlike the unseasonably long and harsh winter in the Parish, it seems that cold has never touched this place. The ground feels firm, but soft. I'm lying on a bed of lush overgrown grass, covered from my chest to my feet in a blanket of leaves that keeps me snug. I can taste the remnants of some sweet nectar on my tongue. My hair feels damp and my skin tingles, as if I've been freshly bathed. My fingers trace the cuts on my body and come away with sticky warmth. I sniff. Crushed plants. An herbal remedy, applied to my wounds like a salve.

The smile on my lips fades. Where's Digory?

I sit up too fast. I'm still feeling a little lightheaded and woozy. My leg bumps against the rucksack Valerian gave me. What was it she said when she insisted I take back the ID tags and Digory's holo?

When you get out of this, you'll thank me.

Digging into the rucksack, I pull out the holocam and stare hard at it for what seems like forever before hitting the activation button.

The air in front of the device shimmers and the holo of Digory appears, still wearing that cold grin he had when he was addressing Cassius. "Tycho signing off," he announces. Then he leans in close to the screen, as if hitting an unseen switch, and the window with Cassius's image disappears.

The moment that happens, Digory slumps back against his chair and lets out a long sigh. His face loses that hard edge, and once again he's the Digory I've always known.

Except now he looks worried. He leans forward, his face practically pressing against the holocam's lens. "If I don't make it back today, I want ... I *need* someone to know—Rafé, Cage, Jeptha, *all* of you—that I never betrayed you. I've been on a rogue mission, making the new Prefect believe I'm a mole within the rebellion. I'm trying to gain his confidence, and gain access to Establishment intelligence in the process."

So Digory never did betray the rebellion. He never betrayed me. Why couldn't I have had faith in the love we had for each other?

I never deserved him.

The holo of Digory is talking faster now. "I've stumbled on something called the Sowing Protocol. Whatever it is, it's dangerous. I think it'll crush the rebellion if we can't stop it.

I'll try to learn what I can and report back. But I've got the feeling Thorn is on to me." His face softens. "If I'm right, and my cover's blown, please do me one last favor and look out for Lucian Spark. He's... he's a good guy. And I think he and his brother are in some kind of danger from Thorn. Promise me you'll take them under your protection, keep them safe."

The holo goes out of focus for a moment, but it has nothing to do with the device.

"If I don't see any of you again, it's been an honor to serve the cause with you." Digory smiles, but I can see how nervous he is. "I'm going to hide this in my quarters when I'm done. Until then, this is Digory Tycho. Down with the Establishment. Protect your families."

The image flickers, then fades away, replaced by an endless stream of static.

That's it. Recording over. I shut it off and stuff it back into the rucksack, even as I place the ID tags around my neck once again.

I was so wrong.

The joints in my knees creak and pop as I haul myself to my feet and take a few steps, my bare soles crunching the leaves beneath them.

I cup my hands to my mouth. "Digory! *Where are you?*"

Trudging deeper into the lush pockets of pink and purple flowers, I hear a sound up ahead. A gurgling sound.

Water.

With both hands, I part a soft curtain of hanging moss.

And there he is.

I let out the breath I've been holding, drunk with relief.

Digory is sitting on the remnants of a small stone bridge, bare-chested, his feet dangling in the water and his long damp hair draped over his shoulders. His eyes are intent on the shimmering brook just below him.

Breathing deep, I wade through the tall blades of grass toward him, fighting a limp, drawing strength from his glowing form. I stop just behind him.

Suddenly, I'm afraid, in spite of all the horrors I've endured up until now.

He whips around to face me, and it's like looking at the sun, a sight so brilliant and warm yet painful all at once.

I freeze. I've been seeing him in my dreams for so long that it still feels so surreal to be standing just a few feet from him again. Maybe it's my mind playing tricks on me, but along with the glint of recognition in his eyes, I sense so much more—fear? Suspicion?

Anger?

I turn away, focusing on the rippling stream shimmering beneath us. "Thanks for the bed. And tending to my wounds. I didn't see you when I woke up. I thought..." My words trail away with the current.

Digory still remains silent and I sit down beside him.

"I tried *so* hard to get back to you. But I thought that you were dead, that it was too late...and then I saw that holo recording." I choke back my anguish, needing to get my words out. "I should *never* have given up on you."

Pivoting, I sit cross-legged, facing him, and force myself to look directly at him. "You haven't said a word to me. I understand, Digory. I won't hold you to anything we might have said in the past." We gaze into each other's eyes in silence, the sound of our breaths harmonizing.

Taking a deep breath and steeling my nerves, I touch his warm, dewy skin. My fingertips graze the contours of his biceps, which, even relaxed, feels like granite, and then work their way to the inside of his elbow.

Digory flinches, and I instantly regret letting my feelings get the best of me. He can't even stand my touch any longer. I feel sick and start to pull away.

But his hand grabs mine and presses it back against the hotness of his skin. I can feel the scabbing in the crook of his elbow. I lean in closer. The entire area is mottled with dark purple bruises, the smooth skin broken by needle marks. I examine his other arm and see the same thing.

It wasn't *me* he was recoiling from.

Ignoring the aches of my own battered body, I sink into him, relishing the heat of his body in the chilled air, my face pressed against the expanse of his chest. All I can hear is the sound of thunderous beating, and I can't distinguish between his heart or mine.

I look into his eyes.

He leans in close, his warm lips grazing against mine, igniting every nerve ending, even more wondrous than I remember.

Our mouths lock onto each other's, tongues exploring, tentatively at first . . . I taste that same sweet nectar on his breath. It feels like I've left my body and I'm floating. All the aching, all the pain, both physical and mental, dissolves in that kiss, a sanctuary against all the darkness that's engulfed my life for so long.

Soon we're rolling in the still-damp grass. What little clothing we're wearing is tossed aside as limbs intertwine, our hands and hearts eager with discovery.

He lets out a small cry. I look up in alarm. But his face is pure bliss.

His arms pull me into him. Then he's planting more warm kisses on my lips. His tongue feels like heavenly fire as it traces down my neck, across the contours of my chest, and beyond.

At that moment, it doesn't matter that he can't speak. His eyes tell me how he feels.

"*Me too*," I whisper.

After what seems like hours, we collapse against one another, slick with sweat, nestling in each other's arms. I can feel Digory's smile against my cheek. Soon, the sounds of his breathing and the steady rhythm of his heart against me lull me into the most wonderfully exhausting grogginess ever. I allow myself to drift into sleep, never wanting to wake from *this* dream.

Ever.

———————

Hours later, we're still lying on our makeshift bed of grass, Digory spooning his body against mine. He fingers the Recruit ID tags I'm wearing, nuzzling his lips against my neck. I take off the ID tag with my name on it and slip it around his neck, so that we both have one, then give him another kiss.

I smile and silently vow to give Valerian the biggest hug and kiss if I ever see her again.

Digory sits up beside me, his eyes wide. He looks around with that almost animal-like instinct, as if he's reaching out with his senses and making sure there's no danger around us.

I give him a peck on the forehead and hug him close. "There's so much that you don't know."

Then I'm telling him everything. My training as an Imposer. Cole being housed in the Priory under Delvecchio's eye. The failed assassination attempt against Cassius and Prime Minister Talon. Our exile to Infiernos and imprisonment in Purgatorium. Everything leading up to our reunion.

Even though he remains mute and I can't be sure how much he understands, I can tell he's hanging on to my every word, grasping the urgency of what I'm saying, if not the specifics. Whatever's been done to him that's traumatized him into silence, there's still that compassionate, gentle Digory brimming underneath.

He'll speak when he's ready, when he's healed—as much as he ever can be.

He wraps his arms tighter around me and I pull away just enough to stare into his eyes. "You know Cage, Tristin, Dru, and Corin, don't you?" I ask tentatively. "You were part of the same rebel cell, weren't you? They were your friends."

He sighs and his fingers interlock with mine. His lips purse and he finally nods.

Of course he's hesitant. After what he gave up for me during that last trial, sacrificing his husband, Rafé—and his entire cause—just so I could get to Cole. The mention of his old allies must be painful. Especially since a part of him might feel guilty for choosing to save Cole's life with so many other things at stake.

"I know you feel you betrayed the rebellion, turned your back on what you were fighting for, all because of me. But I'm sure your friends would understand and welcome you back. They *need* you." I squeeze his hands. "*I* need you. We all do."

He nuzzles my nose.

"I'm so sorry I wasn't there for you," I whisper into his ear. "I should have looked for you. When you wouldn't speak to me after we found each other, I was afraid you hated me for leaving you behind—"

He touches a finger to my lips, capturing my eyes with his own blue prisms. Then he shakes his head slowly. His eyes glisten with moisture. He rests his head on my chest and I squeeze him tightly.

Digory's hands caress my body, reawakening those sensations, sending the blood rushing to every part of me. His fingers trace the contours of my pectorals, squeezing. When he looks up, his eyes twinkle at me.

I can't help but smile. "Yeah, I *have* been working out a little since the last time you saw me. I'm not that scrawny, naïve kid anymore."

The glint in his eye turns to concern. He sits up. With his index finger he traces a shape in the earth. A crude figure of a man. When he's done, he points at the sketch, then back at me.

"I've looked better." I chuckle.

But he's already drawing another shape next to the one representing me. A smaller one.

A child.

He draws a line connecting their hands.

The smile fades from my lips. He knows me too well.

Digory looks up and motions to me, then to himself, before his finger settles on the horizon.

I wipe my eyes. "We have a long journey ahead of us."

TWENTY-EIGHT

The sun burns high overhead as we finish a refreshing swim in the stream—wrestling around, splashing, taking turns dunking each other as if we were children, until we reluctantly get dressed.

Digory scampers up countless trees, using his bare feet and hands with such agility and grace, he's almost a blur as he propels himself up and through the dense foliage. Even with all the Imp training I've undergone over the past year, I can barely keep up with him as I run alongside on the ground, pointing out which berries he should pluck that might be edible based on a few birds pecking at them.

Eventually he drops to the ground in front of me, scooping me over his shoulder while I make a feeble attempt at protest. We finally settle under the shade of an enormous magnolia tree, where he insists on feeding me himself as I rest my head on his lap.

"Mmm." My mouth waters when my teeth sink into the succulent fruit. Sugary nectar drips from the corners of my mouth. "Thith ith delithus."

Digory lifts my head and kisses me.

I kiss him back. "I wish we could stay here forever," I murmur. "Just the two of us. But right now we have to figure out how to get out of here and back to the Parish." I force myself to push away.

But I have no clue what direction to go in, or how to get back to Cole. The transceiver I'd hoped to use to communicate with Cage and the others was damaged in the glider crash and I don't have the tools to repair it. I can only hope they made it out okay.

I stand and offer Digory my hand, savoring the way the muscles in his arm swell as he stretches and reaches for it. Then I'm relishing the feel of his hand in mine as I pull him to his feet.

Our fingers remain entwined like the roots of one of these ancient trees, infusing me with strength. My eyes scan the lush foliage. "What do you suppose this forest is doing, right in the middle of a ruined city?"

Through a gap in the leafy awning shading us, I glimpse several of those enormous buildings, or at least what's left of them, far off in the distance, specters lurking in the mist.

And a plume of dark smoke billowing into the air between them.

"Look!" I point.

Digory's eyes, narrowed to slits, are already glued to the site.

"Could be other survivors from Infiernos," I say. Then another thought hits me. "Or maybe there's *something* living here."

Clutching each other's hands tighter, we trudge off in the direction of the curling blackness.

———————

Once we leave the clearing, our pathway toward the smoke weaves through ever-thickening underbrush, which grows so dense at times that we can barely see a few feet beyond it. Soon both our arms and legs are covered with thin scratches from the whipping branches and waist-high grass.

More than once we stumble over protrusions jutting from the ground. At one point, my foot hits something and I trip, almost nose-diving. But Digory grabs my arm and holds me steady.

"Thanks." I stare down at the metal disc embedded in a patch of dirt. "Looks like a manhole cover."

Digory kicks the earth and shrubs away from it, exposing a series of words surrounding a leaf design.

CITY OF NEW YORK PARKS AND RECREATION.

My forehead crinkles. "City of New ... *York.* I guess the Lady's city finally has a name."

We move on.

So this wasn't a natural forest after all. It was a park. There were once pathways cutting through the greenery, long ago. But in the years since the Ash Wars these paths have been reclaimed by nature, overrun with moss and earth.

And the pathways aren't the only sign of the city's previous inhabitants. Every once in a while we come across the remnants of intricate cobbled bridges, now ensnared by twisting vines. And *that* looks like the remnants of a lamppost.

Digory's leg sinks into a pothole and he grunts.

"I gotcha." I hunch down and help free his foot. Something catches my eye.

More writing. "There's something here!"

Digory stoops beside me, our hands overlapping as we clear the earth and leaves to reveal what's left of a black and gray pattern, made up of tiny stone tiles, with one word at the center: *IMAGINE.*

"Imagine what?" I run my hand over the missing pieces. Digory leans his forehead into mine. He closes his eyes and his lips mutter something undecipherable.

When he opens his eyes again, he almost has a smile on his face. His eyes question me.

"What did *I* imagine?" I ask. "If I tell you, it won't come true." But I can't help but smile myself. "This way," I say, pulling him through another clump of trees.

After about fifteen more minutes of forging through the brushwood, we find the remnants of a statue. At first I think it's a miniature version of the Lady, only without her crown or torch. But this is something different. A beautiful woman with wings—or at least one wing. The other has long since crumpled away. Even so, she retains her dignity, and in spite of her battered condition, she looks like she could still soar through the sky.

An angel.

Maybe she's a sign that what I imagined is true. That Cole is all right after all, and he, Digory, and I will someday be together forever.

We gaze at her for a few minutes, then trudge on through the thicket.

"There it is, over there."

Just beyond another tangle of trees, puffs of dark smoke smear the sky.

In spite of the uneven terrain, we pick up our pace until we're jogging through the undergrowth and finally burst through the last of the trees.

The lushness is gone, replaced by an endless horizon of hollowed-out structures that jut from the sludge of half-flooded streets.

And directly ahead, the mangled carcass of a Vulture craft rests on its side like a felled beast, still smoking and sparking, halfway embedded into the closest of these structures.

Only it's not just any Vulture.

My fingers dig into Digory's arm. "Those markings on the tail end—it's the regal seal. That ship's carrying high-ranking personnel."

Before Digory can react, I'm running toward the Vulture, skirting chunks of debris, my hand over my mouth to avoid inhaling the thick smoke that's already drawing burning tears from my eyes. I peer through the haze and into the Vulture's belly. There's a ragged gash there rimmed with twisted, melting metal, as if the craft's been ripped open and eviscerated.

Careful not to touch the smoking edges, I strain against the haze blanketing the passenger cabin.

A shadow of movement inside. A low groan pierces the crackle and hiss of the flames.

I cough out a lungful of smoke. "We got a live one!"

Digory's hand clamps on my shoulder and I turn to him.

He points to me, shakes his head, then holds out a palm in a *stop* motion. Then he points to himself and motions in the direction of the moans.

"It's okay, Digory. I can go. You don't have to protect me. I can handle myself. Promise." I barely get the words out before I have to stifle another cough.

The muscles in his jaws clench and he shakes his head again.

I wink. "Trust me. I'll be fine." His grip relaxes, but the concern never leaves his face.

I nod and slip from him, gritting my teeth when my skin grazes the steaming hull as I crawl through the opening. Between the gloom and the smog it takes me a few seconds to get my bearings. Then I spot the survivor's silhouette a few feet away and crawl as fast as I can to the person's side.

It's Prime Minister Talon herself.

She's barely conscious. For a split second I'm tempted to leave her behind to burn. But she might be able to provide me with useful information. Maybe she knows where I can hitch a transport back to the Parish. And she'd be a valuable hostage if we run into any Imps.

The smoke and heat start to get to me. I hoist Talon's arm around my neck and lift, half-carrying, half-dragging her to the opening where Digory's waiting to receive my burden.

"Don't let this one out of your sight," I tell him.

"Wait," she rasps into my ear. "There's someone else ... "
She lapses into unconsciousness.

Shoving Talon into Digory's arms, I spin and rummage through the flotsam and jetsam of twisted safety harnesses and toppled supply containers, slinging an emergency medical backpack over my shoulder before finding the other survivor.

Even before I reach him, the sight of his outline lying still strapped to a seat makes me feel like I've been shot by a flare gun. It's not an Imp.

I kneel by the body, grip it roughly, and flip it over.

"*Cassius* ... " I can barely pull the name from my burning throat.

Blood trickles from a gash just above his eyebrow, past a cheek that's already swollen and purple. At first I think he's already dead. But a quick feel of his wrist confirms that there's still wretched life wriggling through his veins with each weak beat of his pulse.

His eyes flutter open. There's a few seconds of blankness as he struggles to focus. Then recognition dawns on his face, and his smile turns my stomach.

"Lucky ... you came back for me. You saved me ... "

He reaches up for me, and I recoil. It's so easy to place my hands around his slimy neck ...

"Can't breathe." Cassius's fingers claw at my hands, snug around his throat. His eyes widen, sprouting thin red blood vessels like a road map to his fear. "Please ... "

I squeeze his throat tighter.

"Lucky ... I know ... where there's ... another ship ... "

Cursing myself, I release my stranglehold and lift Cassius into my arms, dragging his dead weight past Digory. Once I've exited the Vulture, I hurl him to the ground.

Unslinging the medical backpack from my shoulder, I rifle through it. Aside from basic first-aid supplies, there are also some ration bars and a nav-glove that plots coordinates on a small screen embedded in its palm. That might come in very handy. I set it aside for now and pull out one of the first-aid kits before tossing the pack to Digory. "Can you check Talon out? Make sure she's okay? You remember our Recruit training, right?"

A look flits across his eyes. Sadness? Pain? Then it's gone, replaced by blue steel. He takes the bag from me and sets to work without so much as a glance my way.

Pushing thoughts from my head, I leave Digory with Talon and kneel beside Cassius.

His eyes flutter open and he tries to sit up. "You couldn't . . . do it . . . could you?"

He's wrong. I could have finished him off if he didn't have something I needed. After everything I've been through, everything I've seen, I'm almost immune to death. Hell, I killed Renquist with these same bare hands.

I shove Cassius back against the ground.

His body spasms as he coughs, his fingers rubbing the welts on his throat, tears streaming from his eyes. "Maybe you still have feelings for me?"

For a split second, the cockiness in his eyes flickers, replaced by something . . . *else*. Then it's gone like so much static.

And it's my turn to laugh, a hollow sound that echoes through the wreckage before it's strangled by the wind. I lean in close. "The only feelings I have for you are disgust and pity."

The look on his pale face shows I've scored a direct hit.

Digory's shadow falls over us. He's staring at Cassius, and the look on his face is one of pure hatred.

Before I can stop him, Digory lunges.

"Wait!"

Cassius tries to pry Digory's fingers away, but I can tell it's a lost cause. Digory's eyes are blank slates. I definitely get his rage. But we still need Cassius.

I sidle up to Digory, touching his cheek, leaning in to whisper in his ear. "Please. He can get us back to the Parish. I need to get to Cole. For *me*."

His eyes shift toward mine and thaw. He nods and releases.

"It's okay," I say. "I understand."

Cassius hawks up a wad of nasty from his throat and spits it on the ground beside us. "I suppose you know he used to work for me."

Digory takes a step toward him, but I hold him back. "He never worked for you."

Cassius nods. "Right. A rebel spy. But not a very good one. I found out what he was up to—"

"Which is why you had us both recruited that day," I finish. "A lot of good it did you." I grab Digory's hand. "We're both still kicking."

Cassius stares at us. "Yes. I see you two have found your way back to each other. *Touching*."

I shake my head. "Looks like you're just not having a great day, Cassius. First you lose your installation. Then you crash in this dump. And finally I find out that Digory isn't dead like you led me to believe."

He glances at Digory. "Who says the Digory Tycho you knew isn't dead?"

His words hang in the air like a heavy cloud.

I turn to Digory. "How's Talon?"

He shrugs.

"Assuming Cassius is telling the truth about there being a ship that can get us out of here, we can get Talon into a bio-scanner and check for internal injuries. For now, we'll assume it's just a concussion." My eyes probe the bruising horizon. "Time to be on our way."

Digory rummages through the medical pack and pulls out a pair of restraints, which he tosses over to me.

I smile at him. "Thanks."

Cassius strains to sit up. "You won't need—"

"Shut up."

Ignoring Cassius's protests, I cuff him before proceeding to give him a basic med exam. In spite of multiple lacerations and a sprained leg, he seems intact. Good.

I pull him up by the collar. "You're good enough to walk. I'm gonna need you to help carry your fearless leader here."

With Digory's help, we use pieces of debris to fashion a crude travois made of two metal struts from the Vulture wreckage joined by torn fabric from the remnants of a seat's upholstery. In no time, Digory's carried the Prime Minister over and settled her onto the stretcher as I use some torn strips of seat belts to strap her down securely.

"Be careful," Cassius warns. "She shouldn't be moved in her condition."

"She'll live." I glance up from Talon. "Besides, *you're* the one who's going to need to be careful."

Then we're strapping the makeshift litter to Cassius's back, as if he were a caballus or some other beast of burden.

No. That's insulting to animals.

I nod to Digory. "Let's go."

"Which way?" I bark at Cassius.

He shakes his head. "If I tell you the way, you'll have no more need for me and will probably leave me to die."

Digory and I exchange glances. There's no use pretending Cassius doesn't have a point.

Cassius clears his throat. "I'll give you coordinates for the first leg of our journey. There's a beacon not too far from the landing strip that my Vulture was headed to."

He mumbles a few coordinates, which I program into the nav-glove. I decide to tuck the tiny transceiver into the lining of my pants for safekeeping. Can't risk Cassius getting ahold of it and contacting his superiors.

With Digory bringing up the rear and Cassius hauling Talon between us, I lead the way through the ruined city.

TWENTY-NINE

The remnants of half-buried buildings reach up from the earth like the fingers of a giant that's been buried alive. Part of what looks like it might once have been a bridge lies collapsed in a tangle of pylons, whatever water it was meant to traverse long dried up.

I turn to Cassius. "Who built this place? And how was it destroyed?"

But he only shakes his head.

For the next couple of hours we trudge along in silence, the only sounds our feet crunching against the rubble, our heavy breathing, and the ever-intensifying bleeps of the nav-glove. We eventually come to a pile of debris that's just impossible to skirt.

"The beacon signal is close," Cassius grunts.

A soulless eye stares at us from the wreckage, large and unblinking—what's left of a stone statue of a wild beast, surrounded by toppled pillars with vertical grooves cut into their surfaces. The creature's remaining eye is separated from its crumbling mate by a prominent ridge that flares into a pronounced snout, set into a grand jaw.

I wipe the dampness from my brow, unable to look away as I trace its flanks. "Not sure how we're gonna get past this…"

When I kick the nearest column, my foot throbs upon impact. The stone didn't even budge an inch.

Digory grabs hold of my arm, gentle and firm all at once, and pulls me over to a small crater that was partly obscured by debris.

"You found something?" A hint of excitement creeps into Cassius's weary voice.

But Digory ignores him. His shoulder muscles tense as he shoves a clump of stone aside and shines a flashlight inside.

I smile at him. "You just may have found a way through."

He squeezes my hand.

"We're going in."

——————

It takes a while, but between Digory and me we manage to roll one of the pillars into the opening and set it at an angle, at the rim of the crevice, so we can all slide down it. Digory straps Talon onto his broad back and ambles down with ease.

"You know," Cassius mutters, "this would be a hell of a lot easier for me if my hands weren't bound."

I shrug. "Too bad I don't give a damn." I shove him through the opening and he shimmies down, cursing me all the way, before Digory plucks him off and tosses him to the ground.

Then I'm sliding down after them, hopping off near the base and into Digory's waiting arms.

"Thanks," I whisper into his ear. We hold each other tight for a moment, then let go.

The tunnel we're standing in branches off into several different dark channels and multiple platforms. A conduit of rusted pipes twists through the ceiling, and on either side of the trench are raised platforms lined with steel columns. Underneath us, thick metal slats line the ground.

"Looks like some kind of track system." The sound of Cassius's voice echoes eerily throughout the tunnels, then fades into the dark. "The builders of this place must have used it for transport under the city."

"The beacon's close," I say. "*This* way."

We make our way through the tunnel under the dimness of the flickering light, following the tracks, skirting heaps of stone, climbing over piles of rusted and mangled metal. It's slow going, and having to maneuver Talon's stretcher isn't helping.

The pathway ahead of us is moving. For a second I think we must be on some sort of conveyor belt. Until the sound of claws scratching the steel tracks, mixed with high-pitched squealing, makes my skin crawl.

Rats. A horde of them.

Digory's fingers slip between mine, gripping my hand tightly.

I swallow hard, eyes glued to the sea of vermin. "Reminds

me of our first date in the sewers." Eventually, the filthy layer of vermin thins out, scurrying into the cracks in the walls until they disappear.

GONG!

The familiar sound petrifies every hair on my body.

"The Fleshers," I whisper. "The must have followed us from Infiernos."

"Looks like we're not the only ones using these tunnels," Cassius says.

We sprint down the tunnel to our left, leaping over rusted pipes and concrete debris, stumbling in the gloom as fast as we can to get away from that horror. I almost stumble. "The signal's coming from just up ahead!" I yell. "You'd better be right about a ship waiting for you there, Cassius!"

Digory pulls me along faster. We barely avoid crashing into a long, cylindrical vehicle resting on the tracks like a dead behemoth. It's covered in slimy strings of goo.

I tug Digory's arm. "The signal's coming from inside."

He resists, shaking his head.

I whip around to face Cassius. "I should never have listened to you. Tell me where you've brought us or I swear I'll kill you right now."

The platforms on either side are crumbled heaps that'll take precious time to surmount. I stare through the dark gap that might once have been this transport's cockpit, while the Fleshers' unearthly wail echoes behind us.

"*Inside!*" I scramble into the opening, pulling Digory along with me, Cassius dragging Talon right on our heels.

My feet crunch against bone and I freeze.

The interior of the vehicle is a fetid pit jammed with more bones. Only these have been picked clean. Most are intact skeletons wedged into seats, while others lie in heaps along the aisle, or hang from bars jutting from the ceiling.

At the back of the car, the flight crew from a Vulture hang chained together, arms above their heads, half naked, their uniforms in tatters, their skin pale as chalk. I dart forward and check their pulses. They're all dead. Some of their heads are twisted, jaws pried apart in hushed screams.

A powerful rumble rocks the tunnel, the deep bass of a siren that vibrates through the tunnels like the cry of some prehistoric beast. We slip out of the car, staring into the shadows.

The siren is followed by a series of clanks and grinds from some poorly oiled machine, mixed with sickening wet squishes and the clatter of snapping teeth. This is made all the more horrible now that I've seen the monstrosity behind them first-hand.

For a moment the three of us stand frozen, posed like pale statues long forgotten among these grisly ruins, an eternal look of fear plastered on our faces.

Before we can backtrack, that siren blasts louder than ever. Something bursts through the opening of the tunnel ahead, surrounding us in an instant.

A big blur of creepy.

At least twenty Fleshers, looking much like the one that attacked Digory and me at Infiernos, close in on us from all sides. There are some differences among them—variations in facial structures and the skeletal armor encasing their torsos, and in some of the tools on their protruding appendages.

Some are even taller than the one I encountered. But it's obvious that they're the same race of *thing*.

Once in place, the Fleshers' servomotors lock in place and they freeze, fixing us in their sights. As monstrous statues, they're more unnerving silent than when they were clanking and wheezing. Their strobing lights capture their ghastliness like nightmare snippets.

"*What* are you?" My voice echoes down the winding tunnels.

The nearest Flesher's head swivels in my direction.

Digory steps forward, and I can see the thick cords of muscle on his arms and neck tensing as he readies to pounce. That savage look burns like blue fire in his eyes again. His lips curl into a snarl, which births a low growl. A quick reminder of the brutal ordeal that's transformed him.

I grab hold of his granite shoulder. "Wait," I whisper. "There's too many of them."

At the sound of my voice, he relaxes. But he still moves his body in front of mine like a shield.

"Easy now, Lucian. If you hold still they might not hurt you," Cassius mutters behind me.

Their pulsing lights sync into a steady amber glow. I look up at the nearest Flesher. There's something familiar about his face. It's not a resemblance to the Flesher we fought at Infiernos—there's something distinct about this one. Unique. But that can't be right.

My shoulder brushes against Digory's. "I don't know why, but I think I've seen this one before."

Nobody moves. I turn and grab Cassius by the throat. "What's going on here?"

But he just smiles at me, smug.

"*Answer me.*" I spit the words at him through clenched teeth.

"Tycho's been resurrected. You should be thanking me."

Digory snarls and tears Cassius from me, lifting him into the air.

Cassius glares down at me. "You're not the only one with a trained Canid." He shoots the Fleshers a look. "Take them."

In unison, the Fleshers' jaws snap open.

"Digory—"

His name has barely escaped my lips when dark blurs burst from the creatures' throats toward us.

The wind is knocked out of me. Something cold and slimy coils around my body, a wormlike membrane that pulsates, secreting a wetness that seeps into my pores. In seconds, my body numbs and my muscles lock. Some kind of paralytic. I drop to the floor. Luckily, I land on my side. But I can't feel a thing. *I can't breathe.*

"Don't panic, Lucky." Cassius's voice sounds muffled, dreamlike. "It's not going to hurt you. It's a neurotoxin designed to temporarily immobilize you for more efficient transport. The fluids being put into your body are feeding you oxygen and circulating it through your system. Uncomfortable, I know. But don't resist it like your boyfriend's trying to do."

As I struggle in vain to move, I catch sight of Digory thrashing on the ground beside me. Whatever dose of this poison they gave us isn't completely working on him. He's resisting it somehow.

Cassius walks over to him. "Impressive. It appears the Ultra Imposer Program is quite the success."

He signals to the lead Flesher.

Snap!

The Flesher's abdomen pulls apart and an appendage looking like some souped-up version of a neurostim shoots an energy blast Digory's way.

Don't hurt him anymore. I want to scream the words at the top of my lungs, but I can only lie here as they ricochet through my brain instead.

Digory's body spasms, convulsing with seizures, but still he writhes, reaching out his hand toward me even as his movements slow into twitches. His fingertips are just shy of my cheek when he slumps into immobility, staring at me through a cobalt haze.

Cassius stoops beside me and pushes Digory's hand away, stroking my face with his own hand instead. Even though my skin can't feel a thing, it's like a squirming clump of maggots are eating through my brain.

"Sorry I had to do this," he whispers in my ear.

Then he stands and moves out of my field of vision. "Let's go," I hear him tell the Fleshers.

How does he have control over these things? What's the connection?

But my brain's too fried. I look over at Digory, willing every muscle to move, to crawl toward him. It's useless.

I can only stare straight ahead, the chill of the tunnel

harsh against my opened eyes, as I'm hoisted into the air by one of the Fleshers, just like Digory and Talon are, and carried off into the labyrinth.

THIRTY

I'm not sure how much time passes as we move through the tunnels. The journey is a blur of darkness, flashes of light, indecipherable shapes and images. In spite of catching occasional glimpses of Cassius and the still-unconscious Talon, the one image I focus on, which grounds me and prevents me from completely losing my grip on reality, is Digory.

Little by little, I feel the numbness start to lift. At one point I blink against a harsh light.

Daylight.

We're out of the tunnels. More images flash. Concrete rubble. A broken sign that says *Fifth Avenue*.

And then the crumbling spires of a ruin that conjures memories of the Priory. Although most of the wreckage we've passed is barely recognizable chunks of concrete and glass, the architecture of this one is decidedly different, more like what I'm used to from back home.

As we move through what's left of a tall, arched doorway, I catch glimpses of the remnants of a massive door. Strange letters are carved above broken stone figures embedded in its surface. Then we're jostled inside and I panic when I lose sight of Digory. I'm carried down a long aisle surrounded by shards of stained glass, broken statues, and torn pews, past toppled pillars of jagged marble. The whine and purr of the Fleshers' gears and treads grinds over the debris and echoes through the chamber as we approach what looks to be some kind of altar.

Now that the toxin is starting to wear off, my lungs take in a tentative breath of stale, musty air and I nearly choke on the storm of swirling dust flurries.

Cassius's face appears just above mine and he reaches out and strokes my hair. "Don't worry. We're almost there, Lucky." He smiles at me. "Open it," he commands our captors.

No sooner does Cassius move out of the way than I catch sight of Digory again, fidgeting between the grip of two Fleshers. Obviously his body's resistance to the toxin is markedly ahead of mine. What was it Cassius called it in the tunnels? The Ultra Imposer Program.

What have they done to Digory?

A long glistening pincer springs from the forearm of the Flesher on Digory's right and hovers over his neck, zeroing in on his pulsing carotid artery. For a second our eyes connect and I try to flash him a warning look, not sure if my brain's succeeding in getting the message across to my eyes.

I guess it registers, because Digory gives me a nod and his muscles relax. He slumps in the Flesher's grip.

But that pincer doesn't retract.

A hum fills the air, rattling the debris. I'm able to finally shift my head. The floor beneath what's left of the altar parts and a boxlike chamber rises onto the surface, some kind of an elevator. Unlike the ruined state of the rest of this city, the black and silver surface of the car is pristine, gleaming under the strobing lights of the Fleshers' instruments.

What the hell is something so technologically advanced and new doing here, buried under New York City's grave?

The glass doors slide open without a sound.

Cassius movies to stand beside the elevator. "Let's get them inside."

In no time we're herded in, with half of the Fleshers remaining outside since there's no way we're all going to be able to cram into the space. By this time, both Cassius and I are able to stand on our own two feet; the paralysis has almost faded.

All the better to feel the sharp edge of one of the Flesher's sharpened tools digging into the back of my neck.

Then the doors slide shut again and my stomach does somersaults as we drop. My fingers brush against Digory's until we manage to interlock tips. After what we've both been through, I can't think of too many things we won't be able to face as long as we have each other.

"I know you think I'm a monster," Cassius says, shattering the moment. "But maybe you'll understand once you've seen for yourself."

I'm finally able to dredge up enough spit to coat my parched throat. "I think I've already seen enough." I barely recognize my own voice.

The elevator begins to slow and the blur outside the doors becomes discernible.

And I can't believe what it is that I'm seeing. Surely it's got to be the hallucinogenic after-effects of whatever poison they pumped into my system.

The clear tube has descended from the darkness into a vast open area that stretches as far as the eye can see, in every direction. Patches of cottony mist obscure the view as the car plunges through it.

Clouds.

It's the sky. Or more like four different skies, to be exact. It's like looking at an entire day, all at once, that's been carved into four separate pieces. In one direction, the sky's bright with sunshine, rippling with heat as if it's the middle of a hot summer day. Directly opposite, it's almost pitch black, the night sky glistening with thousands of stars that sparkle like gems in perfect synchronicity.

In contrast, the two opposing regions are made up of dawn and dusk respectively, awash in pink, purple, and orange.

I turn to Cassius. "This can't be *real*. We're indoors. *Underground*. But I've never seen holograms on such a massive scale before."

And interspersed among these fragments are huge, mushroom-shaped pods—buildings with windows and balconies. An entire city growing within the entrails of the dead New York.

But unlike the Lady's graveyard, *this* city is very much alive. And the most shocking part of all is that it's not just populated with Fleshers. The entire place is teeming with human life.

All throughout this subterranean metropolis people bustle about, strolling down immaculate promenades, cultivating fields using sleek hovercrafts and laser tech, darting in and out of what appears to be a recycling plant. They're all dressed the same, in stark white jumpsuits with some type of dark band around the arm. I even spot what appears to be a power plant and silos in the distance.

It's too much to take in. A whole society thriving underneath such ruin, hidden from all of us, even the Establishment. If they knew about this place, they'd have plundered it eons ago and claimed its resources.

But obviously, it's not a secret from everyone.

I turn to Cassius. "What *is* this place? And how long have you known about it?"

He nods. "I'm sure you have many questions, Lucky. Be patient. They'll all be answered soon."

The elevator finally eases to a stop and the doors part.

Standing several feet in front of us is a small group of the white-clad inhabitants. The one who appears to be the leader is a tall, silver-haired man with piercing gray eyes, probably in his early fifties but possessing the energy and vitality of someone half his age.

His four companions are actually holograms. They look to be mid-to-late twenties, all very trim and fit. Two of them are men—one olive complected like me, the other with short-cropped fiery hair. Both women are pale skinned—one with hair so blonde it almost looks white, the other with hair as dark as a moonless night.

And they're all smiling at us, which, as unnerving as it is, isn't half as disturbing as their ease in the company of the Fleshers flanking them, which are equally as grotesque and impassive as the ones holding us hostage.

The leader steps forward. "Welcome to Sanctum. My name is Straton. Dr. Sebastos Straton. My four companions here are taking care of matters at another part of the station and are joining us via uplink." He extends a perfectly manicured hand to Cassius. "Brother Cassius, so good to see you again."

Cassius clasps his hand. "It's great to be back, my friend." He turns and gestures to Digory and me. "These are my ... *companions*," he finally says after a prolonged beat.

Straton smiles. "Ah, yes. Lucian Spark and Digory Tycho."

Surprised, I glance at Digory, who stands stoic, eyes scanning our surroundings as if he's assessing weak points, escape strategies. But he squeezes my hand firmly, as if he's sensing what I'm feeling without even seeing my face.

I turn back to Straton, ignoring the grin still plastered on his face. "How do you know who we are?"

"This isn't the first time you've encountered us." He gestures to the Flesher on his right. The thing's gears and motors hum to life as it moves forward. The band around its head where its eyes should be comes to life, igniting with blue like the pilot light on a gas burner. Then a three-dimensional image is projected from it, into the center of our group.

I recognize the footage in an instant. Chaotic shots of us running through the canyon on Infiernos, accompanied by sound bites of panting breaths and shouted warnings. Snippets of Recruit uniforms. The memory of my last Recruit training exercise hits me hard. My chest contracts at the sight of Gideon, Ophelia, and Cypress sprinting for their lives, trying to reach the transport. More shots of Digory and me, the camera zeroing in on our silver ID tags, freeze-framing and enhancing the images until our names are clearly displayed.

The image fades.

Straton signals to the Flesher to retreat and takes another step closer. "Once we had you in custody, it only took a few moments for the subject recognition software to cross-check your appearances with the data in our reconnaissance archives."

I nudge my head in the direction of the Fleshers. "Nice. Your monsters keep a record every time they chase their next meal?"

My words finally succeed in wiping the smug grins off their faces. In fact, they seem mortified, as if I've hurt their feelings.

Cassius grabs my arm. "Lucky, it's *not* what you think—"

I wrench away. "I think that footage speaks for itself. Besides, are you forgetting the little attack we just went through on Infiernos, that one that kind of wiped out all your friends?" I glance at Straton. "Not that I'm complaining."

Straton holds up a hand and shakes his head. "It's all right, Brother Cassius. The young man is ignorant of the truth."

I shake my head. "All I know is that your lot seems awfully comfortable hanging around nine-foot-tall monsters that hunt and eat people, and that doesn't exactly inspire too much confidence on this end. After all, I'm sure they didn't earn the name 'Fleshers' for nothing."

The redheaded male, who up to now has remained silent like the rest of the holographic participants, clears his throat and addresses Straton. "Perhaps we should be the ones to explain, Sir."

"Of course. It's only fitting that it should come from *you*." Straton steps aside.

Red turns back to me and his expression is grave. "When we first came here, from that hell above that you call home, we were as young and ignorant as you are and we thought the same as you do now. But the Fleshers are the perfect synthesis of humanity and technology, achieving the perfection the Begetter intended."

I hold his gaze. "So you basically experimented on hapless victims to create a race of slave drones to serve you."

The blonde woman indicates the thing next to her. "They're *not* our slaves. We coexist. They're our brothers and sisters. Individuals suffering from terminal illnesses, physical and mental challenges. We gave them a chance to live their lives to their fullest."

The brunette nods. "They're more like our guardians and protectors."

My eyes bulge and my brain connects the dots. "You were my age, you said, when you came here from where I used to live. You're…"

The brown-haired man smiles. "Yes. We're the remainder of what you refer to as the Fallen Five."

THIRTY-ONE

I'm still reeling from the shock of learning the identities of the four holographic visitors. Before I can press them for more specifics, Straton whisks me, Cassius, Digory, and our Flesher escort aboard a rectangular glider transport for a tour. At Cassius's request, the still-unconscious Prime Minister Talon is placed in stasis in a medpod and transported to a nearby hospital.

We glide through the city streets, the transport much more fluid than the steam-powered hovercrafts back home. As we wind through marketplaces, outdoor schools, and what appears to be a business district, I can't concentrate due to the logjam of questions in my throat. Finally I lean forward and speak.

"The Fallen Five are a *legend*," I say. "When those Recruits disappeared more than ten years ago, it was the only time the

Trials were ever cancelled since their inception. We need to go back. I *have* to talk to them."

I leave out the part about needing to ask them what the hell happened to the fifth Recruit, Orestes Goslin, that turned him into a crazed cannibal surviving in the wilderness until his gruesome murder.

"Don't worry," Cassius says. "You'll get the opportunity to speak to them."

I ignore him. "Why did those Recruits never go back home?" I ask Straton. "Did they choose to stay here by their own free will or are you keeping them here?"

Straton shakes his head. "Did they look like they are under any duress to you?"

I slump back into my seat in lieu of giving the obvious response. No. They looked to be in excellent health, and happy. Too happy. I can't help but remember the disheveled condition of Orestes Goslin—Cypress's brother—when we encountered him right before that harrowing escape from the Fleshers.

At one point during our tour, we enter a crowded square with a building that appears to be some sort of cathedral. Disembarking, we enter the building and stand in a cordoned-off area in the rear. Despite all the people here, everything is quiet and solemn. The participants bow their heads and kneel as a golden platter hovers back and forth, row after row, dispensing what look to be rectangular-shaped crackers. The worshipers chant their gratitude to an entity known as the Begetter.

"Consume the flesh of the Begetter and become one,"

they recite in unison. Then they place the crackers into their mouths.

The whole ritual conjures images of the Priory, and I shift my weight from one leg to another.

Digory's hand slips into mine again and our eyes meet. I lean into his shoulder, allowing the heat of his body to counter the weariness of my own. Whatever happens to us now, each moment we spend together is a gift I don't intend to waste.

The ceremony ends with the gathering bursting into song, and then we're escorted out and back onto the transport, moving on just as the crowd in the square begins to disperse.

I decide to take a different tact with Straton. "This is quite some eco set-up you have here," I say. "How long have you been down here?"

Cassius answers instead, pursing his lips. "There's a lot about the history of our world that you don't know. That I myself didn't know until I first encountered Sanctum."

I'm intrigued. "All we've ever been told is that the Deity wiped away the old world in the Great Ash Wars millennia ago, because we as a species had become weak and sinful, too dependent on creature comforts and baseless desires. Or some such religious rubbish." Memories of Prior Delvecchio's sermons rush through me, Cassius and me sneaking out of the Priory as children to play in the fields behind the waste treatment facilities instead. A pang hits me as I look at the stranger that Cassius has become.

"On some basic level, that's true, I suppose," Cassius says

now. "But that's more the Establishment's way of dealing with the masses, treating them like children."

I fight the urge to sneer. "You act like you're not a part of them."

"I'm *not*."

Our eyes hold for an uncomfortable moment before I finally break away.

Straton turns to Digory and me. "I think a visit to the archives is in order."

Our vehicle leaves the broad daylight of one quadrant and enters the dark night of another. It's like gliding along a vast dark sea. Up ahead, a sleek, bullet-shaped building lights the way like a lone beacon. The domed roof appears to be an observatory.

"What's with the four regions divvied up by time of day?" I ask Straton.

"It's a constant reminder of the four stages of humanity's life cycle," he replies. "The dawn of life during birth; the peak of day, signifying adulthood; the dusk of old age; and finally death, when we rejoin the Begetter."

I pause to consider this. "So, in spite of all your reliance on science and tech, you still practice your own form of religion just like the Establishment does?"

"Except *our* religion is the one truth." The vehicle glides to a halt. "Time for some answers to your questions," Straton announces.

My suspicions are overridden by my thirst for knowledge.

Cassius steps out of the transport before me and turns

to offer me a hand down. But I ignore it and instead turn to give Digory unneeded help, the two of us striding past Cassius to follow Straton and our Flesher escort into the domed building.

Once inside, we travel down a series of gleaming passages and enter an elevator, flanked by Fleshers standing sentinel. In spite of now having seen so many of them up close, I don't think I'll ever get used to their ghastly appearance.

We exit the elevator and climb a steep spiral staircase, passing through a doorway into the observatory.

The domed room is enormous. Square panels are irregularly spaced throughout the curving ceiling. Directly above the glass in its center, the starfield shines overhead, much like it did on that night so long ago when Digory and I sat overlooking the ocean on the tower during our Recruit training—a lifetime ago, it feels like.

Clathrate Life Extinction Event data selected, a computerized voice announces.

A low hum fills the room and the lights dim.

We're no longer in the observatory. The room has been replaced by a blinding-white, snow-covered tundra stretching impossibly wide in every direction. Animal species I've never seen before populate the horizon, many with snow-white fur. Then the view plunges through the snow and into the sea.

"Buried deep in the seabeds are methane clathrate compounds," Straton explains. "Here, in the Arctic Ocean, because of the lower temperatures and lid of permafrost preventing the escape of methane, clathrates existed in shallower waters."

The images flicker to the surface, where massive ships are tearing their way through the ice. I flinch as chunks of simulated ice are flung in our direction. Soon a montage replaces the ships: massive machines digging through the snow, enormous pipes excavating the surface, destroying all that beauty.

Cassius shakes his head. "Unfortunately, our ancestors became obsessed with exploiting all our natural resources as energy became scarce. This led to rises in sea temperatures and levels, which triggered the sudden release of enormous amounts of methane from the compounds buried in the ice."

I shake my head. "Isn't methane a pretty powerful gas?"

Straton nods. "The effect was like firing a massive gun. Once the methane was released, it created a greenhouse effect in the atmosphere, increasing temperatures even further—"

"And further destabilizing the methane clathrate in the ocean," I say. The awe I've been feeling turns to horror.

"Yes," Straton replies. "It was like a runaway train, warming the planet in less than a human generation." He points to the images, shaky cam shots of dying animals, dead fish floating in the oceans. "Explosions of burning methane covered the planet in smoke, dust, and ash, firestorms that remained in the upper atmosphere for years. Large land masses flooded and created a global cooling that scrubbed out animal life both above and below the surface.

The once-beautiful horizon is now a grit-filled field of darkness and dust. Digory squeezes my hand.

"This lead to a widespread panic and mass food shortages," Straton continues.

Holos of massive crowds and mass chaos surround us. Suffering, dirty faces, all filled with hunger and fear. Even after all the horrors I've witnessed firsthand, none comes close to capturing the utter devastation filling my eyes at this moment.

Cassius sighs. "Due to the raised levels of methane and derivative carbon dioxide flooding the atmosphere, alternating seasons of intense heat and cold rocked the population. Crop production was devastated, and weather patterns were forever thrown into chaos. Back when the city above us was a thriving metropolis, it was blanketed in winter this time of year, while it was warmer the Parish."

Next, it's like we're in the middle of an intense snow storm where I can barely see an inch in front of me. Then the screens shift to images of arid, cracked earth and withered plant-life.

"The less industrialized nations perished first," Straton explains. "But those countries considered super powers in the day fought to horde what was left of the precious resources. Allies turned on each other. There were military strikes. In some cases, there were governments who destroyed their own meager resources rather than see them fall into the hands of another. A series of wars ensued, wars fought in darkness and fire—"

"The Ash Wars," I whisper.

Cassius's eyes meet mine. "Yes. The few who survived came to call it that." He shrugs. "It was a conflict that nobody won. After much bloodshed, the planet settled into quiet, the few pockets of survivors taking refuge underground."

The images fade and the lights come back up. I look

around me, then back at Straton. "This place. Sanctum is— *was*—a refuge against the cataclysm."

"Yes. Our ancestors built it generations ago, one of a nexus of underground bunkers to preserve society. But over the generations, it's become so much more." Straton leads the way out of the observatory and into the elevator. "Scientists, and those deemed to have the technological and agricultural skills necessary to rebuild a society, were chosen to operate these underground installations. They were constructed across what was once known as the United States of America."

"Usofa," I whisper to myself. Digory and I exchange surprised glances.

The elevator begins its rapid descent. "You mean there are other hidden facilities like this one still around?" I ask.

Straton shakes his head. "No. At least not to our knowledge. According to the data that survived from those early days, it seems the nexus maintained communications in the beginning. But after the atmospheric conditions became more intense and the satellites began to fail, many of the installations were either breached during the ensuing wars or destroyed by natural forces. The only documentation we've been able to recover points to a complete loss of communication that was never re-established again."

"But still, there *could* be other installations, isolated, wondering if others survived..." I mutter.

The elevator doors open, interrupting the possibilities swimming through my mind.

Straton beckons with a wave of his hand. "Come." We're

marched out of the archive building and back into the transport.

My mind is swirling with all these revelations. Life Extinction Events. Wars. Hidden pockets of survivors. Except for what I'd learned from those fragments of books in the Parish library, I never knew there was any other life but the Parish and the Establishment. All this time, we've been rotting in our own little world completely oblivious of all this.

My eyes dart to Cassius. At least most of us were oblivious. This new information could change everything.

"What about the *rest* of the world?" I ask. "Did any other countries have survivors after the wars?"

The vehicle begins to glide forward at high velocity. Straton looks back at us from the front seat. "None that we know of. It's possible that some survived in shelters such as this one. If so, they've never made any attempt to contact us, or at least none that I'm aware of."

I grip Digory's hand tightly. Despite my amazement at this place, there's something about all this that just doesn't *feel* right. "I don't get it," I say. "If people have survived in Sanctum all of this time, how is it that *most* of us in the Parish"— I glance at Cassius—"have never heard of you before? How could we have survived without any bunkers, and why have you never come to our aid?"

It's not only curiosity that fuels my question. It's anger, too. All this time, the people under the Establishment's thrall have endured such inhumane and deplorable conditions while Straton and his crew have apparently been living it up down here, with plenty of resources that could have made all our lives so much easier.

It's Cassius who answers me. "It's not like that. The people of Sanctum have had their eyes on us from the very beginning."

My gaze flicks between them. "Tell me everything."

Cassius and Straton exchange a look and the older man nods. He turns to me. "Centuries ago, once the worst of the carnage was over and the atmosphere had become manageable again, much talk occurred here about our eventual return to the surface. The feelings both *for* and *against* were quite passionate—and volatile. A compromise was made. It was decided that a small group of one hundred settlers would be permitted to leave the safety of Sanctum with supplies and provisions in an effort to re-establish a society above ground."

The sky above turns from darkness to soft shades of pink and purple as we zoom into the Dawn quadrant.

Straton clears his throat before continuing. "It was a risky mission, fraught with danger and fear. Those first pioneers had the unenviable task of braving the elements and setting up a new home."

He takes a deep breath. "Because of the dangers, it was decided by the ruling council that each member of the expedition could choose only *one* of their family members to accompany them. The rest had to stay behind. It was a dark time. Families were torn apart. But it was vital to the continued survival of Sanctum that the others remain behind. Of course, the explorers were given as many supplies as could be spared—food, medical provisions—and even were accompanied by a scientist, an agricultural specialist, a tech expert, and a cleric—but it was still a huge gambit. Not all of them survived that first year, but soon they set up a small township and slowly began to thrive under the guidance of their leader, Queran Embers."

"Queran Embers?" My heart rate accelerates. "Small township." I catch Cassius's eye. "The Parish. These *re-establishers* became *the Establishment*, didn't they?"

Cassius nods. "Yes. *All* of us—you, me—everyone we know back home—we're all descendants of those first settlers from Sanctum."

The words gridlock in my throat. I can't stop staring at our Flesher escort, sitting stoic, the soft hues of the newly born sky incongruous against its repulsive features. All that time, fleeing from their touch, I had no idea I was running from our very own past.

And this place, Sanctum—with its Fleshers, four different skies, giant telescopes, and archives filled with information I've always dreamed about—it's not just a wondrous discovery.

It's where we all come from. Our *true* birthplace.

"I can tell you're as surprised as I was when I learned the truth," Cassius says. There's something in his voice that's tinged with empathy, a harsh reminder of someone that doesn't exist anymore—that maybe never did. I huddle against Digory, who puts his arm around me, pulling me close against him.

"If we do come from you," I finally say, "how is it that we've never known about you before?"

This time, Straton's look is stern. "Once the original settlement started to grow, they resented Sanctum's intrusion into their lives. They felt *they* had taken all the risks, and why should *we* reap the rewards? They cut off all ties with Sanctum and became their own entity—the Establishment, as you said. Their leader was consumed by that same greed and lust for power that led to humanity's downfall to begin with. Everything we'd been through and survived—*nothing* was learned from it. Any documentation of Sanctum was destroyed, along with all communication links. As the younger generations were born, our existence was omitted from their histories. The experiment was a failure."

My anger is stoked. "Experiment? You make it sound like we were all a bunch of laboratory rats."

Straton purses his lips. "In essence, your forebearers were just that. Besides seeing if it was possible for human beings to return to the surface after the apocalypse, the mission was also a way of ascertaining whether we could effectively rebuild our race, or whether we'd be doomed to failure yet again. Unfortunately, the latter proved to be true."

He looks away from me. "We've been sending scouts out for years now." He places a hand on the shoulder of the Flesher beside him, who doesn't react at all. "Everything we've seen confirms that our former brethren have become a race of deplorable barbarians, feeding off the lives of those they subjugate for power. Any notions of welcoming them back into the fold would seem to be doomed to failure."

In spite of the harshness of his words, I can't say I disagree with anything he's said about the Establishment. If anything, he's being *too* kind.

Straton locks eyes with me. "While the odds of success are low, we owe it to the Begetter to try to rejoin with our misguided brethren one last time. That is why we invited Prime Minister Talon to our city on a mission of peace. Following our talks here in Sanctum, a retinue from our city shall accompany the Prime Minister back to the Parish to continue negotiations."

"It must have taken an awful lot of persuasion to get Talon to leave the safety of the Parish and venture here," I say.

Cassius smiles. "It's amazing what the prospect of advanced tech and increased food resources can accomplish."

"Of course. Power and greed. The language of politicians." My eyes meet Cassius's. "And you, the poster-boy Prefect for the Establishment, are okay with this?"

"I told you once before that I have plans to beat them at their own game. Nothing's changed."

I cross my arms. "Hmmm. Neither has my opinion of you, especially considering how you're responsible for so much pain—not only to Cole and me, but to the people we care about." I look into Digory's eyes and he kisses me on the forehead. When I look back at Cassius, he seems pained. "From where I'm sitting, you judging the Establishment makes you the biggest hypocrite on the entire planet."

"I did what I had to do to get to this point. I was on my way to Sanctum with Talon to begin peace negotiations when

we crashed and you found us. But you'll understand everything soon enough."

"What's *that* supposed to mean?"

He leans toward me and Digory squeezes his bulk between
us, shoving Cassius back into his seat. Their eyes are dead-
locked—Digory's filled with that savage fury, Cassius's widen
with fear.

"Relax, Tycho," Cassius grunts. "I'm not going to hurt your
precious little Lucky."

Part of me wouldn't mind one bit watching Digory throttle Cassius. Hell, I've been resisting doing much worse ever
since we first ran into him. But now's not the time for that.

I touch Digory's arm, feeling the hot blood pounding
underneath the rock-hard muscle. "Digory, let it go. I'm okay."

Slowly, he settles back down into his chair. But his eyes
target Cassius's face like ice-blue daggers.

The glider transport starts to slow down as it approaches
a series of silver towers surrounding a circular courtyard. Cassius takes a deep breath, rubs his chest where Digory's palm
hit, and shakes his head at us as if he's disappointed. "I would
have thought you two, of all people, would be thrilled by the
prospect of the Establishment's downfall."

My eyes grow wide.

"Just what do you mean?" I ask. "You don't expect Talon
and the Establishment to just throw down their weapons and
make nice, do you?"

He shakes his head. "Get a good night's sleep. Tomorrow
is going to be an eventful day."

Before I can respond, we've stopped at the entrance to

a housing facility and are escorted by silent Fleshers to our quarters.

With all the distance between Sanctum and the surface, I can't help feeling more trapped than ever.

THIRTY-TWO

I can't sleep. Even curled up against the warm contours of Dig-ory's bare chest and listening to the rhythmic lull of his heart, all I can think about is what tomorrow may bring.

What did Cassius mean?

If by some miracle the Establishment can be persuaded to rejoin the fold and the people of Sanctum are willing to share their knowledge and resources with the Parish, it will mean a whole different life for all of us—one free of fear and suffering. No more rebellions. No more war. We can finally have a life where we can dare to hope, knowing that our dreams are within our grasp.

We'll be able to live together as families and grow old together—Digory and I can raise Cole. I feel excited, almost giddy, as I imagine this future. It's an emotion I've never really felt before, and one I never imagined I ever would.

I look up at Digory. Even in the dim light, I take in that

perfectly handsome face, my finger lightly tracing the angle of his jaw. He looks so peaceful in sleep. It's as if the underlying pain that now simmers just beneath his eyes has been wiped clean, leaving a fresh canvas full of possibilities.

My lips brush against his and I feel myself getting even more excited. But as much as I want him, I fight the urge to wake him. He's been through so much. Let him enjoy a restful sleep.

Sliding my body from his arms takes every ounce of willpower I can muster, and once I'm free I slip on some clothes and pad out of the room as quickly as I can before I change my mind.

I spend a few hours using a tool kit I found in one of the closets to repair the tiny transceiver I've kept hidden in the lining of my pants. Not sure it'll work, but at least there's a chance I might be able to contact Cage and Arrah now.

Then I trot up the carpeted steps of the penthouse suite we've been assigned and open the door leading out onto the roof.

I still haven't gotten used to seeing the four different horizons, but the cool, artificially created winds tingling my skin invigorate me. Though we're not housed in the tallest building in Sanctum, we're high enough that I have a bird's-eye view of most of the city.

The streets seem utterly deserted, a stark contrast from the hustle and bustle when we first arrived. Maybe they're all sleeping, but I'd have guessed with the upcoming peace talks, followed by a diplomatic mission to the Parish, there'd be a lot more activity going on.

I shrug and am just about to turn around and go back inside when I spot movement in the night quadrant—what appears to be a procession of white-clad personnel leading a line of gleaming steel cargo containers toward a processing plant. They disappear inside.

The elation I've been feeling shifts into alarm, then suspicion. What was it Straton said when he was giving us a tour of Sanctum? That the plant has been closed for some time, sealed off due to hazardous conditions. Whatever's inside couldn't be too lethal, though, given that no one in the procession seemed to be wearing any kind of protective bio-suit.

My Imposer training kicks into high gear. That gut feeling I had earlier shoves my optimism out of the way. I need to investigate this. If I'm wrong, then there's no harm done.

But if I'm right—

I turn around and my heart almost stops as I plow into Digory. I didn't even hear him come up behind me. I let out a nervous chuckle as he grabs my arms and steadies me, curiosity and concern battling it out on his face.

Throwing my arms around him, I hug him tight. "Sorry if I woke you."

He kisses my forehead, hugging me back. When we finally pull apart, he's looking at me with imploring eyes.

"I think something's going on," I say.

Then I tell him what I saw at the processing plant and how I want to take a look and see what's going on there. He nods and motions to me, then himself, then points at the plant, now silent and cloaked in shadow.

I smile at him. "Sure. You can come. Just try to keep up."

He smiles back.

We slip into a pair of fresh white jumpsuits that have been left for us in the closet. Hand in hand, we scurry down the stairs and make our way to the door of the suite. We glance at each other as I slowly turn the knob and crack it open, peering into the hallway.

Standing sentinel by the elevator doors are two Fleshers, their bulky forms barely able to fit in the cramped space. Their haunting faces stare straight ahead, blank and expressionless as if they were dead.

Why do I get the feeling they aren't going to let us pass if we try to board?

Easing the door closed again, I turn back to Digory. "We're going to have to figure out a way to get past those two."

We look around the room on the off chance that there's another way out, but of course there isn't. At one point, Digory hoists me onto his broad shoulders as I check the ceiling for ducts we might be able to use to bypass the hallway, but the crawlspace isn't large enough and it doesn't appear that there's access to the elevator shafts.

That leaves only one more option.

Opening the balcony doors, I lean against the railing and stare down. Fifteen stories to ground level.

"We've scaled higher drops than this," I say, recalling our Recruit training at Infiernos. Of course we didn't have to worry about being in plain view of anyone who might happen to be looking in this direction.

Digory sidles up to me and grins. Before I can say a word,

he's already grabbed onto the railing and swung his body over the edge in one fluid movement.

"Careful!" I whisper.

He pivots his body until his feet perch on the railing below. Then he steadies himself and releases one of his hands, using it to brace himself against the underside of the flooring of our balcony, which rests right above the balcony below.

I hold my breath, my heart racing as he lets go of the railing with his second hand and drops onto the landing beneath us.

Then he looks up at me with a sly grin, as if he's wondering what's taking me so long.

I shake my head and give him a wink. "Show-off."

Taking a deep breath, I grab onto the railing just like Digory did—well, maybe I'm not as lithe—and in seconds I've joined him on the landing below, where he sweeps me into his arms.

His eyes swell with pride and he kisses my lips one more time before letting go and bounding down to the next balcony. I follow him as before, making sure not to stare at the drop but instead concentrate on him to steady me. Within ten minutes we reach the ground. "Let's move," I say.

We look left and right, then make a diagonal dash toward the processing plant. We reach the shadow of a communications tower, twenty feet or so from a metallic fence that extends the entire perimeter of the plant.

I scoop up a handful of pebbles and fling them at the fence. They're instantly vaporized in a ball of sparks.

"You don't fortify an abandoned plant," I whisper. "This proves they're hiding something, at least."

A low vibration fills the air. Digory and I exchange a quick look, then peer in the direction of the sound.

Whizzing down the path leading to the front entrance of the plant is one of the glider transport vehicles. I barely have time to register it as Digory pulls me into the shadows of the tower.

We wait and watch, trying not to breathe too heavily as the vehicle slows and reaches the gate. There's a burst of static from inside the craft, and a murmur of voices too low to hear. In seconds, the energized hum disappears and the gate begins to open.

Digory's already grabbing my hand and we dart toward the back of the transport, leaping at the last possible moment and grabbing hold of the back fins as it goes through the gate. I grit my teeth and don't dare to breathe, staring wordlessly at Digory opposite me and hoping our maneuver was smooth enough not to attract any unwanted attention.

We're through the fence in seconds and there's a crackle as it's re-energized. We continue to hug the back of the carrier, pressed as flat against its hull as we can. It speeds down a diagonal ramp and disappears into the bowels of the processing plant.

As soon as we're inside, the heavy steel doors slam shut. There's no question they're keeping something in here they don't want anyone to see.

The transport continues its descent, one sub-level after another, as if we weren't already far enough underground as it is. At least it doesn't seem like anyone has noticed we're still hitching a ride. But who knows how long that's going to last.

A few minutes later, the transport begins to slow as it approaches a fork in the passage. I catch Digory's eye, motioning with my head that the ride's over.

He gets my signal and leaps off the vehicle, rolling across the ground and into a darkened side passage. I spring after him and hit the ground hard, banging my shoulder but continuing to unspool into the gloom.

Digory crawls up beside me and together we watch from the shadows as the vehicle stops. Straton disembarks, along with his Fleshers, who surround the transport as he enters a doorway that seals behind him.

Good thing we bailed when we did.

Digory touches my shoulder and I wince. He rests his palm on my cheek.

"It's okay. I'm good," I say.

I risk a peek from our hiding place. "There's no way we can follow him inside." Then I peer into the passage behind us. "But that doesn't mean we can't do some recon of the rest of this place."

He nods and we slink down the passageway. The walls are dark and smooth except for every twenty-five feet or so, where supports jut from the walls all the way up to the arched ceiling like skeletal joints. The farther we go, the more humid and muggy it becomes. I wipe the sweat from my brow as a fine layer of mist begins to obscure the corridor ahead. There's a low vibration in the air, getting stronger the farther we go. My ears detect a pulse, a throbbing sound. The walls become rougher, feeling almost like there's a rough, thick coat on them. It's almost like it's elemental, natural, not man-made. Like a nest.

Or a hive.

I turn to Digory, who's now barely a silhouette in my vision. "Wonder what the hell they're keeping down here?"

We round a corner. The hall dead-ends into one of the most bizarre chambers I've ever seen. It's a cross between the most gleaming, sophisticated tech that I can imagine and a primordial display of pulsing, tentacular appendages blended together in obscene symbiosis.

The center of the room is filled with rows and rows of capsules arranged in concentric circles; they remind me of cryogenic tubes. Their glass surfaces perspire with droplets of moisture, which makes the interiors opaque. Snakelike, scaly tubes descend from a nest of computer terminals suspended from the ceiling and feed into each of the capsules. I approach the nearest one and wipe the condensation away. I'm surprised to find it frosty, considering the heat being generated by all the blinking gauges and equipment in the chamber. Beneath the glass surface, I can barely make out a dark figure lying perfectly still in the thick, swirling cryogenic fog.

At the head of each of these capsules are digital readout displays that seem to be monitoring the vital signs of the patients inside. But these readouts track power levels and electrical impulses, which is odd. The data seems more like the kind of information you'd get from diagnostic and performance tests given to machinery and equipment, not to live human beings.

Digory looks up at me from the capsule he's been examining, a puzzled look in his eyes that I'm sure is reflected on my own face.

"Let's open one," I say.

He joins me and together we comb the surface of a capsule, searching for the release mechanism to spring open its hatch.

After a few minutes of trying in vain, I slam my palm against the glass. "There's got to be a button that opens this thing."

But Digory doesn't seem to think so. He leaps onto the pod and tears out one of the tubes feeding the pod with his bare hands.

I check to make sure no one's coming. "*Or* we can do it that way."

The hose hisses like an angry serpent. Digory wraps it around his fist and pummels the glass shield. A crack appears on the cryotube, which splinters into a thousand crystal streams before it's punctured with an earsplitting crack.

The moment the container is breached, the lid bursts open with an arctic blast of mist, evaporating the sweat pooling on my body in an instant. I wave my hand until the haze dissipates enough for me to peer down at the capsule's occupant.

A familiar-looking face stares up at me. And for a second, I think I've lost it.

It's Crowley. Or at least a *part* of him. His naked torso seems intact, but his arms and everything from the waist down are covered in foul-smelling slime. It's some kind of bio-synthetic cocoon. Wires and tubes slice into his skin as if he were a human pincushion. I can see flashing lights beneath the gooey membranes and hear the sickening *squish* as the substance fuses with Crowley's skin, which has turned from the pale chalk color it was the last time I saw him to a sickly greenish tint.

Cassius announced that Crowley was dead. Seeing him like this, I wish it were true.

I lean closer to get a better look, and that's when his hand darts up in a flash and grabs my arm, pulling me toward him. His eyes spring open, irises milky white.

Digory's at my side in a flash, but I wave him off.

In spite of the horrific condition Crowley is in, there's something truly pitiful in the way he's looking at me, a mixture of fright and complete and utter dread that shreds my insides.

"Spark," he whispers, his voice a thin rasp of its former self. As he speaks, noxious liquid dribbles from the corners of his lips.

I grip the hand that's clutching me. "What have they done to you, Crowley?"

Milky white tears ooze from his eyes. "They're changing me...making me one of *them*..."

His voice trails off, but I don't need him to finish to know who *them* is.

Fleshers.

"We're going to get you out of here." Even as I say the words, my eyes dart across what's left of his body and I feel helpless and frustrated.

He shakes his head. "Too late. No time. This whole place..." His eyes wander for a few seconds. "All of these people...prisoners...Incentives that survived...they change them...turn them into..." His face screws up and an agonized mewl twists from his throat.

My body is racked with the shakes. Crowley is delirious with pain. That's why he's talking such craziness. The Incentives that survived... the loved ones of all the *Imps*... they can't be in this place. I've seen Imposers communicating with their kin at Haven, carrying on conversations in real time. It's the one carefully greased cog in the machine that keeps them following orders: knowing that those they care about are at least being taken care of, living a life they would otherwise have no chance at, all thanks to the sacrifice the Recruits have made. The continued well-being of what, in essence, are Establishment hostages is at the core of its lethally trained forces.

I scan the room, my eyes darting from one control panel to the next. "There must be a terminal—some kind of control panel with a database," I tell Digory, my tone breathless with the possibilities.

Digory takes my cue. Between the two of us, we comb the lab until minutes later he's ushering me over to a keyboard inlaid in an alcove in the far corner.

I scroll through the entries. A list of names I don't recognize at first. But as I near the end of the chronological list, the entries become more familiar to me. Residents of the Parish. Old friends and neighbors. People who served as Incentives for those who were selected in Recruitments just prior to my own.

On a hunch, I search for Cassius's name on the roster. But all details of his own Recruitment are missing.

Did he wipe the information from the system? If so, why? What's he hiding?

By this time the keys are slick with my sweat as I toggle through the names and come across the Incentives of Arrah, Rodrigo, Leander, and Dahlia. I select the names by Arrah—

Her parents. But only one of them is lit in green—her mother, the Incentive who survived the Trials when Arrah was a Recruit.

My heart is at full throttle while I scroll to the option labeled **Begin Interactive Simulation** and press the enter key. A low hum fills the room and an image appears on the computer screen. I see the resemblance immediately. Arrah's mother is staring down at me with a smile on her face. It looks like a real-time video. She's outside somewhere; it's a beautiful summer day with a lake glistening in the background.

I turn to whisper to Digory. "She's supposed to be at Haven, the Incentive compound somewhere."

"Why, of course I'm at Haven. Where else would I be?" she asks, startling me with her cheerfulness.

"You can *hear* me?" I ask.

She nods. "Yes, I can hear you."

It's uncanny. If I didn't know any better, I'd swear we'd actually established a live feed with her. My mind's racing. What if we *have*, somehow? If I could track the location of Haven—

Digory tugs my arm and point at a list of other options.

Age Progression. Time of Day. Location. Health variables.

A rapid clatter fills the room as I select one option after another, watching as Arrah's mother ages—a few years. Ten. Twenty. At the tap of a key, the simulated figure changes location. Outdoor lakes become indoor fireplaces. Day becomes night. Eyes swell as if with a minor cold, then look more sickly, and then look the picture of health.

"*Are you Arrah's mother?*" I finally ask.

She nods. "Of course I am. Have you seen my daughter? I miss her very much."

On the computer, information scrolls by. Line after line of data, information on Arrah and her mother down to the most minute details. All the information one would need to replicate a perfect copy capable of interacting with their loved ones.

All this time, Arrah and the others held on to the belief that those they loved were safe.

But it's a lie.

All this time, the Incentives haven't been safe in Haven. They've been *here*, in Sanctum.

Which means that there are those in the Establishment who are in collusion with Sanctum and what's going on here.

I look around at the capsules crowded in the chamber.

They may as well be tombs.

THIRTY-THREE

I sag against Digory as if I've been struck. He's taken over the keyboard from me, scrolling through the names of prisoners with the designation Incompatible Specimen by their names. As he pulls up their data, my eyes grow wide.

The bodies of those that reject the bio-mechanical synth are broken down for food processing.

Those crackers, passed around and consumed during their religious rites...

Consume the flesh of the Begetter and become one...

I brace myself against the terminal. Bile rises in my throat and I fight the urge to retch. Terror engulfs me. This is even worse than all the horrors I've seen combined.

Digory reaches out to me, but I push him out of the way and type a name in the search field.

Lucian Spark.

Instantly, all the data associated with my Recruitment appears onscreen, along with entries for Mrs. Bledsoe.

And Cole.

Beside Mrs. Bledsoe's name, there's a notation in red: **Subject Shelved. Interactive Simulation inactive.**

I select the entry anyway and her face appears onscreen. The lump in my throat makes it nearly impossible to smile. She's smiling at me like Arrah's mother was, and looking the picture of health, so unlike that ghastly apparition I saw deep in the tunnels of the Skein when I was a Recruit.

"Mrs. Bledsoe," I whisper.

Her eyes light up. "Oh, Lucky! It's so good to see you, boy!" Even through my tears, I can see how she's beaming with pride. "You've grown into quite the young man. I always knew you would."

The simulation must be programmed to respond to my voice pattern, which it does—*too* perfectly. For a second it's like glimpsing an alternate future, one that might have been if it hadn't been so cruelly ripped away.

I tap the next selection before I lose my nerve. Mrs. Bledsoe's face disappears, replaced by Cole's face.

Cole smiles at me. "When are you gonna come see me, Lucky?" he asks.

Digory's hands grip my shoulders, steadying me.

"I'm coming home real soon," I whisper. I toggle through the options, watching Cole age, become a man in seconds before my very eyes, then grow older. The one thing that never seems to change is his eyes, trusting, believing in me.

Unlike Mrs. Bledsoe's, this is a future that can *still* happen.

That *will* happen, if I have anything to say about it.

I scroll further down the menu under my name and see something at the bottom of the list that almost makes my heart stop.

Sowing Protocol initiated on test subject Spark, L.

Digory's eyes grow wide.

"Digory—you mentioned this Sowing thing in your last transmission to the rebels on Recruitment Day," I say urgently. "You found out about it while spying on Cassius and you said it was very dangerous. What did you mean? *Tell me.*"

He grips a fistful of his hair. His eyes narrow and the muscles in his jaw clench. Finally he turns to me, slowly shaking his head.

Whatever they did to him at Infiernos has blocked the memory.

My heart's racing as I try to access the file, but all I get is the same message.

Highly Classified. Access Restricted.

What have they done to me? And what have they already done to Cole?

Crowley's groan of pain mirrors my own. Digory and I rush to his side.

"I don't want to be like *them* . . ." His grips tightens and his eyes grow wide. "Kill me, Spark. *Please* . . ."

I tear myself from his grasp, backing into Digory.

All these capsules . . . they're all people from the Parish. Over the years, countless Recruits have fought for their Incentives' lives, only to be rewarded by having the people they loved most mutilated and transformed into Fleshers.

Digging into my pocket, I pull out the transceiver and make sure it's set to the right channel. I'm not sure of its range, but I have to at least try to transmit the files to Arrah and the others. They need to know what's going on here.

Rifling through the lab, I find a data chip, and in a few anxious minutes have downloaded the information, plugged it into the device and hit transmit. The signal's weak, and there's no way of telling if my message was received, but there's nothing else I can do.

But I don't send anything related to this Sowing Protocol. Not until I find out what it is and what they've done to me.

"Spark, I'm begging you. It hurts *so* much." Crowley begins to sob.

His words feel like a knife carving me from side to side. There's a small part of me that wants to flee. But after everything I've been through, all the suffering I've seen, I understand what it feels like to want to die. If I turn away, I'll awaken every night to Crowley's pleas in my head, knowing I could have stopped his agony and did nothing.

Breathing deep, I take a step toward the capsule.

But Digory beats me to it. He reaches his hands inside and I hear Crowley's cries become muffled. The cords on Digory's neck pulse with the effort. His face turns red, even as his eyes well.

Crowley's gurgling starts to fade. And then it's gone.

Digory bows his head and I rest my hand on his shoulder.

Then the lights on Crowley's capsule begin to flash and the blare of an alarm fills the room.

I'm already pulling Digory away, but we're not quick

enough. Shadows descend around us, dropping out of the ceiling like huge arachnids spiraling down invisible webs. Four huge Fleshers land on the ground, surrounding us. The same four that always escort Straton wherever he goes—except for now.

Digory snarls at them. The muscles in his neck and arms pulse under the strobe of the Fleshers' lights. I assume my own attack stance. Although we're outnumbered and outmatched, I'm not going to go down without a fight. Maybe we can even inflict some damage before we're taken.

There's a series of sharp clicks as flaps of skin on the creatures' arms burst open. Long, metallic appendages squeeze out from the flesh, dripping that slimy dark ooze that passes for blood. The sharpened probes inch toward us...

Game time.

Digory lunges, grabbing the glistening instrument and twisting it away even as he leaps onto that Flesher's shoulders. I whirl and strike the Flesher in front of me with a roundhouse kick. My foot throbs with the impact, but the automaton barely stumbles backwards.

The next few seconds are a blur. Flashes of steel strike my body. I roll, kick, punch as these horrors lash out with their hideous tentacles and sharpened pincers, steel teeth chattering like the whirring blades of meat grinders. At one point, Digory somehow manages to twist the instruments of two Fleshers together, forcing them to engage in a screeching bout of tug-of-war to free themselves.

I'm hurled hard onto my back, which sends a flash of pain through my spine. A blade pistons out from the Flesher's throat. I manage to shove my head aside and, a split second later, the blade smashes into the floor beside me, spraying my face with chunks of cold tile. Before I can roll out of the way, the pincers crash down on either side of my neck, pinning me into position. The cold, slimy metal instrument presses against my throat, making it hard to breathe as it cuts into my skin.

My eyes begin to water. I manage to twist my head to the side, ignoring the pain of the pincers cutting the sides of my neck. It's taken the three other Fleshers to finally overpower Digory and pin him to the ground. Through the blur I can see the fresh cuts and welts on his heaving torso where his jumpsuit has been torn away, leaving only the gleaming silver of my ID tag over his heart, rising and falling with each breath. He goes out of focus for a moment. Then our eyes meet, and I see the mixture of fury and tenderness there.

Whir.

I shift my gaze to the Flesher holding me down. It's face is expressionless as the pincers begin to contract, cutting deeper, squeezing out all my air.

Digory unleashes an agonized cry that wrenches what's left of my soul from me.

I close my eyes, hoping it'll be over soon, waiting for the death grip to cleave my neck in two—

It doesn't happen.

I open my eyes. The Flesher is still staring at me with those soulless eyes. But the pressure around my neck decreases. One if its long silver probes moves toward my chest, a gruesome steel finger. I brace myself as the icy talon grazes my skin, expecting it to tear into my rib cage and pluck out my heart.

Instead, the probe traces a path to my throat. There's a low clink as it grips the chain around my neck—Digory's ID tag—and holds it up. Infrared beams spill from the creature's ocular sensor, bathing the tag in hues of greenish blue.

What the hell's going on here?

I glance in Digory's direction and see the Flesher holding him perform the same scan on the tag around his neck.

The Flesher scanning my chain emits some kind of low rumble.

The four Fleshers' lights blink erratically for a moment before they all sync in a steady pulse.

It's like they're communicating and have reached an agreement of some kind.

The pincers retract.

Digory and I exchange looks of puzzled relief.

A socket in the abdominal cavity of the Flesher above me springs open. The creature pulls something from it, something dripping with dark goo, and dangles it in front of me.

Swallowing hard, I reach up a tentative hand and touch the warm links. Four chains.

Four Recruit ID tags, just like ours.

My heart races as I wipe away the slimy matter to make out the names, already knowing what I'll see written there.

The names of the four remaining Recruits of the Fallen Five.

The holograms of those four people with Straton when we first arrived were illusions. Just like the doctored holograms of the surviving Incentives. Nothing but decoys to distract us and throw us off the scent.

This is what really happened to the Fallen Five. *This* is the grisly fate that Orestes Goslin escaped almost eleven years ago, that drove him mad and turned him into a crazed cannibal.

The missing Recruits were mutated into Fleshers—by Straton and the denizens of Sanctum.

Taking a deep breath, I release the ID tags and squirm out from under my captor, as does Digory. Inch by inch, we crawl our way toward each other, my senses on alert, expecting the Fleshers to attack at any second.

But they remain still.

We help each other to our feet and begin to back away from the foursome. There must be a part of the Fallen Five, still beating within their organic husks, that remembers what they once were—before they became the very first of Sanctum's drones.

As we reach the edge of the lab I take one last look at the Fleshers, still immobile behind us.

A thin, dark trail, starting in its optical sensor, drips a pathway down the face of the Flesher that pinned me.

Oil or blood—or something else. I can't tell.

Then we're running from that terrible place as fast as we can.

THIRTY-FOUR

Sirens blare as Digory and I race through the winding corridors of the hive. Overhead, emergency beacons spiral, creating a dizzying strobing effect that wreaks havoc on any sense of direction I have left. My lungs churn overtime trying to compensate for each ragged breath I manage to take, competing with the throbbing in my chest and ears. Several times we overrun a turn and have to double back to dart down a passage, only to dash in the opposite direction as sinister silhouettes appear just ahead, closing in on us.

By now the entire processing plant must know we're here, and they're probably trying to initiate some kind of lockdown. They can't afford for us to escape and get back to the Parish with everything we know.

Somehow we manage to make it back up to the level we came in on. Up ahead, a sliver of light tantalizes us with the hope of escape.

No. Even if we make it out of here and manage to fight our way to one of the elevators to the surface, that still leaves the problem of transportation. With no ride back to the Parish, we'll be recaptured before we can get a gulp of putrid surface air.

My hand locks onto Digory's arm. "We have to find one of the ships they're gonna use to get to the Parish and get the hell out of here."

Dark shapes appear in the corridors on either side of us.

Without looking back, we race down the hallway ahead to where a lone Flesher stands barring the way.

Digory doesn't even pause an instant. He just leaps and crashes into the thing, pummeling it with his fists. The Flesher's mechanisms squeal and whir as it tries to dislodge him. In seconds, flailing, stabbing instruments whip from its exoskeleton, trying to skewer its attacker.

As valiant a fight as Digory's putting up, he won't be able to hold the Flesher off too much longer. I can already hear the clatter of approaching feet behind us. Pouncing, I grab one of the Flesher's appendages—some type of snapping pincer—and jam it against one of the power cables lining the wall. I let go just as the instrument clips the cable with a loud snap. Sparks bursts, raining mini-fire on my exposed skin. The Flesher bucks and jerks as if it's having convulsions.

There's a part of me that squirms at the idea that this thing, having a seizure in front of my eyes, was a vital human being before Cassius, Straton, and Sanctum genetically altered it in their miserable quest to play the role of gods.

Digory shoves the pitiful thing away from us. Then he grabs me in his other arm and pulls me across a threshold.

My fist slams a panel on the wall just as our pursuers reach us. A steel door crashes closed behind us, cutting them off.

I lean against it, my body vibrating from the heavy thudding coming from the other side. "It's not going to take them long to get through to us," I manage to say through heavy breaths.

Digory's not paying attention to me. His eyes are riveted on something beyond us, and I turn to follow his gaze.

My breath is torn away.

"Looks like we found a ship," I barely whisper.

The entire room is a huge hangar bay, filled with row after row of V-shaped craft. But it's not just the magnitude of the ships that's shocking. It's the ships themselves. Like the Fleshers, each craft is a combination of metal, steel, and organic matter, all fused together in an obscene marriage of biology and machine. Gleaming exhaust ports grow out of slimy, pulsating skins, engines whir even as cockpit doors tear apart with the squish of organic matter in an obscene synthesis. Fuel lines throb like giant umbilical cords, pumping who knows what into each vehicle.

And scurrying around the crafts are legions of Fleshers, thousands upon thousands, some clanking along like living forklifts, others zipping around on wheels, while even others clatter along on all fours like giant insects, their skins splitting open and sprouting vast arrays of gleaming silver instruments as they dart about, servicing their ships.

I almost want to cover my ears to shield them from all the

buzzing, clomping, and snapping that vibrates through the air. Air that smells like a mixture of fuel and the barely perceptible stench of meat that's just starting to go bad.

Then it occurs to me. These are more than just scouts on a diplomatic mission.

It's an army.

A huge screen dominates the far side of the hangar bay. On it is an aerial view of the Parish. It seems that Sanctum has the Parish under close surveillance. They must have spies on the inside, spies within the innermost workings of the Establishment.

I have to warn Cage and the rebels. I grab my transceiver. If they get this message and broadcast it to the entire Parish, there might be a chance to deal a significant blow to the Establishment, Cassius, and Sanctum all at once.

Digory's face is brimming with different emotions. It's as though the footage of our home has unleashed deep feelings inside him, feelings he'd prefer to keep buried forever rather than have to relive the horrors that caused him to block them all out in the first place.

The hangar door blows open and we barely manage to move out of the way in time. Then the Fleshers that were pursuing us swarm in like an insect colony, taking their positions all around us.

There's nowhere left to go.

Straton and Cassius trail into the bay behind them.

Cassius notices my amazement and smiles. "This is how we're finally going to be rid of the Establishment once and for all."

"*This* is your peaceful solution? Hundreds—*thousands*—of innocent people slaughtered in battle? Captured and mutated into these *things*?" My voice is barely audible over the clamor of activity engulfing the hangar bay. I turn to Straton. "Or, consumed for the greater good?"

Straton smiles. "Tomorrow morning our regiments march on the Parish. It is time the experiment be brought to its conclusion."

I ignore him, homing in on Cassius. "Just get it over with quickly."

Cassius cocks his head. His eyes narrow. "What do you mean?"

"Our *deaths*," I respond. My words simmer on their way to boiling point. "You're obviously not going to let us go, not with everything we know. When you murder us, just do it fast, Cassius, if I ever meant anything to you at all, like you claim."

My eyes sync with Digory's. He nods. No trace of fear on his face. At least we can have a few more minutes together. This time we'll die together, the way it should be.

Cassius shakes his head with something akin to pity in his eyes. "Everything with you, Lucian, is always so black and white. Just because the sky is occasionally gray doesn't mean the rain will fall."

My resolve turns to dread. "You're *not* going to kill us?" The thought of what might now be in store for us makes me long for death. I can't help think of this processing plant and what it stands for.

Cassius sighs. "Once again you misjudge me, Lucky." His

eyes bounce between Digory and me. "The both of you are far too valuable alive—oh, I know you're thinking about the limited food resources here in Sanctum and the way the religious choose to *bond* with their enemies." He shakes his head. "That will never happen to either you or Tycho, I promise."

My lips purse. I shift my gaze to Straton and the Fleshers. "So you're not going to let them eat us. I guess I should thank you, but I'm sure that you understand if I don't."

Now Cassius's lips bow into a serpentine smile. "Even though I imagine the rabble would be more than pleased to behold their protector—the great Torch Keeper himself—in the flesh, you'll stay here in Sanctum under my protection while I escort the ailing Prime Minister Talon back to the Parish for some accountability issues. Trust me, Lucian. We both want the same thing. The Establishment must be stopped." He pauses. "As must the insurrection."

My blood turns to ice water. "What do you mean?"

He stares directly into my eyes. "Your friends who escaped Infiernos—that Micajah and his sister, your fellow trainees—they're being tracked by a homing beacon aboard their ship. As soon as they make contact with their fellow insurrectionists, squadrons will be sent to neutralize them."

I'm stunned. Here I thought my friends had a chance. Now, not only they but the rest of the resistance—the very people who are the Parish's last chance—are doomed.

But if they received the data I transmitted, they could still be safe.

I swallow hard. As far as Cassius is concerned, I've learned not to rule anything out as long as there's some detail in need of clarification.

"What about Digory?" I finally dare to ask.

Cassius stares at Digory, then back at me. "It's time to initiate the next phase of his Ultra Imposer Program." He leans in close. "When Tycho didn't die from that virus they injected, the decision was made to study him—to test bio-warfare on his immune system in order to genetically engineer the perfect Imposer. Tycho will undergo the nanotech procedure and become a new breed of Flesher."

THIRTY-FIVE

The walk to nanotech lab is the longest one in my life. Leading us is a squad of armed Sanctum personnel. The four Fleshers who used to be the Fallen Five flank us. I can't help but wonder how they feel—*if* they feel anything at all—as they travel the path that transformed them from frightened Recruits into the lumbering machines trundling beside us, seemingly cold and impassive. Surely there's some remnant of their former selves inside them. The way the one shared the ID tags and let us go, I have to believe the Fallen Five aren't completely dead. If I don't cling to this, I'll have to accept that Digory will be dead within minutes.

And he'll never come back again.

We enter a sector we haven't been to before. I'm still wearing the same jumpsuit, but Digory's been stripped to nothing but a pair of neon white shorts, the contours of his body glistening from the antiseptic solution they dipped him in during the procedure prep.

As we're marched along, I can't stop staring at him, wishing we'd never left that park we landed in. It was the only time since we've met that we were truly free and happy, if only for a short while.

We reach a flight of steps leading up to a triangular platform. In its center, a transparent, bubblelike container is suspended by translucent cables pulsating with glowing light and leading into a bank of flashing, oblong instruments. The bubble descends and splits open like a blooming flower, its interior large enough to encase a body.

My heart forgets to beat.

I feel like a cornered animal. My fight-or-flight instinct is triggered in a mad rush of panic and adrenaline, as if I were back competing in the Trials.

But Digory's face is calm, resolute. He stares back at me with weary eyes, the hint of a reassuring smile on his lips.

The Fleshers prod us closer to the bubble. Cassius and Straton are already waiting there, the flickering light from the cables alternately bathing them in eerie iridescence, which gives their eyes an almost glowing effect, and shadows, which carve their features into hard edges.

I take a step toward Cassius. "Please. Don't do this. He's been through enough. Take *me* instead."

My words break Digory's calm façade. He grunts and pushes forward, trying to shield me with his body.

"*L-Lucky.*" His deep voice echoes through the chamber.

The sound of my name from his lips freezes me in place.

It's been forever since I've heard it. And all at once I'm flooded with joy and grief.

I press my body against Digory's. He pulls me close and our lips press together; we relish our warmth in the coldness of this place. In this one kiss, there's a lifetime of regret—for all that was lost and for what will never be. Hot tears sting my eyes, mingling with his. There's so much I want to say, but the words don't come . . .

The four Fleshers move in closer to us. I catch the gleam of their pincers poised to strike, and this time it's me who covers Digory with my body.

"Digory, listen to me," I whisper in his ear. "There are too many of them. They'll kill us both if we try anything."

His chest heaves and his muscles tense. Slowly, his body relaxes again.

"I'm a-afraid, Lucian," he says, the words coming with great effort.

"Why?"

"Things they've done . . . to me . . . made *me* do . . . not the same person . . ."

I can tell that speaking is a monumental effort for him, but he's determined to get the words out.

Reaching out, I wipe a tear from his eye and he clutches my hand to his face.

"Begin the final phase of the Ultra Imposer Program on Tycho." Cassius's voice is low, emotionless. He may as well be one of the Fleshers himself.

Two of the Fleshers grip Digory while the other two clutch me.

And then we're torn apart.

"Don't let them make you forget," I call to him. *"Never give up."*

This time he smiles. "Never forget *you*."

Then he's dragged into the bubble, his body shackled into a spread-eagled position. All of his muscles tense as the bubble seals shut, trapping him inside.

Cassius and Straton bark orders, but they're nothing but muffled sounds in my ears as I watch the glowing nanotech fluid fill the sphere—crawling up Digory's calves, slithering up the mounds of his thighs, tightening around his waist before swarming over his heaving chest and neck and engulfing his head.

Our eyes meet one last time—a look of longing and pain—before his face is immersed in the fluid.

I can't breathe. I've never felt so helpless. All I can do is watch as his body writhes in the swirling mass of protoplasmic goo.

The minutes stretch into an unbearable blur as his body finally begins to still.

And then it ceases to move completely.

Straton studies the readouts. "He's quite a strong specimen, but it appears his body isn't rejecting the nanotech cells." He looks up from the monitor, his face glowing in the reddish haze. "Assimilation has begun."

The words strike me like a bullet. At first I'm dizzy with emptiness. But that's quickly filled with rage. This time I won't hesitate to kill Cassius.

Cassius nods. "Transfer Tycho's body to a cryogenic tube

and prepare it for transport, along with Talon's medpod. It's time for me to get back to the Parish."

I catch one last glimpse of Digory as the Sanctum techs descend on the bubble to carry out Cassius's orders. Within minutes, the fluid is drained from the sphere and Digory's body is transferred into its new prison, a cryo capsule that's loaded onto a glider transport and carried away, taking what's left of my soul with it.

Straton glances at me, then back to Cassius. "What about *this* one? When can we begin the hippocampus stimulation phase?"

"*This* one," Cassius says, "is *not* to be touched until I give authorization, as per our agreement. Understood?"

Straton can barely hide his anger. "Understood."

I shoot a look at Straton and then Cassius. "Hippocampus is part of the brain, isn't it? Why the hell are you interested in my memories? Does this have something to do with that Sowing Protocol?"

Cassius grips my shoulder. "You'll be safe here until I return. I promise."

Then he's gone, too.

Straton signals the Sanctum personnel, who grab hold of me and lead me out of the chamber.

All I'm thinking about is how little time I have—to break out of these restraints and go after Cassius and Digory—when we round the corner and the four Fleshers attack.

But they don't attack me. They attack the Sanctum guards, skewering them with their weapons until the guards' bodies are nothing but lifeless clumps of bloody pulp.

The numbness I've been feeling is replaced by a surge of adrenaline. The lead Flesher approaches me with one of the sharp cutting blades, raises it—

And cuts through my manacles.

"Which way to the hangar?" I ask.

Then I'm racing after them through the dark maze, burning with the one emotion I'd never thought I'd ever feel again.

Hope.

THIRTY-SIX

The Four lead me through a maze of tunnels that spill out into a smaller hangar bay. I can hear the low thrum of engines even before I spot the sleek lines of the Vulture-class ship prepping for takeoff. The craft is positioned on a circular hydraulic platform that will lift it up a seemingly endless shaft to the surface.

Cassius has his back to me as he gestures to two of the Sanctum escorts, who are busy loading Digory's encapsulated body into the compartment in the ship's underbelly, next to Talon's medpod. I duck behind a terminal as Cassius strides up the boarding ramp, which begins to lift as soon as he disappears inside.

Taking a deep breath, I give the Four a final nod and dart for the ship. I leap and roll into the cargo hold, hoping the sound of the engines have drowned out the sounds of my body bumping the ship.

My muscles tense for a fight as I expect guards to appear in the opening of the hatch any second. But the last sliver of light coming in from the bay disappears with a loud clank as the hatch finally seals. The whine of the engines gets louder. The Vulture is vibrating almost as fast as my heart is.

Then we're moving, and I can feel the pressure as the hydraulic platform shoots up the shaft to the surface. I take a deep breath as the Vulture lifts off from the ruined city and zooms away at full throttle, leaving Sanctum far behind us.

The cargo hold is small and rectangular. There won't be enough room to hide once we land and the hatch is opened. But if I remember the layout of this type of ship correctly, there's a small hatch in the corner of the ceiling that leads to the back of the passenger cabin. Bracing against the turbulence, I reach up and test it. It gives with a loud squeak and I cringe, easing it closed again.

I slide down to the floor of the hold, exhausted. Beside me, I can barely see the contours of the capsule encasing Digory. I crawl past Talon's medpod and over to it, sidling up against the cold hard shell. Inside, Digory is perfectly still, his body floating in the pool of genetic fluid as if he were merely peacefully asleep.

I touch the glass across from his face. "I'm *right* here," I whisper. Then I curl up beside the pod and close my eyes.

I'm not sure how many hours later it is when my eyes spring open. Even with all the jostling from the turbulence, I've managed to sleep on and off, the steady thrum of the engines creating a kind of white-noise effect that makes it easy to give in to my physical and mental fatigue. But it didn't stop the nightmares—horrible images of Digory and Cole morphing into Fleshers. The last one was the worst. I thought I'd woken up and seen a reflection of myself in the glass of Digory's tomb, but something was wrong with my face. The skin was bruised and peeling. When I tried to pull off a flake of dead skin, my flesh began to rip. I couldn't stop myself from pulling and tearing, my face disappearing in bloody tatters and replaced by a biomechanical machine underneath, staring back at me with soulless eyes—

I was a Flesher.

I awoke from this dream in a clammy sweat, despite the ice-cold air that wracks my body with the shivers. It must be the altitude taking its toll. If we don't land soon, I'll die of hypothermia before I ever see the Parish again.

Reaching out a trembling hand, I swipe a clear space in the frosty condensation covering Digory's capsule, which I immediately have to clear again as my breath fogs it up.

He still looks the same.

That's when I feel the ship begin its angled descent.

Springing to my feet, I crack open the hatch just enough to look through the cabin windows. The sky is coated in the pink and orange hues of dusk. Even from the limited vantage point of my perch, I spy the billowing mushroom smog from the factories, soon replaced by the cold gray turrets and spires of the Citadel of Truth. I never thought I'd see them again, let alone be happy at the sight. Whatever else it may be, the Parish is still the only home I've ever known.

And somewhere down there, my brother is waiting for me.

At least I hope he still is.

We're heading for one of the hangars near the top of the Citadel's main building.

I take one last look at Digory. "See you soon."

Then I'm climbing into the main cabin and wedging myself into one of the overhead storage compartments. I'm too big to fit inside completely, but I manage to get the access door closed enough to hide from view just as the ship's braking thrusters kick in and we come to a bumpy stop. I'm counting on Cassius being too preoccupied with his arrival to scrutinize the cabin.

The engines cut out and the exit ramp begins to lower. Cassius bursts from the cockpit and marches down in seconds. I can hear muffled voices and the grind of the cargo hold opening. I wait until the sounds of footfalls die, and then I ease my aching body out of the cramped compartment and slink out of the aircraft as stealthily as I can, pausing at the foot of the gangplank to make sure no one's around.

Cassius has obviously landed the ship in his small, private docking bay in the Citadel's main tower. Rummaging through the hangar's supply closet, I find a flight uniform and helmet that aren't quite my size but will do the trick. I could really use some firepower, but the only thing I come across is a flare gun. Not ideal, long-term, but it can do a lot of damage to a human body up close. Stripping off what I'm wearing, I don the uniform, tuck the gun into my pocket, and exit the bay.

I immediately expect to have to dodge squads of Imps making their rounds, so I'm surprised to find that the corridors are uncharacteristically deserted.

I race through the hallways. Several Imps surprise me when I round a corner, but they're running too and don't bother to stop as they disappear down the far hall.

It's then that I realize that the growing pounding I hear isn't coming from my chest. I pause to listen. The thudding is too uniform to be thunder. It's the sound of impact blasts and alarms, loud enough to vibrate through the soundproof windows of the Citadel and rock its foundations.

Cage and the others must have been tracked to their rebel cell.

The Establishment's strike against the resistance is underway.

I dart down the remainder of the hall to where two Imps usually guard the stairwell that leads to the roof of the Prefect's chambers. But no one's there and I push the doors open, sprinting up the steps and bursting out onto the Citadel's rooftop.

The Parish is in chaos.

Attack squadrons of Squawkers soar through the air, spitting out fiery missiles that streak across the horizon like angry talons, tearing great rents in the sky. Loud concussions transform the tenements of my old neighborhood into billowing plumes of dark smoke. The stench of fire and roasting bodies clogs my nostrils and stings my eyes, which pool with burning moisture that streaks down my cheeks.

Right now, the resistance is scrambling, outnumbered, overpowered. I have no idea if Arrah and the others are already dead. For all I know, I could be looking at the funeral pyre of the rebellion, snuffed out of existence before it ever had the chance to thrive.

As soon as the last of the bombardment's echoes die away, all the jumbotrons across the Parish flicker, cutting off with a burst of static, going black, then coming back to life.

It's Cassius. His face appears saddened, yet stern. Not a trace of arrogance.

"Citizens of the Parish," he begins. "I come to you in the gravest hour our society has ever known. You are all aware of the tide of insurgence that has plagued us for quite some time now. A short time ago, a pocket of these traitors were discovered, and swift justice was meted out." He pauses and inhales sharply. "What you do not know is that these criminals have not been acting alone. While we have been searching for them in every crevice of the bowels of our city, the greatest threat to the Establishment is being perpetrated from within the very core of those ensconced in our ruling body."

The camera angle zooms out to a wider shot, revealing Talon—revived from stasis and looking confused, weak, and haggard—and the members of her cabinet, all being held at gunpoint by Cassius's elite security team.

That image is replaced by a close-up of Cassius's face, visibly distraught as if he's trying to keep his emotions in check.

But I know better. This entire thing is all a ruse.

He looks directly into the camera. "This is going to come as quite a devastating shock to our honored and revered elite Imposers, but evidence has surfaced linking Prime Minister Talon and her cabinet to a plot to undermine the very stability of our society by aligning with the monsters that seek to destroy us."

There's a cut to a montage of the information I discovered in Sanctum, including the simulations of Incentives designed to deceive everyone into thinking the Recruitment process could provide a good life for the Recruits' family members. Cassius narrates the details of the conspiracy, which is intercut with startling footage I've never seen before—the friends and families of winning Recruits being tortured and experimented on, some turned into Fleshers, the ones that don't survive the process dumped into mass graves.

At certain points, there are live cutaways to the faces of Imposer squads throughout the city as they take in the revelation that everything they've sacrificed, all that has made them into the hardcore soldiers they are, the reason for their unquestioning allegiance to the Establishment, has been a great lie.

Cassius is doing the same thing to Talon and her cabinet that he did to *me* on Recruitment Day, masterfully trying and convicting her in front of all to see. I can almost pity her. She's nothing but a pawn, like I was.

Onscreen, Cassius shakes his head. "I cannot stress enough how disgusted I am that the covert actions of so few"—there's another shot of Talon and her crew—"have resulted in such devastation to soldiers who have given so much of themselves and provided services so loyally for years." Cassius swallows hard. "But, my poor citizens, this isn't even the worst of it." He clears his throat. "It appears that Talon and the insurrectionists have established an alliance with a dangerous cult of extremists entrenched in the bowels of the forbidden territories."

Once again, the broadcast switches to a montage. This one depicts the legions of Fleshers attacking Infiernos and readying for combat in the catacombs of Sanctum. Even from way up here, I can hear the gasps of the crowds, feel the fear in the air. And most damaging of all are the images of Talon and Straton. Her smiling as she takes his hand. The huge projection of the Parish map in the Sanctum war room.

So it seems that Talon and Straton met prior to Talon's recent trip to Sanctum. Unless Cassius is using her unconscious body to create another simulation, like those of the Incentives...

The cameras cut back to Cassius, now holding up his hands. "I urge you all not to panic. There's still time to avert this tragedy and restore order to our great nation. But to do this, I need you all to join me in our most desperate hour." The camera starts to zoom in slowly as he speaks. "Despite the differences we may have had, we cannot let the actions of a handful of criminals dictate the survival of our society. It's not too late to protect ourselves. Protect our families. Protect our *children*. Even as we speak, I have already launched a preliminary offensive on those who seek to destroy us," he concludes.

Sanctum. If Cassius is willing to betray them too, it can only mean that he plans on gaining even greater power than he already has now.

The screens fill with images of Squawkers zooming through the skies over the still-smoldering Infiernos. And then the statue of the Lady zooms into view. The Lady who's been such a beacon of the hope and beauty of the old world to Cole and me ever since I discovered her picture in the Parish library.

There's a series of blasts, echoing through the Parish, that may as well be bullets fired directly into my heart. Each missile blasts into the Lady, who remains defiant if just for a few seconds. Her stone eyes dominate the screen and I imagine I see sorrow there—and pity.

And then she's toppling to the ground, her body and book disappearing in a billowing plume of black clouds.

One of the missiles impacts the only part of her still intact—her torch—and ignites it in a huge fireball. Then it, too, shatters into a million pieces. And then the Lady is no more. Just a crumpled pile of smoke and ash.

I feel sick with loss.

An extreme close-up of Cassius's face now dominates every single jumbotron in the Parish. If I didn't know firsthand how treacherous he could be, even I might believe him.

A fierce determination sears his eyes. "I urge you to trust

in new leadership and join me to defeat our enemies—starting with these traitors behind me, whose vile corruption has threatened the very core of our existence, but will do so no more."

In a flash, he whips out a weapon, jams it against Talon's head, and pulls the trigger. The sounds of the shot tears through the city, magnified by every loudspeaker and screen like a violent storm. Talon is thrown back in a bloody mist and her body collapses.

Then the squad of Imposers holding the cabinet members hostage begin firing, not stopping until every single member of the entourage has been assassinated ten times over.

Cassius turns back to the cameras, droplets of blood bleeding down his face. "I promise to end the plague of corruption polluting our country and restore a peaceful, prosperous society. Who is with me?" he shouts.

That's when the chanting begins, low at first, then gaining in strength and momentum until it roars like a hurricane.

"CASSIUS! CASSIUS! CASSIUS!"

He's holding up his hands now, a grin spread across his face, his eyes burning with triumph.

And that's the moment when I know he's won. He's successfully pitted the Establishment against Sanctum and established himself as supreme authority, only having to sit back and pull the strings as everyone he's manipulated wages his personal war. Every Imposer will be on his side now, carrying out his every order. This time not out of fear of reprisals against their loved ones, but bloodthirsty vengeance against those who've wronged them.

Random shots of the crowd fill me with dread. These citizens who have been oppressed, living in squalor and fear, seem to be embracing him, forgetting what they've been through, willing to trust a new order cut from the same cloth as its malignant predecessor, clinging to a false hope that even now is binding them in the links of heavier chains. They're turning against the resistance, the only true chance they have at getting a decent life.

Everything's lost.

Unless I stop Cassius now—finish what I started in Town Square on Ascension Day—before the seeds he's so carefully sown have a chance to grow and mature into a poisonous harvest that's more terrible than everything that's come before.

"Beautiful view, isn't it?" an all-too-familiar voice says behind me.

My hand grips the flare gun still hidden in my pocket and I spin to face Cassius.

The broadcast was on a time delay. He's been waiting for me to come to him. Always one step ahead of me, from the beginning.

And I played right into his hands.

He looks calm and appears to be unarmed, which somehow makes me even more ill at ease.

"Congratulations," I finally say. "Beautifully played." I try to remain composed, even though I'm boiling over with hatred. My sweaty fingers brush against the flare gun, my eyes focused on Cassius's chest.

All I need is one shot, right in his heart, and this madness will be over before it has a chance to unravel.

I pull out the gun and aim it at him. "You *used* me from the beginning. Baiting me by recording that footage of Digory taken alive. Manipulating things so I'd end up at Infiernos. And when Digory and I crashed in the ancient city, you seized the opportunity to get us to Sanctum. You let us find our way into that cryo chamber so we could leak intel about what was going on to the resistance. You didn't have to get your hands dirty while everyone else did your work for you. You've betrayed Talon *and* Straton. All so that *you* could be the Parish's savior."

Cassius shakes his head as if he's pitying me. He makes no move to defend himself. "No need for violence, Lucky. Yes, I've sown the seeds. But it was *your* skill, your *drive*, that was the impetus I didn't have complete control over. Despite what you're thinking, I still—*you* still mean a great deal to me. Why else do you think I had Valerian destroy the forensic evidence that tied you to the attack on the Pleasure Emporiums? And don't you recall how I intervened at Infiernos when you were about to face the Culling? Or once again at Sanctum, when Straton wanted to cut open your brain? There's *always* a place for you in the new regime—if you want it. Once again, you have a choice."

"I choose to kill you before your squad of Imps arrives and kills *me*." My finger applies pressure to the trigger.

Cassius shakes his head. "Who needs Imposers when I have something *better*?"

I'm just about to pull the trigger and end this for good when movement catches my eye. I whip the gun in that direction as a figure emerges from the shadows.

It's Cole.

He looks thinner than the last time I saw him, on the podium in Town Square. His eyes are swollen, either from tears or lack of sleep. But he's alive. My heart leaps. The arm holding the gun drops to my side.

"Cole. *You're okay*."

I drop to my knees as he comes running into my arms. I squeeze him tight, then pull away, cupping his face in my palms. "Did they hurt you?"

He shakes his head.

"I'm sorry I didn't come for you when I said I would," I whisper, "but I'm going to get you out of here now."

His eyes light up and he hugs me tight, pressing his face against my chest.

Just as I'm about to lift him into my arms, something sharp jabs into my side. It's like a million shards of glass piercing my flesh. I can't breathe... everything goes hazy...

Cole tears away from me, the cold steel of a knife blade glinting in his eyes. I stare at the weapon and it takes me a moment to register that the dark liquid dripping from it and spattering on the white marble is my own blood.

I'm too late. The Ultra Imposer indoctrination of my brother has already begun. He'll eventually end up another lab rat like Digory, his mind and body subjected to countless experiments. But Digory was selected because he'd proven himself strong. With Cole being programmed so young, who knows what kind of monster he'll be groomed to be?

I look back up at him. Then I stagger backwards, the flare gun clattering to the floor. And still Cole stares at me, eyes unblinking, as if I'm a total stranger.

Cassius walks up behind him.

"*Stay... away... from my... brother...*" It's more of a wheeze.

But Cassius rests his hands on Cole's shoulders. My brother looks up at him, the way he always looked up at me whenever he wanted my approval.

Another wave of intense pain, accompanied by nausea, almost makes me pass out. My vision blurs...

This can't be happening...

Cassius sighs. "It's *your* rejection that forces me to do this, Lucian."

He looks up at a hovering cam, and then I see his face plastered all over the jumbotrons once again. "Citizens of the Parish, behold. At last I've apprehended the terrorist known as the Torch Keeper, Lucian Spark, who has conspired with Talon and her cohorts to destroy us from within. Behold the face of the most insidious of traitors, revealed at last and brought to his knees on this most momentous of days."

Then I see myself, bloodied and pale, crawling like a wounded animal... and shots of Squawkers on their way to take me into custody, before the screens go dark.

Another wave of anguish wracks me. My back presses against the roof railing and I somehow manage to push myself up. If I'm going to die, I want to do it on my feet and looking Cassius in the eye.

I can barely see from the pain and dizziness and the hot tears streaming from my eyes as I look at the smaller of the two shapes in front of me.

"Cole..." I choke out.

I stagger against the railing, weak, teetering as the cold wind lashes my face.

Cassius's shadow engulfs me. He grips my head, pulling me close. "I tried to spare you this. But my feelings for you are a liability. You can't escape your true nature."

"My true...?"

"The rebellion is lost. Tycho is being purged of his humanity—and his pain—as we speak. And Cole belongs to *me* now." He leans in close, his lips brushing against mine and moving to my ear. "I'll let you in on a little secret," he whispers. "Cole isn't your brother."

This can't be true. I'm delirious. I can remember Cole as an infant. His tiny fist clenched around my finger. The anger gives me a final surge of strength. "You're... lying. Cole is a Spark."

Cassius's eyes deadlock with mine. "But *you* aren't," he says calmly. "*You* aren't Lucian Spark. Your true name is Queran Embers."

Cold envelops me. I no longer know what's real and what isn't. "What the hell are you talking about?"

"The Sowing Protocol. It's the method developed by the original settlers of the Parish, who perfected a physics-based cloning system that can replicate a human being at an atomic level. Every single molecule is copied, preserving not only an individual's physical attributes but also their *memories*. The cloned embryos were to be implanted in future generations, so they could be reborn again and again, achieving an immortality to rival the Deity—or the Begetter—or whatever one chooses to call it. The entire Recruitment process we both experienced is much less random than it appears."

My head's spinning and my body feels like it's been sucker punched. "No. These are just more of your lies and manipulations."

He shakes his head. "All this time, you've been trying to destroy the Establishment. And the irony is ... you are the person that founded it, centuries ago. You built this place, stone by stone, upon the suffering and blood of countless innocents. And now you've been reborn, resurrected as a cloned embryo implanted in your mother during a routine medical examination."

"I don't want to hear anymore ... " I whisper.

His eyes water and a tear streams down his cheek. "All the things I've done since I discovered the truth—some of them terrible—were all in an effort to try to crush the Establishment once and for all and save you, the only person I've ever truly loved. Even though *you* are responsible for all *this*." His arms reach up toward the turrets and spires of the Citadel, then drop limply to his sides. "But I'm starting to realize I can't do both."

It's too much. I just want to shut my eyes and be swallowed by oblivion.

Beside him, Cole lifts the dagger one more time, aiming for my heart.

I push away from Cassius and tumble over the railing, spinning, flashes of color assault my waning senses, just wanting it all to end in that final darkness—

The impact jolts every nerve ending in my body. I expected death to be infinite blackness and peace. Why hasn't the pain throbbing inside me stopped?

"Get him inside, quick!" a voice shouts from far away.

That voice is familiar … I've heard it many times before … but where …

It's Arrah.

I open my eyes and make out Arrah, Drusilla, and Cage pulling and dragging me into a coffin … no … it's a ship … a Squawker …

Then the cold wind stops and I'm inside. A mask is smashed against my face. Oxygen. Someone's at my side. Cloth swipes my side, white cotton turned red with fire.

"We have to stop the bleeding," someone—Arrah again— yells.

The last thing I see, through the cabin window, is a formation of Squawkers heading toward us. Our ship veers and banks wildly, around and over buildings ... and then we're heading into the blackest night of my life.

THIRTY-SEVEN

The convoy stretches over the rocky plain like the winding body of a great caterpillar. Battered glide-craft, rebuilt Squawkers cobbled together from discarded parts, and makeshift transports patched with rust all zigzag through the dying night. Even with the creaking from poor shock absorbers and lack of proper lubricants, it's relatively quiet—considering the thousands of people that are part of this stealth caravan, the remnants of the freedom coalition that have managed to make it out of the Parish.

Cage and Arrah received my transmissions and warned Jeptha, who had just enough time to contact the other resistance cells with warnings and evacuation orders. By the time the first wave of Squawker attacks hit, most of the rebel strongholds were only partially occupied. Still, many were trapped or killed when the squads of Imposers and soldiers sealed the city in the aftermath of Cassius's coup d'état against

Talon and those still loyal to her regime. The clean-up by Cassius's forces was swift and violent—and fortunately provided enough of a diversion for the rebel survivors to slip from the city limits. Unfortunately, Tristin hasn't been seen since. Even though she's probably dead, I find myself uttering a silent prayer to whatever god she believed in to watch over her.

I stare out from the open cockpit of the transport I'm riding in as the first rays of light penetrate that cloak of blackness. With the encroaching dawn, Cassius's forces will come calling, ready to decimate what's left of the resistance. Maybe he has his hands full dealing with Sanctum and that'll buy us some time. In any event, we need to establish a new base of operations soon.

"How're you feeling?" Arrah asks.

I turn toward her, my fingers tracing the outline of the bandages still plastered to my side. The side where—

I wince. "Still breathing."

Her eyes narrow, as if she can't tell whether I'm grateful or bitter.

I'm not so sure which, either.

"Sorry if that patchwork job wasn't exactly up to standard," she says. "It'll probably leave a scar."

"Yeah. I'm sure it will."

She hasn't asked how exactly I got wounded, and I haven't volunteered to fill in the blanks. Maybe someday we'll have that conversation. But I can't. Not now.

The cavalcade begins to wind down into a canyon. The crater's huge, the walls pockmarked with natural niches that have been reinforced by steel beams and girders. I smile. The resistance coalition has been busy over the years, constructing this ersatz base little by little out of supplies and equipment pilfered from the Establishment's carefully recorded inventory.

As we descend, I see that hundreds—no, thousands—have already assembled, bustling around, constructing shelters, soldering equipment, distributing meager supplies of food and clothing.

Amidst the throng, I spot a group of familiar black uniforms and gleaming helmets and my hand reflexively goes to the weapon strapped to my opposite side. But the moment I see the face of their leader, I relax.

It's Valerian.

The closer I get to her, the more I can see that recent events have already started to take their toll. Her face is drawn, mired in cuts and bruises, and her usually pristine uniform is wrinkled and torn.

My transport comes to a stop. I hop off and limp toward her.

She manages a smile. "Spark. That uniform you're wearing isn't exactly up to code, Recruit."

I nod. "Neither is yours, Sir."

"I guess we're all going to need new uniforms now." She glances at her companions. Imposers who, like her, have chosen a side.

"Tim Fremont," she whispers.

"Who—?"

"He was a young man, a Worm peddling fake IDs, who my partner and I caught on the very day you were recruited. I was faced with the choice of killing him outright or taking him into custody and letting him be tortured until he begged for death. I chose the former."

Of course. The poor guy in the alley on the day Digory and my fates became intertwined.

She rubs her weary eyes. "Tim's screams haven't left me. But it was a decision I made for the greater good, one of *many*. Which is why I've left now."

There's always a choice.

And I've made mine.

We grip hands and stare at each other for a moment, until she finally breaks away. "I've got to get back to the Parish before Thorn misses me. I can be much more effective working on the inside. Besides, loading supplies is grunt work for Fifth Tiers." She winks at me.

Then she and her crew are gone, fading into the sea of hustling bodies.

"You should probably get some rest, mate," Cage says. The place where his hand once was has been bandaged meticulously.

I shake my head. "Too much to do. Besides, I need to stay busy." I look away. A particle of dust must have gotten in my eye because it burns, and I try to rub it away. "I'm sure Tristin's okay, Cage."

"Thank you." He grips my arm. "Lucian. I'm not sure what happened to you after Infiernos. But you have to believe, you're not alone now."

I can only nod and slip away from his grasp. Cage is a great man. A natural leader. Maybe someday, when this bloody war is over, he'll meet someone who can appreciate him. That's something I can never be. Not to him. Not to anyone else ever again.

Moving away from him, I lose myself in the crowd and spend the rest of the day working nonstop.

At last, the weary sky gives way to dusk. Without fully thinking about what I'm doing, I grab a flickering torch and move onto the main platform. I raise the flame high over my head, gritting my teeth as I welcome the pain that reminds me I'm still alive—and still have a purpose.

Gradually the sounds fade as people begin to notice me. Finally, a hush falls through the crowd.

"People of the Parish," I say. My voice echoes across the canyon with a power I've never felt until now. "We have *all* felt what it's like to live under the suffocating oppression and tyranny of the Establishment. We've all suffered and lost people that we love." The word catches in my throat for a second. "But I *promise* you, none of what we've experienced shall be in vain. We will fight with every last drop of blood until those responsible cower and drop to their knees. Freedom and dignity are not scraps to be doled out by cruel masters. They belong to every man, woman, and child. They are our *right*. And we won't stop until they *belong* to us!"

The canyon comes alive with roars and applause, a noise that rivals the most powerful thunderstorm. My eyes wander the crowed and I see their faces: Arrah, Drusilla, Cage, Dahlia, Corin, and Jeptha—people who are still alive. People who need me.

Like I need them.

But it's the faces that aren't there that consume me.

As the rumbling ovation and chants continue, I stare into the flame I hold high. Perhaps it's a trick of the light, but I can almost swear I see faces staring back at me through the flickering glow.

A child and a young man.

The fire inside me blazes, rivaling my torch.

"I will win this war for *you*," I whisper.

Somewhere out there, Digory is waiting for me.

And Cole. No matter what Cassius said or what they made Cole do, no matter if Cassius was lying or telling the truth about the Sowing Protocol, Cole will *always* be my brother.

Just like I'll always be who *I* am. Who I've always been.

Who I've become.

Lucian Spark.

The Torch Keeper.

THE END

Acknowledgments

As is often the case, sequels are an extension of the commitment, dedication, and encouragement of all that came before. *The Sowing* is no exception. There are so many wonderful people that have become part of this growing family of supporters of the Torch Keeper series, ever since *The Culling* was released, and I really appreciate all that they have contributed on this magical journey.

Cathy Castelli, I am forever indebted to you for taking the time to record my first book signing event EVER when *The Culling* was first released. You captured a wonderful memory of my dreams coming true that I will treasure for years to come! Also, it was really awesome of you to promote the book in school libraries.

No mention of schools would be complete without a nod to fellow author, Jennifer Lavoie, a teacher who has championed *The Culling* and introduced it to her students, while whetting their appetites for *The Sowing* in fiendishly clever ways. You tease!

Much thanks to Micah Dawson and the members of the Chaos Reads forums for embracing the Torch Keeper series, spreading the word of its existence, and starting its very first fan forums. I can't tell you how amazing it felt the first time I saw a fan site featuring discussions of stories and characters of my own creation, and realizing I had actual fans!

And speaking of fans, I'd like to give a special shout-out to Chloe Hill, Marie White, Mel Longchamps, and Michele Cantwell, who befriended Lucian, Digory, and the rest of *The Culling* gang when no one had a clue who they were, and who have continually raved about the Torch Keeper series so that other readers might discover it and enter the dark worlds in my head. Hope this book settles the "Digory" questions. You guys ROCK!

My warmest thanks go out to my friends Adam Magee and his partner, Chad Michaels, for their encouragement and countless tweets, even before *The Culling* was ever released. ChAdam, Shantay, you STAY!

I also appreciate Frank Garcia and his partner Pedro Aguas including me in a full-page color spread in *What's Happening Magazine*. Thanks guys! Next time, maybe I can have a center-fold?

Dawn Sorokin-Tschupp, you did a great job making my mug look presentable for my author photo. You must use a wand instead of a camera to work that kind of magic!

Thanks to Luis Contreras for featuring me in my very first YouTube videos, and helping to promote *The Culling* and the Torch Keeper series to the vast world of social media.

Extra shiny props to Keri Mcdaniel, whose selfless efforts are responsible for beaucoup sales of *The Culling*. Girl, I can't tell you how much all you've done means to me and I hope to have you head up my marketing team some day!

And, as always, to my wonderful partner, Jeffrey Cadorette, who helps keep me grounded when things seem overwhelming. It's always amazing what a little TLC can do.

About the Author

Steven dos Santos was born in New York City and moved to Florida at the tender age of five. He wrote his first book, *The Enchanted Prince*, when he was in second grade.

Steven has a BS in Communications but spent most of his career in law, even going to law school before realizing he wanted to be a writer. *The Sowing* is his second novel with Flux.

Visit the author at www.stevendossantos.com.